Pagan Themes in Modern Children's Fiction

Pagan Themes in Modern Children's Fiction

Green Man, Shamanism, Earth Mysteries

Peter Bramwell

First published 2009 by
PALGRAVE MACMILLAN

Palgrave Macmillan in the UK is an imprint of Macmillan Publishers Limited, registered in England, company number 785998, of Houndmills, Basingstoke, Hampshire RG21 6XS.

Palgrave Macmillan in the US is a division of St Martin's Press LLC, 175 Fifth Avenue, New York, NY 10010.

Palgrave Macmillan is the global academic imprint of the above companies and has companies and representatives throughout the world.

Palgrave® and Macmillan® are registered trademarks in the United States, the United Kingdom, Europe and other countries.

ISBN-13: 978–0–230–21839–0 hardback
ISBN-10: 0–230–21839–3 hardback

This book is printed on paper suitable for recycling and made from fully managed and sustained forest sources. Logging, pulping and manufacturing processes are expected to conform to the environmental regulations of the country of origin.

A catalogue record for this book is available from the British Library.

Library of Congress Cataloging-in-Publication Data

Bramwell, Peter, 1966–
      Pagan themes in modern children's fiction : green man, shamanism, earth mysteries / Peter Bramwell.
         p. cm.
      Includes bibliographical references and index.
      ISBN 978-0-230-21839-0
      1. Children's stories, English – History and criticism. 2. Paganism in literature. 3. Shamanism in literature. 4. Children – Books and reading – English-speaking countries. I. Title.

PR830.C513B73 2009
823'.914093829994—dc22   2008050836

10 9 8 7 6 5 4 3 2 1
18 17 16 15 14 13 12 11 10 09

Printed and bound in Great Britain by
CPI Antony Rowe, Chippenham and Eastbourne

For the female line –
Wendy, Wendy and Zoe –
and in memory of
Derek John Bramwell (1932–2008).

Contents

List of Figures

Picture Acknowledgements

The author and publisher wish to thank the following for permission to use copyright material:

Random House Group, for the illustration from *Willy the Wizard* by Anthony Browne, published by Julia Macrae; the illustration by Edward Mortelmans from *The Boy with the Bronze Axe* by Kathleen Fidler, published by Oliver & Boyd; both reprinted by permission of The Random House Group Ltd

The Society of Authors, for the illustration by Judith Masefield from *The Box of Delights*, reproduced by permission of The Society of Authors as the Literary Representative of the Estate of Judith Masefield

Oxford University Press, for the cover illustration by David Wyatt for *The Stones are Hatching* by Geraldine McCaughrean (OUP, 1991), reproduced by permission of Oxford University Press

Walker Books Limited, for the illustration from *The Snow Queen* retold by Naomi Lewis and illustrated by Angela Barrett, © Angela Barrett, 1988. Reproduced by permission of Walker Books Ltd, London SE11 5HJ

Wooden Books, for the illustration from *Once Upon a Winter's Turning*, written and illustrated by Trystan Mitchell (Wooden Books, 2000), reproduced by permission of Wooden Books.

Personal Acknowledgements

I am grateful for the interest, encouragement and advice I have been fortunate to receive, at various stages from conception to completion, from Charles Butler, Chris Clark, Nikki Gamble, Debbie Mynott, Pat Pinsent, Diane Purkiss and Kim Reynolds. My thanks go to Paula Kennedy at Palgrave, who saw the potential and encouraged me to achieve it in a more purposeful way. I never would have got anywhere without the understanding and support of my wife Wendy Martin and our daughter Zoe, and I am indebted to Wendy for her patient assistance with the edit. Any faults are of course entirely my own.

Introduction

The argument of this study is that some recent children's fiction has been making significant formative contributions to fashionable but controversial aspects of modern Paganism. The Green Man, shamanism and earth mysteries are all notable for their responsiveness to environmentalist anxieties. However, the Green Man could be criticised as a patriarchal figure imposing apocalyptic teleology upon the Pagan cyclic view of time; the integrity of indigenous shamanism is threatened by decontextualisation and cultural theft; and earth mysteries interpretations of prehistoric monuments can simultaneously construe them as a manipulatable technology and impose narrow ecological rhetoric. Children's fiction reflects these concerns and comes up with innovative and exciting reformulations. The witch figure is the most evident, pervasive and studied aspect of Paganism in children's literature and culture (see Stewig 1995, Purkiss 1996, Pearson 2002b, Stephens 2003), and witches, wise women and cunning men do make appearances throughout this book.

The first chapter prepares for and anticipates the subsequent thematic chapters by introducing the critical perspectives to be drawn on, and by maintaining an emphasis on close reading of primary texts. Sacred place and cyclic time coalesce in the Pagan chronotope, manifestations of which are analysed in a selection of children's novels. Encounters between children's literature and modern Paganism add distinctive accents to gender-conscious approaches, ecocriticism and critical linguistics. Exploring mixed Pagan attitudes to magic, and the types and uses of magic in children's fiction, leads into discussion of autonomous and developmental models of childhood, children's spirituality and reflexive narration. The cumulative argument of the chapter is that Pagan elements in children's literature merit disciplined critical scrutiny.

Herne the Hunter and the Green Man have contended to succeed Pan as the foremost literary Pagan god. Writers in the 1970s and 1980s struggled to evade or redefine Herne's association with hunting and the specific location of Windsor. The Green Man has proved more of a blank sheet on which to inscribe current ecological preoccupations. There are, however, many tensions in his portrayal, such as between the cyclic and the apocalyptic, between patriarchy and feminist Goddess-centred Paganism, between developmentalism and childness. The texts particularly honoured in Chapter 2 are those that balance the masculine and feminine, and question teleological narrative and developmental models of childhood, such as Geraldine McCaughrean's *The Stones are Hatching* (1999) and Susan Cooper's *Green Boy* (2002).

Representations of shamanism in children's fiction contribute to debate about such issues as decontextualisation, cultural integrity and appropriation, and gender roles. Chapter 3 concentrates mainly on novels set in north Eurasia, from where the term 'shaman' originates. There appears to be, very roughly, a trend that the more recently a text is written, the further back in time it is set, as if the possibility of depicting shamanism in appropriate historical and cultural contexts is receding elusively. There is also a tendency to depict female shamans as authentic and male shamans as charlatans, more than overturning the disputed claims made by some scholars that shamanism is a male preserve. Chapter 3 also covers such areas as Sami shamanism in children's fiction, texts that re-vision Heathen (Anglo-Saxon and Norse) traditions, historical novels in which European migrants encounter indigenous shamanic societies, and the Aurora Borealis as a signifier of northernness and focus of beliefs.

The final chapter compares Pagan with other constructions of prehistoric monuments – New Age, earth mysteries, heritage – and takes Penelope Lively's *The Whispering Knights* (1971a) as the starting point for exploring the relationships in children's fiction of prehistoric monuments with witchcraft and environmentalism. Antiquity is conferred on witchcraft, whether presented as evil or dualistic or in a Wicca-friendly manner, by association with prehistoric henges and menhirs. I argue that, since its peak in the 1970s, the linking of environmentalism with prehistoric monuments in children's fiction has declined or gone underground as a result of being colonised by earth mysteries ideology, so that motifs of shamanism and the Green Man currently respond better to ecological concerns. The chapter closes with a celebration of the integration of a prehistoric monument with shamanism and the Green Man in Catherine Fisher's psychologically profound *Darkhenge* (2005).

1
Locating Paganism

Modern Paganism can be 'located' in several senses. Its beliefs and practices need outlining before its manifestations and functions in children's literature can be identified and scrutinised. To do this effectively, a kind of 'Pagan poetics' can be defined, by drawing on a range of theoretical perspectives and occupying a critical space. And, quite straightforwardly, a sense of place permeates fictional uses of Paganism. This chapter starts, then, by combining this sense of place with the Pagan cyclic view of time to define the Pagan chronotope, manifestations of which are analysed in a selection of children's fiction. Looking at the Pagan chronotope leads into discussion of tenets of Pagan belief: pantheism, animism and polytheism. Gender-conscious approaches are introduced by comparing the Pagan chronotope with Maria Nikolajeva's ideas about female and male chronotope (Nikolajeva 1996), and with Starhawk's rhetorical theory (Foss et al. 1999).

The environmentalist credentials of modern Paganism, and ecological tropes in selected children's novels, are then examined. Ronald Hutton's four languages of Paganism (Hutton 1999) are outlined and discussed, and a critical linguistic approach to issues of language, power and agency is advocated. I go on to explore relationships between magic and Paganism, and types and uses of magic in children's literature; enumerating uses of magic bridges into discussion of autonomous and developmental models of childhood (Hollindale 1997), children's spirituality, and reflexive narration. The chapter concludes with arguments favouring the foregrounding of Pagan elements in children's fiction for critical attention. The current chapter prepares for and anticipates the subsequent thematic chapters by introducing the critical perspectives to be drawn on, and by maintaining an emphasis on close analysis of primary texts.

* * *

'Chronotope' is the term used by Mikhail Bakhtin for 'the intrinsic connectedness of temporal and spatial relationships that are artistically expressed in literature [...] it expresses the inseparability of space and time [...] spatial and temporal indicators are fused into one carefully thought-out, concrete whole' (Bakhtin 1981: 84). The 'connectedness' of chronotope makes it more than what the traditional term 'setting' can cover; as Rosemary Ross Johnston explains, the concept of chronotope 'can help us to read beyond the mechanics of "setting", and to re-think depictions of narrative time-spaces in ideological terms, as subjective, changeable, and interwoven with the observer's positionality' (Johnston 2002: 137). I shall seek to define and explore Pagan chronotope, a holistic outlook on time and space found in the language of today's Paganism and in modern children's fiction, the latter exemplified here principally by *The Lammas Field* by Catherine Fisher (1999), *Spin of the Sunwheel* by Elizabeth Arnold (1999) and *The Grey Dancer* by Alison Fell (1981).

Especially characteristic of contemporary Paganism is celebrating the eight-spoke Wheel of the Year. Four of the eight spokes, the 'quarter days', are commonly given Celtic names: Imbolc (Candlemass, 1/2 February), Beltane (May Day), Lughnasadh (1/2 August) and Samhain (Hallowe'en). A comparatively early example in children's literature of the quarter days being named and observed is in *The Kelpie's Pearls* by Mollie Hunter (1964). Morag the wise-woman's grandmother 'used to light the great bonfires that were burned every year on the hill at Beltane in May and Hallowe'en in October' and

> four times a year she baked a cake that was called a quarter-cake for it was made each quarter-day at Candlemass, Beltane, Lammas and Hallowe'en. Then she would go out on to the hill-side and break the cake into pieces [petitioning predators to spare her farm animals]. (Hunter 1964: 41)

The quarter days are intersected by summer and winter solstices, and spring and autumn equinoxes. Undoubtedly, 'equinox celebrations [...] were added to the cycle of festivals in the modern period' (Harvey 1997: 9). Following Ronald Hutton (1996), Joanne Pearson asserts that

'The calendar is most likely an academic construction dating from the eighteenth and nineteenth centuries' but adds that 'nevertheless the Wheel of the Year is now of profound importance to Paganism' (Pearson, in Pearson (ed.) 2002: 5). Some of the importance invested in and arising from the Wheel of the Year can be seen in how its annual cycle has been conjoined with the daily cycle and the cycle of human life (see Crowley 1996: chapter 5): 'nature religion involves the re-ritualisation of the stages of human existence from birth, through growth and maturity, to death, which intersects with natural annual and cosmic cycles' (Pearson et al. 1998: 2).

The Wheel of the Year is the aspect of Paganism most frequently found in children's literature, as will be apparent in the chapters that follow. To give one more example for now, *The Roundabout Horse* by Rosemary Sutcliff (1986) is a pony story that revolves around the magic of Midsummer. Jenny's personal chronology coincides with a turning point of the Wheel of the Year:

> Jenny had been born on Midsummer's Eve, very late. And of all the times in the year, Midsummer's Eve is the time that belongs to the Fairies. It is a magic time to be born, and so she was not quite like other little girls. (Sutcliff 1986: 10)

On Jenny's sixth birthday, everyone is too busy to take her to the fair, so she steals away to ride on her favourite roundabout horse, which is not made of beech like the others, but elder, which 'is a Fairy tree, as everybody knows' (6). Being 'Midsummer's Eve and beginning to get dark and magic, they could talk to each other' (20). At dawn on Midsummer Day the wooden horse breaks free of the roundabout and becomes a real pony for Jenny.

So far, I have considered only temporal aspects of the Pagan chronotope. Looking at two quite recent examples of children's fiction will serve to show just how sophisticated literary realisations of the time and space of Pagan chronotope can be, and will then lead into discussion of the significance of place in the Pagan chronotope.

The very title of *The Lammas Field* by Catherine Fisher (1999) combines time and place: the August corn-harvest festival is held in a field of Stokesey Hall, of which Mick's father is the estates manager. Mick's ambitions to be an exceptional flautist are exploited by a mysterious woman who appears at night on a white horse with silver bells, proffering him a silver branch. She reappears at the Lammas folk festival as Rowan, intending to repeat legend and ballad by enticing Mick to the

Land of the Young – she tells him: 'it's what all artists and musicians really want [...] To step out of the world. [...] I've known so many of them down the ages. Thomas and Tam Lin, Taliesin, Conle, Oisin' (118). With Rowan's coming, time and space work together malevolently. 'In the time between day and night something had happened to the wood' (25): it fills with leering faces and ensnares Mick. Earth mysteries phenomena proliferate: earth-lights and crop circles are associated with Rowan and her faery folk, and the overgrown long barrow in the wood is 'a hollow hill' (78), according to Alex, a harpist and previous victim of Rowan.

Saving Mick from his Mephistophelean pact with Rowan falls to Alex and to Mick's friend Katie. Alex passes to Katie a disc necklace, made of iron for protection from faery, decorated thus: 'one side had a cross inscribed, with a circle round it. On the other, worn smooth by fingering, was a wheel, or maybe a sun, spokes of light radiating' (128). Both symbols, like the Wheel of the Year itself, embody the temporal solar cycle in a spatial image. A genuine Pagan symbol, the quartered-circle has a literary pedigree through Susan Cooper's *The Dark is Rising* (1973) back to John Masefield's *The Box of Delights* (1935). The sunwheel is also used contemporaneously with *The Lammas Field* in *Spin of the Sunwheel* (Arnold 1999, considered shortly).

To Katie, 'the Lammas field was [...] ancient and unchanging, a small world of its own [...] the old songs and dances and customs [...] the Ritual, regular as the harvest' (30). For this Ritual, a wooden henge is raised 'stark and ominous, rearing up in the twilight, a survivor of some lost prehistoric mystery, the protection and sorcery of the harvest' (Fisher 1999: 158). The sacrifice of the Corn King forms the climax of the novel, and occurs at Lammas under a full moon, so that lunar and solar cycles coincide. The place of Lammas in the Pagan chronotope is strongly anticipated and signalled throughout the narrative; for example, in Tom the groundsman's earthy wisdom, 'The year has cracks. Gaps. That's when there are ways between worlds. [...] Lammas is one. The harvest, the turning of the year' (123).

Rowan's imprisonment of Katie on the eve of the Ritual leads to a bifurcation of narrative time and space: the same event is seen from Katie's, then Alex's, point of view. Trapped in the cellars of Stokesey Hall, Katie scrabbles an opening and grabs a hand. From Alex's viewpoint, he ventures into the barrow which 'had been the entrance to all his dreams and ambitions, a place very like this one, miles away, but just the same, leading to the same darkness, the same surrender of his own existence' (153). The artefact and its effects are the same, the time and place different but merged. Alex finds Katie in a chamber of the barrow, and his point of view is privileged as she realises the cellars were a faery glamour. Ultimately, what releases Mick from Rowan's spell is the longed-for affirmation from his father of his musical gift and ambition. Rowan has more than a hint of the Triple Goddess about her, shimmering between youth and middle age, and playing the Hag in the Ritual. But, unfortunately, with her green dress and eyes, her cold beauty, her terrifying changes of mood, she is the familiar villainous Green Lady (compare Chapter 2).

The Triple Goddess is invoked all the more overtly in *Spin of the Sunwheel* by Elizabeth Arnold (1999). The complicated rivalries and infidelities of Romano-Celtic deities and legendary ruling families are resolved by reviving the Celtic river Triple Goddess Brigantia to address the ecological crisis of the current new millennium. Following an apparent accident at a canal lock, present-day boatee Gwen is accompanied by Brigid up the Thames and the Severn, through the past and towards the future. It is through this river journey, and through the symbol of the sunwheel, that the Pagan chronotope in *Spin of the Sunwheel* is realised.

Gwen has a sunwheel printed on her sweatshirt, and Brigid wears one around her neck, in which Gwen glimpses three-in-one faces of the Goddess, one of which is the legendary Guendoloen, who she is becoming. The sunwheel stands for the cycle of time and millennial renewal. Environmental neglect and degradation have made the sunwheel 'sluggish and hard to turn' (133). 'Slowly she cools, slowly she dies' (85; it is by no means unusual to personify the sun as female – see McCrickard 1990) and so she commands Brigid and Gwen's journey 'to restore the earth to balance. With Brigantia ruling, the sunwheel has its best chance of spinning eternally' (Arnold 1999: 135). Past, present and future are combined in Gwen/Guendoloen, and in the three aspects of the Goddess Brigantia: Habren is the past, Guendoloen the present and Brigid the future.

The description of Brigantia as 'the triple goddess of the rivers of life that the sunwheel turns' (161) shows how much significance the novel condenses into rivers: deity, life, the cycle of time. As far as chronotope is concerned, spatial movement along the rivers is also anachronic movement. Encountering working people from the past, Gwen realises that she is 'steering *Brigantia* [the name of the boat as well as the Triple Goddess] along waters I knew no longer existed' (61). What is more, the beginning and end of the journey are marked by important points in the Wheel of the Year. The odyssey starts at Samhain (Hallowe'en), when

'The river's mood was eerie. [...] I was not into pumpkins and witches, but somehow I felt wary, expectant' (8). And it ends – though the voyage could not have taken so long in 'real time' – at the Winter Solstice. As with *The Lammas Field*, solar and lunar calendars coincide climactically, when Nodens (Brigid's river-god father) is summoned at full moon, and Habren, Goddess of the River Severn, is resurrected at new moon, the fortnight between full and new moon being compressed. Place is as crucial as time, for the final destination at the Winter Solstice is Lydney Sands, where the Severn Bore tidal phenomenon is imbued with apocalyptic power. Highly original and challenging, *Spin of the Sunwheel* will be revisited later in this chapter as Arnold's novel raises the recurrent issues of ecology and of control.[1]

So, in these two texts, *Spin of the Sunwheel* and *The Lammas Field*, non-linear time – cyclic, backwards, different periods synchronously – depends upon space: place, movement, direction, bilocation. 'Bakhtin's concept of "space" [...] includes not just description of place as a geographical location, but the *perception* of place' (Johnston 2002: 140), and a sense of place is as defining of modern Paganism as the outlook on time represented by the Wheel of the Year. The word 'pagan' has been taken variously to mean 'country dweller', 'civilian' (as opposed to *miles Christi*, soldier of Christ) and 'follower of the religion of the locality' (Pearson 2002a: 16–19), with the last being 'by far the most popular among modern pagans', for 'modern pagans [...] perceive themselves to be creating links with the energy of the land at a local level, celebrating their rituals with reverence for the *genius loci*, the spirit of the place' (Pearson 2002a: 20, 19).

Underlying the importance of place are fundamental Pagan beliefs: pantheism, 'a view that divinity is inseparable from nature and that deity is immanent in nature', and animism – 'all things are imbued with vitality' (Adler 1986: 25). Animism is especially prominent in fictional depictions of shamanism (see Chapter 3), and erases the 'apparently precarious dividing line between animate and inanimate objects' (Armitt 1996: 50) which is one of Freud's categories of the uncanny: what may be *unheimlich* and defamiliarised for the reader is naturalised in the cosmology of the fiction. Pantheism and animism entail that all places are sacred... however, some are more sacred than others! As Prudence Jones puts it, 'Venerating nature [...] regularly extends to a strong sense of the spirit of the place, of the sanctity of particular locations' (Jones 1998: 78). This has been called ' "topophilia": the belief that certain locations are inherently powerful and exude a heightened sense of place' (Bowman 2000: 91). Some of these sites have human-made monuments such as hill-figures and standing stones, the topic of Chapter 4. Others 'are natural formations. Places where two elements meet are often considered particularly sacred' – mountains; seashore; springs; waterfalls; caves; and trees and groves are sacred (Crowley 1996: 107).

A birch tree is axial to *The Grey Dancer* by Alison Fell (1981): the eponymous Grey Dancer, the tallest tree in the wood, stands by a confluence in Laggan Burn (Loch Dee, Scotland). Both the tree and the stream are places that knot together different times and stories. The affinity Annie Latto feels with the Grey Dancer in 1953 is shared by Isobel, over a century earlier. In this earlier time, when Lal, Isobel's partner, speaks up against the laird's proposed clearances, Isobel finds herself arraigned as a witch, though she says in her defence: 'It is a healer I am. And it's the few skills I've learned I give to all who ask. [...] I'm no magician' (55). She perishes in a suspicious fire at Lal's cottage on their wedding night, but Lal preternaturally lives on, right into Annie Latto's present, waiting by Laggan Burn every Midsummer to be reunited with Isobel.

The Grey Dancer is where Isobel and Lal become engaged on May Day, and get married at Midsummer. The wedding is Pagan, with Isobel in 'a plain green gown' (58) taking the lead. As with Mollie Hunter's *The Kelpie's Pearls* (see above), Pagan ways are presented as old, and passed on through the female line: 'in the way she'd learnt from her grandmother [...] She took the lower branches of the big tree [...] and twisted them together to form a wreath' inside which she and Lal kiss (Fell 1981: 58). She calls on 'Bride, goddess of the old religion' to witness, and chants 'some ancient blessing, of wedding or of harvest' which describes Bride as 'The mother of birch trees [...] The mother of landslides [...] The mother of rainbows' (59). As will be evident by now, this intense concentration of sacred place and time, ritual and deity is typical of the Pagan chronotope.

A difficulty with the Pagan sense of locality as expressed in children's literature is how to avoid mere parochialism and attach broader significance. One answer, one that can strain credibility, it has to be said, is to explode a local event into one of global, epochal change, as happens at the climax of *Spin of the Sunwheel*.[2] A particular place can be made to stand for wider history, as does a part of Sussex in Rudyard Kipling's *Puck of Pook's Hill* (1906). I have argued elsewhere that Kipling is not straightforwardly an 'apologist for Empire' in *Puck of Pook's Hill*, but rather 'the edifices of British history and empire [...] are questioned and deconstructed by themselves and by a more inclusive and coherent mythology of the land and the spirit' (Bramwell 2002a: 27). *Puck of Pook's Hill* was Simon Schama's favourite story as a child, his own equivalent to Pook's Hill being the Thames: 'the idea of the Thames as a line of time as well as space' (Schama 1995: 3) resonates with the river-journey-through-time in *Spin of the Sunwheel*.

Another way of transcending localism is to connect localities which are physically distant from one another: 'nature religion currents frequently stress that genuine human existence should refer primarily to the local place, but with the explicit assumption that others around the world are doing the same with reference to their own places' (Beyer 1998: 19). In Susan Cooper's *The Dark is Rising* (1973), while Herne is firmly placed as the *genius loci* of Windsor and the surrounding area, connections are made to Jamaica through a mask (*The Dark is Rising* is analysed in more detail in Chapter 2).

Space in the Pagan chronotope is not only a matter of location, but also of direction and movement, as we have seen with the journey west and back through time in *Spin of the Sunwheel*. Similarly, in Catherine Fisher's *The Soul Thieves*, 'they travelled in time, as well as distance' (Fisher 1996: 98), only in this case the direction is north. Jane Yolen's *The Wild Hunt* describes north as 'the greatest of the compass points' and 'the polar hinge of the universe' (Yolen 1995: 28, 124), and it is well-known that a portal between worlds is opened at the North Pole in Philip Pullman's *Northern Lights* (1995). Northern settings, from which, more tellingly, journeys further north are made, are common in children's novels featuring shamanism (considered in Chapter 3), but northward orientation is not exclusive to Heathen (Anglo-Saxon and Norse) and shamanic traditions – Wicca is located and faces north too. Joanne Pearson (2002b: 144) reports the view that: 'Wicca is more popular in Northern European, Protestant countries, where people lack any focus for the divine feminine (i.e. the Goddess), rites of passage and a sense of ritual, factors that remain popular in the Catholicism of southern Europe and the Mediterranean (Crowley 1998: 171).'[3] Furthermore, in the Wiccan ritual circle, where 'cyclical time is celebrated above linear time' (Harvey 1997: 46), the focal and climactic direction is north. All this could be seen as amounting to a radical reorientation in spiritual geography, from other religions facing and making pilgrimages eastwards (from a European and North American perspective), to Paganism looking north.

I wish now to relate the Pagan chronotope to Maria Nikolajeva's concepts of female and male chronotopes (Nikolajeva 1996), and to prominent Wiccan Starhawk's feminist rhetoric (as analysed by Foss et al. 1999). This will lead into reflecting on the implications of Pagan polytheism and vexed questions of gender polarisation and essentialism.

Pagan chronotope combines, or confounds, Nikolajeva's female and male chronotopes, for Pagan time is cyclic, as in the female chronotope, but Pagan space is outdoors, as in the male chronotope. Nikolajeva distinguishes 'male space' which is 'open [...] outdoors' from female space which is 'closed and confined. The action mostly takes place indoors, at home' (Nikolajeva 1996: 125). Pagan focal places are out of doors: in our key examples from children's fiction, a field, a waterway, a tree. In the female chronotope, 'time is circular, follows the cycle of the moon, and consists of recurrent, regular events of death and resurrection, seasonal changes, and so on' (Nikolajeva 1996: 126). If the essentialism of this were not evident enough, Nikolajeva later goes further when describing *kairos* (sacred, cyclical, mythic time):

> The female body follows the lunar cycle, which is closely associated with the idea of death and rebirth, the waning and waxing of the moon. The cardinal function of the female body is reproduction. The female initiation myths involve repetition, rebirth, the eternal life cycle. [...] Connected with essential life mysteries such as menstruation and birth (both involving blood), female myths are more secret and sacred than male myths. (Nikolajeva 2002: 126)

Connecting lunar and female cycles is significant in Wicca, so perhaps it is surprising that followers of the Wiccan path do not appear to have resisted the Wheel of the Year for its solar rather than lunar basis. It is notable that some of the children's fiction we have been considering – *The Lammas Field* and *Spin of the Sunwheel* – makes moves to combine stages in the solar cycle with lunar phases at climactic moments. Furthermore, the solar Wheel need not be seen as a patriarchal colonising intrusion if it is taken into account that sun deities are often personified as female (see McCrickard 1990), as is the case in *Spin of the Sunwheel*. However, I would suggest that millenarianism (more appropriate to New Ageism, as its name indicates, than Paganism) and ecological apocalypticism are uneasy intrusions of the male chronotope's linear time into the Pagan chronotope.

Starhawk's rhetorical theory, expressed not least through her novel *The Fifth Sacred Thing* (Starhawk 1993), sets the world of the Goddess against the currently dominant patriarchal world order: 'the patriarchal world reifies hierarchy, power-over, self-hate, and estrangement, [whereas in] the world of the Goddess [...] immanence, connection, and community are central' (Foss et al. 1999: 187). Such egalitarian Goddess-centred values are upheld by intrapersonal 'power-from-within' and interpersonal 'power-with', as opposed to patriarchal 'power-over'. Mystery and ritual are pivotal: mystery 'involves resistance through the creation of new ways of seeing and being in the world, accepting uncertainty and even randomness, and deciding to engage and act in the world' and ritual can 'change the individual consciousness, which then changes the larger social structure' (Foss et al. 1999: 179, 180). Starhawk rejects essentialism and 'suggests that for feminism to be effective, individuals must recognize and embrace both female and male dimensions'; the Goddess is 'among other things, an energy field that contains both maleness and femaleness' (Foss et al. 1999: 171). Even so, Starhawk's feminist rhetoric, and the Pagan chronotope as I understand it, seem to be predicated on a binary opposition between feminine and masculine in which the feminine is valorised. This position is both reflected and questioned in the literature on Paganism, especially when polytheism is discussed.

Whether it is taken to refer to external, psychological or poetic reality, polytheism is a defining characteristic of Paganism. Margot Adler rejects the notion that polytheism 'is an inferior way of perceiving that disappeared as religions "evolved" toward the idea of one god' (Adler 1986: 26). Indeed, modern Paganism often upturns theories of social evolution and individual development, by privileging and attempting to recreate supposed prehistoric polytheism or Goddess matriarchy, and by valuing children's spirituality.

Plurality of deities entails diversity of belief. Vivianne Crowley asserts that 'most Pagans believe that for wholeness the Divine must contain images of both female and male' (Crowley 1996: 59). For Wiccans, this might be seen as resolving into duotheism, 'conceiving of deity as the Goddess of the Moon, Earth, and sea, and the God of the woods, the hunt, the animal realm' (Adler 1986: 35). There may be a slant towards female deity, as when Prudence Jones stresses that 'Pagan religions recognise the female face of divinity, called by modern Pagans the Goddess' (Jones 1995: 34). Moreover, 'Feminist Witches are often monotheists, worshipping the Goddess as the One' (Adler 1986: 35). Belief is so varied that Graham Harvey comments, 'there are apparently Pagan mono-, duo-, heno-, poly- and a-theists' (Harvey 1997: 168). The abundance of labels in effect reinforces a key argument of Harvey's book, that modern Paganism is about experience rather than systematic theology. Harvey contends that 'The worship of divinity, of whatever gender and number, is not the primary experience of Paganism. Celebration of Nature is more central' (Harvey 1997: 133).

Polytheism may be perceived as implying 'a world of multiplicity and diversity, a world that concentrates on processes rather than goals'

(Adler 1986: 38). At the same time as these values align with the Pagan chronotope, and with Starhawk's Goddess order, they can also provide a means of questioning imbalances in gender and power. Thus the next chapter, on the Green Man, resists patriarchal and monotheistic tendencies in his portrayal, favouring balance and narratives that interrogate goal-oriented quests. Chapter 3 shows how assertions about shamanism being a male preserve, and about modern Heathenism being patriarchal and intolerant, are redressed by more inclusive representations in children's fiction. And in the final chapter I contrast 'power-over' attempts to manipulate earth energies with 'power-with' experience of ancient sites.

Monotheistic tendencies, be they towards a God (such as the Green Man) or a Goddess (such as the Triple Goddess in *Spin of the Sunwheel*) – especially when yoked to ecological apocalypticism – can all too often involve submission and loss of agency for child characters. A critical stance on issues of ecology, power and language is further developed next.

* * *

As nature religion, Paganism would appear to be self-evidently environmentalist, but the extent and depth of its 'greenness' is contested. The premise of Graham Harvey's *Listening People, Speaking Earth* is declared in the opening sentence: 'Paganism is a religion at home on Earth, an ecological spirituality' (Harvey 1997: vii). Harvey later adds that Paganism 'is fundamentally "Green" in its philosophy and practice, taking seriously the understanding that "everything that lives is holy"' (126). Likewise Vivianne Crowley asserts that 'Paganism is a green religion. It encourages us to live in love and kinship with the natural world' (Crowley 1996: 18).

Yet the specific connection between modern Paganism and environmentalism has not always been so clear. Revealingly, Margot Adler locates a rise of consciousness and campaigning in the early 1980s: 'there is a lot more political activism among Pagans and a lot more concern with ecology issues than there was when *Drawing Down the Moon* was first published [in 1979]' (Adler 1986: 412). The timing could result from the fuel crises of the 1970s and a dawning awareness of climate change, though Adler also sees a radicalising reaction against the rise of the Christian right as significant. Adler perceives 'a deep split between Pagans whose commitment to ecological principles was strong and practical, and those whose commitment was limited to a religious vision' (Adler 1986:

400), in which she evidently aligns strongly with the former. Perhaps it need not be seen as a split, when direct action is inspired by religious vision and 'the eco-magic of Pagan ritual [that] can be activated towards environmental, social and spiritual change' (Hardman, in Harvey and Hardman (ed.) 1995: xv) can be performed *in situ*.

Still, modern Pagans' 'response to nature' can be criticised for being 'often confused, revealing both intimacy and distance as they shape nature with the Wheel of the Year' (Pearson, in Pearson (ed.) 2002: 9). Diane Purkiss is all the more trenchant:

> rituals celebrating the wheel of the year are invariably tied to images of preindustrial nature. [...] The rhythms of urban life are almost never incorporated into invocations, rituals or spells; what is celebrated is a rural calendar which does not exist in the countryside either, and never really did. This idealised rural cycle floats free of any need to worry about drought, early frost or disease. (Purkiss 1996: 48)

One can discern a clear affinity between contemporary Paganism and modern children's literature by comparing this Pagan fantasy of nature with Stephen Thomson's (1998) argument that the canonisation of texts such as *The Stone Book* (Garner 1976) indicates a flight to the supposedly timeless countryside, supported by a construction of the child as 'primitive' and 'natural'. Innumerable children's books present the countryside as other, mediated to implied (sub)urban readers through protagonists who move from their home cities to old country houses, haunted by ghosts which are convenient devices for unveiling heritage. The range and distinctiveness of rural readers' responses has hardly been researched, apart from anecdotes such as 'John, a serious little boy of about seven or eight' reacting to *The Tale of Peter Rabbit* thus: 'Never mind poor old Peter Rabbit. It's Mr McGregor I feel sorry for – trying to grow his vegetables with a lot of 'ungry rabbits all ovver t'place' (Phinn 1998: 51, 52).

The fantasy of the countryside shared by modern Paganism and children's literature could be potently retrogressive and reactionary, perhaps the greatest impediment to the innovative role I claim for children's fiction in redefining controverted aspects of Paganism. For, to a large extent, Pagan motifs in contemporary children's literature are confined to rustic settings, whereas ecology in the city is devoid of spirituality, as in Judy Allen's *Awaiting Developments* (1988) and City Farm Stories (1990–1991) – all the more telling when Paganism and ecology are conjoined in the rural settings in Allen's earlier novels (discussed

later in Chapter 4). A singular exception to the Pagan country/despir-
itualised town divide is Bel Mooney and Helen Cann's *The Green Man*
(Mooney 1997a), in which the Green Man is instrumental in the community getting together to green a grey city environment. Mooney and
Cann's picture book is notable for making the urban pastoral, and for
not succumbing to the impulses of more apocalyptic narratives to globalise the local and to gothicise the city (this text is analysed further
in Chapter 2).

None of the four ecological literary tropes identified by Greg Garrard
(2004) are unproblematic as vehicles of Paganism. One, the 'Georgic
model of dwelling', might appear the most appealing, but again nature/
culture dualism intervenes, so that ' "We" apparently cannot dwell in
working harmony with nature, but perhaps other cultures are able to do
so' (Garrard 2004: 120). Ecological integrity is wishfully projected onto
'primitive' people such as shamans. The other three ecological literary
tropes – Pastoral, Wilderness, Apocalypse – are, as Garrard observes,
'heavily indebted to the Euro-American Judaeo-Christian narrative of
a fallen, exiled humanity seeking redemption, but fearing apocalyptic
judgement' (Garrard 2004: 15). The apocalyptic mode is most worrying since it can do violence to the Pagan chronotope and rob child
characters of agency and identity, as we shall see by returning to the
example of *Spin of the Sunwheel* (Arnold 1999) shortly. Chronotopes
'may be interwoven with, replace or oppose one another, contradict one
another or find themselves in ever more complex interrelationships'
(Bakhtin 1981: 252), and so the Pagan chronotope and the apocalyptic
chronotope clash. Perhaps it is inevitable that the cyclic, rural Pagan
chronotope will clash with something – if not necessarily with apocalypticism – in narrative or in its reception: with the linear imperatives
of plot and character development, or with readers estranged from the
Pagan chronotope's fantasy of nature.

Spin of the Sunwheel is a jeremiad of ecological crisis, given voice
throughout by Brigid. Gender, human and divine, is polarised: 'Men have
become greedy and infertile. Women want everything but can't cope'
(Arnold 1999: 58); the remedy to 'the destructive forces of man' (129),
and the detachment of a patriarchal God, is Goddess hegemony – 'in the
new millennium Brigantia will be made all powerful' (133). A Malthusian
approach to population is given mystical sanction:

> Populations are controlled by nature. Too many people and births
> must be reduced, a suitable culture usually evolves. If it doesn't,
> then sooner or later a catastrophe occurs leaving too few homes for

Otherworld souls. Then the birth rate rises again to compensate. That's how the wheel of life turns. It's always seeking equilibrium. It never quite gets there, so onwards it spins. (Arnold 1999: 93)

The solution put forward to the supposed problem of overpopulation is not redistribution of wealth and equal and sparing use of resources, but culling. This is achieved at the apocalyptic climax through the divine retribution of a deluge:

Enough will survive to make life good. Those that die will not give their lives in vain. It is their sacrifice that gives us hope for the new millennium. [...] The people must learn the hard way how to subject themselves to the needs of Mother Earth who provides for them. [...] A few must die for the good of all. (Arnold 1999: 157)

This pronouncement of Brigid's is all the more objectionable in the wake of the death and misery caused by the flooding of the Severn and other rivers in Britain in the summer of 2007. Horrendous culling presented as necessary sacrifice throws out all the previous careful, if unpersuasive, equivocations about the role of sacrifice in ancient Paganism, such as: 'Sometimes Nodens took a drowning soul. He *never* asked, but sometimes he accepted the gifts that were offered. He never wasted a soul. It was always rested in the Otherworld so it could be used later for a greater purpose' (63). In Brigid's assertion that 'Sometimes life demands the odd sacrifice, steals the odd body, but the gods don't ask for deliberate death' (132), the repeated 'odd' is chillingly casual.

Brigid's voice dominates the narrative, though Gwen rails against her and is consistently aware that she is being controlled: 'The more I looked for choice the less I found' (141). There is a rare, child-centred moment when Nodens says, 'it's often the innocent voice of a child that drops the pebble that starts the ripple that builds into a flood of good intent' (138), though the sentiment, expressed in rhythmic right-branching house-that-Jack-built syntax, might cloy. It is worse than cloying if one compares the metaphorical 'flood of good intent' with the later, literal flood that brings death. Gwen finally relinquishes control when Brigid confers the sunwheel on her and they are apotheosised into aspects of the Triple Goddess: 'In that moment I understood at last why choice was not mine. I took their hands and let Guendoloen rise for ever' (160). Becoming a Goddess could be seen as the ultimate empowerment, but it is simultaneously the annihilation of 'Gwen, a boatie of no importance' (164). Brigid's attitude to death, that 'Dying is just a journey. You go to the Otherworld, you come back. What is there to fear?' (154), is as alarmingly nonchalant as that notorious line from *Peter Pan*, 'to die would be an awfully big adventure.'

The Grey Dancer (Fell 1981) is tinged with the apocalyptic, though more subtly than *Spin of the Sunwheel* and without overtly making local events take on global significance. The hydroelectric scheme, which gives Annie Latto's father work, is not presented as a bad thing for the environment in itself; rather, human meanness and negligence are the threat, as Annie's father warns, 'It's no safe, ye ken. The machines arenae maintained right. They willnae employ enough men' (30). The weather breaking 'with a vengeance' (76) is presented as the action of the Goddess Bride, mother of landslides and rainbows. When a landslide destroys the poorly constructed hydro tunnel, Lal accepts the flooding fatalistically, as a mechanism finally to reunite him with Isobel. As men in Annie's time cannot control the element of water, so their malicious use of the element of fire when they set Isobel's cottage ablaze in the time of the Clearances is redressed by Isobel's last words: 'mind that Bride is the mother of fire. Of the fire that transforms' (62). The narrative implies by parallelism that the Clearances and the hydro-electric scheme are both motivated by men's selfishness and hubris.

As an eleven-year-old child, Annie's play unconsciously projects her concerns and reproduces the adult world in microcosm, when she spends an hour 'perfecting the earthworks on her dam in the burn' (25). She grows in assertiveness, though she very much depends on Lal for her independence. Defying her cruel and sarcastic teacher, she gains confidence by thinking of Lal: 'She took a breath and concentrated on getting a picture of Lal in her head, for she needed an extra dose of courage for this deed' (42). Lal, shapechanged into a golden eagle, saves Annie from the attentions of the ghillie's son, and defends her when she hits back at her violent teacher. Contentiously, Lal predicates Annie's positively valued qualities on race: 'you have it in you to stand firm and brave. And I see in your eyes the wildness – and the longing too, of the old Gaels' (38).

According to Peter Barry, 'ecocritics reject the notion [...] that everything is socially and/or linguistically constructed [...] For the ecocritic, nature really exists' (Barry 2002: 252), though this 'should not be taken as implying that ecocritics hold a naive "pre-theoretical" notion of nature' (252), as they do acknowledge that 'social inequality [can be] "naturalised"' (253) and that 'the meaning of the word "nature" is a key "site of struggle"' (254). Greg Garrard goes further, aiming 'to balance a constructionist perspective with the privileged claims to literal truth made by ecology' (Garrard 2004: 10). Indeed, I would say that a critical linguistic approach is very necessary, to interrogate the 'privileged claims' made by ecological rhetoric in children's fiction, as the foregoing analysed examples have shown.

Critical linguistics (see Fairclough 2001, Stephens 1992, Hollindale 1988) regards language as a socially situated generator and vehicle of ideology and power relationships, and seeks to expose and question the workings of these. It is a mode of analysis that pervades this volume, which is particularly concerned with how the language of children's literature with Pagan themes controls or liberates child characters and readers, often with regards to gender roles, and in some cases in the dynamics between human and divine beings. Both green politics and politically committed Paganism, such as Starhawk's, would place importance not just on individual agency but also on interpersonal and collective agency (Goodin 1992, Foss et al. 1999).

Ronald Hutton (1999) has identified four languages of Paganism. The first is the 'savage', Paganism 'as a religion of gloom and gore' (11). At the service of imperialism and evangelism, this language says that 'pagans are people who bow down to idols, offer up blood sacrifices, and represent the religious aspect of human savagery and ignorance' (5). Hutton's second language is the 'classical':

> a religion which had been associated with magnificent art, literature and philosophy, and was deficient to Christianity only in its ethics and in its lesser component of divine revelation. This avoided any direct confrontation with the first, in that it referred to a different culture; not to modern or prehistoric tribal societies, nor to the exotic civilisations of the East, but to the familiar, beloved and respected world of ancient Greece and Rome. (Hutton 1999: 11)

While the first two languages 'were traditional and conservative' the remaining two 'posed a self-conscious challenge to prevailing religious and cultural norms' (17). The third language, then, depends 'on the notion that there had once existed a single great world spiritual system, based upon divine revelation' (17–18). Often this prehistoric world system is inflected as a benevolent matriarchy, though Diane Purkiss cautions:

> The myth of a lost matriarchy is disabling rather than enabling for women. To relegate female power in politics or religion to a lost past,

to associate it with the absence of civilisation, technology and modernity, is to write women out of the picture. (Purkiss 1996: 42)

Hutton's fourth language of Paganism is classical, but unconstrained: 'Like the second language, it lauded the culture of classical Greece and Rome, but it demolished all constraints placed upon admiration of their religions' (Hutton 1999: 18).

Children's authors discussed by Hutton include R. M. Ballantyne, Kenneth Grahame, Rudyard Kipling and Rosemary Sutcliff. But Hutton's claim that 'It was the fourth [language – classical unconstrained], without mixture, which was to become the language of late twentieth century paganism' (31), whether or not it is true of Pagan practice, does not hold for late twentieth-century – and early twenty-first- century – children's literature. Certainly there has recently been a classical revival in children's fiction – such as Adèle Geras's *Troy* (2000) and *Ithaka* (2005), Tobias Druitt's Corydon series (2005 onwards) and Ann Halam's *Snakehead* (2007) – but classical settings do not necessarily entail a classical language of Paganism. For example, the Amazons' worship of the Great Earth Mother Maa in Theresa Tomlinson's *The Moon Riders* (2002) may be interpreted as partaking of the pre-classical universalism of Hutton's third language. The persistence of southern classical gods in the northern imagination is commented on by Charles Butler's description of statues in the grounds of Lychfont in the novel *Death of a Ghost*: 'Zeus and the Olympians were mildewed and rather sombre [...] Yet still they hung on in the alien northern air' (Butler 2006a: 23).

In the following case studies of children's books involving the Green Man, northern shamanism and earth mysteries, the most common language of Paganism I find is not classical but one that exalts native spirituality, though 'native' need not entail 'primitive'. This might involve 'portraits of tribal religion [...] being projected backwards on to the ancient European past' (Hutton 1999: 7) as in Hutton's first language, though viewed much more sympathetically than in earlier literary portrayals. Or it might involve eclectic appropriation of spiritual techniques from aboriginal cultures. As Joanne Pearson observes, often in modern Paganism 'a past golden age or the spiritual practices of indigenous peoples are held up as being more ecologically sound or close to nature' (Pearson, in Pearson (ed.) 2002: 9) – two alternatives that can be seen as corresponding, respectively, to Hutton's third language, and to a positive re-evaluation of his first 'savage' language. Yearning for 'a past golden age' should be tempered with Margot Adler's discovery that her respondents looked to the future as much as the past, and that 'while they may take inspiration from the past, they do not want to return to it' (Adler 1986: 392). However, the Pagan in children's literature predominantly looks backwards, through a process which Mikhail Bakhtin (1981) calls historical inversion, locating the ideal not in the future but the past. The Pagan chronotope bears a number of resemblances to Bakhtin's description of the folkloric chronotope as cyclic and ritualised, unified in space and time, and close to nature (Bakhtin 1981). Bakhtin equates the folkloric chronotope with the coming of agriculture – that is, the neolithic era, so we may discern an underlying reason why neolithic monuments in children's fiction act as foci of Pagan perceptions (see Chapter 4).

Modern Paganism being 'tribal' rather than 'credal' (Adler 1986: x) has possible repercussions which are problematic and troubling. It cuts both ways: spiritual practices being stolen from indigenous cultures, decontextualised and watered down, by contrast with racial exclusivity sometimes being advocated for northern traditions (Anglo-Saxon and Norse Paganism, also known as Heathenism). Furthermore, as forbidden – often erotic – fantasies have been located in the orient (see Said 1978, Kabbani 1986), savage aggression is retrojected into the northern Heathen past. By analogy with Orientalism and Occidentalism, perhaps a shorthand for literary conventions and fantasies of the north could be the term Borealism. In Chapter 3, I argue that representations of Heathenism in contemporary children's fiction make positive interventions in fraught areas of Borealism by interrogating and overturning assumptions of racial or violent bases for northern traditions.

Greg Garrard points out that the crucial fallacy in the concept of the primitive is that 'it transforms a geographical differentiation into an historical and evolutionary one, so that Indians and aborigines can be seen as being *behind* Europeans in an inevitable progression from a natural to a civilised state' (Garrard 2004: 125). Therefore, if so-called primitivism is seen as coexisting equally with 'civilisation' rather than being an earlier evolutionary stage, it need not imply denial of civilisation, or regression to the past. The value Paganism attaches to native traditions and to children's spirituality (the latter will be explored shortly) does not entail primitivism or infantilism, but does invert developmental models of human societies and of childhood. Native traditions are then seen as situated in sophisticated societies with complex religious practices, including European native traditions, which some scholars reclaim as being neither primitive nor wholly in the past. Prudence Jones maintains that 'in considering the European native tradition we are not simply fleeing to a primitive dreamtime of

simple nature-worship [...] but owning our inheritance of vast civilis-
ing influences' (Jones 1998: 86). Similarly, Simon Schama in *Landscape
and Memory* sees nature and civilisation not as mutually exclusive but
as inextricably and felicitously intertwined through history right into
the present. Schama argues that:

> our entire landscape tradition is the product of shared culture, [...]
> a tradition built from a rich deposit of myths, memories, and obses-
> sions. The cults which we are told to seek in other native cultures [...]
> are in fact alive and well and all about us if we only know where to
> look for them. (Schama 1995: 14)

Inflections of nativism, languages of Paganism, and uses of ecological
rhetoric will require and repay critical scrutiny in the case studies of
Pagan themes in children's fiction in the following chapters.

* * *

Relationships between magic and Paganism, and types and uses of
magic in children's literature, are analysed next. Enumerating uses of
magic leads into discussion of models of childhood and children's spirituality, and also reflexive narration and response to Pagan elements in
children's fiction.

Pagan animistic and pantheistic beliefs that everything is alive
and sacred entail that everyday life is in a sense ' "magical": significant, imbued with value, sacred or paradoxically suffused with tran-
scendence' (Harvey 1997: 87). However, this by no means implies that
using magical techniques is a necessary part of modern Paganism: as
Vivianne Crowley (1996: 119) states, 'Not all Pagans practise magic and
for many this holds no appeal.' As with so much Pagan belief and practice, views on magic are very diverse, so that 'Some groups may extol
the efficacy of magic, deeming it to be a requisite part of Paganism,
while others eschew magic and follow instead a path of different inclination' (Pearson, in Pearson (ed.) 2002: 3).

Likewise, what magic is for is understood variously. In a way that
chimes with Starhawk's Goddess system of power-with through ritual
and mystery (see above), Crowley emphasises group bonding and shared
purpose: 'Magic as practised by Pagans involves uniting the minds of
a group to a common purpose and visualizing that coming about by
an act of focused will' (Crowley 1996: 119). Of the 'two facets of magic:
attempts to change things or situations and attempts to change the

practitioner' that Graham Harvey (1997: 88) identifies, he sees the latter as predominant: 'Western magic [...] is primarily a means of personal growth and self-expression' (Harvey 1997: 89). To an extent this accords with Margot Adler's definition of magic as a range of mental and emotional techniques used 'to effect changes in consciousness' (Adler 1986: 8), though the consciousness changed need not be only individual, but can be of a group and, further, can permeate wider society, which brings us back to the social and political activism possibly implied by Crowley and certainly openly advocated by Starhawk.

In children's fiction, three types of representation of magic are common, it seems to me. Firstly, there is ceremonial magic, depicted as practised by power-hungry individuals, with a christianised Satanic tinge which of course has nothing to do with Paganism, as texts frequently make clear by counterpointing selfish ceremonial magic with vraisemblant folk belief. Examples include Richard Carpenter et al. (1990) *The Complete Adventures of Robin of Sherwood*, Michelle Paver (2006) *Soul Eater* and, earlier, John Masefield (1935) *The Box of Delights* (see, respectively, Chapters 2 and 3 of this volume, and Bramwell 2002b). Secondly, some children's fantasy fiction opposes Old and High magic, the former presented as primitive, amoral and matriarchal, the latter as civilised, morally dualistic and patriarchal. This is the scheme of Susan Cooper's (1974) *Greenwitch* (see Chapter 2 below), and of Ursula le Guin's *Earthsea* trilogy, though in subsequent instalments of the series le Guin radically redresses her earlier assumptions (see Hunt and Lenz 2001: chapter 2).

The third type of representation of magic is the magic of wise women and cunning men, independent-minded people living on the edge of communities which need but also fear and persecute them. This magic is largely a matter of superior knowledge of natural remedies. Although Ronald Hutton argues that much of modern Paganism is a recent invention, he concedes that the activities of cunning people and charmers have 'not altered in essentials from early modern times' (Hutton 1999: 84), though they take different guises in the present day: 'demand, and supply, still exists, but the suppliers are no longer likely to be called charmers, but be identified with the one of the techniques within the burgeoning fields of natural healing and therapy' (110). In children's fiction, the tendency is for cunning people either to appear in historical novels, or to be in the living memory of an older generation in contemporary stories. *Carrie's War* (Bawden 1973) bridges the two: Carrie as an evacuated child meets the Welsh wise woman Hepzibah Green within living memory during the Second World War, and as an adult meets her again in the present of the story. Hepzibah is an early example in children's fiction of witch as wise woman, a herbal healer with a piercing gaze and 'spell-binding voice'. It is explained that her methods are religion, not magic, rooted in sacred landscape of the once world-wide old religion.

Wise women in children's historical fiction, such as Monica Furlong's *Wise Child* (1987) and *A Year and a Day* (1990), and Theresa Tomlinson's *Forestwife* trilogy (Tomlinson 1993, 1998, 2000), maintain a female line through adoption of adolescent young women as apprentices. Herblore and other knowledge (rather technological in the case of Juniper in *Wise Child*) enables them to act as healers and midwives, and to make interventions in the cause of social justice. They have a syncretic and tolerant attitude towards Christianity which is not always returned; if their knowledge and actions are misunderstood and mistrusted, they face persecution. These wise women live at the edges of their societies, mirroring both adolescent liminality for the young adult audience, and the perception of some modern Pagans that theirs is 'the forgotten or suppressed religion of the marginal [...] such marginalisation from the dominant power structures is interpreted precisely as a warrant of greater authenticity' (Beyer 1998: 18–19). But, as Diane Purkiss (1996) argues, the myth of the marginalised and persecuted witch is hardly empowering. And indeed it is noticeable that Furlong's and Tomlinson's wise women are very like 'the midwife-herbalist-healer-witch [who] seems a spectacular collage of everything which feminist historians and others see as the opposite of medieval patriarchy' (Purkiss 1996: 19), and who can also, Purkiss observes, resemble 'the fantasy superwoman heroine of the 1980s and 90s' (20), a professional and domestic goddess with an idyllic country retreat.

Two examples of children's novels with contemporary settings concerned with, respectively, wise women and a cunning man are *Summer Witches* by Theresa Tomlinson (1989) and *Yaxley's Cat* by Robert Westall (1991). In *Summer Witches*, Sarah's friendship with elderly Miss Lily Morgan causes her to revise her assumptions about witches, who are shown to be wise women, healers steeped in herblore; magic is in the rhythm of the seasons and in healing acts. Miss Lily is deaf so that, as with Sherryl Jordan's *The Raging Quiet* (2000), a parallel is drawn between countering prejudice against deafness and against witchcraft. Sarah and a friend turn an old air-raid shelter into a witches' den, with herbs, a witch's board and a crystal ball, which 'could make you see the whole world as a better, magical place' (Tomlinson 1989: 87). Miss Lily returns to the shelter where she and her sister Rose used to play, but which she has guiltily avoided since her mother was killed in an air-raid. This prompts Rose to comment to the girls, 'Well, you two witches have really done a bit of healing, a bit of magic' (90). It is ironic that the publishers deemed it necessary to retitle *Summer Witches* as *The Secret Place* on paperback release (in 1990), when the book is a plea for tolerance and understanding of wisecraft.

John Stephens (2003) sees *Summer Witches* and *Wise Child* as examples of the wise-woman schema displacing crone and sorceress schemata. While he praises Diane Purkiss's *The Witch in History* (1996), he seems not to take into account her critique that there is a side to the wise woman figuration that can be a limiting, essentialist idealisation, especially when he lists oppositions including: 'she [...] privileges the other over the self, [...] emotion over reason, intuition over knowledge, [...] nature over culture' (Stephens 2003: 197). Representations of cunning men are altogether rarer than those of wise women in children's fiction. Though the cunning man in *Yaxley's Cat* (Westall 1991) has much in common with fictional wise women, he is less idealised, more ambiguous. Rose flexes her independence by taking her son and daughter to a rented cottage in the Norfolk countryside, the previous owner of which disappeared mysteriously seven years earlier. Sepp Yaxley had been an autodidact and cunning man. In a hand-made book, he kept account of wart charms, herbal remedies, finding lost items, putting on and taking off crop blights, curing women of unwanted pregnancies. It turns out that the villagers killed him because of an unsuccessful treatment. Sepp Yaxley's fate underlines the perilousness of the cunning person's role, the contingency of the community's regard. Taking payment in cash rather than kind for some questionable services, Yaxley is a more morally compromised figure than the wise women discussed above.

In the current volume I shall continue to apply the categorisation of uses of magic I have employed before (Bramwell 2005b: 144, repeated below with some alterations). By contrast with Nikolajeva's formalist Magic Code (Nikolajeva 1988), it constitutes a functional paradigm, concerned with meaning more than structure, a pragmatic approach for which I claim no particular rigour or originality. It is a commonplace, for example, to say that magic in fantasy is associated with confrontations between good and evil, though perhaps complications of morality in fantasy fiction with adolescent protagonists and readers are less often emphasised (Use of Magic 5).

Uses of Magic in Children's Fiction

1. Maturation: children's fiction uses magic as a metaphor for personal development; the fictional protagonist's maturation offers a model for the reader's own growth. The magical transitional object becomes dispensable when a maturing character takes ownership of her/his abilities and realises that a prop is no longer needed.

2. Imagination: magic is also a metaphor for the child's imagination and capacity to tell stories. While these abilities are defined and honoured as being characteristic of childhood, they are often presented as being important to preserve and adapt into adulthood, not least because authors of children's fiction are themselves imaginative, story-telling adults (which links to self-conscious narration, see 4. below).

3. MacGuffin: magic may serve as a plot device, to get into and out of scrapes! But since magic is never *essential* to driving the plot, its presence upholds a magical view of reality (see 6. below). The ambiguities of prophecy and divination thicken the plot, but they also disrupt its linearity, so they are an aspect of:

4. Metafiction. Authors of magical fiction may foreground definitions and functions of magic, and 'spell out' analogies between magic and narration, both of which can play tricks with words and alter perception. Fiction involving magic lends itself to self-conscious narration, alerting the reader to the artifice of fiction and alternate ways of telling.

5. Morality: good, evil and false magic are differentiated, though in a more blurred and complex way in writing for older readers. Good magic tends to be portrayed as communal, evil as solitary and divisive. Exposing false magic – trickery – lends credibility to 'true' magic.

6. World-view: magical thinking need not be outgrown, because magic can be used in fiction as a vehicle for an outlook on the world, including politics and spirituality. Magic is defined in terms of this world-view – often magic is used to confound arbitrary distinctions between natural and supernatural, and to express a sense of wonder in nature.

While the presence of magic is not in itself adequate for elusive and unfruitful generic definitions of fantasy, the uses of magic in children's fiction do correlate with characteristics of the fantastic which Lucie Armitt (1996) identifies, including: hermeneutic hesitation (after Todorov 1970), border-crossing, metamorphosis and defamiliarisation. Another parallel that can be drawn between the fantastic and magic is their potential for subversion: Armitt declares that 'we can look at the fantastic as a form of writing which is about opening up subversive spaces within the mainstream rather than ghettoizing fantasy by encasing it within genres' (Armitt 1996: 3), and John Stephens maintains that:

Not just for characters within fictions, but for authors and audiences as well, it is possible that any kind of magic will be problematic because of what it might symbolize: the subversion of religion, rationality, patriarchy, sanity, and science. (Stephens 2003: 200)

For the remainder of this chapter, I shall use a selection of the uses of magic enumerated above as the basis of wider discussion. The first and second uses lead into exploration of models of childhood, children's spirituality and the transitional object. From the fourth use of magic arise some examples of texts which define magic in their own terms and use reflexive narratological techniques. Following on from the sixth use of magic, this chapter closes with arguments in favour of foregrounding Pagan elements in children's fiction for critical attention.

The first and second uses of magic correspond to two models of childhood: respectively, 'childhood as essentially preparatory and developmental, a long and gradual rehearsal for maturity' and 'childhood as an autonomous part of life [...] enabling the child to be a child' (Hollindale 1997: 13). Philip Pullman's *His Dark Materials* trilogy unites these poles – Lyra is a child who becomes an adolescent, but not too quickly, and her growth involves loss, as her protean daemon stabilises. Daemons can be seen in Jungian terms, as if 'each person's *anima* or *animus* were an embodied presence' (Lenz, in Hunt and Lenz 2001: 139), but the fluidity of children's daemons in Lyra's world upholds an autonomous model of childhood and so questions the developmentalism that might otherwise underlie Jungian readings of children's literature.

Carl Jung also has a prominent but questionable status in modern Paganism. It would be a challenge to find a book about Paganism which does not mention Jung within the first few pages; Joanne Pearson observes 'the use of terminology borrowed from Jungian psychology in popular books on Wicca' (Pearson, in Pearson (ed.) 2002: 6). But in practice not all Pagans feel the need for quasi-scientific validation from Jungian psychology:

the 'sitting by the fire' type of Pagans generally devote less energy to contemplating themselves and their personal growth than Pagans on more initiatory paths. [...] 'fireside' Pagans primarily focus on celebrating Nature with little reference to Jungian archetypes or the individual's 'true self.' (Harvey 2000: 159)

The flawed arguments of Richard Rudgley's *Pagan Resurrection* (2006) show how pernicious invocations of Jung can be. Rudgley's very first sentence asserts that 'The major cultural figure who must be placed at the very epicentre of the pagan revival is Jung,' who reportedly identified 'the northern god Odin [...] as the most important archetype of the Germanic mind' (Rudgley 2006: 3). Here and throughout, Rudgley conflates Heathenism with Paganism, when Heathenism (the Northern Tradition, including Odinism) is just one of many Pagan paths. Rudgley does succeed in raising issues about the problematic racial basis of some strains of Heathenism, though he talks down any direct Heathen influence on Nazism, and a lot of what he discusses for the 'first Odinic experiment' in Germany is more to do with the esoteric, Theosophy and the like, than with Heathenism. All sorts of frenzy, irrationality and – sensationalistically – serial and mass murder are attributed to the Odin archetype, when they could just as well be associated with gods from other pantheons, such as Dionysus – if they have to be given a theistic or archetypal basis at all.

Rudgley advocates a positive, alternative Heathenism consisting of shamanism, rune divination and runic exercises, which relate to northern tradition but have parallels with Native American shamanism, the I Ching and yoga. Such multicultural syncretism addresses the racial exclusivity of some Heathenism, but could also be seen as an eclectic New Ageish mishmash. Only at the very end of the book does Rudgley at last concede the crucial counter-argument to the Odin archetype which has been obvious but unmentioned all along: 'Odin is but one element in the pagan [i.e. Heathen] system; it is only if the power of this god is seen as part of the pantheon that the holistic nature of paganism [i.e. Heathenism] can be truly understood' (281).

Jungian psychology is combined with structuralism by Maria Nikolajeva (2000, 2002) in a three-stage model of children's fiction and child development, 'from texts involving nonlinear time, typical of archaic or mythical thought, toward linearity, typical of contemporary mainstream literature' (Nikolajeva 2000: 1), the intermediate second stage being the time-out of carnival. Nikolajeva calls the first stage variously Arcadian, prelapsarian, utopian and idyllic, and the third stage postlapsarian or collapse, and defines the time of the former as *kairos*, cyclical and iterative, and the time of the latter as *chronos*, linear and singular. Her connecting of *kairos* with archaic Paganism and *chronos* with Christianity needs qualification, I would say: while Christ's once-and-for-all sacrifice is singular, and the anticipation of his second coming is linear, the eucharist is iterative and the liturgical calendar is cyclic.

Nikolajeva subsumes autonomy under developmentalism by in effect making autonomy the initial developmental stage, and she resorts to a questionable elision of ontogeny and phylogeny: 'small children can be compared, in their apprehension of time, to archaic man, while older children and adults have a "modern" view of time' and 'the Arcadian time of individual childhood is similar to the mythical time of the childhood of humankind' (Nikolajeva 2000: 6, 10). Furthermore, an unfortunate implication of Nikolajeva's association of the Arcadian with the sacred is then that the sacred is somehow infantile and lost to adults and to modernity. Arcadian fiction carries the seeds of its own destruction, because adults' 'nostalgic idealization of childhood's innocent bliss' coexists with their 'almost compulsory need to socialize the child' (Nikolajeva 2002: 118), a developmental imperative which can be seen in Rosemary Ross Johnston's characterisation (in the same volume) of 'the chronotope of childhood in narrative' as 'the creation of a present that has a forward thrust' (Johnston 2002: 146), 'inherently [...] focus[ing] on change, growth and becoming' (148).

The linear, postlapsarian narrative, according to Nikolajeva, confronts death and sexuality, and 'unity is disturbed, resulting in polyphony (multivoicedness), intersubjectivity, unreliable narrators, multiple plots and plural endings' (Nikolajeva 2002: 129). However, the presence of the Pagan chronotope (Arcadian) in young adult novels (postlapsarian), which we have already observed and shall see again and again in later chapters, disrupts the sequencing of Nikolajeva's categories, and can be seen, depending on one's point of view, as a reconciliation or a deconstruction of autonomous and developmental models of childhood, as a regression to prelapsarian idyll or a subversion of teleological developmentalism.

Contemporary Pagan views of childhood are a mixture of developmental and autonomous. The maturational model of the first Use of Magic appears to be corroborated by Graham Harvey's statement that at Paganism's 'centre is a metaphor for transformation and growth: [...] magic as a means of self-discovery and personal growth' (Harvey 1997: 209), though he may be referring to adult rather than child or adolescent development. Helen Berger (1999) sees Neopaganism as a New Religious Movement which is being adapted for children born into it: 'changes are occurring in rituals [...] to both accommodate children and acknowledge their life cycles' (15). Berger perceives that what was a diverse, individualistic counterculture is thus becoming more conservative and routinised, so that 'children who are raised in this new religion, much like children raised in traditional religions, are less spiritual seekers than passive recipients of their families' traditions' (13).

The developmentalism of rites of passage rituals being created for Pagan children would appear to be in tension with the autonomy of children 'believed to more easily access the divine' and 'believed to be born in synchrony with the spiritual world' (Berger 1999: 15, 24). Such privileging of childhood spirituality seems to be a widespread Pagan belief. Margot Adler says that adult Pagans endeavour to 'maintain a childlike wonder at the world' (Adler 1986: 382) and Graham Harvey imputes animism to children: 'To many children, perhaps all of them before they are taught otherwise, the world is profoundly alive. Trees speak, rocks move, there are giants beneath the hills and the clouds have faces' (Harvey 1997: 133). Again a clear similarity can be discerned between a Pagan view of childhood and the construction in children's literature of the child as primitive, connected with nature and the past, which Thomson (1998) identifies and critiques.

However, the Pagan perception of childhood spirituality does chime with research into children's spirituality conducted by David Hay with Rebecca Nye (1998). They maintain that adults could learn from 'the child's more inclusive and all-pervading sense of relation to the spiritual' (137), and they argue that children's environmental consciousness

> may in part derive from an animistic tendency to attribute or project their own emotions and thought on to animals and things, as noted by Piaget. This so-called childish phenomenon may in fact be a tool in advancing a shift from seeing things primarily from the perspective of personal gain and worth, to apprehending a wider, holistic perspective. (Hay with Nye 1998: 71)

By contrast, what children are learning from adults is that 'there is a social taboo on speaking about spirituality' (143) and that 'The adult world into which our children are inducted is more often than not destructive to their spirituality' (22). Tellingly, Nye finds that children are enabled to express their spirituality through the languages of fiction and play, which allow 'personalized and creative expressions of the child's ideas and feelings' in words 'of their choosing, not imposed by any particular tradition' and which afford 'considerable flexibility – that is, playfulness – with the material itself' (Hay with Nye 1998: 127).

Although the autonomous model of childhood may be a wishful invention of adults who value imagination and spirituality, many of the fictions discussed in this volume could be regarded as giving children a language to talk about spirituality; for example, a ten-year-old reader of Michelle Paver's *Chronicles of Ancient Darkness* series told me that she enjoys them because they show her other people's beliefs. While beliefs that can be framed as Pagan are currently not short of representation in children's literature, other traditions that have the potential to privilege and empower the child – Nonconformist Christianity's child prophets, Spiritualism's adolescent mediums – are largely untapped in contemporary children's fiction.[4]

Both autonomous and developmental models are implicated in the use of the magic object, which is transitional in two senses. Firstly, the magic object is a transitional object in the psychological sense of being a developmental prop, which gives comfort at one stage, but needs to be outgrown. There is a hint of this when Snape coaches Harry Potter, 'You must remain focused. Repel me with your brain and you will not need to resort to your wand' (Rowling 2003: 472). Secondly, the magic object can partake in the magic passage fantaseme (see Nikolajeva 1988: chapter 4), facilitating transitions in space and time, thereby standing for the power of imagination. But, while the object may prompt imagination, it may also come to limit it and so again must be dispensable; imagination transcends any artefact. The magic object takes protagonists and readers into 'transitional space':

> a term invented by the English psychoanalyst Donald Winnicott. It is intended to describe the all-important realm *between* illusion and reality, in which many of the most significant human experiences, such as creative and religious impulses, appear to find expression both in childhood and adulthood. (Hay with Nye 1998: 46–47)

The act of reading itself could be regarded as entering into transitional space, a liminal state between absorption and critical attentiveness.

Once more, Philip Pullman reconciles autonomous and developmental models of childhood, when Lyra finds, on reaching adolescence and discovering love, that the alethiometer will no longer work for her: in future, truth will be more hard-won. Xaphania explains that travelling between worlds will still be possible, through imagination: 'You can learn to do it, as Will's father did. It uses the faculty of what you call imagination. But that does not mean *making things up*. It is a form of seeing' (Pullman 2000: 523, original italics). Pagan chronotope can be also be discerned when Lyra and Will pledge to return to the same bench in the Botanic Garden in their respective parallel Oxfords at midday on Midsummer's Day every year.

The magic object and its dispensability do not pertain only to adolescence but also to other transitional periods. Anthony Browne's *Willy the Wizard* (1995) straddles younger stages of Reader as Player and Reader as Hero (see Appleyard 1991). Willy loves football but cannot afford boots, and never gets picked for the team. In the magical in-between time of evening, he has a kick around with a ghostly stranger who is 'wearing old-fashioned soccer gear, like the clothes Willy remembered his father wearing' – in a photograph in the background of a later illustration, Willy's father does indeed look like the footballer. The stranger gives his boots to Willy, who plays fantastically and gets picked for the team. On the day of the match, Willy wakes up late after a restless night and in his hurry forgets all his getting up and not-stepping-on-the-cracks-in-the-pavement obsessive compulsive routines. Arriving at the football ground, Willy finds he has forgotten his magic boots. But in the style of Roy of the Rovers, he single-footedly snatches victory from the jaws of defeat: 'Willy was magic.' The magic boots have encouraged him to practise hard, but ultimately the magic object is not needed as Willy's own skill comes through. He walks home, a smile on his face, his shadow adorned with a wizard's hat, oblivious to, and unharmed by, stepping on cracks, and walking under a ladder and past a banana skin (see Figure 1.1).

Figure 1.1 From *Willy the Wizard* by Anthony Browne

Source: Anthony Browne's *Willy the Wizard* (Julia MacRae Books 1995 ISBN 1856816613).

As fascinating as the functions of magic objects are instances where authors include within their fictional worlds definitions of magic, which can also be reflected in multi-layered and self-conscious narration (Use of Magic 4). In *The Ghost Drum* by Susan Price (1987), the old witch trains her apprentice Chingis in the three magics of (oral) word-magic, the magic of writing, and the magic of music. The magic of words is in the power of persuasion, as the old witch demonstrates by imagining a Czar talking his people into fighting 'a war, a stupid war, a war that should never have been fought' (36). Using the same oratorical techniques as she attributes to the Czar, the old witch ambivalently raises metalingual awareness at the same time as she subjects Chingis to the force of rhetoric. This epitomises the bind into which critical discourse analysis of children's literature gets itself – improving child readers' ideological awareness is something done to them for their own good by texts selected by the adult critical vanguard:

> when texts are recommended because they are said to *teach* this critical disposition, there is a clash between the message and the way it is being taught: the reader's imagined relationship to the text that is said to coach her into freedom sounds dangerously passive. (Thomson 2004: 145)

The magic of words in *The Ghost Drum* continues into the following narrative, as Chingis begins 'to study words: the sound of them, the use of them, the shock, the smart and soothing cool of them' (Price 1987: 37) – the iambic rhythm, the tripartite structures and the dense assonantal and consonantal sound scheme conspire to enhance and go beyond meaning and suggest a musical magic of form and patterning. The narrative is as many-layered as a *Matryoshka*, a Russian doll, with the Czar's words nestled into the old witch's presentation of them as an elaborated example of word-magic, headed by Chingis being exhorted to learn word-magic, and tailed by her doing so, while the whole story is framed by a story-telling cat. The cat is referred to in the third person, implying another narrator, who may be Chingis herself, as 'she practised her arts and slowly, sentence by sentence, wrote her own book' (63). (For more on *The Ghost Drum*, see Chapter 3 below, R. Johnston 1995, Stewig 1995 and Bramwell 2002c, 2005b)

In Kevin Crossley-Holland's second Arthur book, *At the Crossing-Places* (2001), the thirteenth-century adolescent narrator, Arthur de Caldicot, deliberates on types of magic, calling them 'degrees', which might suggest a hierarchy of initiation. The first is mere conjuring and

trickery; the second depends on learning, such as knowing the properties of herbs and medicines (compare wise women and cunning men,
discussed above). 'The third degree is when a person concentrates and
finds a force inside himself or within an object, and releases it' (203), in
which words can have a role: 'I know some words are magical. Charms
and prayers, maybe. The way they sound' (204). Magic of the fourth
degree is 'God's magic': the miraculous. Placing the Christian God at
the top but using the language of magic is consistent with the High
Medieval syncretism of the book, an ecological holism: 'Humans and
animals, plants and trees as well. We're all one fellowship. We can use
them as we need them, but we must respect them with the old words
and the old customs' (238). With a tinge of Celtic Twilight, Pagan animism is particularly associated with the Welsh characters.

Like *The Ghost Drum*, *At the Crossing-Places* sees a magic in words, which
is embodied by the narrative. The scriptorium is its own chronotope, 'a
world inside our world, with its own language and methods, even with
its own time' (279). The title itself has a plethora of meanings, as Arthur
'takes the Cross' and leaves the borderland of the Welsh Marches to
fight the Saracens, Muslims whom he cannot see as the 'enemy of God'.
Kevin Crossley-Holland is conscious that in his novel there is 'a whole
range of crossing places, between child and adult, between England
and Wales, between century and century, certainly between the world
of actuality and the world of the imagination' (Gamble 2002). And
he makes the character of Arthur self-conscious too, as Arthur says:
'Fords and bridges and the foreshore; the place where England ends
and Wales begins; midnight, and New Year's Eve. [...] places and times
where changes can happen. [...] I'm between my child-self and my
man-self' (Crossley-Holland 2001: 191). The Pagan chronotope can be
discerned in these meeting places of elements (earth and water) and
turning points of day and year, mirroring Arthur's transition from
child to adult.

For younger readers, *The Magic Hare* by Lynne Reid Banks (1992) is a
collection of 12 tales. One of them has the hare outwitting a dragon by
exploiting its vanity, in the manner of an Aesop's fable, so that the hare
comes to the realisation Snape urged on Harry Potter (cited above): 'He
had defeated the dragon without using any magic at all, just brains!'
(Banks 1992: 74). Another story challenges the association of black with
evil and white with good by featuring a witch who is ethnically black:
'instead of being a white witch in black clothes, she was a black witch
in white clothes' (78). When the hare challenges, 'I suppose you'll tell
me you do black magic to bad people and white magic to good people!'

she replies, 'No, no. The other way round' (80). A good black spell she is working on is 'to close up the hole in the ozone layer' (83). In the final tale, the nature of magic and the magic of nature are explored. To the hare, the mundane is magical: a cow turning grass into milk, a hen laying eggs, and a sheepdog and a horse understanding human commands are all magic. The hare wonders if he should abjure his own magic, as it is too easy and can have unforeseen consequences. But he cannot, for it is in his nature, just as the other animals' 'magic' is in being themselves.

The sixth Use of Magic states that 'magic can be used in fiction as a vehicle for an outlook on the world' – though this outlook need not of course be Pagan; indeed it is often Christian, as with the Deep and Deeper Magic in *The Lion, The Witch and the Wardrobe* (Lewis 1950). Yet some critics see Aslan's sacrifice as Pagan: 'Aslan's death and resurrection – a performance of the ritual of the returning god, with its pagan rather than Christian meaning – restores the cyclical time' (Nikolajeva 2002: 121). John Goldthwaite – who regards make-believe that 'do[es] not intimate the one immanence of a creative and self-revealing God' as 'specious and [...] vain' (Goldthwaite 1996: 352) – decries Aslan's 'crucifixion' for its very Paganism: it is, Goldthwaite asserts, 'specious, a transmogrification of the Passion into a pagan sacrifice with sado-masochistic overtones' (236). The Pagan critic might echo the words of the Christian Priest Father Mac in Catherine Fisher's *Darkhenge* (2005): 'Why the fixation with [...] sacrifice?' (111). While Christ's once-and-for-all sacrifice is pivotal to Christianity, the shedding of blood – present but by no means pervasive in ancient Paganism – has no part in today's Paganism. A Pagan reading of *The Lion, The Witch and the Wardrobe* might, then, be less concerned with sacrifice than with, for example, exploiting Lewis's 'playing at polytheism' (Goldthwaite 1996: 325) to wrest the carnivalesque Bacchus and other Roman gods and mythological creatures towards Ronald Hutton's fourth language of Paganism, classicism unconstrained.

Thus, as always, there is scope for the reader to negotiate with and interrogate authorial intent, stated or implied. This particularly struck me, and provided a major impulse for writing this book, when reading Geraldine McCaughrean's declaration at the front of *The Stones are Hatching*:

> All the creatures, dangers, legends, and magics
> described in this book were,
> until very recently,

accepted as real and true by ordinary people
living and working in a civilized and Christian Europe.

(McCaughrean 1999)

Equivocally, 'civilized and Christian' implies that folk belief is uncivil-
ized and unchristian, at the same time as it legitimates and tolerates it
but subsumes it under Christianity. But crucially, it seems to me likely
that many readers would have neither the resources nor the inclination to frame the Pagan elements in *The Stones are Hatching* within a
Christian world view. (McCaughrean's complex take on Paganism in
The Stones are Hatching is examined further in the next chapter.)

Fiction, especially fantasy, science fiction and children's fiction, has
a peculiar importance to modern Pagans. Margot Adler's observation,
based on interviewing, that 'Most Pagans are avid readers, yet many of
them have had little formal education' (Adler 1986: 37) is reinforced
by Diane Purkiss saying that 'Many, perhaps most, modern witches are
passionate autodidacts, often bibliomaniacs whose houses are stuffed
with books' (Purkiss 1996: 43), and by Ronald Hutton's comment that
among Pagans there is 'a greater than usual love of reading and a commitment to constant self-education' (Hutton 1999: 402). Hutton also
thinks that those who in recent years have 'adopted a self-conscious
Pagan identity [and have] said that to do so felt like coming home'
may have been influenced by reading in their youth such authors as
Mary Renault, Henry Treece and Rosemary Sutcliff (Hutton 1999: 285).
Joanne Pearson's (2002b) survey of the witch in literature, television
and film includes the young adult novels *Wise Child* by Monica Furlong
(1987) and *The Earth Witch* by Louise Lawrence (1981), as well as Marion
Bradley's *The Mists of Avalon* (1982) and Terry Pratchett's Discworld
novels, which have a cross-over readership of adolescents and adults.
The Mists of Avalon and the Discworld novels of Terry Pratchett are cited
so often that they might be regarded as the core of a Pagan canon of fiction. If there is such a thing as a Pagan canon emerging, one aim of the
current volume is to widen the canon, possibly destabilise it, by going
beyond the witch figure and the Wiccan path, and the comforts of rec-
ognition and induction, to other more contentious aspects of Paganism
in which contemporary children's literature makes numerous and significant interventions.

The Paganism of some earlier children's literature texts is well known
and has been vigorously debated, whereas in other cases the Pagan has
been overlooked or marginalised. An example of the former is *The Wind
in the Willows* (Grahame 1908). Humphrey Carpenter believes that ' "The

Piper at the Gates of Dawn" is an error of judgement on a grand scale'
(Carpenter 1985: 169) and Neil Philip calls it 'pallid Edwardian paganism [...] it was his [Grahame's] unique achievement to reduce the savage
god to a sort of woodland nanny' (Philip 1989: 309). Nevertheless, I
would argue that 'The Piper at the Gates of Dawn' is thematically integral to *The Wind in the Willows*. The story as a whole allows, but also
severely circumscribes, wider experience. Goldthwaite expresses it in
terms of the 'conflict between a man's need for the familiar hearthside
and his longing for new horizons' (Goldthwaite 1996: 322). 'The Piper
at the Gates of Dawn' episode accords with this theme, as Mole and
Rat abandon their comfortable aimlessness for a 'quest', a widening of
spiritual horizons. Yet they are returned to the mundane through the
device of forgetfulness, fading echoes.

There is potential to discern the Pagan, perhaps surprisingly on
first impressions, in texts where previous interpretations may not
have emphasised it. Tom Brown's pre-school days are spent in the
sacred landscape of the Vale of the White Horse, which, despite some
Christian hedging, is described as 'a place to open a man's soul and
make him prophesy' (Hughes 1857: 12); later (in the third chapter), a
cunning man's ministrations are recorded. As folktales can be interpreted as containing traces of Paganism (see Yovino-Young 1993), fiction featuring magical animals can be argued to do the same. In Mrs
Molesworth's *The Cuckoo Clock* (1877), the magic feather mantle, with
the aid of which the cuckoo transports Griselda to the Country of the
Nodding Mandarins, has something of the shaman's coat about it. The
cuckoo itself can be compared with a shamanic power animal: in 'a
Khaka shaman's description of the figures on his drum [...] The cuckoo
maintained contact between the shaman and the earth when he was in
the heavenly sphere' (Hultkrantz 1991: 15).

Humphrey Carpenter argues in *Secret Gardens* that 'almost without
exception, the authors of the outstanding children's books that appeared
between 1860 and 1930 rejected, or had doubts about, conventional
religious teaching' and 'attempt[ed] to find something to replace it'
(Carpenter 1985: 13). Thus texts such as *The Water-Babies* and *Peter Pan*
move towards the creation of an 'alternative religion' (41, 181) – arguably
nascent modern Paganism if it is taken into account that 'a struggle to
adapt or reject Christianity, by mixing in or substituting concepts associated with ancient paganism, was one feature of the literary culture of
the time' (Hutton 1999: 161). Another century has turned, and modern
Paganism is coming of age, with children's literature as a key site of
struggle over Paganism's current and future meanings and directions.

This chapter has attempted to suggest the new accents a Pagan poetics might give to a broad collection of concepts and methods, including: chronotope, gendered approaches, ecocriticism, critical linguistics, types and uses of magic, models of childhood, reflexivity, and reader response. These are applied selectively in the following chapters, which consist of case studies of how topics which are somewhat contentious in Paganism – the Green Man, northern shamanism and earth mysteries – are presented in recent children's literature.

2
Herne the Hunter and the Green Man

The Green Man currently appears to be becoming the pre-eminent literary Pagan god, a role occupied by Pan a century ago. For a period, Herne the Hunter contended for this position. In this chapter, after briefly considering the decline and yet survival, even recent resurgence, of Pan, I concentrate on his successors, Herne the Hunter and the Green Man. From Herne's appearance in *The Box of Delights* (Masefield 1935), through *The Dark is Rising* (Cooper 1973) and other children's fiction of the 1970s, to the 1980s television series *Robin of Sherwood* (Carpenter et al. 1990) and beyond, there have been attempts to extend Herne's role and location beyond haunting and hunting in Windsor Great Park. Yet his defining characteristic of hunting, however it is evaded or redefined, limits his appeal. By contrast, the Green Man is a blank slate on which current concerns can be inscribed, notably the desire to get in touch with the rhythm of nature and to act against ecological degradation. I look separately at the Green Man and then the Green Lady, and finally I consider texts that balance the Green masculine and feminine.

The section on the Green Man briefly considers his origins and then progresses chronologically from the 1960s onwards, starting with Kevin Crossley-Holland's picture book retelling of a folktale, *The Green Children* (1966), and John Gordon's novel *The Giant Under the Snow* (1968). Gail E. Haley's words and pictures for *The Green Man* (1979) depict the cycle of the seasons and a succession of young men taking the role of the Green Man. The burgeoning of the Green Man in recent children's fiction is illustrated by close readings of Mooney (1997a, 1997b), Gardam (1998) and McCaughrean (1999). Green women are rarer than green men, and portrayed less kindly: Helen Cresswell's Green Lady in *Stonestruck* (1995) is an antagonist; the Green Lady in Caldecott (1989) is too often deprived of agency; and Susan Cooper's *Greenwitch* (1974) is lonely and pettish – but, as a powerful representative of matriarchal Old Magic, she keeps patriarchal, dualistic High Magic in check. The Green masculine and feminine are carefully balanced in *The Oak King and the Ash Queen* by Ann Phillips (1984); Theresa Tomlinson's *The Forestwife Trilogy* (Tomlinson 1993, 1998, 2000) pairs Marian and Robin Hood and their successors in roles as May Queen and Green Man; and stories in Datlow and Windling (ed.) (2002) give equal attention to green men and green women. Finally, in Susan Cooper's *Green Boy* (2002) the Green Man depends for his being on the Goddess Gaia and on children's imagination and play.

This structure of looking at the masculine, the feminine and balance is an attempt to raise and address the concern that there is the potential in the rise of the Green Man for him to become a monotheistic, patriarchal, interventive and controlling figure, very much against the pluralist, feminist and egalitarian spirit that has heretofore inhabited modern Paganism. It all depends on how female and male deities are inflected – Diane Purkiss (1996) argues that, through the horned god, Margaret Murray (1921) turned the tables 'on all those men determined to see the goal of the spiritual quest as a passive feminine muse. By reinventing the chief deity as male, Murray could install women as active worshippers and desiring subjects' (Purkiss 1996: 37). A number of the texts analysed below attempt to maintain a balance between masculine and feminine, and moreover uphold childness and child characters' agency. Less resolved are the tensions between the Green Man as an embodiment of the cyclic seasonal Pagan chronotope, and his eschatological function in environmental apocalypse.

* * *

A century ago, Pan was the pre-eminent literary Pagan god. 'In a hundred novels his cloven hoof left its imprint on the sward,' observed Somerset Maugham, quoted in both Patricia Merivale's (1969) study of Pan in literature and Ronald Hutton's (1999) history of modern Paganism. Pan appears in the work of E. M. Forster and D. H. Lawrence as well as early twentieth-century children's literature such as *The Wind in the Willows* (Grahame 1908), and *The Secret Garden*'s (Burnett 1911) close-to-nature, pipe-playing Dickon. What is relevant here is to consider reasons for the decline of the literary Pan, and to observe how he does live on in some more recent children's novels, perhaps enjoying a resurgence.

Pan became overused to the point of absurdity and emptiness. He was 'the poetaster's cliché with which nothing new could be said' (Merivale

1969: 134); in fiction, his appearances in English parks and countryside were all too easy to ridicule. I would suggest, though, that Pan came to be rejected because of a wider reaction against the classical paradigm. As the British Empire declined through the twentieth century, so did the cultural authority of the Roman Empire as a model for it. Both Empires superimposed their deities on those of subject peoples. As British colonies gained their independence, so in Britain the invasive gods of the Roman conquest were abandoned in favour of searching for – even inventing to a great extent – native gods such as Herne and the Green Man.

Yet Pan lives on. Panchit in *Panchit's Secret* (Wayman 1975) is as diminutive as his name suggests, a bronze statue in a wild, walled garden who becomes flesh to befriend two children. He uses his pipes to lead sheep, to bring back a lost goat, and to liven up a church service. Enid Richemont's *The Enchanted Village* (1999) has classical deities vibrantly reappearing in a travelling fun-fair in modern-day Cornwall. Mr Pan is a musician, healer, wise fool and trickster. *Corydon and the Island of Monsters* by Tobias Druitt (2005) restores Pan from English pastoral to a mythical ancient Greek setting. Still, there are contemporary resonances: most obviously, Perseus's recruitment campaign satirises advertising techniques. More profoundly and universally, there are themes of prejudice (against 'monsters' and witches), the cost of conflict, and subversion of theocracy.

Corydon has inherited from his father Pan a leg shaped like a goat's, as well as an aptitude for theft and subterfuge. When they meet, Pan's face is 'mischievous and smiling, but with a great well of sadness and solemnity behind the laughter' (Druitt 2005: 87). Chthonic and liminal Pan exhorts Corydon to resist the hegemony of the Olympian sky-gods, a message that is complemented by his companions' words of wisdom. Early on, Medusa chides, 'faith in them [the gods] keeps you passive' (9). Another Gorgon says that knowledge is power: 'Zeus wants us to forget. His power rests on our ignorance. Any knowledge – even if it seems useless – is a menace to him' (66). And the Sphinx advocates plurality: 'already you know that the world is not single. There are no answers, only conversation' (126).

Not only does *Corydon and the Island of Monsters* revive Pan, it also includes wild hunts led by Artemis and Hades, and places a green man in a classical setting. On one of Corydon's journeys to the Underworld, he encounters:

a man as tall as a cyclops [...] carrying a huge branch of olive wreathed in ivy in one hand and an axe in the other. [...] And everywhere the giant stepped, the snow melted away from his feet, leaving huge and spreading patches of greenness. (Druitt 2005: 243)

Later, it is hinted that this is one of Pan's many guises. Thus the presence of a green man in *Corydon and the Island of Monsters* has two very different significances. On the one hand, it corroborates the pervasiveness of the Green Man as the current literary god. On the other hand, making a green man an aspect of Pan contests the ascendancy of the Green Man and defies the tendency in some children's fiction of the last 30 years for him to subsume other gods.

Pan and the Green Man both appear in Sophie Masson's second Thomas Trew story, *Thomas Trew and the Horns of Pan* (Masson 2007a). Thomas, a Rymer who can partake in both the Obvious and the Subtle World, is now settled in the quaint Hidden World village of Owlchurch, but the village comes under the spell of the hypnotically beautiful, sweet-tongued Frodite Peree. The villagers defer to her because she holds the Horns of Pan, the Hidden World's highest award for magic, and Thomas travels to Arkadia to meet the great god Pan and check out Frodite's credentials. Thomas returns to find that Frodite has taken over the Dream Emporium, casting a fog around it. Only the Green Man can tear through the mist and so allow Thomas to confront and expose Frodite.

Pan, who rules over 'beautiful, but rather dull' Arkadia (104), is described as 'a bit of a stick-in-the-mud' (31), indolent but subject to instantaneous rages, 'whimsical, selfish' (124), but he does repent of taking matters too lightly, and praises Thomas. Reflexively, Thomas says 'in my world, people still tell stories about the great lord Pan' (115), though dwindling belief in Pan has thinned him – as Thomas's friend Pinch puts it, 'Pan might not be what he used to be – what people used to look up to' (123).

The Green Man, also called Vertome,[1] is the father of Thomas's friends the twins Pinch and Patch. He lives deep in the wild forest, and the doorway to his green and gold furnished hall is in a tree on which 'It was as if every season was happening at the same time' (54). Like Pan, he is initially reluctant to get involved, and he is not what he used to be: he is an outlaw because 'the springtime of the world has gone, mischief no longer forgiven' (59). Yet when his help is needed he is an apocalyptic figure:

suddenly, from out of his hands, long snaky vines sprouted, thick and strong. His legs thickened, his neck bulged with cords, a creaking, groaning sound came from all of his muscles as he started to shed his human shape and become more and more like a giant tree. [...] [His voice] was a deep, roaring sound, full of huge, inhuman force, as if the forest itself was speaking. (Masson 2007a: 174)

Though this Green Man has an apocalyptic guise, his action is limited and not of global ecological significance, and, as with Druitt's green man, no claims are made for him combining and subsuming other gods.

* * *

According to legend, Herne the Hunter was a keeper at Windsor Great Park under Richard II. Herne interposes himself between a deer and the king, saving the king but receiving a mortal goring himself, though he is revived by horns being placed on his head. Antlered Herne later commits suicide hanging from an oak which is blasted by lightning, and thereafter his ghost leads a vengeful Wild Hunt (see Fitch 1994). Eric L. Fitch discerns shamanic elements to Herne's ritual death and rebirth on an axial tree, and observes that both Herne and the Green Man are 'symbols of regeneration and [...] the wild, untamed side of nature' (120). *The Merry Wives of Windsor* mentions Herne, and William Harrison Ainsworth's novel *Windsor Castle* (1843) details and embellishes his legend.[2]

There are numerous variants of the Wild Hunt, as Charles Butler observes: 'Wild Hunt traditions are extremely various and widespread, involving a complex overlay of Celtic and Saxon sources, of pagan and Christian beliefs, of national myth and local legend' (Butler 2006b: 184). Butler finds the Wild Hunt 'paradigmatic of the way in which mythological and folk material has been utilized within British children's fantasy' (ibid.), taking as his examples *The Moon of Gomrath* by Alan Garner (1963), *The Wild Hunt of Hagworthy* by Penelope Lively (1971b), *The Dark is Rising* by Susan Cooper (1973) and *Dogsbody* by Diana Wynne Jones (1975). Out of these four texts, the Wild Hunt is overtly associated with Herne only in *The Dark is Rising*, which is considered below along with John Masefield's *The Box of Delights* (1935), William Rayner's *Stag Boy* (1972), Richard Carpenter et al.'s *The Complete Adventures of Robin of Sherwood* (1990), Jane Yolen's *The Wild Hunt* (1995), Christopher Golden and Nancy Holder's *Buffy the Vampire Slayer: Child of the Hunt* (1998), and Patricia A. McKillip's short story 'Hunter's Moon' (in Datlow and Windling (ed.) 2002). Authors and many readers might struggle with Herne's defining characteristic of hunting,[3] which is often either evaded or redefined, and so this could be one reason why the Green Man currently looks more likely than Herne to be Pan's literary successor. Herne's confinement to Windsor is more easily overcome: Susan Cooper does retain Windsor but makes connections to the Caribbean, whereas other writers simply transfer Herne to other locations.

One of the most celebrated episodes of *The Box of Delights* (Masefield 1935) – for example, Diana Wynne Jones includes it in her anthology of *Fantasy Stories* (1994) – is when Herne leads Kay through a series of metamorphoses in the wild wood. Looking at the first page of the Book of Delights inside the Box of Delights, Kay is transported to a forest where he anticipates 'there's someone wonderful coming' (Masefield 1935: 84) – Herne. Herne knows Kay's wishes without having to be told, and grants three of them. Kay becomes a stag, then he and Herne are ducks and fish, but all the time they are pursued, by wolves, hawks and a pike.[4] Thus Herne is not hunter, but hunted, though he is alert to predators and evades them. At the end of the adventure, Herne merges into 'a great ruined oak-tree, so old that all within was hollow, though the great shell still put forth twigs and leaves' (87). The vectors of Judith Masefield's illustration for this chapter (see Figure 2.1) suggest both Herne leading Kay and Kay evolving into Herne. Throughout the book, Kay's magical and mystical experiences are presided over not only by Herne but also the Lady of the Oak Tree. Herne and the Lady could be seen in Jungian terms as projections of Kay's animus and anima, or in more outright spiritual terms as mediating and balancing the masculine and feminine divine.

Figure 2.1   Kay and Herne in Judith Masefield's illustration for Chapter Four of John Masefield's *The Box of Delights*

Source: Judith Masefield at the head of chapter 4 of John Masefield's *The Box of Delights* (Heinemann 1985 ISBN 0434950505).

Like *The Box of Delights*, Susan Cooper's *The Dark is Rising* (1973) and *Silver on the Tree* (1977) feature Herne the Hunter and a Lady. Cooper's Lady wears green, is unnamed and elusive, has healing powers, and appears to be the most powerful of the Old Ones: in *The Dark is Rising*, Merriman speaks of 'the full midwinter power of the Dark, which none but the Lady can overcome alone' (Cooper 1973: 219); likewise, in *Silver on the Tree*, Merriman says, 'without words from the Lady, the last height of power cannot be reached' and Will describes her as 'the greatest of all, the one essential' (Cooper 1977: 622, 639). The Lady's ultimacy is comparable with the role of Gaia in Cooper's later novel *Green Boy* (2002), discussed later in this chapter.

The sacred time and place of the Pagan chronotope are central to *The Dark is Rising*. Will Stanton's birthday falls on the midwinter solstice, during a season when the power of the Dark waxes strong, according to Merriman. Will is highly conscious of the Pagan significance of the Yule log and protective holly, and when the church of St James the Less is besieged by the Dark he ponders his dual identity:

> But in a church? said Will the Anglican choirboy, incredulous: surely you can't feel it inside a church? Ah, said Will the Old One unhappily, any church of any religion is vulnerable to their attack, for places like this are where men give thought to matters of the Light and the Dark. (Cooper 1973: 280)

Where *The Dark is Rising* pivots around midwinter, *Silver on the Tree* is its complementary opposite, midsummer being the moment in the yearly cycle in which different eras converge: 'time and space merged as the twentieth and fourth centuries became for a Midsummer's instant two halves of a single breath' (Cooper 1977: 620).

Cooper's sacred landscape is precisely located in Buckinghamshire and Berkshire. 'The shape [...] cut through snow and turf into the chalk beneath the soil [...] a circle, quartered by a cross' (Cooper 1973: 204) that Will sees among the Chiltern Hills is likely to be adapted from Whiteleaf Cross, or possibly the Bledlow Cross (see Marples 1949). An 'Old Way' connects Will's home near Hunter's Combe to Windsor Great Park, where Herne and the Wild Hunt ride on the eve of Twelfth Night. That the Park is 'peopled with creatures neither of the Dark nor of the Light' (Cooper 1973: 337) implies that Herne and the Yell Hounds are of the Old Magic, and Will is troubled by how 'the Hunter's [face] told instead of cruelty, and a pitiless impulse to revenge. Indeed he was half-beast' (340). Contrary to the legend, Will is capable of looking Herne in the eye and resisting enchantment – perhaps (though it is not stated) because of the strength of Will's will as an Old One. Otherwise, Cooper is very faithful to the legend of Herne the Hunter and its setting, but avoids parochialism by broadening the perspective: the mask that comes to life when Will presents it to the shadowy figure under Herne's Oak has been sent from Jamaica. As Will realises, 'the circle stretched all the way round the world. But of course it did, there would be no point in it otherwise' (273). Though this means that the Old Ones come '[f]rom every land, from every part of the world' (347), it does not globalise Herne himself.

Merriman rather than Herne in *The Dark is Rising* is the functional equivalent to Masefield's Herne, as mentor, though there is a great deal more exposition from Merriman than from Masefield's Herne. Cooper's Herne does serve to deliver the third and final verse of the prophecy that drives the three further instalments to *The Dark is Rising* quintet. He also vanquishes the Dark without resistance – as Merriman states, 'Nothing may outface the Wild Hunt' (Cooper 1973: 343). Thus Herne is no more than a *deus ex machina* who 'conveniently wraps things up in *The Dark is Rising*. He disposes of the Dark, but it is unclear why he hunts the Dark and why the immortal Rider should fear him' (Jones 1997: 107). Herne's motivation and power may be insufficiently explained, but at least his appearance is carefully anticipated in *The Dark is Rising* (though not in *Silver on the Tree*). To Will's perception, 'the branching tops of small trees and bushes jutt[ing] snow-laden from the mounding drifts [...were] like white antlers from white rounded heads' (Cooper 1973: 202) – a sight like which 'gave [Cooper] the impulse to begin the book' (Butler 2006b: 188). When Will has a succession of visions under Merriman's auspices, 'the brightest image of all' is a Herne-like figure.

Stag Boy by William Rayner (1972) uses Herne and other antlered men to explore power relationships between the sexes, and the nature of sacrifice. Jim Hooper returns from Wolverhampton to the Porlock area where he spent his earlier childhood. On an ancient hill fort, he sees a man wearing antlers who leads him to a passage grave (which is later not to be found). There Jim discovers 'the iron framework of a helmet, with scraps of old hide still clinging to it, and stranger still, a pair of stag antlers riveted to its iron sides' (35). He cannot resist trying it on, and is transported into a dreamlike state in which his senses are heightened. His revulsion at modern farming is also heightened. Previously he has been unimpressed that Mr Rawle 'was a farmer of tourists now – tourists and battery hens' (15). Once Jim has tried on the helmet, he is all the more revolted at the conditions of the battery hens; he hears a voice in his head declaiming 'Men are eating the flesh of misery. They should only eat the flesh of joy' (48). Jim sets the battery hens free, and he attacks the tourist campers. A parallel is drawn between factory farming and urban living: 'Rage shook him at the memory of Wolverhampton, the endless maze of streets, the houses like cages, that world of hutches and batteries and stunted lives' (136–137). Jim's attitude to hunting is more mixed: '[t]he meet was a gay occasion and the chase was gallant' (20), but the kill repulsive. The antlered helmet enables him to meld with a stag and taunt and outwit the hunt, though this only gives 'extra relish to the chase' (50). New-found confidence soon becomes arrogance: when Jim's spirit enters the stag, he causes it to prance down Porlock high street, and to chase, tease and humiliate a rival for the affections of Mary Rawle the farmer's daughter.

In an unusual twist on the dispensability of the magic object (see 'The Uses of Magic' in Chapter 1, above), Jim discovers that though he does not have to put on the helmet to inhabit the stag, this does not make him more independent; rather, he is subject to its control at a distance. At first Jim thinks he can control the stag, but:

> There were forces stirring in him which made common cause with the blood-driven will of the stag, and the two together threatened to take all control away from him. Sometimes he was tempted to let that happen. (Rayner 1972: 131)

In stag form, he feudally dominates other stags, and the sexually charged moonlit encounters between Jim-as-stag and Mary are likewise pervaded by his dominance and her submission. Mary responds to Jim's new confidence with docility, and seems content to do so. Moreover, Mrs Yeandle (with whom Jim is staying) encourages Mary to collude with the oppression embodied in the hunt: 'It's not for us to think we can meddle in such affairs. I tell you, it is not a thing for women. You must learn to bide still and bow your head' (156). To Mary, the antlered helmet is 'meant for bigger hands than hers, a male possession' (79). But finally she asserts herself and saves Jim. To appreciate the significance of the climax it is necessary to consider the role of Herne the Hunter in the novel.

Introduced through the well-worn device of Jim dipping into an antiquarian book, Herne only features in one chapter, but this chapter is thematically central. In answer to the key question 'Why does the hunter wear the horns?' (64), Herne is associated with the prehistoric horned man of the caves at Trois Frères. The animals around the dancing, antlered figure seem 'to be painted out of a deep understanding, even a love – and yet the lives of mankind had depended on the deaths of these lordly creatures, on their sacrifice' (65). The dancing man asks Jim a litany of questions about sacrifice, starting with 'What sanctifies the holy man?', to which in every case Jim replies 'Blood.' At the end, Mary answers differently. Despite hearing 'a booming voice in her head [saying] who was she, a woman, to break in on this mystery?' (157), she puts on the helmet and defies the ancient horned man, 'his brutal arrogance, his animal power' (158). She realises there is another answer to the litany: Love not Blood. When she offers herself as a sacrifice in Jim's place, the helmet and its spell break. Evidently the theology is *Stag Boy* is ultimately Christian, feminised by Mary taking on Christ's role of loving self-sacrifice. Prehistoric Paganism is thereby presented oppositionally as being brutally masculine and built on blood. Historians might dispute this; modern Pagans certainly would regard it as a travesty.

The version of Herne which has reached the widest audience comes from the three 1980s television series of *Robin of Sherwood*, novelised by Carpenter et al. (1990) as *The Complete Adventures of Robin of Sherwood*. Richard Carpenter distinctively grafted the supernatural onto the Robin Hood stories, adding both lurid diabolism and more vraisemblant earth religion, centred on Herne and the wild wood. This Herne is a shamanic figure (compare Chapter 3, below), a man who becomes the god Herne '[w]hen the Horned One possesses me' (Carpenter et al. 1990: 37). In his antlered form, as Lord of the Trees, Herne subverts the King's authority over forest and deer. It is Herne who gives Robin a mission of social justice, and mentors and protects him. His equivocal prophecies sometimes frustrate Robin, but they contribute to the hermeneutic code which engages the audience. Under Herne's auspices, Robin sees visions, sometimes induced by hallucinogens – an unnecessary move, as it is clear that Robin is capable of foresight and farsight without such stimulants, before and while he knows Herne.

Herne is not attended by the Wild Hunt, which instead is displaced to The Hounds of Lucifer, possessed men disguised as demons who terrorise the forest people. They are led by a Pan-like Lucifer, 'a tall shape, with cloven hooves, horns and a baleful glare' (208). The Cauldron of Lucifer speaks the language of charismatic Christianity – 'Praise his name!' (193) – and uses a nunnery as a cover. Morgwyn of Ravenscar's satanism has nothing to do with Paganism; it is a Christian invention and inversion:

She and her followers believed that the Devil, whom they called Lucifer, was the real creator and ruler of the world, and that he had been unjustly banished from heaven. It was their belief that Lucifer would eventually overthrow God and rule in Heaven eternally, replacing good with evil. (Carpenter et al. 1990: 172)

This supports the observation that 'Christianity and Diabolism are depicted as opposite means to the same ends; that is power, dominance, material wealth' (Stephens and McCallum 1998: 186). However, Christian characters are presented more sympathetically when they preach liberation theology and defy the organised church's function as an ideological apparatus of the state. Friar Tuck is the obvious example, but in Series Three there are also the monks of Croxden Abbey, 'holy men who were just as dedicated to serving the poor as Robin and his friends. The Abbot of Croxden preached fearlessly against de Rainault's iron-handed regime' (Carpenter et al. 1990: 486). Christian sacraments also underlie some of the Pagan rites in *Robin of Sherwood*: the eucharistic sharing of mead that recurs rhythmically throughout, and Robin and Marion's marriage before Herne, of which Stephens and McCallum say, 'The Christian ceremony is present here as a palimpsest [...] evoked in order to be displaced by the setting (both time and place), by dress, and by the presiding deity' (Stephens and McCallum 1998: 187).

The most sustained and authentic depiction of earth religion centres around the festival of the Blessing in the second series. As a forester explains, it is 'to celebrate the coming of summer. [...] nothing can be killed during the few days before the Blessing. No blood must be shed' (Carpenter et al. 1990: 214). This taboo procures Herne's blessing on the harvest, and means that cunning must be used to defeat enemies without bloodshed. It is a time of guile, guising and carnival; Robin and his band mum as Saint George, Saracen, man-woman, hobby-horse and doctor. In a 'forest clearing sacred to Herne' (227), a village elder and Robin share a chalice and Robin pledges 'This seals the bond between us, between we of the forest and you of the villages. Between the outlaws and the oppressed. Blessed be!' (228) – 'Blessed be!' is a phrase used by modern Pagans. When Herne appears, dramatic tension is provided by Guy of Gisburne's intent 'to kill their god in front of them!' (229). A Brabancon mercenary does wound the man-god Herne in the thigh, a mythic echo of the Fisher King's dolorous blow, and an ash tree sacred to Herne is hacked down by Gisburne: the coincidence of injuries to Herne and the tree suggests they are somehow homorganic. Gisburne mistakes Robin for Herne and chases him 'through bushes and briars that seemed to trip and tear at him almost deliberately [...] Panic seized him' (230). Despite the seriousness of Gisburne's offence and punishment, carnival comes to the fore again when Robin quips, 'I led him a merry dance' (231).

The forest people's sincere and light-hearted Paganism contrasts with both the (Christian) diabolism of Morgwyn and, in Series Three, the savage Paganism of Owen, Lord of Clun and his magician Gulnar. This savage Paganism (Ronald Hutton's first language, see Chapter 1 above) and Owen being exotically other (he is Welsh, which is an Anglo-Saxon word meaning foreign, other) are suffused with forbidden libido. Having drugged and hypnotised Marion, Gulnar declaims, 'Hail to thee, Arrianrhod, Earth Goddess, Mother of Men. Be faithful in the embrace of the All-Father. Hail to thee, Marion! Kneel and worship thy Lord!' (413). The combination of Celtic Goddess and Norse or Anglo-Saxon God (the All-Father is Odin) may simply be confused. But then again Owen, a Marcher lord, has betrayed the Welsh to embrace English gods and ally himself with the Normans, the latest invaders. The forced marriage symbolises the attempted subjection of native people and traditions to conquest, though Marion escapes.

Alongside the interpretation that *Robin of Sherwood* 'evokes a transcendent essential Englishness which is embodied as a pagan spirit of place' (Stephens and McCallum 1998: 186), it needs to be emphasised that this Englishness is hybrid. Though not an overt theme of the series, the hybridity can be teased out. For example, a focal point for the villagers and outlaws is a stone circle called Rhiannon's Wheel: the English preserve a Celtic name for a pre-Celtic centre of ritual. Rhiannon's Wheel is of great significance because it is central to the Pagan chronotope of *Robin of Sherwood*. Circular itself, it represents a cyclic view of time: repeatedly returned to by Marion and Robin, it is a place where Herne heals, even resurrects. On an occasion when Marion is miraculously healed from a mortal wound, Robin senses the stones whirling around him, 'calling to him, trying to tell him a secret. If only he could understand them, the knowledge of all things would be his in a single moment' (Carpenter et al. 1990: 161). Herne's gnomic utterances imply that time is cyclic: 'There is no end and no beginning. It is enough to aim' (249); 'In the past lies what is to come' (364). When the first Robin dies, Marion goes full circle, remembering the very first words he said to her, 'You are like a May morning' (28, 331). Though one Robin is dead, Herne adopts another son – the role of Hooded One is renewable. Thus, as with Doctor Who's regenerations, *Robin of Sherwood* had the potential for longevity, by working through the historical contenders for Robin Hood.

The problems of the second Robin are acknowledged at the start of the third and final series: Robert of Huntingdon, as the only son and heir of an Earl, hasn't endured the trauma that Robin of Loxley did. Robert at first resists Herne's calling, and the outlaws are also resistant to Robert. His prowess in fighting is what wins them over: Little John 'had thought of Robert as no more than the offspring of nobleman. But the boy had spirit. And he knew how to fight' (387). An aristocratic Robin is just one way in which the third series is more conservative. Marion's options are severely circumscribed. She and the new Robin arrange a Christian marriage, but do not go through with it; instead Marion withdraws to a nunnery. Even so, the Pagan cycle of the year is spelled out more explicitly than ever: after Robin has defeated a golem double of himself at Rhiannon's Wheel, he realises:

> the deeper meaning that lay behind his conflict. For he was the Summer King. He had to die. That was the final ritual. [...] But Herne had found a way. Robin had killed Robin. A substitute victim had been found and the Year would turn again. (Carpenter et al. 1990: 625)

Richard Carpenter's Paganisation of Robin Hood could well have influenced Theresa Tomlinson's *Forestwife Trilogy* (discussed later in this chapter), though instead of Herne appearing to Robin, Tomlinson's Robin takes the guise of the Green Man. Indeed, I have found only a few writers taking up Herne since *Robin of Sherwood*: most notably Jane Yolen (1995), and there is also a *Buffy the Vampire Slayer* novel (Golden and Holder 1998) and a short story by Patricia A. McKillip (in Datlow and Windling (ed.) 2002). More recently, in Sophie Masson's Thomas Trew stories, all Herne has is a drive-on part as a Hidden World limousine chauffeur (Masson 2006), the role of flying huntsman being filled by the ancient and feral Euryon who is 'bigger even than the Green Man' (Masson 2007b: 122).

The chapters of Jane Yolen's elegantly constructed *The Wild Hunt* (1995) are tripartite, moving between Jerold's isolated house, Gerund's 'same house, but in a different time or perhaps in an alternate world' (14) in the 'Sort of' chapters, and the wintry outside in the 'Almost' chapters. There are metafictive, intertextual and metalingual manoeuvres: Jerold reads a book called *The Wild Hunt* – 'Unlike the other books he had read, this one had no comfort in it at all' (10) – and this book later falls open of its own accord to reflect the action of the story in which it appears; the heroes 'Ged Sparrowhawk, Aragorn Strider, Will Stanton,

Arthur Pendragon' (25) are alluded to, putting the work of Le Guin, Tolkien and Cooper on a par with the Matter of Britain; and much is made of Gerund being named after a part of speech.

Jerold and Gerund are swept up in the endless annual playing out of the contest between 'the Queen of Light and the Hunter of Dark' (133), which always ends in a draw. Control and balance are at issue: 'the Summer Queen, the Lady of Light, the White Goddess' (40), who is 'She Who Is Ever. She Whose Word Is Law. The Now and Future Queen. Maiden, Mother, Crone' (55) will never let the Horned King have the mastery over her that he craves. Jerold and Gerund stand up to the Queen, questioning her bloody game with the Horned King and her polarised characterisation of herself as peace and light, and the Horned King as force and darkness. Not until near the end of the story is the black armoured, coal-red eyed, horned man on a white horse named as Lord Herne, and naming his true name, if it is such, only serves to limit and diminish him.

In the *Buffy* novel *Child of the Hunt* (Golden and Holder 1998), Buffy's Watcher Rupert Giles's job as a librarian allows swathes of background research on the Wild Hunt to be served up, including Goethe's poem 'The Erl King'. Hern (*sic* – the terminal 'e' seems to have migrated to the 'Renaissance Faire'), accompanied by hosts of hellhounds and dark faerie, slays vampires, who are his competitors for the lost souls he captures. By joining the hunt, some of these lost souls find a place and purpose they have never known before. Thus the Wild Hunt impinges on Buffy's territory with the more blurred morality of ancient magic. As Hern's successor explains in the denouement:

> the Wild Hunt will always ride, and the hopeless and foolish will always join us whether they wish it or not. We are part of the fabric of the night, Buffy. Neither the Lord of the Hunt nor the Slayer is powerful enough to alter that. (Golden and Holder 1998: 320)

Herne is named in the Author's Note to Patricia A. McKillip's 'Hunter's Moon' (in Datlow and Windling (ed.) 2002: 118–136), but not in the story itself. Talking about the deer-hunting season in the Catskills, McKillip explains, 'I wondered what Herne, the ancient guardian of the forest, would make of all this.' Her answer in the story is to redefine hunting. Oakley Hunter, with his deer-like eyes and movements and his gentle, terse speech, joins an autumn gathering of Hunters whose hunt is a symbolic game. These are 'Hunters who loved animals, who hated to see them suffer, who understood the language of trees' (133).

It is telling that McKillip's Herne-inspired Hunters appear in a collection entitled *The Green Man*: the Green Man has displaced Herne as the literary Pagan God. Herne has declined, partly perhaps because his apotheosis in *Robin of Sherwood* is a difficult act to follow, but mainly because his role as a hunter is insurmountably problematic, no matter how it is evaded or redefined. By contrast, the Green Man is virtually a *tabula rasa* onto which current sensibilities can more easily be inscribed.

* * *

Only about seventy years ago was the term Green Man first controversially applied by Lady Raglan (1939) to the foliate heads found in churches. She regarded them as a fertility symbol and, in the style of Frazerian anthropology (compare Frazer 1922), subsumed under a single idea diverse figures from legend and folk custom, including Jack-in-the-Green, Robin Hood and the May King. Lady Raglan's thesis and analogies have been disputed ever since, on such grounds as the recency of some folk rituals, the tenuousness of the analogies, and the unlikelihood of a Pagan symbol being tolerated in Christian churches. There is a distinct lack of documentary evidence for Pagan interpretation of ecclesiastical foliate heads, though the same is true of their Christian symbolism, which has to be deduced speculatively. Kathleen Basford considers that foliate heads in church contexts are more likely to represent demons, lost souls and sinners than the May King. She points out that 'very few [are] benevolent or serenely smiling; more typically they frown' and appear 'eerie and macabre' (Basford 1978: 7). Mercia MacDermott notes the selectivity of reproductions of the Green Man: 'The foliate heads most frequently copied and displayed are the quizzical face leaf-masks and the tranquil disgorgers of greenery. The more hideous Gothic images and the impersonal, stylized Italianate heads are usually shunned' (MacDermott 2003: 193), but William Anderson's Green Man as ecological archetype can be fearsome: 'The ferocity of his expression is one of warning against neglect of Natural Law' (Anderson 2000: 115).

While Anderson admits that links between the Green Man and folk customs are 'patchy', he devotes plenty of space to them, and to elaborating the view that the Green Man is an image of death and renewal originating in the supposed 'matriarchal religion of the Neolithic period' (34; compare Hutton's third language, and Murray 1921). The Green Man is being rediscovered now in the wake of the re-emergence of the

Great Goddess, Anderson thinks. In believing that the Green Man is an archetype, Anderson side-steps issues of proof and disproof: 'an archetype such as the Green Man represents will recur at different places and times independently of traceable lines of transmission' (Anderson 2000: 25). Anderson combines two aspects of the Green Man that MacDermott has identified and critiqued: the environmentalist icon, and the 'green umbrella' for 'the maximum number of religious and folkloric phenomena' (MacDermott 2003: 6). For modern Pagans, as for Anderson, the Green Man signifies seasonal renewal and ecological awareness; these connections are prominent in literary portrayals of the Green Man, especially in the plethora that appeared around the turn of the millennium. Some texts relate the Green Man to the endless, cyclic Wheel of the Year, whereas in other texts – or indeed the same texts, with some tension – he reawakens once-and-for-all to bring about eschatological eucatastrophe. In children's novels, short stories and picture books, the Green Man may also be used as a model of maturation (see Chapter 1, Use of Magic 1), particularly for young men, which raises the same issues of control as young women's apprenticeship to wise women (compare Bramwell 2005a, 2005b). This section starts by comparing two versions of the legend of the Green Children of Woolpit, but thereafter is confined to the Green Man, while the next section considers Green Lady figures, and the following section examines stories that attempt to balance the Green masculine and feminine.

Kevin Crossley-Holland's *The Green Children* (1966) tells of how a green girl and boy from a twilight land are discovered in a wolf-pit in Suffolk. In Peter Hill's view, 'it is likely to be a garbled and degenerated form of fertility myth' (Hill 2004: 179).[5] Indeed, it can be read, in part, as fertility myth. The children are found during the corn-harvest, which would be around the festival of Lughnasa or Lammas, though Crossley-Holland does not specify this. Through autumn the boy declines, and then dies in the winter. He does not revive, but the green girl grieves through winter and recovers in spring. So, seasonal fertility myth can be found if one is minded to look for it – but I do not think that a folktale first recorded in the twelfth century, and presumably older in origin, can be dismissed as 'garbled and degenerated' just because it does not fit the picture of the Green Man that has been created in the late 20th and early 21st centuries.

It is revealing to compare Crossley-Holland's *The Green Children* with Judith Stinton's later retelling, *Tom's Tale* (1983). The latter begins when the wolves are running in snowy midwinter, rather than high summer, so that the green boy lives through a full cycle of the year. In both, the green children are found by humble people: by cottars in Crossley-Holland; and by Tom, one of seven children who share one bed, in Stinton. Crossley-Holland portrays a feudal and ecclesiastical society sympathetically: Sir Richard de Caine is thought by the cottars to be 'a just lord, and a generous one, though his moods were as variable as the weather'; the cottars pray to the saints and cross themselves, and an old priest educates and baptises the green children, as 'They may be green but they still have souls.' This is all appropriate to a 12th-century setting, but Stinton writes it out, perhaps assuming it might not be very palatable to a modern audience, but also giving the past of 'Long, long ago' (the opening and closing words of her story) more of a fairytale indeterminacy. More definite is Tom's naming of the green children, Griselda and Martin, a speech act which can be seen as attempting to control them and make them more like him.

Diane Purkiss suggests looking at the story of the Green Children as 'a way of telling in reverse-angle shot what it might be like for a human child to visit fairyland. The children cannot eat human food, just as we must never eat fairy food' and '[t]hey are frightened by difference' (Purkiss 2000: 63). Such a dual perspective is sustained in both retellings: thus the green girl in Crossley-Holland's version says, 'If you were surprised to see green children, think how astonished we were to see pink men'; and in *Tom's Tale*, when Tom claims to have rescued the children from the pit, Griselda counters that they rescued him from wolves. And yet, despite the shifting points of view and apparent upholding of difference, the ultimate message is: assimilate or die. The green boy will not change his green appearance or green diet, and so fails to survive. The girl lives on because she eats other food and joins a household; in Crossley-Holland she marries and moves away, and in Stinton she becomes part of Tom's family, helping with the chores. She gains acceptance by her skin colour changing: 'And slowly her skin lost its green tinge, her hair became fair' (Crossley-Holland 1966); 'She was no longer green, she was as white as he and Ellen were' (Stinton 1983: 41).

Thankfully, the green girl's difference is not entirely whitewashed. In Crossley-Holland's story, she continues to pine for her homeland, 'And nobody knows – unless you do – whether the green girl lived on earth to the end of her days; or whether, one day, near the Wolfpits, she simply disappeared.' Crossley-Holland leaves the ending open, and, as Gail E. Haley does at the start of *The Green Man* (1979; discussed shortly), invites the reader to tell alternative tales. *Tom's Tale* is more closed – definitively, 'Griselda never did go back' (Stinton 1983: 42), but she does retain one aspect of her otherness: her bright green eyes, which 'keep the wolves from the door' (44).[6]

In John Gordon's *The Giant Under the Snow* (1968), Jonquil Winters is on a mound shaped like a giant green hand when she discovers a buckle that portrays 'a man standing upright with his legs together and his arms outstretched' (12) – a stance like those of the only two surviving human hill-figures in England, the Cerne Abbas Giant and the Long Man of Wilmington. Jonk's friend Bill links the green hand to legends of the Green Man being chased from Wiltshire to the east, and the ageless wise woman Elizabeth Goodenough explains that the buckle is a focus for the battle between her power to protect the land and the evil of an ancient warlord. She gives Jonk, Bill and their friend Arf the gift of flying to aid them against the warlord and his leather men. An industrial wasteland inside the walls of a town is the warlord's territory; as we shall see, such a questionable, conservative opposition between urban evil and rural good reappears in later depictions of the Green Man.

When Bill is flying below Jonk, he appears to merge into the green giant:

> He seemed motionless below her, like somebody sprawled in sleep. His head was on the horizon and his shape was as dark as the earth beneath, but huge; his hand covered a whole field. When he moved to begin climbing again it was as though he dug himself from the earth in which he was embedded. (Gordon 1968: 116)

At the climax of the novel, the Green Man rouses to defeat the warlord and find his own rest. This partakes more of a teleological Christianised chronotope than a Pagan cyclic one: the giant reawakens at dawn on Christmas Day, rather than at the winter solstice, and his resurrection is an apocalyptic one-off rather than a yearly occurrence. As Elizabeth Goodenough says, 'there was a struggle between great powers that was never properly ended. But now it has been resumed, and you have become involved in the final act' (78). Once the warlord is defeated, the sad-eyed Green Man becomes himself, but only to find his final rest:

> the caverns of his eyes closed and the landscape of his face became gentle. [...] the tower of earth [gave] up its life. It began to collapse, a huge structure from which all strength had gone [...] A great door seemed to have slammed shut. (Gordon 1968: 174–175)

The Green Man of *The Giant Under the Snow* resolves an ancient battle between good and evil, but he does not then go on to have an abiding presence in the world.[7]

Gail E. Haley's picture book *The Green Man* (1979) has a strong developmental message: an 'arrogant, vain, and selfish' aristocratic young man, who is dismissive of belief in the Green Man, finds himself taking on the role. After a year's time out, he returns home changed: 'Now he was hospitable to travelers. He cared for his animals. And each night Claude set out food and drink for the Green Man.' The front cover depicts a Green Man in harmony with plants and animals. He is dressed with ivy, acorns and oak leaves, bark and ears of corn, and carries a basket of root vegetables, an axe and a sprouting staff. A squirrel hangs on to his moustache, butterflies circle his head, and a hare bounds along looking up to him. The reader is invited into the book by the Green Man's direct gaze and by his striding from left to right.

In four tableaux representing the seasons, the frontispiece anticipates the cycle of the year that Claude spends as Green Man. In spring, the man in green cradles a lamb and has his arm around a unicorn – an association picked up later, not in the main story, but in the afterword, 'Who is the Green Man?' The summer picture shows a ploughman and the man in green in discussion. Root vegetables and a sheaf of corn are gathered by the man in green in the autumn; his beard is in plaits similar to corn dollies; on the ground, a cornucopia overflows with fruit. The snow-laden winter scene looks forward to an incident in the story when Claude as the Green Man orders a boar away from a frightened girl and boy. At the centre of these four pictures is a foliate head sprouting tendrils which frame the scenes, making the turning of the seasons and the Green Man an organic whole. The man in green in the seasonal scenes has hair not leaves on his head, so a distinction is established here which is maintained through the book: the central foliate head represents the everlasting Green Man, whose role is taken by specific individuals such as Claude from year to year.

This balance between the universal and the specific is clear in the opening words of the verbal text: 'The story you are about to read may have happened just this way – or perhaps it came about in a different way in some other place entirely.' Thus the reader is invited to make up alternative stories. The bustling activity and the buildings of the accompanying double-page illustration establish a medieval setting. Haley appears to have painted onto coarse cloth, giving a warp and weft to the texture, like tapestry. A young man's brash red cloak stands out, as he approaches the Mermaid and Bush inn (again, it is the afterword that explains the heraldic link between the Green Man and mermaids). On the next page, inside the inn, the young man, Claude, looks out and mocks the people's belief in the Green Man, but the landlord explains that 'the Green Man keeps their animals healthy. He protects their children if they stray into the forest. Without him, the crops would not grow, nor the seasons turn their course.' This is a precise outline of what the Green Man is shown doing in the rest of the book.

A hunting expedition takes Claude deep into the forest. He is incongruous and oblivious. His red outfit clashes with the green background, he wears spurs and carries sharp, angular weapons. The rigid falling diagonal of Claude's leg in the stirrup suggests trouble to come. His head in profile is arrogantly upturned and his eyelids are half closed – the same expression as he had on the title page, where he had his back turned to a foreboding foliate head capital. He grumbles, 'I haven't seen an animal all day!' but there are many frowning animals, plus the Green Man, looking on from the undergrowth. When he goes for a swim to cool down, he does not notice 'a thin bony hand reaching out of the bushes'. A sequence of six wordless pictures shows a naked old man taking Claude's clothes and riding off, tucking into Claude's lunch. The verbal text resumes with Claude improvising leafy clothing, eating strawberries and settling in a cave for the night. He fears shapes and movement in the cave, but the reader is safely distanced by seeing that they have rational explanations. The morning and the next page-turning reveal the cave to be stocked with utensils and supplies. Claude feeds a nanny goat and some roosters and they provide food for him. When Claude's father comes with men and hounds to look for him, he hides from them. The illustration shows the horn-blowing men and braying dogs to be an intrusion, the hounds' vicious claws extruding from the picture frame. After this, 'Claude lived on in the cave, growing leaner and stronger every day.'

He grows happy and confident with his new identity as 'Milker-of-the-Goat, Feeder-of-the-Hens, Friend-of-All-Wild-Animals [...] Gatherer-and-Preserver [...] Gleaner'. He is depicted picking apples, and on either side anthropomorphised sun and moon smile down as he picks grapes by day and harvests wheat by night. The curved picture frames suggest his contentment and cycles of day and night and the seasons. In preparation for the winter, he makes the cave much more abundantly well stocked and homely than he found it. He performs good deeds such as rescuing a calf stranded by a flood, and ordering away a boar that threatens a girl and a boy who are collecting acorns. The latter episode demonstrates Claude-as-the-Green-Man's authority, but also his humour, as he calls the creature 'a selfish swine' and an 'old boar'. This is also the moment when Claude acknowledges his identity as Green Man, in answer to a question from the girl. The perspective of the picture is from her point of view: the conspicuously foreshortened Green Man, wearing a necklace of acorns, towers above and stares down at the viewer. The text says that 'He seemed as ancient, green, and moss-covered as the oak tree that towered above them.' The Green Man has his arm protectively or proprietorially on the young boy's shoulder, perhaps suggesting that when the boy reaches adolescence he may take his turn as the Green Man.

As winter draws in, Claude becomes lonely and is torn between home-sickness and his duty in the forest. He accepts the food offerings he was so dismissive about at the start. The picture shows a snow-covered street with the warm yellow light coming from a door on the left inviting him back. His hair repeats the shape of a bare windswept bush. Finally in spring he returns home. The cycle repeats in a triptych: a young man, destined to be the next Green Man, goes swimming, and Claude takes the clothes, cuts his hair and returns to his parents. In the first picture, the viewer's eye is drawn to a tree breaking out of the top of the frame. It has two trunks twisted together, which may stand for the changeover from one individual to the next in the single role of Green Man. The interior of the home to which Claude returns contains hints of the forest: the cracks in the floor paving look like branches, there is an acorn ceiling boss, and a column capital is decorated with a foliate head. This last is an echo of the foliate heads at the start of the book, on the frontispiece and title page; the repetition reinforces the circularity of the Wheel of the Year and renewal of the persona of the Green Man every spring by a different youth.

The worthy didacticism of Haley's *The Green Man* may provoke resistance from some readers, and there are instabilities in the text to be exploited. Claude takes time out to act as the Green Man as a young man, and is replaced by a young man, but this is not always the pattern as it is an old man he replaces. Although we are told that Claude has spent a 'year away', there is some inconsistency in the order of events. The incident with the children and the boar occurs between Claude's autumnal preparation for winter and the coming of snow. Yet when he appears to the children, the oak trees are in full leaf, whereas the same incident has been depicted in snowy winter on the frontispiece. The apparent inconsistency can be explained in a number of ways. Claude's acknowledgement that he is the Green Man is given power by surrounding him with green foliage. The story has a pattern of alternation between Claude's gradual adaptation to the seasonal cycle, and 'one day ...' incidents, such as with the calf or the boar, which are not necessarily presented chronologically. It is also possible that what Claude perceives as a year may be indefinite 'fairy tale' time.

As I indicated earlier, some details of the illustrations are not explained until the afterword, 'Who is the Green Man?' Here Haley also claims that 'The Green Man had many names: Woodwose, Jack-in-the-Green, Wild or Savage Man, Woodhouse, and many others. Robin Hood and Puck were surely Green Men.' She goes on to associate the Green Man with Merlin and Arthur's knights, 'Amaethon, the Celtic god of vegetation' and 'Dionysus, Osiris, and Gilgamesh'. This is a comparatively early example in children's literature of the tendency to make the Green Man absorb and supplant all manner of wild men and gods, especially those that seasonally die and are reborn. Whatever we make of Haley's assertions in the afterword, the sophisticated interplay of verbal and visual in the main text presents a paradigm of maturation and a vision of the Green Man. By learning to live in harmony with nature, the young man also becomes more considerate of others. The Green Man is ageless, benevolent and good-humoured, and lives in rhythm with the Wheel of the Year.

In the last decade or so, appearances of the Green Man have proliferated in children's books. Before turning to those in which he is prominent, I shall mention three works in which he is more peripheral. In *Timon's Tide* by Charles Butler (1998), Daniel's drawing of an owl-eyed green man anticipates glimpses of his lost brother Timon in the woods. At one point in Catherine Fisher's *Corbenic* (2002), Merlin takes on the semblance of a green man. Arthur de Caldicot's father in Kevin Crossley-Holland's *The Seeing Stone* (2000) buys a tile adorned with a green man from a pedlar. Later, in *At the Crossing-Places* (2001), Arthur finds that the eyes, 'Sometimes [...] kind, sometimes angry', reveal his own dual human nature: 'They make me think how I'm only a little lower than the angels; but they also make me feel little better than a hideous beast. Beautiful and horrid. Both' (34). The Green Man is central to the novels and illustrated stories analysed in the rest of this section: Bel Mooney's *The Green Man* (1997a) and *Joining the Rainbow* (1997b), Jane Gardam's *The Green Man* (1998) and *The Stones are Hatching* by Geraldine McCaughrean (1999). (Theresa Tomlinson's *Forestwife* trilogy (1993, 1998, 2000) and Susan Cooper's *Green Boy* (2002) are discussed later, in the section concerned with balancing the green masculine and feminine.)

In Bel Mooney and Helen Cann's *The Green Man* (Mooney 1997a), the Green Man inspires the greening of a grey urban environment, and this is anticipated by Cann's cover illustration. The top half of the picture, the 'given' information, depicts in grey, blue and white a city skyline of tower blocks, and a dome which looks like St Paul's, making the city specifically London. The 'new' information in the bottom half of the picture shows the Green Man against a green background, facing the viewer with eyes and mouth wide open. His hair consists of green leaves and red berries, and his eyebrows, moustache and jacket are also made of leaves. One leaf is placed on his forehead like a 'third eye', and vines curl on his cheeks like tattoos. From his smiling or laughing mouth, tendrils emerge. His brown hands are like wood, grained and knotted, and from them leaves, flowers, berries and insects float upwards. This upward movement indicates that he is on the rise, in the ascendancy, as do other upward vectors: his foliate hair breaks through the straight bottom line of the semicircle framing the title; this semicircle obscures much of the cityscape, and its curved top edge again suggests upward movement. Amongst the buildings are trees, and a couple of the tower blocks have green growth climbing up them; leaves hang down in the top corners.

Mooney's verbal text opens bleakly: it is winter, and through the window Luke sees 'the world all grey'. The words 'grey' and 'greyish' are used five times in the first two paragraphs. Window boxes are empty, the flowers indoors are plastic. The illustration shows Luke looking at a view of the angular squares and oblongs of flat-roofed tower blocks with only a small patch of mottled grey sky showing. There are several signals of change for the better to come: Luke's form interrupts the rigid, dark grey double border; he faces right, looking forward; the layers of his brown hair resemble dry leaves or wood shavings; the patch on his blue jeans is green with a swirling brown pattern.

Luke repeatedly encounters the Green Man in unexpected places, though his mother is dismissive. The Green Man's face appears in the lichen on a tree trunk, looking fierce. A supermarket cabbage blinks at Luke, and in the picture the Green Man's eyes are downcast and his mouth sealed by a barcode sticker. In the car returning from the supermarket, Luke begins to notice how ugly his urban environment is. His stance in the illustration echoes the Green Man on the cover: face on (despite the side-view of the car), hands upraised. His hands are shaded like knotted wood and he wears a green jacket. Luke sees the Green Man again, friendly and talking, in a bush by the path to the flat, and then 'in the swirling brown grain' of the sideboard indoors.

Luke dreams of the Green Man breaking through the concrete pavement – like the tree on which Luke first saw the Green Man's face. The picture shows the Green Man's size: though sitting, his head intrudes into the frame, and his foot is planted outside of it, and his sleeve looks like a patchwork of fields. Luke is barely taller than his knee, but Luke has more agency in the picture than in the words, which say that the Green Man holds out a hand and commands 'Come with me.' In the picture, Luke puts his hands to the Green Man's thumb and wrist to help him up. While the verbal text rationally relegates the Green Man to a dream, there are no visual cues (as there could be) to indicate unreality.

The next day Luke once more spots the Green Man's face in the peeling green paint on an old shed. An old woman sees the Green Man too; she is dressed 'with all the colours of the rainbow' and introduces herself as Lily. 'Her hand was as rough as bark', and in the picture it has the wooden texture that the Green Man and Luke's hands have displayed before. The grey tendrils of Lily's hair echo the green tendrils hanging from the picture frame. Lily is a wise old woman who mediates Green Man to Luke: the Green Man helps her grow fruit and vegetables on her allotment, but he is fierce because he has been forgotten and ignored, though he 'will never go away'. The old woman claims 'He's the oldest spirit in the world [...] he's all growing things in one, and everything grows because of him.' When Luke sees the allotment, he feels 'something spring up inside him, as if a green shoot was growing there,' and Lily explains that the Green Man has chosen him to help him. In the illustration, Lily authoritatively looks down on Luke and points her finger at him.

A running visual footnote is a line of pots, jars and cans with flowers growing in them. At the moment when Luke moves from reaction to action, these flowers reach full bloom. The hard work does him good: 'His hands were dirty, and his back ached a bit – but he felt very happy.' Luke's Mum and Dad join him and Lily in planting and nurturing seeds, while people in the ground-floor flats look on, happy or astonished. Generations, family and community are brought together by the Green Man, or by Lily's understanding of him. Finally, Luke plants seeds in his window box, and they wondrously flower overnight. He hears the Green Man telling him, 'you can make things different!' The fringe of ivy around the window is 'just like the hair of the Green Man', and the last picture very precisely reflects the cover illustration. The border is the same design, and the blue and grey bricks echo the buildings. Surrounded by flowers and insects, Luke has the same face-on, hands-raised pose as the Green Man; the fingers are splayed identically. Luke has been inspired by the Green Man and, through acting to improve his environment, has become him.

Mooney's 'Author's Note' is consistent with the main text in emphasising the Green Man's ambivalent character, 'as soft as rain on crops, as hard as winter [...] friendly, but fierce'. Like Haley, Mooney creates a mythology and antiquity for the Green Man: 'when churches were built, country people believed in the Green Man – a belief older than the Christian faith. So the priests let them carve him all over the place – just to be sure, you see.' But the 'country people' would not have been likely to make the connection between foliate heads and the name 'Green Man' that Lady Raglan first applied in 1939. Mercia MacDermott rejects 'the popular but anachronistic idea that the Green Man was smuggled into churches by recalcitrant, underground pagans' (MacDermott 2003: 163) and argues that 'foliate heads either played a neutral, decorative role [...] or else were recruited [...] to press home some Christian teaching' (165).

The importance of Mooney and Cann's *The Green Man* is in introducing the Green Man to a contemporary, urban setting, though in a rather schematic and idealised way. The inner city is not necessarily as grim and ungreen as Mooney, for the sake of contrast, makes out, and the harmonising of generations and families in a common cause is very optimistic. Lily could be seen as the Jungian grandmother archetype and as the Crone aspect of the Triple Goddess, balancing the Green Man and interpreting and mediating him to Luke. While Luke is arguably empowered by becoming the Green Man at the end, along the way, as we have seen, there are tensions between words and pictures as to how much autonomy and agency the boy has in relation to the Green Man and the old woman.

Mooney's view of the Green Man in *The Green Man* accords with that in her young adult novel *Joining the Rainbow*:

> He forces his way up with the daffodils in the windowbox in the heart of the city; he lurks in the weeds which penetrate the stony wasteland. He is the wounded bark of the old tree in the park. (Mooney 1997b: 100–101)

It was expedient for the church to tolerate his images; he has been forgotten, but is now 'Awakening', in an essay 14-year-old Kaz writes in the first person as the Green Man. Kaz gets involved with a protest against a road bypass, and with the protester Ash, who has escaped a violent and abusive background, changed his name, and found a new 'family'. The title *Joining the Rainbow* has multiple references:

- Kaz joins the protesters' diverse alliance;
- Ash has an optimistic vision of the rainbow having no end and always being there: 'Suppose the ends just go on, so that it joins

up beneath the earth, and it's a beautiful great circle of light and colour' (78);

- 'joining the rainbow' complements Keats's critique of science 'unweaving the rainbow': Kaz knows that a rainbow is not 'merely the refraction of light in drops of crystal rain. Science did not have all the answers' (240).

Joining the Rainbow is unusual among fiction featuring the Green Man in having a female focaliser. To Kaz, the Green Man is a resurgent god, a *genius loci*, and – in Kaz's relationship with Ash – an animus projection. The Green Man's literary predecessor is alluded to when Kaz and her mother first visit the protesters. They hear 'the thin, clear sound of a pipe, the tantalising notes dancing up and down the scale in no familiar tune, but a wild sound, such as the great god Pan might have played, deep in some untamed wood' (27). Ash first appears to Kaz in the guise of the Green Man, his face painted in a wild mask that is to her initially ugly and hostile. Perhaps improbably, Ash is unconscious of adopting the role of Green Man, but when he is made aware, he welcomes it: 'I just did this because we're all about being green, saving the planet. Now you tell me I'm a mythical pagan figure – a real Green Man – and I'm right into that!' (91). To Ash, the Green Man is angry and vengeful about environmental despoliation, and promises victory in their campaign. It is only a moral victory, for the developers move in, and when Ash moves on, Kaz writes to him, 'I remember you as my own green man' (262).

The Green Man presides over the map at the front of the book. To Kaz, he is embodied in an ancient oak scheduled for felling, from which he calls to her and welcomes her. The novel is structured around the Wheel of the Year, with sections called Winter, Spring, Summer and Autumn, but Kaz does not envision the yearly death and resurrection of the Green Man so much as the impending, apocalyptic reawakening that we have seen in *The Giant Under the Snow*, and shall encounter again. There is an emotional complexity to the Green Man and Kaz's reactions to him. He can be sorrowful and pained, fierce and triumphant. Kaz tells Ash, 'I used to think of him as scary, but not now. Sometimes he's friendly, but mostly sad' (170).

When Kaz's face is painted, she feels liberated: 'It was somebody powerful, not just a schoolgirl. For a second she heard ancient drums in her blood, tribal rhythms, which made her forget herself, so that she could do anything' (106). This partakes of Ronald Hutton's 'savage' language of Paganism, but redefines it. Instead of being located elsewhere and condemned, it is regarded as historically native to Britain, and revived and celebrated. Such a post-colonial re-evaluation and nativisation to Britain of 'savage' Paganism looks set to become the dominant language of Paganism, in literature and practice (as argued in Chapter 1, above). Hutton's fourth language of Paganism, as a universal, prehistoric matriarchal religion, underlies the protester Skye's belief that 'all beliefs, in all cultures, go back to the great fertility goddess. This is her hill we're sitting on!' (204). But Kaz disagrees: 'No. I think it's the Green Man's hill. I think he's watching everything that's happening. I think when they cut a branch with a chainsaw he feels it like I'd feel a cut in my arm' (ibid.). She is unsure about the Goddess but is convinced that the Green Man will act.

It is a bold move to portray such a clash of Pagan beliefs, showing that fictional representation of Paganism has matured beyond extremes of condemnation and idealisation to something more realistic. Kaz defies what might be called Pagan orthodoxy in refusing to subordinate the Green Man to the Goddess, but although Kaz appears to win this argument, a school friend has previously warned her: 'You're like one of those born-again religious freaks who's seen the light and thinks everybody else is blind!' (174). Skye has formalised her faith, and Kaz, after raw spiritual experiences such as feeling 'the whole universe [...] compressed into the small patch of rough bark trembling beneath her fingers' (59), is also imposing order on her beliefs.

Jane Gardam's story *The Green Man* (1998) originally appeared in a collection for adults, but has since been published separately in an edition illustrated by Mary Fedden, which I have seen in children's sections of bookshops – though a book being illustrated does not necessarily make it a children's book... Unusually in the current publishing climate, a story for adults seems to have crossed over to children, rather than the other way round. Gardam's tale of the cycle of the Green Man's year is, like him, lyrical and ludic, earthy and elusive. Gardam's sophisticated writing and dry wit bear repeated reading. She emphasises the Green Man's humanity, but his divinity is there too, in his antiquity, cyclic rejuvenation, and encounters with the Devil and Christ. As a man, Gardam's Green Man is like a crotchety farmer, shouting 'get off my land.' He has a house which he uses when he feels the cold, though he keeps all the windows and doors open. Plagued by mice, he buys some poison, but then realises he can expel the mice rather than kill them: 'The Green Man can make mistakes, for he is a man' (16).

In relation to time, he is ancient, but governed by the cycle of the year. In winter, he is seen as a 'shadow', then a 'stump', then a 'scarecrow' until he begins to appear fully around Easter and then reaches his peak in summer. He declines with the fall of the year, but some years later, a green-eyed child and a shadow in the fields suggest he lives. Time is protean in this story, which is encompassed by the cycle of a year, and yet the children playing in the present tense in the opening chapter are grandparents later in the story. The Green Man's constant refrain is 'each to his element.' When his possessions are stolen, he is not particularly bothered, for, as his daughters comment, 'He is in his element when he's away from plenty' (38). Mermaids, though associated with the Green Man in heraldry, confuse him because they have 'No sense of their element. Neither wet nor dry' (17). He abducts two mermaids and contemplates slicing them up, though his daughters rescue them. In a self-conscious comment on the contested folklore of the Green Man, his eldest daughter says 'And *you* thought to be a conservationist!', to which he replies, 'I don't know why, most of it's guesswork' (21).

'For all his stillness he is given to rages' (9), and he is very threatening when he raises his axe high in both hands, only to hand it over pacifically to the loss-adjuster's woman. He is also enigmatic: 'it is hard to get near. Now you see him, now you don't' (9) – Gardam often uses the second person, with some ambiguous slippage between generalising and direct address. The Green Man thinks that 'when I am noticed everyone sees someone different [...] yet nobody knows who I am' (30). Different generations vary in their perceptions of him: old people know his antiquity and that he has many names, and children hug and tease him; but the adult generation in-between dismiss him as a pub name or a drug addict from the Sixties. To his own grown-up sons he is elderly and of unsound mind. When the Devil taunts, 'Nobody believes in you. You're kidsbook stuff' (26), the Green Man responds that children, the old corn chandler and animals do believe.

The Devil is presented as the Green Man's twin and shadow, who tempts him to destroy the earth and start afresh with the moon. The Green Man only just resists, saying, 'You're nothing but my shabby self. You're the dark side of my soul' (27). In a reversal of the interpretation of disgorging heads generating greenery, but in accordance with Basford's observation that 'Sometimes the leaves appear parasitic, drawing their strength from the wretched head which bears them' (Basford 1978: 19), the Devil argues that 'You are strangled by the living green. [...] It is eternal sorrow that stares through the leaves. Sad and bound is the Green Man' (Gardam 1998: 24). The Green Man shares this perception when he attends a harvest festival: 'The Green

Man's head, so beautiful, so passionate, tormented, ardent is being eaten up by oak leaves' in 'the church which is his prison' (30). But while carvings and buildings contain the Green Man in a rigid image, working in the open air he is at one with the greenwood, 'his face dappled by the flickering leaves that caress his cheeks, and sweep out from around his eyebrows' (35).

The Green Man meets Christ in a dream. Christ's 'figure is much like that of the Green Man' and the Green Man thinks 'This is myself' (45). When Christ says 'Today you will be with me in paradise', the Green Man retorts, in characteristic simple, existential sentences:

> I'm the Green Man. The earth is my element. That is my tragedy. You know this. I am not yours. I am bound and tied. I am from some other old place. The very meaning of me is not known. You do not include me. (Gardam 1998: 45)

At this point, the story's epigraph 'The Green Man is no enemy of Christ' (attributed to Ronald Blyth) is repeated; like the epigraph to *The Stones are Hatching* (McCaughrean 1999), it is an uneasy attempt to place the Green Man within a Christian world-view. The Green Man may be no enemy of Christ, but neither is he an equal in Gardam's story: when 'The Green Man falls to his knees, but Christ raises him up' (45), both actions subject the Green Man to Christ. Some readers may not be comfortable with this, but otherwise Gardam's Green Man is a complex, enigmatic character placed in a rural setting which is depicted without romanticism but with affection and humour.

In Geraldine McCaughrean's *The Stones are Hatching* (1999), 11-year-old Phelim Green is hailed as 'Jack o'Green' by a domovoy who warns 'Every moment the stones are hatching, the Worm is waking' (9). The Stoor Worm (from the northern Scottish folk tale – see Manning-Sanders 1976) has been woken by the guns of the Great War, and it is Phelim's quest to defeat the Worm and her 'hatchlings', the mythical creatures the Worm is bringing to life. Phelim is aided, indeed propelled along, by the mumming figures of a Fool (Mad Sweeney), a Maiden (Alexia) and a Horse (Obby Oss). As one might expect from Geraldine McCaughrean, not only is the style beautifully textured, but also the characterisation is complicated and psychologically convincing. Quest narrative is interrogated through Phelim's extremes of resistance and euphoria, and by the moral ambiguity of the outcomes.

Mad Sweeney of the Trees is the Fool who addresses Phelim as 'Green Man' and whose wisdom leads him. Sweeney has been traumatised by war and knows that it is war, not himself, that is mad. But Phelim believes that Sweeney and the others all want something from him, and he resists: 'I'm a boy, not a man. And I'm not Jacko Green. I'm Phelim Green, and I'm not going to fight any Worm' (McCaughrean 1999: 76). Only when he encounters the faeries of Hy Brasil, who relish and take advantage of the bloodshed of human wars, does he adopt the name and role of 'Jack o'Green'. The moment of change for Phelim rings psychologically true because the trigger seems random and trivial: a dead man's shoe banging boat timber sets off a memory of Phelim's bullying sister and absent father. He becomes resolute and authoritative, defeats the faeries, and then pledges to stop the Worm waking: 'The others stared at him, this altered, confident Green Man of theirs' (127).

However, confidence turns into drunken arrogance in the ersatz Pagan revival of 'burning the bush'. His companions have to save him: first the Oss and then, at the cost of her life, Alexia. Even after death she helps, her bones providing a Witch's Ladder for Phelim to climb the Worm. When Sweeney boils up her bones in an oil-drum cauldron, she is reborn. Thus Phelim as the Green Man depends on the feminine, Alexia, for his survival, and it is she, rather than he, who takes the Corn King's death and resurrection role. Phelim completes the quest, but is 'repelled by what he [is] doing [...] the kill-or-be-killed pettiness of it all' (156–157). He feels not triumphant, but compromised: 'In fighting her, he could only become what she was: malevolent, destructive' (157); fighting a monster makes him monstrous. David Wyatt's cover illustration of *The Stones are Hatching* (see Figure 2.2) suggests the same ambiguity by placing the Green Man and the Maiden among the hatching stones, their supposed foes.

The greatest challenge for Phelim is not the flawed heroic quest in the outside world, but asserting himself at home against his bullying sister Prudence. He has realised that he is 'the Stoor Worm in her landscape' (157), and he returns not in triumph, but to feel 'the old helplessness come slurrying down on him, pinning him to the spot, pressing his shoulders into a stoop, oppressing his heart into speechlessness' (174). The root of Prudence's resentment is Phelim's resemblance to his father, a storyteller who refused to enlist, whom Prudence has had committed to an asylum. Phelim summons an ushtey to take Prudence away, though he is 'left with the same kind of emptiness as after killing the Worm' (179). Nevertheless he is at last no longer pressed into maturing, but is allowed to be a boy. Phelim has struggled with the role of Jack o'Green because, it is hinted (and spelled out at the end of the extended US edition), he has been mistaken for his father. Out of

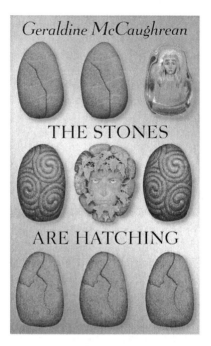

Figure 2.2   Jack o'Green hatches at the centre of David Wyatt's cover illustration for Geraldine McCaughrean's *The Stones are Hatching*

Source: David Wyatt for Geraldine McCaughrean's *The Stones are Hatching* (OUP 1999, ISBN 0192717979).

the shadow of his sister and father, with Aisling ('dreamer'; formerly Alexia, 'helper') for a companion, Phelim can be *not* a Green Man but a Green *Boy*.

The Stones are Hatching presents the Old Ways as harsh, but rues their passing, whilst satirising artificial revivals. The opening sentences of the novel express Phelim's view of magic – that, if it exists, it is not conjuring tricks, nor is it supernatural, but it is the wonder of nature: 'Sometimes, when the winter air turned into a puff of smoke in his mouth, or hail reclinkered the garden path, he suspected there was magic at work' (1). When Phelim claims that people have progressed beyond belief in fairies and the like, the Oss asserts the Pagan cyclic view of time:

So why do Monday come round to Monday, and May to May and zummer to zummer and dawn to dawn? Generation to generation?

Janner, lad! How do a man look at the great wheel of Time and zee a straight line? (McCaughrean 1999: 75)

The Oss regrets the thinning of the old beliefs, even though these beliefs are presented as entailing sacrificial tributes and bribes. When Phelim cuts down the last sheaf of a field of wheat, the harvesters think he should pay in blood:

They had fallen back on the bloody ways of their ancestors. [...] The hot excitement gripping their bowels made them feel more vital and alive, convincing them still further that Old Magic was at work. (McCaughrean 1999: 130)

Though the tone is sceptical about their belief, the assumption that 'the bloody ways of their ancestors' is historical fact is reinforced by the Oss asking 'So, Green Jack. Do you still like the Old Ways?' (131). Saturating the Old Ways with blood could be argued to be a Christian smear on Paganism, whereas blood sacrifice is central to the Judaeo-Christian tradition: 'without shedding of blood is no remission' (Hebrews 9 v. 22). Modern Pagans would emphasise the celebratory over the placatory.

McCaughrean's only use of the word 'paganism' is satirical: 'a splendid day's paganism' (138). The day is organised by the librarian Mr Basil Pringle and is based on rootless book-learning; he is even 'unable, without his reference books, to give a correct name to the Obby Oss' (137). Although there is an anti-war strand to the book, and Phelim's father refuses to join up, Mr Pringle is belittled for being excused service through ill health. The festivities are fabricated, their leader improbable: 'Mr Pringle had reinvented Old Ways which had never even been practised in Storridge. [...] Mr Pringle had taken on a virility and authority no one had ever suspected in him' (136); 'Not since the opening night of the Storridge Players' *Charley's Aunt* had he felt such a surge of adrenaline' (139). The procession through Storridge might be seen as resembling a Worm, and indeed the 'frenzied, terrified joy' (136) turns bad. When the villagers decorate Phelim, a very emotive comparison is drawn – 'They made him as anonymous as a Ku Klux Klansman' (140) – and his participation, intoxicated by attention and drink, is what leads to Alexia's death. Mr Pringle is the unmitigated hate-figure of the book: when Phelim brings himself to kill the Worm's soul-mouse in vengeance for Alexia, he imagines the mouse is Mr Pringle. Pagan readers may react to Mr Pringle's travesty of Paganism as some Christians do to

Philip Pullman's satirical version of the church in *His Dark Materials* – as not resembling their own faith, but still representing a possible danger that they would equally condemn.

* * *

It makes sense in terms of Pagan duotheism that if the Green Man is (an aspect of) the God, then there must be a Green Woman who is (an aspect of) the Goddess. Examples of the Green Woman in children's fiction are much rarer so far than the Green Man, and she tends to be called the Green Lady, as in Helen Cresswell's *Stonestruck* (1995) and Moyra Caldecott's *The Green Lady and the King of Shadows* (1989).[8] Cresswell's Green Lady is a villain; Caldecott's Green Lady is victim, victor and Triple Goddess. In Susan Cooper's *Greenwitch* (1974), matriarchal Old Magic and patriarchal High Magic collide.

In *Stonestruck* (Cresswell 1995), Jessica Weaver is evacuated from blitz London to Powis Castle. Looking over the valley, Jessica thinks, ' "It's green gone mad!" And she felt a stir of excitement, as though something in herself, too, were greening over' (23). Her new environment stimulates and projects the adolescent psychic drama of widening horizons and dislocation: 'the world had at a stroke become wide and dangerous. [...] she was no longer herself, was cut adrift, floating in time and space' (29). Children are being snatched by the Green Lady and her other 'stonestruck' children in a sinister game of chain-tag. When Jessica incautiously wishes she were back home, her shadow self joins the ghostly children. By conquering her fear she reunites with her shadow (the story would be very amenable to a Jungian reading). Jessica bands together with the other evacuees to release the stonestruck children and triumph over the Green Lady.

Jessica's struggle with the Green Lady is about control and agency, and about childhood and adulthood. The Green Lady's offer of perpetual childhood is a terrible trap, which Jessica escapes so that she can mature and 'becom[e] used to living in a world of uncertainties' (119). Despite being 'given a part she did not want to play' (80), she gains ascendancy over the Green Lady: first by seeing through her disguise as Priscilla ('ancient'), the old woman who entraps children; and, ultimately, by leading her fellow evacuees in beating the Green Lady at her own game of chain-tag. There is an echo of Snow White in Priscilla tempting Jessica with an apple, and sometimes Jessica does see herself as a fairytale protagonist. Searching for a girl locked away in a previous century for fear of being taken by the Green Lady, Jessica pretends that she herself is 'the prince out of Sleeping Beauty and the castle's been enchanted a hundred years' (127).

Although Jessica matures and has no desire to remain a child for ever, grown-ups are criticised. Billy, another evacuee, exclaims that adults are a ' "Bloomin" 'orrible lot! Shoving kids on trains, locking kids in rooms!' (161). In the past and present of the story, overprotective parents incarcerate children, depriving them of freedom in order to keep them safe, imposing another kind of abuse because of the perceived threat of abduction. What is more, the adults' reticence about the disappearances and their avoidance of counting children amount to a conspiracy of silence and passive complicity with abuse. It is in being free agents that the parentless evacuee children are able to vanquish the threat.

Cresswell's Green Lady is not a very well realised character. Her motivations are sketchy; she is simply a malevolent force to be destroyed. As Priscilla, she is wicked stepmother and hag witch; as Green Lady she is an alternative witch stereotype: 'beautiful and terrifying [...] cold and careful' (78) with a 'heart of stone' (65), who acquires children rather than producing them. A beautiful, powerful woman cannot possibly be a good mother seems to be the reactionary 'can't have it all' covert ideology lurking here.

The Green Lady and the King of Shadows by Moyra Caldecott (1989) is set in sixth-century Glastonbury. The orphaned novice monk Lukas finds himself dreaming about and re-enacting a Celtic legend from the Mabinogion: the yearly contest between the hero Gwythyr and Gwynn ap Nudd, the King of Shadows, over Creiddylad, the Green Lady. Allied with the hermit Collen, Lukas/Gwythyr releases Creiddylad from imprisonment under the ground, and the three of them confront Gwynn ap Nudd. Like Persephone in Greek myth, Creiddylad spends winter in the underworld and is released for the summer. Every Beltane (May Day), Gwythyr wins Creiddylad back and on Glastonbury Tor they enact the life-renewing marriage of Earth Goddess and Sun God. In Lukas's vision of the ritual, he becomes Gwythyr and sees that 'the white disc of the full moon stood like a bride. The bridegroom, the burning sun, stood beside her' (36). Thus earth and moon goddesses are fused, or just confused. Caldecott's Sun God/Moon Goddess gendering follows a convention that has been challenged by an extensive survey of Sun Goddess/ Moon God myths (McCrickard 1990; from the same publisher as *The Green Lady and the King of Shadows*, as it happens).

Caldecott presents Christianity as absorbing and supplanting Paganism. 'Four times a year, at the turning point of the seasons, the monks wound through the forest, circling the base of the Tor, chanting prayers of exorcism' (11): whilst trying to exorcise the Old Religion, the monks still follow the Wheel of the Year upon which the Creiddylad story revolves. Gwynn ap Nudd, Lord of the Wild Hunt and megalomaniac villain of the piece, is frustrated that that he has 'been pushed aside by the new religion as though he were some sort of outgrown toy' (56). The hermit Collen describes Gwynn in terms of both Judaeo-Christian and Celtic mythology, and as a Faust figure:

> Some call him Lucifer, once a great and mighty Archangel of light - now a dark and bitter shade. [...] Some call him the King of Shadows, Gwynn ap Nudd, Lord of Annwn, and fear him as a god or demon left over from pagan times. Some say that he is no more than an ordinary man, deep into the study of the black arts. (Caldecott 1989: 63, 64)

Like some of the Green Man texts we explored in the previous section, *The Green Lady and the King of Shadows* imposes the teleological on the cyclic. The seasonal enclosure and emergence of Creiddylad, the Green Lady, are broken when Gwynn abducts her indefinitely, and then Lukas releases her permanently. Lukas has an apocalyptic vision of the noisy and noisome future, comparable with Pangaia in Susan Cooper's *Green Boy* (discussed below); and in both novels green growth cracks open and reclaims the endless city.

The Green Lady and the King of Shadows is a revised version of *The King of Shadows* (Caldecott 1981), and it is not only the change of title that reflects Caldecott's developing thinking about the Green Lady. In a vision not in the original version, Lukas follows a stream through a pair of crystal trees to a fair land, where he sees a young woman 'so beautiful that [...] he was unable to take his eyes off her. [...] She was like a princess in an ancient tale' (Caldecott 1989: 25). Then she is a mother 'waiting for him beside the hearth' (26), then an old woman. These three aspects of the Triple Goddess are reified as merely objects of Lukas's desire: 'He had desired her body when she was young, her comfort when she was middle aged, and now he desired her wisdom' (ibid.).

Creiddylad, the Green Lady, goes through the three phases of Maiden, Mother and Crone, but not in order: first, imprisoned, she is the old woman; then, released, she is transformed into young woman; finally, she is 'the Mother of the Earth, the bringer of Life and renewal' (109). Though we are told that Lukas desires the old woman's wisdom, he rejects the grandmother archetype in favour of embracing his anima projection. When he first sees the shackled old woman, he goes on to dream 'that he saw not an old woman upon the floor, but a young woman of great beauty and delicacy, with gold hair falling almost to her feet' (17). And when Lukas/Gwythyr comes to rescue the Green Lady, the 'old, old crone, thin as a skeleton, grey as dust, sagging forward from her chains' metamorphoses into 'petal soft flesh, [...] vibrant strength of life coursing through her limbs' (92).

As an old woman, Creiddylad has no agency or power, but becoming a younger and younger girl she holds 'her head high and walk[s] ahead as though she were choosing of her own free will to do so' (101). The 'as though' is significant: her will is only effective insofar as it conforms to her destiny. She finally comes into her own, leading Lukas and Collen, in the climactic show-down with Gwynn ap Nudd, the King of Shadows, on Glastonbury Tor. The defeat of Gwynn ap Nudd is also, however, a questionable victory of young woman over old woman, beauty over maturity, youth over wisdom.

It may appear wilful to include Susan Cooper's *Greenwitch* (1974) in this section on the Green Lady, when Jane Drew[9] 'had always thought of witches as being female, but she could feel no *she* quality in the Greenwitch' (33). A possible unfortunate implication of Jane regarding the Greenwitch's elemental power as transcending gender is that the feminine is thereby dissociated from power. In any case, Jane's perception of the itness of the Greenwitch may surprise the reader, given the evidence to the contrary. In the spring fertility rite of making the Greenwitch, 'only women are allowed to be present' (23), and these women refer to the Greenwitch as 'she', as I shall. The Greenwitch represents ancient, amoral, matriarchal Wild Magic, by contrast with dualistic patriarchal High Magic. She is 'outside Time, boundless, ageless, beyond any line drawn between good and evil' (34); her moral neutrality is projected through the form that her control of the weather takes: 'It seemed neither night nor day. The sky was grey all around' (49). Wild Magic is 'not permitted' to take sides in High Magic's Christianised confrontation between Light and Dark. This is 'the Law', the origin of which is not specified.

Wild Magic and the deep sea are the realm of the goddess Tethys, the Greenwitch's mother, whereas High Magic is the province of males – Merriman and Will Stanton for the Light, an unnamed male painter for the Dark. While Merriman comes to realise that he cannot command the Wild Magic, the painter does succeed in summoning the Greenwitch, only to find that she furiously refuses to obey him. Even so, this refusal effects a further lurch towards the Dark, as the Greenwitch appears 'as a great mass of black absolute darkness, blotting out all light' (99). There is carnivalesque anarchy to the Wild Magic, 'which is without discipline or pattern' (106), and the Greenwitch knows that it 'besets the minds of men, calling up all the terrors they have ever had, or their forefathers have ever had' (122).

This is one telling instance where it is questionable whether 'men' includes all humankind, or refers only to males; 'forefathers' would suggest the latter, and therefore that Wild Magic is feminine, and more fearsome for men than for women. When the Greenwitch claims that men have nothing to do with her, Will retorts: 'Men have everything to do with you. [...] They make you, each year. Each year, they throw you into the sea. Without men, the Greenwitch would never have been born' (116). Will's generalising hides the clear distinction in sex roles: women alone make the Greenwitch, and men alone throw her into the sea. In reply, the Greenwitch asserts that she is not made by men, but 'given real life only by the White Lady' – Tethys (117). When the Greenwitch accuses, 'You are all self-servers, Light, Dark, men' (ibid.), it is again open to interpretation whether the criticism applies generally to the human species, or exclusively to the male sex and the patriarchal order of the High Magic.

Both Tethys and the Greenwitch are hugely powerful, but isolated, so that Jane feels for the Greenwitch 'a terrible awe, and a kind of pity as well' (34). Tethys and the Greenwitch are also similar in their abrupt rages, and the Greenwitch is portrayed as impulsive, petulant and pettish, 'clutching at something for comfort, like a child with a toy' (51). Though the Wild Magic endures, it is presented as childishly primitive and arbitrary. It is possible to question such a pejorative, developmental view of childhood, and its yoking to the feminine and to an evolutionist model of religion. Indeed, Cooper goes on to take a very different perspective on childhood in relation to the Goddess and the Green Man in *Green Boy* (2002), discussed in the next section.

*   *   *

Having looked in turn at texts which feature either the Green Man or the Green Lady, now we move on to those that combine the Green masculine and feminine. Some of the stories already considered do mediate and modulate the Green Man's power through female characters: Alexia in *The Stones are Hatching*; the wise old women Elizabeth Goodenough in *The Giant Under the Snow* and Lily in Mooney and Cann's *The Green Man*. But *The Oak King and the Ash Queen* (Phillips 1984), *The Forestwife Trilogy* (Tomlinson 1993, 1998, 2000), short stories from Datlow and Windling (ed.) (2002), and *Green Boy* (Cooper 2002) go much further, making a central theme of balancing masculine and feminine.

As its title signals, *The Oak King and the Ash Queen* by Ann Phillips (1984) is concerned with balance: among the trees and in the natural world; between the sexes, the elements and the seasons. This scheme is exceptionally well worked-out and thought-provoking. The story starts like a fairy tale. Similarly to lady Heurodis in 'Sir Orfeo' (see Tolkien 1975), 12-year-old Dan accesses another realm by falling 'asleep under an oak tree in the middle of the Forest in the hottest part of the day' (Phillips 1984: 1). The Oak King allows three questions a day, and is averse to metal and to revealing his 'true' name; Dan is at first wary of eating with his host in case he is trapped permanently. The enchantment for Dan and his twin sister Daisy is bounded by the fairy tale period of a year and a day.

Time and place partake of a Pagan chronotope. The Forest's antiquity and physical centrality are emphasised when Bramble explains, 'of all the old forests, it's the one nearest to the middle of the kingdom' (117). The novel is divided into sections that run through the seasons, from summer to summer again. The forest people celebrate two Turnings (Midwinter and Midsummer) and two Changes (May and November: Beltane and Samhain). These festivals are about maintaining balance between the seasons. In the November fire festival, the Oak King willingly allows Holly, the Winter King, to behead him and take his place, while the Ash Queen relinquishes her elemental symbols to Ivy and joins Oak on the fire. At the winter solstice, also Daisy and Dan's birthday, the winter people reign; they are more inclusive and informal than the summer people, and hold lively games of female–male rivalry. The revival of Oak and Ash at May Day is accompanied by joyous sport.

Trees and seasons correspond to elements. Oak has dominion of earth, while Ash holds air and water. Fire they share, as Oak explains: 'It is essential and appalling; a terror and a need. The end and the beginning. Neither of us could possess it alone' (18). The elements link to the Wheel of the Year, as Mistletoe spells out: 'Water at mid-summer; earth in autumn; fire at midwinter; air in spring. Times and seasons. You people used to understand and celebrate with us' (30). Oak too maintains that tree people and human people once shared a primal, global religion (Ronald Hutton's third language of Paganism) of 'The rising of the sun, the turning of the year, the growing of things; and their death and burial' (17), which has since been Christianised.

Oak tells Dan, 'if you don't believe that your religion knows about me, look carefully in your church. My likeness is there' (73). The likeness, which Dan finds 'fierce' and 'forbidding' (158), is a foliate head. It is only Dan and Daisy's older sister, a Christian, who refers to the head as the Green Man, whom she regards as 'pagan', 'heathen', 'the demon king appearing in the woods'. Dan argues against her: 'It isn't pagan. It's to do with the creation part of religion. The rising of the sun and the turning of the year' (85). It is noticeable that for Dan, as well as his older sister, 'pagan' is a bad word, and that Phillips treats associating ecclesiastical foliate heads with the Green Man as suspect.

Religion for Oak is a matter of balance: 'we are all in the Rising and the Falling. That's God. [...] that which is perpetually making and unmaking, and itself being made and unmade. The very heart of balance' (73). Balance pervades the narrative: between the sexes, represented by the Oak King and the Ash Queen; between winter and summer. The balance is maintained through ritual conflict, in which Daisy and Dan become involved. Daisy and Dan are themselves balanced, as twins of opposite sexes with birth names which are anagrams of each other: Diana and Aidan. Gender, and thus each side in the Forest War, is assigned meticulously to trees, birds and beasts – not according to biological sex, but by a kind of elemental essentialism. Oak explains that maleness is associated with 'The trees which hold with the dominion of earth choose the things of the earth. They choose rootedness, or might; they choose standing; they choose the heel,' while femaleness is associated with 'The trees which follow water or air choose leafiness, or light; they choose dancing, they choose the hand' (53). Though Dan and Daisy take opposite sides, they both become green children, 'grimed by earth, mud, moss and the dust in the bark of trees; [...] scratched by rough branches and thorns, and bits of leaf and twig got into their eyes and mouths' (49).

Daisy overcomes her initial resistance to fighting to find it glorious and absorbing: she become adept with bow and arrow, and enjoys the tactics of patience and stealth that frustrate Dan. On her 13th birthday, the start of the teenage years and a symbolic threshold into adolescence, Daisy insists that she be called by her given name, Diana: 'Queen and huntress, chaste and fair' (110), as her father hails her (quoting Ben Jonson). When peace is established, Diana misses 'All that lovely fighting!' (169). Ash has previously said to Daisy, 'What world is it where females don't fight! It must be a world devised by males, where they can triumph unopposed' (33) – but alternatively, males could refuse to fight!

The outcome of the mock war between the male and female sides of the summer people is a draw, as it needs to be to preserve balance. A real threat to the balance comes from the winter people, led by the Holly King and the Ivy Queen, who, like Caldecott's Gwynn ap Nudd, intend to overturn the order of the seasons permanently. In the ideology underlying this conflict, conservational and conservative values are worryingly elided, and these conservative values are literally 'naturalised' by being tied to the seasons. Humans are culpable for cutting down 'the old jumbled forests, oak and birch and beech and ash and hazel' (81) and replacing them with winter evergreens, 'fast-growing trees – not the trees of our native soil' (88): the conservation message is confused with a parochial rejection of the non-native, with all that implies in human terms, for example in the treatment of immigrants and asylum seekers. Once the rebellion has been crushed, Oak declares 'you must include only the true foresters, and shut the extra people out' (150).

Holly offers power-sharing, by contrast with being 'vassals of Oak and Ash', and there is a Marxist dialectic to his assertion: 'Of course there must be balance: but balance means extremes' (124). Dan and Daisy have a flash of sympathy for the winter trees, as 'a despised minority' and 'outcasts' (66), but ultimately do not trust them. Like the stoats and weasels in *The Wind in the Willows* (Grahame 1908), the winter people are anarchic revolutionaries against whom the old order must be upheld. A disappointing aspect of the resolution of the novel is how Mistletoe, a most interesting, liminal character, becomes fixed. Previously he has slipped between Oak King and Ash Queen, and between summer and winter courts, as go-between, interpreter and spy. In an echo of the Norse myth in which Loki slays Balder with a mistletoe dart, Mistletoe has attempted (but failed) to assassinate Oak. Mistletoe does not want to choose between summer and winter – 'I grow on oak and apple, summer trees. I'm greeny-gold all winter. I have to be both' (151) – but Oak assigns him to 'watch the balance in the winter court'. Confining Mistletoe to one place makes the balance frigid rather than fluid.

Robin Hood is mentioned on the first page of *The Oak King and the Ash Queen*, and is known to the tree people as Robin Wood; and Daisy has heard of the May Queen and Green Man, but this is not overtly linked with Ash and Oak's May Day rebirth and festivities. Marian and Robin Hood, and their guises as May Queen and Green Man, are at the core of Theresa Tomlinson's *Forestwife Trilogy* (1993, 1998, 2000). These roles are what I concentrate on here, as I have considered elsewhere

(Bramwell 2005a) the Forestwife wise women, and the ways in which the narratives embody a female and Pagan chronotope.

The epigraph to *The Forestwife* is an extract from the Grimms' fairytale 'The Old Woman in the Forest' in which a tree turns into a handsome young man. It transpires Marian's nurse has told her this and other stories, including Marian's favourite, 'the tale of the green lady, the beautiful spirit of the woods, who walked through the forest, blessing the trees with fruitfulness, hand in hand with the green man' (Tomlinson 1993: 6). When Marian first sets eyes on Robert (Robin), she finds 'her mind drifting into a dream of the green lady and her forest lover. It seemed he was part of the woodland itself; grown from the trees, the bracken and the rich dark earth' (54). This picture of Marian and Robert as green lady and green man seems to uphold the belief held by some Pagans that the Robin Hood legends 'originated in Pagan myths of the Green Man of the forest who wandered the woods accompanied by the Goddess, guarding and cherishing the life there' (Crowley 1996: 75).

The sequels to *The Forestwife* make May Queen and Green Man proper nouns and extend the roles from Marian and Robert to Magda and Tom, their successors as Forestwife and Hooded One. It seems that the May Queen represents the youthful aspect of the Forestwife and the maiden face of the Triple Goddess, while the Green Man is the youthful aspect of the Hooded One. Paul Young's striking cover art for the second part of the trilogy, *Child of the May* (1998), depicts the May Queen dressed in white standing in front of a towering, glowering Green Man, evoking oppositions of light and dark, beauty and beast. I am not sure that such stark oppositions are corroborated by the text, which nevertheless does to an extent redefine the gender roles of Maid Marian and Robin Hood: though largely confined to the forest, Marian is more effective in righting wrongs than Robert, who wanders widely but achieves little. *The Path of the She-Wolf* (2000), the conclusion to the trilogy, goes further by exchanging roles: Tom is experienced in midwifery, and Marian acts as the Hooded One.

Earlier I looked at Patricia A. McKillip's story 'Hunter's Moon' from the collection *The Green Man: Tales from the Mythic Forest* (Datlow and Windling (ed.) 2002). This important anthology seems to be aimed at teenagers, many of the protagonists being adolescents. In Delia Sherman's 'Grand Central Park', for example, the narrator's perception of the 'Green Queen' is framed by youth language and cultural references, and concern with appearance: 'Next to her, Britney Spears is a complete dog' (Datlow and Windling (ed.) 2002: 27). The Green Queen is changeable, and can become 'less street kid, more like Mom' (29) or 'like somebody's Aunt Ida from the Bronx' (32). As with Mooney and Cann's *The Green Man*, Sherman finds a green space in the heart of the city; likewise Midori Snyder's 'Charlie's Away' is set in 'a piece of wild wood left in the city' (Datlow and Windling (ed.) 2002: 139). The 'mythic forest' also appears in the desert (Emma Bull's 'Joshua Tree') and in a backyard grove of plastic bags (Kathe Koja's 'Remnants'). Terri Windling's introduction partakes of the trend to absorb into the Green Man other figures and gods, including Jack-in-the-Green, the Green Knight, Dionysus and Cernunnos; similarly, Windling sees goddesses such as Artemis and Sheela-na-gig as aspects of the Green Woman. Male and female divinities and spirits are balanced throughout the collection as a whole, and within some individual stories.

When missing artist Frank Spain encounters Lily in 'Somewhere in My Mind There Is a Painting Box' by Charles de Lint, the artist at first mistakes her for the Lady of the Wood: 'It was the wild tangle of your red hair – the leaves in it and on your sweater. But you're too young and your skin's not a coppery brown' (Datlow and Windling (ed.) 2002: 60). A carving of the Lady in a cave in the forest portrays her thus: 'Her hair was thick with leaves and more leaves came spilling out of her mouth, bearding her chin' (73) – 'bearding' perhaps making her somewhat androgynous. In search of her, Frank Spain disappears again, but Lily decides not to follow him into another world but to remain in the wonder of this one, taking to heart the Apple Tree Man's observation: 'Sometimes people need fairies and fancies to wake them up to what they already have' (67–68). The Lady of the Wood and the Apple Tree Man may be seen as balancing feminine and masculine, but they have different roles in the narrative: she is the object of a quest, never directly encountered, whereas he can interact and has a voice.

Midori Snyder's 'Charlie's Away' is inspired by Irish epic 'Sweeney in the Trees' (as is the character Mad Sweeney in McCaughrean's *The Stones are Hatching*, discussed above). In Snyder's story, Charlie takes time out from his parents and from grief for his dead sister by climbing his favourite oak tree and entering the huge Greenwood. There he is greeted by a woman who says, 'I'm known by many names, Charlie, most your mouth cannot say. But you may call me the Greenwoman, and I will answer to that' (Datlow and Windling (ed.) 2002: 151). By contrast with de Lint's story, the protagonist is male and the mentor female, but, as well as the Greenwoman, a horned man appears later in the story, and both are essential to explaining the mystery of Charlie's sister's birth, life and death.

Jeffrey Ford's 'The Green Word' focuses on three connected Green Men, who are presided over by a line of witches who revere 'the great green mind that flows through all of nature' (359–360). The story is set in a high medieval world, in which King Pious persecutes the rebellious people of the forest. Moren Kairn, condemned to be executed, is visited by a crow from the witch of the forest, and given a seed which he swallows. His perceptions alter so that he sees the people of the royal court as a thicket of trees, and he too becomes green. His final thought when he is beheaded is of 'himself, a thousandfold, flying on the wind, returning to the green world' (356). From the spot where Kairn's blood falls, the witch pulls up a mandrake, carves and animates it into a second Green Man, who reveals his name is 'Vertuminus' (compare the Roman god of seasonal change, Vertumnus, possibly the origin of C. S. Lewis's Mr Tumnus – see Ford 1994).

Vertuminus's heart is a blue fruit that 'contains the green word. It is what gives me life' (Datlow and Windling (ed.) 2002: 374). King Pious removes it, and the second fruit that grows in its place, and has Vertuminus destroyed. The King compels the Moren Kairn's daughter to eat one fruit, and he eats the other. To him, the green word is 'a single syllable comprised of two entities, one meaning life and one death, that intermingled and intertwined and bled into each other' (379). When he hears that the stockaded rebels have escaped with the aid of a tree that grew overnight, the king becomes the third Green Man, spewing vines which turn the palace into a forest. Kairn's daughter becomes the latest avatar of the witch and plants the seed of the blue fruit, which links the three Green Men: her father, Vertuminus and King Pious. 'With her new powers came new responsibilities as the forest people looked to her to help them in their bid to rebuild their village and their lives' (381–382); to her, the green word is love. The ways in which Ford's Green Men depend on the witch for their being is similar to the relationship between the Green Man and the goddess Gaia in *Green Boy* by Susan Cooper (2002).

Green Boy is narrated by Trey Peel, whose sex is never specified. Trey's environment in the Bahamas is threatened by an ecologically disastrous tourist development. At the suspended moment between tides, Trey and her younger brother Lou access another world. Whether Pangaia is a parallel, future, or past (lost civilisation) world is deliberately left unclear, but what is clear is that Pangaia's overdevelopment writes large the present-day ecological warning. Trey observes that in Pangaia 'Everywhere we had been, the land was paved or concreted and built-over, jammed with people. The air was hazy and the water was brown, and no stars shone' (Cooper 2002: 91). There is an Orwellian tinge to Cooper's dystopia: people do not talk to each other, but are constantly exposed to television pictures of war. The only green is the Wilderness, but this harbours fearsome mutants from genetic engineering and cloning. Pangaia is a self-regulating organism with a mind called Gaia, according to Bryn, one of the ecowarriors in an underground movement fighting a 'Greenwar'. Bryn then strays from the Gaia hypothesis of James Lovelock (1979) by claiming that Gaia elects human agents such as himself. As we shall see, this is not the only mistake Bryn makes about Gaia.

Trey's seven-year-old brother Lou cannot speak and has seizures, but is exceptionally sensitive to animals. In Pangaia, he is 'strange and special' (Cooper 2002: 19); according to underground member Annie, 'he is magical, he is predestined. We have been waiting for him. Only he can save this world, only now and only here' (40).[10] Lou is homophonic with Lugh, the Celtic God of light, and a number of the rebels have Celtic names – Math, Bryn, Gwen. Charles Butler thinks that 'it is hard to feel that the power of such associations is increased by being placed so far out of their traditional context' and that the 'specifically Celtic element is largely subsumed within a modern "myth" of genuinely global significance, that of Gaia' (Butler 2006b: 231). Annie thinks that Lou has come to fulfil an ancient prophecy from Gaia which predicts that Lugh will save Pangaia at his feast of Lughnasa, 1 August (one of the Pagan festivals of the Wheel of the Year). A quest through a chthonic labyrinth (a symbol of the Goddess) leads to an encounter with Gaia, 'a woman with kind eyes and a strong mouth' who speaks 'like the voice of the whole earth' (Cooper 2002: 144).

Bryn expects Gaia to demand sacrifice, but he is mistaken. The Goddess rejects both heroism and sacrifice: 'You mistake me always. You dream of monsters, who will kill your heroes. No! No monsters are needed. I ask not for sacrifice, but for renewal' (ibid.). There is no blood when the Green Man is called up, but red flowers flow out of his mouth, along the streets and into the sea. Cooper's Green Man is huge, unstoppable, and full of laughter. Like Mooney and Cann's Green Man, he erupts into and transforms an urban landscape: 'sharp green sprouts came breaking up out of stone and concrete and brick, bursting up, cracking the paved ways' (Cooper 2002: 152).

Cooper's Green Man only has life and power through the wisdom and direction of Gaia, and she places children at the centre: 'the weaver of his rebirth [...] is a child. [...] Children weave story' (145). Children's tag games and chants summon the Green Man, and Trey perceives that:

> We all have these rhymes and games that we learn from other kids when we're small, and the younger ones learn them from us, and so on. But when we grow up, we forget them. Only the little ones keep carrying them, only the little ones know them. (Cooper 2002: 150)

Like McCaughrean, Cooper rejects the model of childhood as a developmental stage to be got through, which is the drive of the quest narrative these authors interrogate. For them, magic is a metaphor for the child's unique imagination rather than for maturation (see Chapter 1, Uses of Magic 1 and 2). Trey's thoughts affirm the model of childhood as a distinct culture, 'an autonomous part of life, [...] its passage [...] entailing some losses' (Hollindale 1997: 13).

Back in Trey's Bahamian home, a hurricane puts paid to the development of the tourist resort. Trey interprets the hurricane as an echo of the Green Man:

> In Pangaia he had destroyed the works of humans and reclaimed the land for Nature. Here, Nature wars erupting to claim land and sea for itself. Himself. Herself.
>
> Herself seemed the most right, somehow. Maybe Nature was just another name for Gaia. (Cooper 2002: 163)

The Green Man does not appear directly in the primary world; the focus is all the more on the earth Goddess, Gaia. Trey expresses the pantheistic belief that Nature (with a capital 'N') can be equated with divinity, but privileges Gaia: Trey thinks 'Maybe Nature was just another name for Gaia' – not 'Maybe Gaia was just another name for Nature.'

Cooper's Green Man is one whose rebirth is a single, apocalyptic event to redress ecological crisis, yet his resurrection is tied to the repeating seasonal festival of Lughnasa, and the flow of red flowers suggests feminine cyclic renewal. In Pagan theology, the Green Man is often regarded as Great Mother Goddess's son and consort, dependent upon her for his rebirth (see Crowley 1996). This dependency is rarely depicted in fiction, but *Green Boy* shows it. *Green Boy* is just as distinctive in making children's imaginative play essential to the Green Man's rebirth. In many texts, the Green Man is confined to locations in

England; Susan Cooper's Caribbean and parallel world settings broaden his role and relevance.[11]

*   *   *

This is an exciting time to be observing the emergence of the Green Man as a new literary God. The tension in many Green Man texts between the cyclic and the apocalyptic may well reflect the perception that global warming is wrenching the seasons out of joint and the only remedy is radical change. 'Think globally, act locally' is the ecological slogan, and placing local environmental concerns in the context of global vision should prevent the search for – or invention of – native deities from becoming parochial and inward-looking.

Presenting the Green Man as intervening, globally or in individual lives, can be regarded as circumscribing human autonomy and agency. Some texts present rather earnest didactic models of (usually male) maturation, pressing towards adulthood and not allowing the child to be a child. And there is a risk of perpetuating and recreating patriarchy when the Green masculine is not balanced by the feminine, although many of the texts that have been discussed above attempt this balance in some way. The tensions and ideological traps associated with the Green Man in fact serve to provoke very fine, original writing, such the childhood-centred, quest-questioning narratives of Geraldine McCaughrean's *The Stones are Hatching* and Susan Cooper's *Green Boy*. The most recent stories move away from the Green Man as eco-apocalyptic figure and subsumer of all manner of gods and traditions, attempting instead to put him into more coherent mythological contexts: Tobias Druitt's *Corydon and the Island of Monsters* and Sophie Masson's *Thomas Trew and the Horns of Pan* revive Pan and relate the Green Man to him, while Catherine Fisher's *Darkhenge* (discussed at the end of Chapter 4, below) places a Green Man figure in Celtic mythology. The Green Man has not yet stabilised into a literary convention, and I hope that he will not, but will continue to be depicted with imaginative diversity.

3
Shamanism and the Pull of the North

A shaman is someone who is capable of entering into trance and journeying in spirit to other realms, returning with knowledge beneficial to the community. The trance can be induced by various means: 'music, song, dance, pain, traditional hallucinogenics and stillness' (Maclellan 1995: 140). The soul-journeying shaman is accompanied by, works with, and can even transform into, a 'power animal'. Becoming a shaman involves an initiatory crisis of psychic death, dismemberment and reconstitution. The popular cultural currency of shamanism is demonstrated by the scene in *The Simpsons Movie* (2007) in which Homer arrives at an epiphany under the ministrations of an Alaskan Inuit woman. She gives him a bubbling liquid, throat sings with him (the chant and Homer's dance moves are more likely derived from stereotypes of Plains Indians than Inuit practices), and breathes into his mouth to facilitate soul-journeying, represented as psychological through the ballooning of Homer's head and the back of it opening up. Through mental landscapes of frozen staircases and speaking totem poles, Homer arrives among trees with twiggy hands which dismember him and only reassemble him once he gets his epiphany: 'In order to save myself, I have to save Springfield! That's it, isn't it?' ... though the notion of personal salvation is an imposition on shamanism.

A whole book could be written about shamanism in children's fiction, so for manageability and focus this chapter will have to be selective. As the term 'shaman' is Siberian in origin, and as it can be argued that 'circumpolar culture [...] has been a continuous whole, not only with regard to historical content, but also for its ecological integration of culture and religion' (Hultkrantz 1991: 10), I shall concentrate on stories set in North Eurasia and a few that cross between Europe and North America. The essential argument of this chapter is that representations of shamanism in children's fiction make significant interventions in current controversies about shamanism over issues such as decontextualisation, personal development, cultural integrity, and gender – debates which will now be outlined.

One criticism of some contemporary neo-shamanism is that it is just too casual and easy. This could be the reaction to Nevill Drury observing that 'within an hour or so of drumming, ordinary city folk are able to tap extraordinary mythic realities that they have never dreamed of' (Drury 2000: 9). However, others emphasise that shamanism is a perilous calling: it 'is not merely a weekend of entertainment [...]. Rather, it is a very powerful and dangerous practice to which one is called, at times against one's own desires' (Versluis 1993: 52). Children's fiction featuring shamanism does often show the toughness of a shamanic vocation. In *The Bearwood Witch* by Susan Price (2001a), the practices of the eponymous shaman in present-day Birmingham have 'nothing to do with pretty crystals or scented candles' (that is, the New Age); rather, 'A shaman's way was often cruel and ugly, and it took courage to follow. Those who weren't strong enough often turned back in disgust and fright' (Price 2001a: 156). Examples discussed later in this chapter frequently show shamanism to be an unbidden, even resisted, and harrowing calling.

Modern Western Pagan shamans are different from historical shamans – 'more individualistic [...]. They have *chosen* to experiment with "techniques of ecstasy" mediated by anthropologists, rather than being *compelled* by a powerful initiatory experience' (Harvey 1997: 111, original italics). Such individualistic shamanism can amount to 'a self-conscious, counter-cultural, reversal of attitudes dominant in western societies' (Hutton 2001: 159). Against the elective individualism of neo-shamanism, prominent contemporary shamans stress the shaman's role in the community: Geo Cameron maintains that 'the social role of the shaman is to use the spiritual power he [or she] gains to help the community' (Cameron 1997), and Gordon Maclellan believes that 'the shaman is empowered to act by the community [...] Shamans belong to their people' (Maclellan 1995: 142).

These oppositions – compulsion and choice, individualism and community, conformity and subversion – are very much the concerns of young adult fiction and literary criticism of it. Shamanism in the stories analysed in this chapter is the focal point for adolescent characters' self-realisation as individual subjects and agents in society, in heightened tension with the compulsions of shamanic vocation and apprenticeship. Shamanism's subversive and countercultural potential is realised, for example, in Susan Price's *The Ghost Drum* (1987), where it is used to empower the powerless, to give voice to the voiceless, and so to defy the established order; to privilege the female over the patriarchal, the poor over the rich, the provincial over the central, the diverse over the monolithic, the wild over the controlled.

Neo-shamanism may run counter to dominant Western values, but at the same time it has been accused of running counter to the cultures from which it borrows – or steals. Speaking of Westerners 'wanting to be Indian', Myke Johnson warns of the trap in which 'Indians become the "utopic other" holding the dreams we wish were true' (Johnson 1995: 282). 'Utopic' is a resonant term: there is not only the sense of the ideal(ised) society, but also of 'no-place', implying that neo-shamanism can be rootless and decontextualised. The children's fiction discussed in this chapter places shamanism in vraisemblant prehistoric and historic milieux, often at key moments of contact and conflict, such as early modern European privateering and colonialism in North America.

While the integrity of Native American traditions has been asserted against cultural dilution and theft (Johnson 1995, Mumm 2002), Heathen traditions (Norse, Anglo-Saxon) have been accused of taking cultural integrity to an extreme of racial exclusivity. J. R. R. Tolkien despaired of Nazism 'Ruining, perverting, misapplying, and making for ever accursed, that noble northern spirit, a supreme contribution to Europe, which I have ever loved, and tried to present in its true light' (cited in Rudgley 2006: 160). Any reading of the use of Norse and Anglo-Saxon mythology in children's fiction has to contend with the widely reported reputation of some present-day Heathenism for right-wing and even neo-Nazi ideology. Margot Adler admits that she avoided Norse Paganism in the first edition of *Drawing Down the Moon*, and, when she did open this 'can of worms' for the second, she found Heathen groups to be patriarchal in structure, and that 'In general, Odinism attracts people who are more politically conservative than the majority of Neo-Pagans. They are uncomfortable with feminism, anarchism, and diversity in sexuality and life style' (Adler 1986: 279).

Christopher Partridge corroborates that 'some Heathen groups [...] teach that gay and lesbian relationships are "unnatural, confused and no part of Odinism"' (Partridge 2001: 169). Partridge observes that 'extreme right-wing' views are 'particularly evident within Heathenism [...though] it should also be noted that there are many Heathens who cannot be considered sympathetic to fundamentalist-like, right-wing extremism' (168). Graham Harvey takes a similar line, 'that Heathens are likely to be politically right-wing and generally conservative in their views [...unlike] many other Pagans, who tend to be politically left-wing and generally liberal or radical in their views' (Harvey 1997: 65), though he is sure that there is still some diversity of political belief among Heathens. Some books on Heathenism, such as Svenson (1998), are very quick to distance themselves from 'a popular misconception that Northern Traditions are misogynist' (Svenson 1998: iii) and from 'misguided racist elements [...] steeped in National Socialist philosophies of a so-called "Master race"' (2), though Svenson describes himself as 'a purist' (v) who will have nothing of 'New Age pick-and-mix' (back cover). Jennings (1998) has a chapter on 'The Hard Questions', in which he argues that 'the Northern European peoples are a mixture [...] and the idea of a pure race [is] laughable' (72), and asserts the Viking achievement in 'democratic government and women's rights' (73).

Of the novels, discussed below, which include Norse and Anglo-Saxon settings and beliefs, Robert Leeson's *Beyond the Dragon Prow* (1973) attempts most directly, though with the displacement of a historical setting, to confront the racial prejudices attributed to some present-day Heathens, by credibly including an African character. Although shamanism is involved in both Norse and Sami (Lapp) traditions, the Viking main character of *Beyond the Dragon Prow* goes to the Sami nomads for healing and wisdom, whereas Susan Price's Ghost World trilogy (Price 1987, 1992, 1994a) problematically grafts Norse mythology onto Sami/Siberian shamanism. *Beyond the Dragon Prow*, the Ghost World trilogy, and *Elfgift* and *Elfking* (Price 1995, 1996) have an egalitarian spirit and interrogate the fighting ethos. These texts also challenge polarised constructions of gender roles. This is a potential the Norse tradition has, for not only is the god Odin a shaman figure, so is the goddess Freyja (Eliade 1964, Crossley-Holland 1980). Any rigid division between '*seidr*, that intuitive, and largely feminine-based, magic of the Norse Tradition' (Jennings 1998: 55) associated with the *völva*, or female seer, and *galdr*, male rune divination, does not hold for these novels, nor for Catherine Fisher's Snow-walker trilogy (1993, 1995, 1996), wherein both shamanism and rune magic can be practised by either sex.

More broadly, questions of shamanism and gender have been much debated. Ward Rutherford (1986, *passim* but especially Chapter 2: 'The Eternal Conflict') is adamant that shamanism is a male preserve with 'a profound and remorseless antipathy to the feminine' (29). Such a view is easily countered, by avoiding global generalisations and looking at individual cultures. In Siberia, 'A shaman could be of either sex or even of indeterminate sex' (Riordan 1989: 18). Colin Thubron (1999) observes that 'In Kyzyl's museum [...] a map shows that in 1931 Tuva had

725 shamans, 314 of them women' (Thubron 1999: 99). Ronald Hutton (2001) uses the same figures and concludes that 'What is very clear is that female shamans were found throughout Siberia' (Hutton 2001: 105). There is, however, a lack of consensus on the sex of Sami shamans. Juha Pentikäinen argues that 'the shaman drum was taboo for women' and that Sami shamanism was 'a male institution' (Pentikäinen 1987: 142), and yet Bo Lundmark (1987) counters (at the same Symposium) with documented examples to disprove such an assumption. Thus, across cultures or within them, generalisations about gender and shamanism are difficult to establish, just as shamanism itself as a 'category simply does not exist in a unitary and homogeneous form, even within Siberia and Central Asia' (Atkinson 1992: 308). Shamans of both sexes appear in the children's fiction considered in this chapter, though it has to be said that male shamans are more likely to be depicted as villains or charlatans.

The organisation of the rest of this chapter is as follows. After taking a look at Rudyard Kipling's 'Quiquern' (1895), with its quite sceptical take on Inuit shamanism and belief, the following four sections explore some notable depictions of northern shamanism in children's fiction published in the last 20 years or so. There appears to be, very roughly, a trend that the more recently a text is written, the further back in time it is set, as if the possibility of depicting shamanism in authentic historical and cultural contexts is receding elusively. Michelle Paver's ongoing *Chronicles of Ancient Darkness* series (2004 onwards) shows Torak's trials as a spirit-walker, and Renn's resistance to becoming a Mage, as they withstand the Soul-Eaters' ambitions to impose a new religion in prehistory. *North Child* by Edith Pattou (2003) and *The Snow Queen* by Eileen Kernaghan (2000) elaborate on northern European fairy tales, foregrounding shamanic aspects and characters, and quests further north. Catherine Fisher's Snow-walker trilogy (1993, 1995, 1996) also has a northward quest, and the accent of its presentation of Norse shamanism and sorcery is on the psychological and the uncanny. Susan Price's lyrical and visceral Ghost World trilogy (1987, 1992, 1994) pits shamans against a tyrannical Czarist state.

The remaining sections of the chapter pick up on particular topics. As indicated above, Heathen traditions are radically reimagined in *Beyond the Dragon Prow* (Leeson 1973) and *Elfgift* and *Elfking* (Price 1995, 1996). Sami life is shown contemporaneously with the time of writing in *The Reindeer and the Drum* (Kerven 1980), *The Summer of the White Reindeer* (Pohlmann 1965) and *The Twins of Lapland* (Jenkins 1960), though these texts vary in the extent to which they present Sami shamanism and pre-Christian belief being remembered, if at all. *The Abduction* by Mette Newth (1987) and *Witch Child* and *Sorceress* by Celia Rees (2000, 2002) show European and indigenous North American cultures in contact and conflict in the 16th and 17th centuries, while young adult characters connect across the divides. Finally, the phenomenon of the Northern Lights is shown to be a focus of different world views in several of the novels already analysed (making the term I proposed in Chapter 1 for representations of northernness, Borealism, particularly apt), and witches and shamanism in Philip Pullman's *His Dark Materials* (1995, 1997, 2000) are also briefly considered.

* * *

Rudyard Kipling's short story 'Quiquern' (1895), from *The Second Jungle Book*, is set 'far away to the north [...] on the north shore of Baffin Land' (Kipling 1895: 133) among a band of nomadic Inuit. The poem that prefaces 'Quiquern' says that the People of Eastern, Western and Southern Ice are being corrupted by contact with the white man, 'But the people of the Elder Ice [are] beyond the white man's ken' (131) – though of course the story does place them within the white man's ken. And it is a particular sort of gaze, romanticising the Inuit as prelapsarian, pre-adult even: 'a very gentle race [...] who did not know exactly what telling a real lie meant, still less how to steal' (138). The knowing narration rationalises their beliefs, and mocks the egoism and showmanship of their *angekok*, or shaman.

'Quiquern' centres on Kotuko, a young man of 14 'tired [...] of helping the women [...] while the men were out hunting' (135). He also longs to join the hunters in 'the *quaggi*, the Singing-House', where the *angekok*'s antics are described in terms redolent of Victorian table-rapping séances: 'the *angekok*, the sorcerer, frightened them into the most delightful fits after the lamps were put out, and you could hear the Spirit of the Reindeer stamping on the roof' (ibid.). Kotuko's father finally acknowledges his son's development by naming a dog for him, and, as in *Black Beauty* (Sewell 1877), there are parallels between child and animal being 'broken in'.

During an exceptionally harsh winter when dog-sickness takes hold, Kotuko's dog and another dog run off, and Kotuko hears the voice of a *tornaq*, the woman-spirit animating a rock, telling him 'I will guide you to the good seal-holes' (Kipling 1895: 143). Rational explanations are offered: exhaustion makes Kotuko suggestible – 'the hunger, the darkness, the cold, and the exposure told on his strength' (142) – and as for the *tornaq*: 'In summer thaws the ice-propped rocks and boulders roll and slip all over the face of the land, so you can easily see how the idea of live stones arose' (ibid.). With the *angekok's* blessing, Kotuko heads north, as the *tornaq* directs, and is accompanied by an unnamed girl of his own age.

The Quiquern of the title is an ominous, two-headed eight-legged dog-like phantom which follows Kotuko and the girl, and leads them to safety from shifting ice. Again there is a rational explanation, realised by the girl this time rather than provided by the narrator, but Kotuko holds fast to his belief that 'the *tornaq* did not forget us. The storm blew, the ice broke, and the seal swam in' (152). He is also sure that the *angekok* song that he howled caused the winds to abate and the ice floe to begin to break up, unseasonably early. On Katuko's and the girl's return, the *angekok* claims credit for their successful quest: 'My body lay still in the *quaggi*, but my spirit ran about on the ice, and guided Kotuko and the dogs in all the things they did. I did it' (153). Now that Kotuko's people are cosy and well-fed, none of them gainsays the *angekok's* pompous self-aggrandisement.

'Quiquern' is carefully researched, containing many genuine Inuit terms, probably derived from a Smithsonian publication (see Lycett 1999), but the mocking tone of the narration even extends to the provenance of the story in a reflexive postscript. The elaborate peregrinations of the piece of ivory on which Kotuko 'scratched pictures of all these adventures' (Kipling 1895: 153) are a pretence of verisimilitude that undoes credibility. Authenticity is further subverted in the final sentence, wherein the narrator appears in the first person for the only time to find the inscribed ivory 'under some rubbish in a house at Colombo' and, impossibly, translate it 'from one end to the other' (154). The more recently published texts analysed in the rest of this chapter are not so playful, and take a much more serious and earnest attitude towards shamanism in indigenous northern cultures.

* * *

Michelle Paver's *Chronicles of Ancient Darkness* series is set in the Stone Age with an imaginary geography, based on north-western Europe. I wanted to start with this series simply because it is new and ongoing (at the time of writing the first four of a projected six instalments had been published), and because it is very thrilling and thought-provoking, thereby being on the cusp of Reader as Hero and Reader as Thinker (see Appleyard 1991). Paver confers most of the shamanic attributes – soul journeying and soul retrieval, foresight and farsight – to Clan Mages, but Torak is exceptional in his world in discovering he can spirit-walk into animals.

In the first book of the series, *Wolf Brother* (Paver 2004), Torak's father Fa, with his dying breath, tells Torak to go north in order to defeat a demon-possessed bear which, against taboo, kills for fun and is menacing the Wolf Clan. The bear was sent against Fa by one of seven power-hungry Soul-Eaters. Fa had been the Wolf Clan's Mage but became estranged from the Clan and kept Torak away from it. Torak must acquire three artefacts to complete the quest and save the clans from the possessed bear. Torak travels through mixed terrain – forest, river, cave, glacier – in a narrative packed with incident and cliffhangers. To take an early example, 'Torak had to make a fire. It was a race between him and the fever. The prize was his life' (25): short, simple sentences, the first with high modality, the other two existential, convey the urgency.

Torak's companions are Renn and Wolf. Renn of the Raven Clan learns Magecraft from her Clan Mage, but prefers to hunt using her skill as an archer. The same age as Torak, 12 winters, she is 'incredibly brave' (148) and she propels Torak onwards with the quest; at crucial moments she proves more knowledgeable than he is. Torak, who was fostered by wolves, has an instinctive understanding of his wolf companion, and to Wolf, Torak's 'eyes were silver-grey and full of light: the eyes of a wolf' (20). For Torak, Wolf is a kind of actualisation of the shaman's power animal and spirit guide. Parts of the story are told from Wolf's defamiliarised point of view, and without doubt Wolf is a very big part of the series' appeal, wolves featuring prominently in Michelle Paver's promotional talks and readers' questions to her.

Torak's character develops through the quest. He acts heroically, but as circumstances dictate he has to use guile rather than force. Fin-Kedinn, leader of the Raven Clan and a mentor figure to Torak, perceives that Torak's great qualities are listening and using his wits. Torak's moral growth hinges climactically on a terrible choice between going after Renn or preserving himself. The test is 'Not whether you could find the third piece of the Nanuak. But whether you could risk it for a friend' (188). Torak's agency is paramount: he has to act when no longer hearing the voice of his dead father, and 'The World Spirit would only help him if he tried to help himself' (215).

The cosmology of *Wolf Brother* is fascinating. Every individual partakes of three souls: the name-soul, the clan-soul, and Nanuak the world-soul. Parts of meals are offered for the clan guardian. Trees and rivers, plants and animals are all animated by spirits and connected by the world-soul, which is addressed before taking anything. There is a prevailing ecological ethic of 'not wasting a thing. That was the age-old pact between the hunters and the World Spirit. Hunters must treat prey with respect, and in return the Spirit would send more prey' (42). The world-soul 'link[s] to all other living things: tree and bird, hunter and prey, river and rock' (12) but it is located in the far north. 'Nanuak is like a great river that never ends. Every living thing has a part of it inside them. [...] Sometimes a special part of it forms, like foam on the river. When it does, it's incredibly powerful' (102): this comparison is highly redolent of the river image David Bohm (1980) uses for his theory that matter (life and non-life) and consciousness are aspects of a holomovement of limitless dimensions.[1]

At one point in *Wolf Brother*, Torak reflects on what he knows and does not know of his people's world view. He contemplates demons, clan guardians and ghosts, and the Hidden People who 'live inside rocks and rivers' and 'seem beautiful until they turn their backs, which are hollow as rotten trees' (Paver 2004: 32). And then he thinks about the World Spirit:

> Until now he'd never even thought about it. It was too remote: an unimaginably powerful spirit who lived far away on its Mountain; a spirit whom no-one had ever seen, but who was said to walk by summer as a man with the antlers of a deer, and by winter as a woman with bare red willow branches for hair. (Paver 2004: 32)

Previously, Torak has had practical concerns and spirituality has not been openly discussed much, yet he knows more than he thinks he does; perhaps all this constructs and positions the implied reader in a similar situation.

Those who perform shamanic functions in *Wolf Brother* are called 'Mages: people who can heal sickness, and dream where the prey is and what the weather will do' (53). Renn knows that sickness is usually caused by eating 'something bad. But sometimes it's because their souls have been lured away by demons. The sick soul needs to be rescued' (159). She has observed her Clan Mage Saeunn tying 'little fish-hooks to her fingertips to help her catch the sick souls; then she takes a special potion to loosen her own souls, so that they can leave her body and find the [demons]' (ibid.). The Mage puts on body paint and a mask to hide her own souls from the demons, and Rann uses a similar technique to disguise and protect one of the quest artefacts: 'she'd made a little box of folded rowan bark, and smeared it with wormwood and red ochre. Then she'd put the stone tooth inside, and tied it up with locks of her own and Torak's hair' (160). Knowledge and power are contested between Clan Mage and Clan leader. When Mage Saeunn favours a trial by combat involving Torak and a stronger opponent, Fin-Kedinn, leader of the Raven Clan, opposes her but has to give way. Fin-Kedinn later prevails by telling Torak what Saeunn kept secret: Torak's unique role and destiny. Knowledge is power, but once known, it cannot be unlearnt. Only as the series progresses does Torak discover the gift and burden of exceptional abilities.

Spirit Walker (Paver 2005), the second volume in the series, again immerses the reader in the world of six thousand years ago through Torak's senses. Animism and ecology remain integral to Torak's outlook. When he builds a shelter, he is 'uneasily aware that he'd caused the death of three saplings. He could feel their souls hanging in the air around him: wistful, bewildered; unable to understand why they'd been robbed of their chance of becoming trees' (50). And when he makes a kill, he knows that 'the oldest law of all' dictates that 'you had to treat the prey with respect, and use every part of it. That was the Pact which had been made long ago between the clans and the World Spirit' (63).

The story is packed with thrilling incidents, such as a formerly friendly boar turning against Torak, and Torak having to stitch his own wound; Torak being trapped in a seal net; and a vertiginous climb for a root to cure the fatal illness that is decimating the clans. This sickness has exposed the limitations of Saeunn the Mage, revered as 'the oldest [person] in the clan by many winters' (17), whose magical and shamanic techniques have proved ineffectual. Torak, impulsive and courageous, determines to find a cure. First he goes into the Deep Forest, to the Forest Horse Clan, a kind of green people (compare Chapter 2 above):

> The men's beards were dyed green, like the moss which hangs from spruce trees. The lips of both men and women were stained a darker green; but most startling of all were the leaves on their faces. Torak saw that these were dense greenish-brown tattoos: oak leaves for the women, holly for the men. (Paver 2005: 66)

Among this clan, Torak finds not a cure, but the cause, as the Leader whispers, 'Tokoroth.' Tokoroth are children brought up deprived of light, warmth, food and friendship to be vessels of demons; a tokoroth 'knows no good or evil. No right or wrong. It is utterly without mercy, for it has been taught to hate the world' (76). If the reader is so minded, this chilling foe raises issues to do with child abuse and children's capacity for evil.

That Saeunn does not know why tokoroth are causing sickness again shows limitations to the Mage's knowledge, which unnerves Renn. Renn continues to prefer hunting to what Saeunn calls her 'destiny' of becoming a Mage: 'people cast her the same wary glances they normally reserved for the Mage. More and more, they regarded her as Saeunn's apprentice. She hated that' (73). Torak, too, struggles with his destiny. He discovers he has the exceptional ability of spirit-walking, the spirit needing to be loosened by stimulation such as smoke inhalation or near-drowning, circumstances which he has not willed. When he learns that a Spirit Walker 'sees, and hears, and feels, just as the body into which it has strayed – and yet remains himself. [...] Spirit-walking is the deepest of mysteries. [...] it is very hard, and very dangerous' (217), Torak is resistant: 'This is a curse. I don't want to be different. It's a curse' (218).

Torak, Wolf and Renn go west to the Seal Islands in search of a solution to the sickness. The Seal Clan honours the Sea Mother, whose arbitrary and amoral Old Magic recalls Tethys in Susan Cooper's *Greenwitch* (1974; discussed in Chapter 2 above). As Tenris, the Seal Clan Mage, explains: 'the ways of the Mother are far harsher, less predictable, than the ways of your Forest' (Paver 2005: 136). When Torak is trapped in a seal net, he thinks he hears the Sea Mother murmuring: '*I am beyond pity or malice, beyond good and evil. I am stronger than the sun. I am eternal. I am the Sea*' (162, original italics). The final showdown of *Spirit Walker* takes place at a turning point of the Wheel of the Year. Not only is Midsummer 'the night of greatest change' (137) and so 'The most potent night for Magecraft' (239), it is also Torak's birthnight, suggesting his potential power as a Mage. And it is abuse of power, the evil of the Soul-Eaters, that Torak has to resist when tempted: 'To know the hearts of others! *Think* what you could do if you learned this! You could discover such secrets! [...] You could gain such power...' (219). Torak embraces the possibility of death rather than submit to his foe's power.

Soul-Eater (Paver 2006), third of the *Chronicles of Ancient Darkness*, begins with Wolf being abducted. Torak ties a lock of hair to a fallen spruce and prays to the Forest for Wolf's safety, then sets off single-mindedly in pursuit: 'Torak's need to find Wolf was all-consuming' (93). Torak is both impelled and repelled by prophecies: from an elder of the Inuit-like White Fox Clan who foresees 'a boy with wolf eyes [...] about to do a great evil' (55); and from the idiot savant Walker, who, like Tolkien's Gollum, always refers to himself in the third person. The Walker has appeared before in *Wolf Brother* and there are other echoes: in the northwards quest, in Torak's and Wolf's dreams and memories, and in an encounter with a bear (white rather than brown this time). What is new is that Torak has to confront no fewer than four of his mortal enemies, the Soul-Eaters, who plan to unleash demons to terrorise the clans and so impose their power and a uniform religion. To do so they intend to break the ultimate taboo (as shocking as intercision in Philip Pullman's *Northern Lights*) by sacrificing animals that hunt, including Wolf and a human.

The by-now familiar beliefs are still present, but a new direction is also taken. Thus the White Fox Clan, when they hunt and kill a seal, release its soul and thank it, in accordance with beliefs already firmly established in the series. And once the reader is attuned to animism, personification becomes more than a literary device, as when 'those trees that remained awake leaned closer to the fire, warming their branches and listening to the talk' (Paver 2006: 245) and an 'oak was slumbering too deeply to feel [a breeze], but the beech trees sighed, and the alders rattled their tiny black cones, chattering even in their sleep' (250). But the new direction is the intrusion, mainly through the Soul-Eaters, of a Christianised outlook and language. There are hints of Christianity in the Soul-Eaters' ceremonial and sacrificial high magic, and in their aim of imposing, through fear, a powerful and standardising priesthood – even though, as Fin-Kedinn says, 'Nobody speaks for the World Spirit' (242). Original sin is incorporated into the mythology:

> The World Spirit fought a terrible battle with the Great Auroch, the most powerful of demons. At last the World Spirit flung the demon burning from the sky; but as it fell, the wind scattered its ashes, and a tiny speck settled in the marrow of every creature on earth. Evil exists in us all. (Paver 2006: 135)

Nef the Bat Mage, a Soul-Eater who, against expectation, shows tenderness and compassion, has a theological turn of phrase. The value of redemptive sacrifice underlies her pronouncements that 'You'll have to take on the burden of sin for the good of the many' (115) and 'the innocent must die for the good of the many' (120). When a climactic sacrifice is made, she cries, '*The debt is repaid!*' (235, original italics).

Torak discovers through Nef that someone who is supposedly bad can have some good in them, the converse of finding previously, in *Spirit Walker*, that an apparently trustworthy person can be villainous. The other three Soul-Eaters are all cruel. Seshru the Viper Mage is a *femme fatale*, using her beauty sadistically: 'One long forefinger caressed his cheek: gently, but letting him feel the edge of her nail' (Paver 2006: 221). Thiazzi the Oak Mage is a malevolent Green Man figure (compare Chapter 2 above) – 'The eyes that bore into his were a fierce leaf-green' (111) – who takes pleasure in torturing weaker creatures. Eostra, the cruellest of all, can shapechange into an eagle owl, the creature of ill omen that appears to Torak at the very start of *Soul-Eater*. The name Eostra is very close to Eostre, the Anglo-Saxon Goddess of dawn whose title is retained in Easter, the Christian spring festival of sacrifice.

Torak's shamanic destiny, and his becoming like the Soul-Eaters in order to defeat them, catalyse his weaknesses and taint him. The Walker and Renn warn him, and 'It wasn't only the evil of the Soul-Eaters which Finn-Kedinn feared. It was that within Torak himself' (135). The danger of moral pollution is also apparent in another boy, one who aspires to be a Soul-Eater. Renn challenges the boy, 'And for this you'd break clan law by catching hunters for sacrifice? For an empty promise of a power that will never be yours?' (105). Disguising himself as the boy, Torak breaks taboo by killing a hunting creature, an owl. He is also forced to eat a trance-inducing root, but later he chooses to take the root again for his own ends. Earlier in the story he has fasted and used soul-loosening paste and smoke potion to spirit-walk at will, but it is questionable how requisite hallucinogens are for inducing trance states and soul journeying, and so Torak may be tainted by resorting to drugs. However, when he electively eats the root and spirit-walks into a bear, he does resist further temptation, for 'if he killed the Soul-Eater now, then, truly, he would become as one of them' (235). Yet defeating the Soul-Eaters on this occasion has all too high a cost, as Torak breaks the taboo against killing hunting animals and is even forcibly tattooed with the mark of a Soul-Eater.

Torak keeps secret his Soul-Eater mark until it is exposed in a fight with another boy in *Outcast* (Paver 2007). Saeunn, the Raven Clan Mage, is implacable in insisting that clan law be upheld and Torak cast out, while Renn speaks up for Torak, summarising his achievements – 'He destroyed the bear. He rid the Forest of the sickness. This winter we would have been overrun by demons if it hadn't been for him' (31) – but to no avail. Torak's mother made him clanless, it is revealed; now the Wolf Clan, to which he has always thought he belonged, cannot defend him. So Torak is made outcast, 'as one dead. Cut off from everyone. Hunted like prey' (20). The Forest, which Torak honours, helps him to survive; willows whisper, '*You belong here. In the Forest*' (44, original italics). Cast out and clanless, he is not friendless: Renn and Wolf take great risks to be with him.

The sickening task of cutting out the Soul-Eater tattoo must be done with correct ceremony, so that, 'For the first time in his life, he [Torak] was going to do Magecraft. He was going to meddle with the forces which Mages use to see the future, heal the sick and find prey: forces he didn't understand and couldn't control' (55). Renn explains the principles to him: 'It's a way of getting deeper. A way of touching the Nanuak itself. But you've got to be careful' (54). The typology of magic she gives, and the importance of the four cardinal directions and elements, bear more than a passing resemblance to modern Wicca: 'There are five kinds of Magecraft. Sending. Summoning. Cleansing. Binding. Severing. The one for this rite will be cleansing. And – severing. You'll need something from each of the four quarters of the clans: Forest, Ice, Mountain, Sea' (55). As instructed by Renn, Torak performs the rite under a full moon, at the confluence of two rivers – that is to say, in harmony with the sacred time and place of the Pagan chronotope.

But the rite does not work. The purifying drink involved, left out in the moonlight, is poisoned by Seshru the Viper Mage, who controls Torak through the excised Soul-Eater mark and through his name-pebble. Seshru causes Torak's spirit to walk while he sleeps (he knows that is not the way spirit-walking should work), inhabiting an elk which attacks 'the person he cared about most' (65), Renn. Torak realises that 'There is something inside me I can't control' (ibid.) He goes from bad to worse, neglecting offerings and reverence for the Forest, and leaving a pursuer to drown (as Torak assumes). Torak is driven east to Lake Axehead in an episode that is, in Nicolette Jones's words, 'dark and hallucinatory' (Jones 2007). Swirling mists, shifting walkways and sinister totems disorient Torak; 'in this nebulous half-world which was neither land nor lake, he was losing his very self' (100). He forgets how to hunt, how to speak with Wolf, how to listen to the Forest. Saeunn regards it as soul-sickness, the varieties of which she expounds to Renn:

> If your name-soul falls sick, you forget who you are. You become like a ghost. If the canker attacks your clan-soul, you lose your sense of good and evil. You become as a demon. If your world-soul becomes palsied, you lose your link with other living things – hunter, prey, Forest. You become as a Lost One. (Paver 2007: 113)

Naturally, readers with a different world view are likely to look for alternative psychological explanations, perhaps breakdown after Torak's extreme heroism in previous instalments of the *Chronicles of Ancient*

Darkness, or adolescent and depressive feelings of incapacity, alienation and loss of identity.

Seeking Torak, Renn arrives at the Otter clan village, where she is unnerved to find that the Otter Mage consists of twin children, who tell her to go east for what she seeks. There is Delphic equivocation to this, and 'Renn knew better than most that the prophecies of Mages are tricky things, and can have many different meanings' (142). Being sent in the opposite direction from Torak forces Renn to employ the gift for Magecraft that she has previously resisted and denied. Using locks of Torak's hair and howling a charm in the face of a storm, Renn invokes 'the power of the guardian of all Ravens' (145) and sends it after Torak. Taken out of himself by looking after a pair of fledgling ravens, Torak starts to recall offerings, words for things, tracking skills. The Forest forgives him, as 'trees live longer than people, and are slower to anger' (159). Reconciled with Wolf and the pack, Torak's mood swings to 'a thrill of pure happiness. [...] For a moment he felt his world-soul reaching out to the world-soul of every living creature, like threads of golden gossamer floating on the wind. [...] He could live like this for ever' (169) – except he now yearns for his friends.

Torak kept his Soul-Eater mark secret even from Renn, but when Renn's own secret is revealed, Torak cannot accept that she never told him. With her secret out, Renn need resist Magecraft no longer, so she uses her power to find an explanation for the signs she has been seeing and the sickness of Lake Axehead. The methods she uses are shamanic: grinding pebbles and rocking back and forth, she works herself into a trance, assisted by juniper smoke, her eyes stung shut by alder juice. Asking the spirits of the four quarters for guidance, she soul-journeys to the bottom of the lake, to a healing spring, to a nearby glacier, and has a moment of revelation. I shall not detail the climactic confrontation with Seshru the Viper Mage, or other final twists to *Outcast*; I would just like to pick up on some of Fin-Kedinn's typically wise words in the denouement. Talking of his own youthful passions, Fin-Kedinn tells Torak: 'Growing up can be a kind of soul-sickness, Torak. The name-soul wants to be strongest, so it fights the clan-soul telling it what to do' (252). Evidently this struggle between subjectivity and duty also applies to what Torak has been going through, and – even though Fin-Kedinn's words are appropriately framed in his culture – generalises to the implied reader.

Physical signifiers of Torak's and Renn's pubescence are prominent in *Outcast*: 'Torak thought she looked older than her thirteen summers, and beautiful' (31), and Renn notices Torak's muscular body and breaking voice. Saeunn refuses to help Renn interpret signs on the grounds that 'Your first moon bleed has brought a fearsome increase in your power – but it is raw, untried!' (111), caging the untamed power of Renn's emerging womanhood. In another way though, Renn is not ready and willing to take on an adult identity – when Fin-Kedinn tells her, 'You're no longer a child, Renn. You're old enough to make your own choices,' she thinks, 'No I'm not! [...] I need you to help me! Tell me what to do!' (116). Renn's and Torak's adolescence underlies the most remarkable developments – Torak's dark night of the soul, Renn's use of Magecraft, the joys and difficulties of their relationship – in the fourth of the *Chronicles of Ancient Darkness* series.

* * *

North Child by Edith Pattou (2003) is a substantial novel based on the Norse fairy tale 'East of the Sun, West of the Moon' (Asbjørnsen and Moe 1849), with elements of other fairy tales such as 'Beauty and the Beast'. There are indications that the story takes place in the 16th century: early modern, 16th and 17th-century settings are not uncommon in novels analysed in this chapter, a period in which European exploration, trade and colonial expansion brought contact with, and damage to, indigenous cultures. Pattou gives names to, and develops the characters of, the 'lassie' and her family in 'East of the Sun, West of the Moon', and reader sympathies are complicated by having five narrators: Rose; her brother Neddy, scholarly and fond of stories of Norse Gods; their father, a cartographer who reverts to subsistence farming in hard times; the White Bear, whose impressionistic and poetic narration, mostly minor sentences, becomes continuous prose when he is turned into a man; and the Troll Queen, giving the antagonist's point of view. Comparing *North Child* with 'East of the Sun, West of the Moon' would prove a lengthy study in itself – here I pick out just one episode as exemplary of significant contrasts, before going on to look at the pull of the north on Rose, and the presentation of Inuit shamanism.

In her variations from 'East of the Sun, West of the Moon', Pattou adds explanations, complicates motivations, and gives more agency to the girl she calls Rose. In the original fairy tale, when the bear comes to take the girl away, she and her mother resist but the father agrees; *North Child* reverses all this. Pattou has the bear offering improvement not only in material circumstances, but also in Rose's ailing sister's health, and it is on this that the family divides. Father asserts, 'I will not sacrifice one daughter for another' (Pattou 2003: 87), but Rose does agree to go, through mixed motivations of love and obligation to her family, and a yearning sense that it is her destiny to go, which her mother affirms. But then Rose's mother is more disposed to believe in magical bargains and fate, her tenacious superstition being mocked by her son Neddy. There is room both for Mother's superstition and for Neddy's rationalism in the change of fortunes that follows Rose's departure. A kindly landlord saves the family from eviction, gets a doctor for Rose's sister, and nurtures Father's map-making hobby into a business. To Mother, this is evidence that the bear has kept the deal; to Neddy, it is 'coincidence, nothing more. Harald Soren, a flesh-and-blood man, brought about our good fortune, not the bear' (213). Neddy, just as much as his mother, resists evidence that does not fit into his outlook: 'I did not actually want there to be talking animals and mysterious requests on storm-tossed nights. Such things were for stories and ought to remain there' (94).

Characters' scepticism about magic, and constraints to its use in the narrative, can in fact serve to make it more credible. Rose thinks:

> even though I was living with a talking white bear in a castle inside a mountain, my mind rebelled at the whole idea of magic. After all, I hadn't seen any mystifying transformations, things flying through the air or anything like that. The unlightable darkness of my bedroom and the lamp that went out for no reason were the only real signs that anything supernatural was going on. (Pattou 2003: 240)

Yet the extinguishing of lights by magic – an addition to the source fairy tale – seems an arbitrary and unnecessary intrusion of the supernatural, only confirming what Rose realises later as she learns seafaring the hard way: 'how much more complicated life is without the benefit of magic. [...] magic lets you skip over the steps of things. [...] But [...] the steps of things are where life is truly found, in doing the day-to-day tasks' (344). However, a Pagan view of magic might be that it is not about *ad hoc* disruption of natural laws, but is to be found precisely in the wonder of the mundane.

Rose learns seafaring while she is taken north in a longship by a drunken 'Viking' sailor who calls himself Thor and is of the opinion that 'If something remains of magic in the world, I believe it would lie in the far north' (347). Rose's pursuit of the bear northwards to the Troll Queen's palace has a clear analogy in the Norse story she treasures and has told the bear, about Freya searching for her husband in an ice palace in the far north. Rose admits to herself: 'I had always had a secret desire to someday go to the lands of the far north. [...] it was in my nature, the direction I naturally gravitated towards' (307). Despite her parents' resistance, she has always had a wandering spirit and a northward inclination, from birth and even before. There was an 'extraordinary amount of movement from the baby [... which] had taken it upon itself to explore every last corner of [the] womb' (39), and Rose is born facing north, though her mother denies it, because North Children are 'Wandering and wild and very ill behaved' (24).

Father colludes with the denial, embroidering a lie – a fabrication – about Rose's birth direction into the cloak he makes for her, depicting the compass rose for which she is named. Thus, although the stereotype of weaving and needlework being 'women's work' is broken by Rose's father, he uses it for false signification. However, Rose's own passion for weaving and sewing empowers her with independence and agency: for example, of the three gowns of silver, gold and moon-thread she weaves in the white bear's castle, two are later used to barter her passage north, and the third disguises her in the troll ice palace. This upholds Kathryn Sullivan Kruger's argument that, while weaving appears to confine and suppress women, what is woven can be revolutionary and enable women to shape their own destiny (Kruger 2001). The relation between textile and text, especially regarding female voice and agency, is foregrounded in a number of the novels considered in this chapter, and so will be revisited.

North, Rose's true birth direction, is where magic survives. The Troll Queen's magic is malevolent and misguided – it cannot make the bear love her. Contrasting with the Troll Queen's evil magic is the benevolent magic of Malmo, the Greenland Inuit shaman who generously equips Rose for the journey further north to the Troll Queen's palace, and accompanies her for a perilous part of it. Malmo and her people are located in Inuit mythology, having 'lived on that land since Sedna, the Mother of Sea Beasts, came to guard the oceans' (365),[2] and Malmo explains the spiritual ecology of hunting for survival:

> We are not separate from the animals or the sea or the ice but part of the whole. And so we must treat the animals, the sea, the ice with respect. [...] We must hunt to survive. Disrespect would be to hunt when you are not hungry and then to treat the dead in a wasteful, unclean way. The words I sing are to ask forgiveness for taking the seal's life, and to send its soul safely to the spirit world. (Pattou 2003: 390–391)

As a shaman, Malmo has a power animal and believes in dreams and portents. Much of her power is in her 'penetrating black eyes' (358), which can read a person's soul; she combines her gaze with song and speech to charm a white bear that attacks Rose. Having guided Rose to the ice bridge, Malmo suddenly disappears: 'I saw Malmo lift her arms to the sky, and then she was gone. There was a white petrel riding the wind directly above the place she had been' (408). Rose asks herself, 'Was it possible that Malmo had turned herself into a petrel, or had she merely skied down the other side of the slope? I didn't know' (ibid.). Once again, as with Rose's family's change of fortunes earlier, Pattou leaves interpretation open: magic is a possibility, and so is a more rational explanation.

Eileen Kernaghan's *The Snow Queen* (2000) is a novel-length reworking of Andersen's pre-text (1846), and also draws on the Finnish epic *Kalevala* (Kirby (tr.) 1907). In interview, Kernaghan observes that 'Andersen subverts the traditional fairy tale plot by having the heroine set off on an epic quest to rescue the boy,' and declares her own intent:

> to celebrate a classic of fantasy literature with uniquely independent female characters. [...] I decided that what the future should hold for Gerda was not marriage to Kai, but a life of travel and adventure. [...] Reworking the story also gave me the chance to expand the role of the Little Robber Maiden, who has always been my favourite fairy tale character. (Kernaghan 2002)

A striking innovation, and the focus of the current discussion, is Kernaghan's Ritva, who is the daughter of a robber father and a Sami shaman mother, and so is not only the Little Robber Maiden, but also absorbs the Lapp-woman and the Finnmark woman of Andersen's tale (see Figure 3.1). Ritva is focalised in the first chapter, and her story alternates with Gerda's until they meet and join forces in their heroic quest. Repelled by her mother's shamanism, Ritva nevertheless cannot resist what is a harrowing vocation, through which she achieves individual self-realisation and empowerment – more in line with Gerda's and the implied adolescent reader's culture than the indigenous role of shaman as community functionary and psychopomp.

'In her shaman's robes Ritva's mother possessed a frightening dignity' (Kernaghan 2000: 14), and she makes spirit-journeys, induced by drumming, to the Land of the Dead to recover the lost souls of the sick. Ritva loathes 'the whole business – the monotonous drumming, the writhing and shaking and frothing at the mouth. [...] Most of all she hated the reminder that one day this power, and this dreadful obligation,

Figure 3.1 The Lapland woman depicted by Angela Barrett in Hans Christian Andersen's *The Snow Queen* translated by Naomi Lewis

Source: Angela Barrett on page 31 of *Hans Christian Andersen's The Snow Queen* translated by Naomi Lewis (Walker 1988, ISBN 0744506212).

would be hers' (13). Offering dried cranberries to a bear skull wedged in the crotch of a tree, Ritva seeks advice: 'When did I ask to inherit her power? I don't want it. I want to live by myself in a hut by the river. I want to ride south, to where it's always summer' (23). The skull replies, 'Child, you may not turn your back on the gift the great god Aijo has given you. Nor on the obligations birth has placed upon you' (ibid.). Thereafter, Ritva's calling as a shaman impends: she dreams of being dismembered, and of an antlered man who is an anthropomorph of her power animal, the white elk; her dead grandmother comes to her singing a shamanic chant telling her to seek and confront the Snow Queen. What finally tips Ritva into initiatory crisis is her concern for Gerda, who is pining away for Kai. Ritva wanders in the woods until she is exhausted, and a bear tears the flesh from her bones, which she numbers and names. She is 'flooded with calm, and lightness, and power; freed of everything that was transient, unessential; pared down to the hard imperishable bone' (82). She returns ready to take over her weary mother's drum, and therewith the shamanic skills of soul-journeying, foresight and farsight. Although the forest spirits gave her contradictory advice, Ritva is full of zest for the quest.

In the face of Gerda's Christian monotheism, Ritva declares her own pantheism – 'They are everywhere. They live in the forest, the river, the hearth fire, in the rocks and bushes – everything has a god in it' (76) – and tells Gerda how 'the God of the southerners' countenanced the persecution of her ancestors, killing shamans and destroying drums. Kernaghan prompts the adolescent 'Reader as Thinker' (Appleyard 1991) to hesitate between Ritva's Pagan outlook and Gerda's Christianity, stereotypically wild versus civilised, uninhibited versus inhibited, and also between their different understandings of the Snow Queen: to Ritva, 'a powerful wizard'; to Gerda, a wily, non-magical manipulator, 'a woman, like any other – though cleverer, perhaps, and able to seduce people into doing what she wants. But I don't believe she has magic powers' (91). Thus readers and characters 'hesitate between a natural and a supernatural explanation of the events described' (Todorov 1970: 33).

The Snow Queen sets Ritva three tasks: catching cold fire, catching a fish, and making dye and embroidery. These involve, respectively: cunning; music magic; and courage, skill and perseverance – a mixture of personal qualities and the magical. The three tasks derive from the Kalevala, and Kernaghan has Ritva proudly identifying herself with the hero Väinö. Success in these tests is not enough for the Snow Queen, who demands sacrifice, but Gerda refuses to kill Ritva's reindeer. Magic takes over: Ritva's 'slumbrous music' (functionally equivalent to invisibility) covers their escape. When Ritva drums, mumbles and sings herself into trance to create reef and mountain from moss and flint to protect their flight, Gerda realises 'the true nature of Ritva's power. This was no illusion, no conjuror's trick, but real stone, solid and impenetrable, created out of a bit of flint, and air, and sea-spume' (149). At the end, Ritva emphatically rejects domesticity in favour of a powerful shamanic identity: 'Can you see me darning trousers, and stirring the stewpot? I am a shaman [...] I am a woman of power. I have travelled to the spirit kingdom. I have defeated the Dark Enchantress' (155).

* * *

The Snow-walker Trilogy is a fantasy pervaded by Norse and Anglo-Saxon legend and mythology; the chapter head quotations in *The Snow-walker*, *The Empty Hand* and *The Soul Thieves* (Fisher 1993, 1995, 1996) are taken, respectively, from 'Hávamál', *Beowulf* and 'Völuspá'. Despite some schematic gender polarisation – good female shamans, bad male shamans; a Wicked Witch of the North figure competing with her son for power – *The Snow-walker Trilogy*'s psychological depth of characterisation anticipates the remarkable achievement of Catherine Fisher's *Darkhenge* (2005 – considered at the end of the next chapter).

Jessa, the spirited third-person focaliser of *The Snow-walker's Son* (Fisher 1993), and her cousin Thorkil, both now 'old enough to be dangerous' (8), are sent under escort into exile in the north, 'a wilderness of trolls and spirits on the edge of the world' (14) by a usurping Jarl. This Jarl has been put into place by his wife Gudrun, the snow-walker, a beautiful malevolent snow queen figure from the far north. On their way north, Jessa and company enter Trond, a Pagan republic (compare Susan Price's *Foiling the Dragon*, mentioned in the next section) where there are 'no chieftains [...] no one man better than the others' (Fisher 1993: 47). Trond's 'shamanka' is a wise and wizened old woman, who, typically of fictional shamans, lives liminally on the edge of the community and yet has a central role. She has the power to protect her people from Gudrun: 'I have spread my mind like a bird's wing over this kin. Here, we are safe. She cannot see us' (52).

Completing her journey into exile, Jessa encounters Kari, son of Gudrun the snow-walker, and he is not the monster she has been led to believe: 'This was not the terrible creature of the stories' (79). Like Odin, Kari is associated with two ravens, which have shadowed Jessa and her party all along. Kari's ability of far-seeing is something Jessa shares to an extent, and she is also addressed at one point as 'little shamanka' (132) by the pedlar and skald – pedlar of words – Skapti Arnsson, a Cole Hawlings type of character (compare Masefield 1935). Kari's magical gifts – such as invisibility, presented as perceptual shift – are unlearned, spontaneous. He scares even himself when he conjures an arch of light.

What is more, there is a moral ambiguity to his use of his powers, shown in his dealings with Jessa's cousin Thorkil. Through Kari's empathic magic and vicarious suffering, 'Thorkil began to breathe easily and freely. At the same time Kari shivered, as if something had chilled him' (95). But when, soon after, Thorkil attacks Kari, Kari sends him into agonies: 'Kari scrambled up and looked down at him, his eyes cold and amused, like Gudrun's' (106).

Gudrun has incarcerated Kari, regarding her son as a rival and threat, like Margaretta with her nephew Czarevitch Safa in Susan Price's *The Ghost Drum* (see next section). And, like Chingis and her foe Kuzma in *The Ghost Drum*, Gudrun and Kari can be seen as the splitting of a single personality. Kari's face is identical to Gudrun's, and, while he has no reflection, she, as the shamanka knows, 'fears her mirror. [...] Gudrun never looks in a glass' (53). As Lisa Sainsbury argues, doubles and mirrors, as aspects of Freud's notion of the uncanny, intimate both death and immortality, and are used in adolescent fiction to deny 'a unified and stable sense of self, offering instead a range of subject positions manifested in uncanny confrontations with the double' (Sainsbury 2005: 130).

The final climactic showdown between Gudrun and Kari combines a thrilling magical duel with psychological insight. Jessa is struck again by the likeness of mother and son, and Kari says to Gudrun that the reflection she fears is 'not the one in the mirror. I'm your reflection' (Fisher 1993: 145). She dismisses his magic as 'Tricks played on fools. Not the real spells, not the twisting of minds, the webs of fear and delight' (ibid.), but when she draws a rune in the air to rack him with pain, Kari retaliates, without rune, with the pain to which he has been subjected, the mental anguish of nightmares and silence and fear. He declares, 'It's over – your time of power. There are two of us now – a balance' (147). Apparently defeated for now, Gudrun curses Kari with power:

> I will do you the greatest harm I can. I'll give you what you want. [...] I leave it all to you. With this curse. They will never love you, never trust you. Power like ours is a terror to them. (Fisher 1993: 149–150)

Sure enough, Kari's power does provoke distrust and fear in *The Empty Hand* (Fisher 1995), an analogue of *Beowulf* in which Gudrun creates a rune-beast 'out of spells; deep spells and runes and cold, out of snow and the dark between the stars. Out of her anger with us' (62). Kari is hero and beast: as Gudrun's actual son he is as much the Grendel figure as the rune-beast, and Kari identifies with the rune-beast, for Gudrun has inflicted emptiness on both of them.

The restored rightful Jarl, Wulfgar, has his mind poisoned against Kari by the ambitious charlatan shaman, Vidar Freyrspriest. Through Vidar and Gudrun, Catherine Fisher inverts the association in the Norse tradition of *galdr*, rune magic, with men and *seidr*, shamanic divination, with women, though the inversion is compromised by Gudrun using magic malevolently, and by Vidar being false. Vidar has all the trappings and practices of a shaman: the coat, the vision quest, the prophetic trance assisted by hallucinogenic toadstools. His prophecies contain a grain of truth, and are ambiguous, as prophecies tend to be – 'Freyr spoke obliquely, as the gods do' (90), he says – but they are also manipulative and self-serving: he foretells Wulfgar's death, which he later attempts to bring about himself! Vidar's pronouncement, 'It comes from the north – a pale thing, evil, a creature of runes!' (57), equivocates between Kari, who immediately appears, and the rune-creature.

The depiction of Vidar in trance – 'Firelight danced on him, black and red, and on the great image above him, and both their eyes were dark gashes; they were fragments of faces, masked with smoke' (56–57) – partakes of the 'savage' language of Paganism (Hutton 1999, and see Chapter 1 above), as does the description of Freyr's image as 'unknowably ancient, centuries old; a crude, wooden shape, seamed and split with time and the rain' (Fisher 1995: 54), itself redolent of Weland's image in *Puck of Pook's Hill* (Kipling 1906). And yet, Fisher also conveys the jubilation of a seasonal festival of fire and fertility:

> fires burned for the god's journey. The image of Freyr, keeper of the harvest, lord of boars and horses, was coming [...] on his gilded wagon. All through the last of the winter the god had travelled, bringing spring with him, dragged from [...] village to village [...]. Every year Freyr visited his farmers and brought them luck, and heart; the promise of plenty. (Fisher 1995: 52)

The threat of the rune-beast brings superstition and faith to the fore. Hearing reports of the creature, 'the men of the hold felt amulets and thorshammers discreetly' (40), and the thrall Hakon, when pursued by the beast, prays to Odin for help. The 'empty hand' of the book's title is Hakon's, frozen into paralysis by Gudrun's touch, and healed at the end of the story by Kari, who says he has done 'The opposite'. Kari and Gudrun both know that they are the same, yet opposite, maintaining the theme of doubling from *The Snow-walker's Son*.

Kari's meetings with the rune-beast reveal his empathy with it, as well as the potency, ambivalence and temptation of Kari's magical abilities. From his time of incarceration, Kari knows 'the emptiness, the darkness, without faces, without language, without warmth' (Fisher 1995: 163) that the beast feels, and 'for one piercing second' Kari makes the people in Wulfgar's hall feel the same: 'empty, without heart or thoughts or memories, so that inside each of them was a black, raging nothing that swelled out and engulfed them' (88). The final confrontation between Kari and the rune-beast is full of ambiguities. The snakeskin bracelet from Gudrun that Jessa has been so wary of Kari taking, he proffers to the beast, saying 'Take it. Let it feed you. Then both of us can break free' (164). The creature is released, but it is left open whether it dissolves away or becomes fully human. And Kari, while he has done good by simultaneously abjuring greater power and showing compassion, appears fearful even to Jessa:

> all the darkness and tension spread from him, and the danger too, and for a moment of sharp fear she knew he had them all in the power of his mind. Her vision shifted; for that time he was not the Kari she knew. He was someone else. A stranger. An alien. (Fisher 1995: 164–165)

Like *The Snow-walker's Son*, *The Empty Hand* ends with a curse from Gudrun, this time on Jarl Wulfgar: 'I lay this fate on you, my lord. The thing you love best, that thing I will have, one day' (Fisher 1995: 166). It is fulfilled in the third book of the trilogy, *The Soul Thieves* (Fisher 1996). On the eve of Wulfgar's Midsummer wedding, Gudrun sends fog and frost and steals the bride's soul. Kari, Jessa and their companions travel north, through prehistory and Norse myth, through Ironwood and across the rainbow bridge and through the aurora to Ginnungagap and beyond, to 'The land of the soul. The place beyond legends. The country of the wise' (14), where Kari and Gudrun have their final confrontation. As Kari and the others depart Wulfgar's hall on their epic expedition, they hear 'A drum beat[ing] quietly from the corner of the hall; an old man in a shaman's coat of feathers chanted luck-songs and charms in a quavering voice' (44) – the sole exception to the bad male shaman/good female shaman duality of the trilogy which will only be reinforced later in this story.

The season changes from summer to winter, and the epoch reverts to the Iron Age, as the travellers enter a village on a lake where bog sacrifices are made (compare Glob 1966). The village is presided over by the

Speaker, 'our shaman to the dark' (115). Deceitful as Vidar, the Speaker fixes the lots to decide who will be sacrificed to 'the dark one': Skapti is chosen, and knows very well that 'I wasn't chosen by any earth-goddess, but by the shaman' (139). A village girl explains 'His blood will enrich the land. He'll nurture our crops; feed our cattle. Because of him the dark one will be pleased' but 'if the dark one isn't given her choice there is famine, death, disease' (129). Controlled by a male sha-man who carries a phallic wooden staff of office, this is far from the utopian prehistoric Goddess matriarchy of Hutton's third language of Paganism; it is the savage language, unameliorated (see Hutton 1999 and Chapter 1, above). Skapti is rescued, but the sacrificial system is impli-citly upheld, because the Speaker replaces him, falling into the bog: 'a blackness seemed to rise and gather from [the marsh], covering him as he screamed and struggled, bending over him, a dark form' (136).

Very different from the Speaker is the skraeling woman the compan-ions meet, all the further north and near to the end of their quest. Comparable with the Finnmark woman in Andersen's *The Snow Queen* and Malmo in Pattou's *North Child*, the skraeling woman explains, 'I am the memory-keeper, the story weaver. Here I weave the happenings and hangings of my people' (154). Her weaving includes elements from the Finnish epic *Kalevala* (Kirby (tr.) 1907): 'An old hero made the earth from an eggshell, made a kantele of pike-bones and sang the trees and clouds and mountains into being' (Fisher 1996: 161). Skapti the poet attempts to appropriate textile to textual practices: 'All poets weave this web, lady' (ibid.). The skraeling woman is perceptive about Kari. She sees that 'He has an emptiness deep inside; a blank space where his childhood should be' (156), and asks, 'How can he defeat her [Gudrun] without using the same powers as she does?' (157). Jessa has also become concerned that Kari's strength and power have grown as they have trav-elled further north, towards his mother. In the final confrontation, Kari does indeed play by Gudrun's rules, like for like, as they battle to steal each other's souls. His restraint and inability to kill his mother may in effect be more cruel than compassionate, leaving her to an uncertain eternity: 'I stole her soul and locked it into a crystal, locked it deep, with tight spells. [...] Now she's neither dead nor alive' (213).

* * *

I have written at length before (Bramwell 2002c, 2005b) about Susan Price's *The Ghost Drum* (1987); here I would like to look at selected issues across the Ghost World trilogy: power relationships between the sexes, between shaman and apprentice, and between ruler and people; and Price's construction of shamanism and her use of Norse Heathen mythology. The Ghost World trilogy is bound together by all three parts having word-for-word exactly the same openings and closings, both concerning the narrator cat. The names of the books, *The Ghost Drum, Ghost Song* (Price 1992) and *Ghost Dance* (Price 1994a), signify the main 'techniques of ecstasy' (Eliade 1964: subtitle) which a shaman can employ to facilitate entering into an altered state of consciousness to journey in spirit.

The Ghost Drum (Price 1987) is set in the frozen north of a historical fantasy Czardom, where, on Midwinter Day, a witch takes a new-born slave to raise as a Woman of Power. The witch teaches her apprentice, Chingis, herblore and the three magics of spoken and written word, and song. Meanwhile, the evil shaman Kuzma grows jealous. The Czar's scheming sister Margaretta makes the Czar fear his own son, so that he has him incarcerated in the highest tower of the Imperial Palace. Chingis hears when the lonely boy Safa's distressed spirit cries out and, singing herself invisible, she sets him free. A whole new world opens up to Safa as he leaves his room and the palace.[3] When Margaretta becomes Czaritsa, she wants Safa found and killed, and Kuzma is keen to oblige. Chingis is lured into confrontation with Kuzma, who neutralises her magic and kills her, transfixing her to the ground. Safa is taken and returned to the tower. Chingis's spirit travels to the ghost-world, where she meets the spirits of her witch-grandmother, and Safa's dead mother and maid. Together they return to earth, trap Kuzma's spirit, and take over his body. John Stewig (1995) succinctly spells out the significance: 'Thus the four women working together are able to overcome Kuzma's solitary evil' (Stewig 1995: 123). Inhabited thus, 'Kuzma' rescues Safa from execution and Czaritsa Margaretta meets her end. To be with Chingis in the ghost-world, Safa chooses death by biting an ice-apple. He thereby renounces Czardom, and becomes something greater: 'now he is a shaman and not a Czarevich, I think there are no doors closed against Safa that he cannot open' (Price 1987: 164). Five hundred years later, in a village in the frozen north, at Midwinter, the spirits of Chingis, her grandmother witch, Safa, and Safa's mother and maid enter five babies. The first three become shamans, the other two live ordinary lives.

The Ghost Drum opens and closes at Midwinter. This is the time in the Wheel of the Year for storytelling, and for celebrating 'the birth of the Sun Child, the Child of Promise' (Crowley 1996: 103) – Chingis in this case. A further dimension is added if one takes into account the theory that Sami 'drums were orientated to depict the night sky at the winter solstice' (Sommarström 1987: 238). In any case, Susan Price deliberately makes use of 'hinges of the year': *The Ghost Drum* is 'set at the Midwinter Solstice (and *Ghost Song* at the Midsummer Solstice) [when] the borders between worlds are supposed to wear thin, and you can step into another world without knowing that you have' (Price 2002b). With respect not only to time of year, but also gender and control, the premise of *Ghost Song* (Price 1992) systematically inverts *The Ghost Drum*:

> *The Ghost Drum* had been about what happens when a night-walking female witch comes in the midst of winter and successfully begs the new-born daughter of a slave-woman from her. So what would happen if a male witch came at mid-summer and begged that the new-born son of a slave be given to him – but the father refuses? (Price 2002a)

Ghost Song, then, opens on Midsummer's Day, with the shaman Kuzma (for it is he) coming to take a new-born boy child as his apprentice. The father refuses, but as the boy Ambrosi ('Immortal') grows, he is haunted in dreams by Kuzma. Ambrosi gets a drum which he decorates, and finds that his singing and story-telling hold hearers spellbound. Finally he reveals his true name to Kuzma, but still refuses to become a shaman until after his beloved father is dead. Ambrosi's father is killed by people turned into werewolves by Kuzma, and Kuzma traps the dead man's soul. To allow his father's ghost to rest, Ambrosi accompanies him to the Ghost World. Kuzma offers Ambrosi the choice of becoming a shaman or ceaselessly being tortured by spirits. Ambrosi rejects both options by eating a Ghost World apple and thereby choosing death, saying 'Only change is everlasting, Grandfather. I choose everlasting change' (Price 1992: 142) – 'Only change is everlasting' is a refrain of both *Ghost Song* and *Ghost Dance*. The ending of *Ghost Song* amounts to a further inversion of *The Ghost Drum* because, whereas Safa chooses death to become a shaman, Ambrosi chooses death in order *not* to be a shaman.

In *Ghost Dance* (Price 1994a), the Northlands are being devastated by overfishing, overhunting and deforestation. The Lapps are to be killed or enslaved. Shingebiss shadows the anxious, restless Czar, trying to affect his decisions, which, however, only become more harsh: he approves of the despoliation of the Northlands, and shuns pity. Having before rejected a shamanic vocation, Shingebiss decides after all to travel to the Ghost World and thus become a shaman, through the force of her own will and courage. She returns to find that an English magician has persuaded the Czar that her blood is needed for an elixir of life. Shingebiss sings and dances to summon Loki, the First Shaman. Loki absorbs Shingebiss and ensures that the magician and the Czar meet their ends. The only way that Shingebiss can save the flora and fauna and people of the Northlands is by transferring them through a portal to the Ghost World. In the Iron Wood, the dead Czar's spirit dreams cruelty into the world, so that 'the Northlands come to that desolation Hel desired' (216). Like its predecessors, *Ghost Dance* portrays shocking deaths. It also presents the exploitation and destruction of the Northlands as unstoppable: an ecological apocalypse with no prospect of a eucatastrophe. Susan Price defends this bleakness thus: 'I'm afraid it goes against the grain with me to be optimistic. It doesn't seem to make sense of the world as it is' (quoted in Hunt 1994: 14). Furthermore, 'For me, a fantasy story will always have extremes – beauty, horror, cruelty, sacrifice. If you read my books, I warn you, there won't always be a happy ending' (Price 2002a).

Price's presentation of gender is far from straightforwardly polemical. In *Ghost Dance*, there is sustained ambiguity about Shingebiss's sex. While Chingis, her 'grandmother' and the villainous Czaritsa Margaretta in *The Ghost Drum* are powerful female characters, Price balances and foils feminist interpretations by making the three leading characters of *Ghost Song* male. Moreover, there are many ways in which a schematic opposition of good female shaman Chingis/evil male shaman Kuzma can be destabilised. Matching Kuzma for malevolence is Czaritsa Margaretta, whose puericidal intentions in turn shadow Safa's maid's protectiveness. Susan Price (2002b) reveals that 'In the earliest versions [of *The Ghost Drum*] Chingis was both heroine and villain, but that gradually changed, and Kuzma became the villain.' Seeing Kuzma as a projection of Chingis's own bad side might encourage a Jungian interpretation in which he is her shadow. If a Jungian reading is taken further, with Safa as Chingis's animus, then Chingis achieves personality integration with shadow and animus catalysed by 'Shamanic awakening', which can be described in Jungian terms as 'a time of individuation, when the male and female principles [...] come together into an androgynous whole' (Jamal 1987: 175).

The dynamics of Chingis's relationship with Safa are significant. Though the old witch's death and Safa's rescue are in the same chapter of *The Ghost Drum*, between the two events Chingis spends an indeterminate spell independent and alone, an iterative summary telling of her reading, writing, travelling and observing the great variety of nature. But she learns that 'nothing in the world is content to be alone' (Price

1987: 64). Reversing male gaze and possession, on seeing Safa she thinks him beautiful and declares, 'Here is my apprentice' (69). Safa is not a bright pupil, though: 'the boy was unteachable, and could not learn even the simplest word-magic' (95). Instead, teacher learns from pupil 'to see anew things which even a witch comes to think of as ordinary' (94). Chingis breaks all the rules by taking 'an apprentice, though she was still so young herself. And [...] a male apprentice! And one who was not new-born!' (94).

Chingis's defiance of the rules exposes what the rules are and the tension that runs through the Ghost World trilogy between the empowerment of becoming a shaman and the subjection of being apprenticed. In *The Ghost Drum*, shamanic vocation is liberating to a great extent, especially for women who are poor. When the old witch first appears, she declares, 'I know all the magics, and am a Woman of Power, yet I was born a slave too' (Price 1987: 5). Someone born in provincial poverty and powerlessness can subvert the central political authority, as the villain Kuzma knows very well when he challenges Margaretta: 'You call yourself Czaritsa, and you have power – but she [Chingis] is a Woman of Power' (111–112). Whereas shamanism is mostly presented as being emancipating in *The Ghost Drum*, its successors in the Ghost World series interrogate the disempowering aspects of the shamanism created in *The Ghost Drum*.

In *Ghost Song*, Kuzma becomes a little more sympathetic as he seems to resent having no choice about becoming a shaman, about losing his childhood, and about being alone. Kuzma tempts Ambrosi's father, 'Give him to me and he will be freer than your Czar' (Price 1992: 11), but Ambrosi's father asserts, 'More treasure I have here than lies in all the Czar's storehouses!' (45), and will not allow the boy to become Kuzma's apprentice. Although Ambrosi has aptitudes to become a shaman, he refuses, even unto death, to submit to Kuzma. *Ghost Dance* rejects the apprenticeship paradigm altogether by having Shingebiss enter the Ghost World independently, without tuition.

While a great deal of internal consistency is maintained throughout the Ghost World trilogy as to what constitutes a shaman, this deviates significantly from external definitions. A witch is someone who has 'learned all the magics', but to become a shaman involves in addition the ability to 'venture into the ghost-world, where the dead go and the unborn wait, and when you have explored that world, and know all the ways to and from it, then we shall call you a shaman' (Price 1987: 41, 34). Price is very clear that soul-journeying to worlds other than the ghost-world does not amount to shamanism: Safa's spirit travels 'to places in this world, and to places in other worlds' but he is categorically not a shaman because 'He turn[s] back only from the gate of the ghost-world' (128). This differs significantly from definitions in other sources, which talk about soul-journeying in other worlds, but do not make travelling to the world of the dead the exclusive criterion for shamanism. I would suggest two reasons for the narrowness of Price's definition, 'To be a shaman, you must travel the ghost-world' (159). Firstly, the ghost-world is major contributor to the thematic prominence Price gives to death: sudden unjust death or else the choice of death as the ultimate act of defiance; the endurance of the soul; reincarnation and retribution. Secondly, since only access to the ghost-world is exclusive to shamans, all other worlds are by implication open to all: anyone may journey in dream, in imagination and in reading.

In declaring that 'The pre-eminently shamanic technique is the passage from one cosmic region to another – from earth to the sky or from earth to the underworld,' Mircea Eliade (1964: 259) implies a hierarchy of otherworlds. Shamans have commonly reported experiencing seven or nine levels above and the same number below the earthly realm. Price rejects such hierarchy by not stratifying her otherworlds; and the portals of the ghost-world appear to be on the same horizontal plane as the 'primary' world. According to Eliade, 'the chief methods of recruiting shamans are: (1) hereditary transmission of the shamanic profession and (2) spontaneous vocation' (Eliade 1964: 13). For Chingis, it is neither: she is freed from a life of slavery when she is dramatically chosen at birth by the old witch, who declares, 'I am to make you a shaman before I leave this world' (Price 1987: 32). This does accord, however, with what Mervyn Jones says: 'Each *noaidi* [Sami shaman] chose and trained his [/her] successor' (Jones 1982: 6). Whilst any discussion of shamanism ought to include Eliade's renowned work, this is one instance of his habit of 'imposing an ideal type on a very diverse and complex set of phenomena' (Hutton 2001: 123).

Whether the vocation is hereditary, spontaneous or co-optative, becoming a shaman involves a psychic crisis. This typically consists of journeying in the other world whilst in an ecstatic state of dream or trance, and experiencing a dissolution and reconstitution of the self through figurative suffering, death, dismemberment and reconstitution. Then 'ecstatic election is usually followed by a period of instruction, during which the neophyte is duly initiated by an old shaman' (Eliade 1972: 110). Again Chingis is different. She receives her training from an old shaman without having first gone through the spiritual trial. Only *after* learning the magics does Chingis gain the ability to make soul-journeys on earth and in other worlds in dream and trance, including visiting the ghost-world: 'Chingis's spirit came and went through a thousand worlds; and passed a thousand times through the ghost-world' (Price 1987: 41). What is extraordinary is that the mystical experience of shamanic initiatory 'death' is actualised for Chingis: she really does die, is cut up and staked down. But death is not the end, and in spirit she and the other dead women achieve justice.

In *Ghost Song*, Ambrosi does undergo initiatory dismemberment: sable spirits 'are biting me to pieces! They bite off my fingers and hands; they are in my head, hollowing it out- !' (Price 1992: 110). Kuzma, in bear form,

> ripped him with its claws and opened him up, bit his head, and his arms, and his legs from his body, and would say, with a man's voice, 'When you are put back together, you will be a shaman.' (Price 1992: 126–127)

Ambrosi thinks he has been dreaming, but 'then he would find the scars around his fingers, around his wrists and ankles, around his elbows, where he had been sewn together' (127). The psychic crisis has a physical reality and is effectively torture, as it is imposed by Kuzma, whose power and control Ambrosi defies by refusing to become a shaman.

Jane Atkinson shrewdly exposes Eliade's assumptions about shamanism, gender and power:

> The classic shaman defined by Eliade [...] is the master of spirits, not their puppet. [...] Male practitioners predominate in the traditions to which Eliade assigns the label shamanism, whereas women are conspicuously present in traditions relying on possession. (Atkinson 1992: 317)

Susan Price effectively rejects such a gendered power-over model in favour of power-with. In *The Ghost Drum*, Chingis neither controls spirits, nor is controlled by them, but she negotiates with them, for example persuading the spirit of an ageing bear to give its body in an easy death to feed people starving in the forest.

The shaman's power in the Ghost World trilogy is through art, not force, through words and music, and most of all the two combined in song.[4] The old witch explains to Chingis that 'when a shaman sets words to music, nothing in which a spirit lives can resist. When a shaman twines the two strongest magics together, all within hearing must do as the shaman wills' (Price 1987: 40; similar statements are made in *Ghost Song* and *Ghost Dance*). The old witch sings to make a snow baby, and she sings and drums for a year to make baby Chingis grow to 'a young woman of twenty years' (31). When the old woman chooses death, she sings 'of every step a spirit must take on the way to the ghost-world' (63). Chingis is able to sing dawn into Safa's chamber, and she can sing herself invisible, as Shingebiss also does in *Ghost Dance*. The way one shaman can rob another of power and identity is by undoing song magic, as Kuzma does by using 'patternless din' (Price 1987: 124) against Chingis.

The power of song is described and enacted through the words of the narrative. On the first page of each story in the trilogy, the narrator cat walks one way round an oak to tell a story; if it walked the other way it would sing. The magic of song is mysterious and elusive, and the words of song magic are rarely given, though an exception is Shingebiss's song of invisibility, with its rhetorically forceful repetition, syntactic inversion and parallelism, and groups of three:

> White hare on white snow, you see me not, you see me not. White fox on white snow, you see me not, see me not, see me not. One flake of snow lost in the drift, see me not, see me not. (Price 1994a: 90)

What Susan Price has herself called the 'chanting rhythms' (Price 2002a) of the Ghost World narratives are very similar in technique to shamans' chants: I now compare an example from *The Ghost Drum* with how Pal Simoncsics (1978) and Mongush Kenin-Lopsan (1997) analyse Siberian shamanic verse.

When the spirits of Chingis and three other dead protagonists capture Kuzma's spirit, their reported song magic is conveyed through rhymes and syntactic patterns, binary forms characteristic of folk tale and Pagan ceremony (compare Yovino-Young 1993): 'They trapped it, wrapped it, in nets of hair and air, in words and music' (Price 1987: 147). A sense of magic chant, 'in words and music', is given by the change of rhythm and sounds that pivots around the comma after 'wrapped it': in 'They trapped it, wrapped it', there are short vowels and unvoiced plosives (/p/ twice, /t/ four times); then 'in nets of hair and air, in words and music' has mostly long vowels and diphthongs in stressed syllables.

Analysing a Nenets magical chant, Simoncsics finds parallelism, chiasm and embedded symmetry at phonological, syntactic and discourse levels. He concludes that form enacts meaning, the symmetry of the incantation reflecting 'the shaman's journey to the otherworld and his return from there' (Simoncsics 1978: 400). Kenin-Lopsan dem-onstrates that 'Tuvan shamanic verse is synharmonic in nature, based on rhythmical syntactical parallelism' (Kenin-Lopsan 1997: 142), and discerns a narrative syntax to shamanic texts: 'we see that the seance is a complex and well-structured event, where one can discern a pro-logue, exposition, plot, author's digression, culmination, denouement, and epilogue' (110). Kenin-Lopsan's overview is that 'shamans told their listeners of their impressions and actions. It might be said that shamans created worlds through words' (ibid.). Creating 'worlds through words' is just what writers and their readers do, so that in a way authors are shamans, as shamans are authors. A comparison can be made with the centrality Neil Philip attributes to shamanism in Alan Garner's work (Philip 1981a, 1981b, 1997), and the suggestion 'that Garner sees his own function as author as in some ways akin to that of the shaman' (Philip 1981a: 102), as does Russell Hoban (Hopkin 2002).

Just as Sami yoik chanting may be interpreted as expressing individu-ality and diversity (Somby 1995), so may song magic in the Ghost World trilogy. This fits the wider picture we have seen, of Price's construction of shamanism being about power, agency and equality. Furthermore, diversity and interconnectedness are honoured. Everyday diversity is celebrated: 'the variety and beauty of the world were shocking; and the shock never ended. [...] The real, the ordinary, outdid all imagin-ation. [...] Difference, difference in everything' (Price 1987: 92–93). Interconnectedness is expressed by Chingis in terms redolent of chaos theory: 'Nothing can be altered without altering everything that touches it' (97). There is a similar philosophy in *Ghost Dance*: 'You can-not change one thing alone; you will always change many things, and you cannot tell what might become of that' (Price 1994a: 16). Diversity, interconnectedness and individual worth are also upheld by the ani-mism of the Ghost World stories, whereby all people and animals have spirits.

People's Paganism underpins these egalitarian social values, whereas the Church operates as the apparatus of the totalitarian state. In *The Ghost Drum*, Margaretta while still a Princess prays in her chapel for the death of her brother, and bargains with God: 'Let me ascend to the Czar-chair, dear God,' prayed Margaretta, 'and I will serve Thee truly and faithfully, and all Thy commandments shall be kept in my Czardom' (Price 1987: 77). Shortly afterwards, when the Czar does die, the bells of all the churches in the kingdom are rung. Czaritsa Margaretta declares, 'I am God on earth in female form' (88) and 'I have a mandate from God! Nothing I can do is wrong!' (138). The Church legitimates her actions, Safa's execution being attended by 'priests in tall hats and stiff black robes' (151). In *Ghost Dance*, in 'many, many churches in every part of the city [...] the priests cried, "Obey the Czar, our God on Earth!"' (Price 1994a: 26).

In much of Susan Price's work, Paganism and Christianity are opposed. In the light-hearted *Foiling the Dragon* (Price 1994b), Dragonsheim, a Pagan republic, is set against Angamark, a Christian monarchy. More violent and visceral are *Elfgift* and *Elfking* (Price 1995, 1996; considered below), and *The Wolf-Sisters* (Price 2001b). Christianity is unsympathetically portrayed in *The Wolf-Sisters*, the Abbess's notion of 'saving' the 'Wood Demons' being to kill one of the Wolf-Sisters with a silver knife which has been concealed in a crucifix. But then the Dionysian excesses of the two remaining Wolf-Sisters and the renegade novice Kenelm are shocking, as they slaughter and gorge themselves on the monks. Kenelm, who 'had stayed stubbornly loyal to his own Gods through all his years in the monastery' (Price 2001b: 19), is both entranced and repelled: perhaps the implication is that there is an exhilarating, terrifying wildness lurking in us all – Kenelm 'was afraid of the wood and he was afraid of himself' (144).

The possibility of a more tolerant and syncretic relationship between Paganism and Christianity is explored in Theresa Tomlinson's historical fiction. Women's solidarity overcomes religious differences in *The Forestwife* (Tomlinson 1993) as an itinerant group of nuns, who 'took their own services, preached their own sermons, held their chapter meetings without the advice of a priest' (74), work with the Forestwife and partake in Pagan celebrations. Sister Fridgyth in *Wolf Girl* (Tomlinson 2006), 'a strong, practical lay sister' (40) at Whitby Abbey in the seventh century, will not give up her residual Paganism: 'I may still cast the runes, but I do try hard to be a Christian' (45). Another Sister says of Abbess Hild's reputation for wisdom: 'Some say it comes from the Christian God [...] but I would say that a little of it comes from Nelda in her forest lair' (166). Nelda is a wise woman whose blessings invoke a mixture of angels, Woden and Brig. Similarly, Wolfrun, the lead character and Wolf Girl of the title, prays to and thanks both Freya and the Christian God.

There are human and animal spirits in *The Ghost Drum*, but no gods, which reflects Siberian and eastern Sami belief (see Riordan 1989). In the sequels to *The Ghost Drum*, Norse gods become more prominent: in *Ghost Song* and *Ghost Dance*, Loki is referred to as the First Shaman, who made the world; and Hel, the queen of the dead, appears in *Ghost Dance*. This is more in line with western Sami belief, the direction of influence between Sami and Norse cosmology having been contested for some time (see Spencer 1978). Even though Norse gods do not appear in *The Ghost Drum*, the ghost-world gate and the World Tree already do, and they derive in part from Norse mythology.

The ghost-world gate, a variant of the door to the world of the dead fantaseme (see Nikolajeva 1988), shows how Susan Price creatively synthesises a variety of inspirations. One influence is 'a description of a Viking funeral, given by an Arabic trader' (Price 2002a),[5] and then there is 'the quote from Norse Myth, where Valhalla is said to have a thousand doors' and '*The Duchess of Malfi*, where there is a line about the door of death having such quaint hinges that it can open a thousand, thousand different ways' (Price 2002b).[6] Thus in *Ghost Song*, the Gate (now capitalised) is described as having 'hinges on all sides, for this Gate opens in many ways' (Price 1992: 135).

The World Tree appears as follows: 'At the centre of Iron-Wood you may see them [new bodies for shamans] growing, on the ash' (Price 1987: 134). *Ghost Song* conveys the scale of the Iron Ash: 'its roots go down into chaos, and it spreads its iron leaves among the stars' (Price 1992: 147). A bridge (Bifrost) and a squirrel (Ratatosk) are mentioned, too, and Ambrosi's father's head by the pool is like Mimir's head. Norse mythology is used all the more in *Ghost Dance*: the Well at the World's End, the stone squirrel, the eagle, Hel's hall. *Ghost Song* and *Ghost Dance* both allude to the story of Balder and Loki. Loki is presented as the First Shaman, a lonely shape-changer and trickster with whom Kuzma identifies: 'Kuzma had Loki's heart in his breast, Loki's breath in his mouth' (Price 1992: 147). At the climax of *Ghost Dance*, Shingebiss summons and becomes Loki.

It is difficult to disentangle the Norse cosmology of the Ghost World trilogy from Sami and Siberian shamanism because Norse mythology has so many shamanic resonances, at the heart of which is the World Tree, Yggdrasil. Susan Price observes that the World Tree is 'an extremely ancient symbol that's also found in the myths of the shamanistic Siberian tribes' (Price 2002b), and H. R. Ellis Davidson reports 'the widespread shamanistic idea that the tree is the source of unborn souls' (Davidson 1964: 195). Bo Sommarström makes a sustained comparison between Sami depictions of the Tree of the World and the Nordic Yggdrasil, including '*The tree as centre of the world and principle of organisation*' and the '*Bridge of death*' (Sommarström 1987: 222, 223, original italics).

The world tree or *axis mundi* is the means by which the shaman ascends and descends through layers of worlds; it 'is indeed the centre of the shaman's cosmology, as it is in the world of the northern myths' (Davidson 1964: 144). Odin's hanging on Yggdrasil for nine days to obtain wisdom can be interpreted as a shamanic initiation. Moreover, '*Ygg* means "the terrible one" and *drasill* means "horse", and it is now generally accepted that this compound noun must mean "Odin's horse"' (Crossley-Holland 1980: 187) – that is, it is a vehicle for his shamanic soul-journeying, as is his eight-legged horse Sleipnir. In his ability to shapechange and travel between worlds, including Hel's realm, Odin is a shaman. 'Odin' seems to derive from words meaning excited, intoxicated, and ecstatic (Davidson 1964: 147), suggestive of the shaman's trance state.

This association of Odin with the World Tree and shamanism, and Odin's presence in much of Susan Price's other work (Price 1986, 1995, 1996, 2005, 2006, 2008), then begs the question – why Loki and not Odin in the Ghost World trilogy? Perhaps Odin as head of the Norse pantheon, a kind of Czar of the gods, would be too invasive for the Sami/Siberian setting. When one finds out that the raven is the creator and trickster spirit in some circumpolar cultures (Riordan 1989), Odin's companion ravens, Thought and Memory, could represent a subjection of these cultures and erasure of the thought and memory of them. By contrast, Loki is a subversive outsider, more in keeping with the anti-authoritarian ethos of the Ghost World trilogy.

* * *

Having considered how the Ghost World trilogy uses Norse mythology in a Sami/Siberian milieu, I turn now to three novels set in the Anglo-Saxon and Norse past, two by Susan Price and one by Robert Leeson, which radically rework Heathenism. Susan Price recasts Heathen mythology creatively and critically in *Elfgift* and *Elfking* (Price 1995 and 1996) by exploiting unstable oppositions: Christian and Pagan, divine and human, feminine and masculine. Elfgift is a man of two worlds, born of a human father and an elfin mother. From the latter come 'feminine' and otherworldly qualities that disturb the conventional masculinity of Elfgift's half-brothers: Elfgift is preternaturally beautiful and has gifts of healing and prescience, but can be arbitrary, cold and impulsive. These stories are bloodthirsty and violent, steeped in the revenge ethic, but also questioning of it. Elfgift is fated to become king – though that would be 'a great sin' (Price 1995: 9) according to a Christian priest – and Elfgift's three half-brothers try but fail to murder him, one of them dying in the attempt. A chain of revenge is thereby triggered, but ultimately neither Elfgift nor his half-brother Wulfweard want to kill each other. Their confrontation is narrated from Elfgift's then Wulfweard's point of view, a bifurcation that partakes of the non-linear Pagan chronotope (compare the discussion of Catherine Fisher's *The Lammas Field* in Chapter 1, above) and enacts the warp and weft woven by weird (fate).

Price decided 'to make Elfgift a champion of paganism, fighting against encroaching Christianity' (Price 2002a), and so Christianity and Paganism are opposed, and often defined in terms of attitudes to fighting. A Valkyrie trains Elfgift, emphasising the role of the feminine in battle in Heathen mythology. Elfgift's uncle rejects Christianity because 'any man who prayed to a Prince of Peace who had advised his followers to invite another blow when someone struck them, was a coward and a weakling' (Price 1995: 12). War is presented as being integral to Heathenism, whereas fighting in the name of Christ is hypocritical: 'Ing bore a sword, Thunor a war-hammer, and Woden a spear, but Christ hated weapons of war – except when the war was led by Unwin' (Price 1996: 259–260). Unwin, Elfgift's other surviving half-brother, is frequently satirised for advocating violence in the name of Christianity; like Czaritsa Margaretta in *The Ghost Drum*, his prayers are an entirely selfish projection of his own ambition.

Though Unwin's militant version of Christianity is a distortion, it is the one gaining ascendancy, wreaking cultural and ecological disaster. Monotheism is bound to monarchy in an imperialism that annihilates diversity: '"One God above," said the Christians, "one king below." [...] Little countries, with their own Gods, their own customs, their own laws, couldn't hope to survive' (Price 1996: 77). The Goddess Lady Eostre employs apocalyptic ecological rhetoric to warn that Unwin's followers are destroying the earth, 'clearing the forests, draining the marshes, damming the streams' (Price 1995: 203), and asserts her own dominion. The Lady Eostre is more prominent in *Elfgift*, Woden in *Elfking*, so that the feminine and masculine of the Heathen pantheon are balanced over the course of the two books into a kind of duotheism, and the dual nature of each is also emphasised. The Lady brings both 'warm days and flowers' and 'ice and darkness' – she is 'a loving lady and a hard-hearted hag' (Price 1995: 202, 244); Woden has 'one blue eye that looked on life and growth, and the blind, gouged hole that looked into darkness and the world beyond Death' (Price 1996: 27). They complement each other, according to the Lady: 'I am Life and Death; He is Death and Life. I choose the slain; He chooses those to live' (66).

Susan Price recalls that 'when I was writing "Elfking", [it] felt as if I was reinventing paganism (and very good fun it was)' (Price 2002a), and elaboration of theology and festival is noticeable in the sequel to *Elfgift*. Obscure twin gods come to be embodied by Elfgift and his brother Wulfweard, now an ally. Unwin's wife leaves him and his faith to return to Paganism; visiting the God-house with her sons, she observes the depiction of Ing, Thunor and Woden: 'A three-fold God – just as the Lady was Maiden, Mother and Crone, so here was the Lord: Youth, Warrior and Elder: Sword, Hammer and Spear' (Price 1996: 165–166). In this attempt to match male and female trinities, the female side is not so adapted to the Heathen pantheon but is more of a generic triple Goddess, though Heathenism is framed as organic and mutable: 'New Gods arose, and old Gods sank back into the shadows of the God-house walls and the darkness of forgetfulness' (167). Unwin later has the God-house destroyed, but the religion is more than the temple.

Three seasonal feasts are described in *Elfking*, reflecting the preference of some modern Heathens for three festivals over the eight of the Pagan Wheel of the Year (see Harvey 1997). In line with Price's narrative scheme, there is an emphasis on the death and resurrection of the corn God Ing, and on the Goddess Eostre. Ing's feast is the autumn fire festival, 'when Ing, in defiance of the dying all around, offered Himself as a target and spread wide His arms to receive the spears' (Price 1996: 59). Jul's feast (Yule) falls at midwinter, after which the sun and life will return, and is celebrated with cakes and guising. At Eostre's feast, people share dyed eggs to celebrate the return of Ing from Hel's domain. *Elfking* pivots around Jul, the peace of which Unwin breaks, declaring: 'No truce I make with a devil can bind me. I am working for Christ and His Victory' (161). Elfgift is killed, but brought back as the God Ing by Woden's shamanic rites. Woden transforms a rubbish tip outside the borough fortifications into the World Tree, drums 'a rhythm to the Tree's song' (244) and recites a rune song. Elfgift's spirit climbs the Ash from the underworld, dismembers his own mutilated corpse, puts it in a cauldron and eats. He lays out his bones and Woden orders, with grim humour, 'Now name your bones. Pull yourself together!' (251). Elfgift's ghost lies among bones, covered with ash leaves, when Woden breathes life into him and the Lady Eostre embraces him.

By the end of *Elfgift*, Elfgift is a king, and by the end of *Elfking*, he is a god. Susan Price confesses, 'I sort of fell out with Elfgift. I'm a republican, so writing about people fated to become kings goes against the grain with me,' and she was all the more perturbed by his deification (Price 2002a). Price's discomfort with the direction of her own stories generates some fascinating developments within them, as kingship and godhood are subverted. When Elfgift places his foot in the hollow of a stone, 'a valkyrie shriek' acclaims him 'the Goddess-chosen king' (Price 1995: 239).[7] He claims Unwin's borough and reinstates the Heathen Gods, but his is a carnivalesque kingship. Part androgynous Queen of the May, 'with his striking beauty, his atheling's hair, his sweaty field-hand's clothes, his crown of flowers' (143), he is a 'decrowning double' (Bakhtin 1984: 127) of Unwin; his court is 'a fairground' in which the social order is inverted: 'In hearing after hearing, he found for the farm-ers and against the nobles' (Price 1996: 172). Goddess-chosen, he has never controlled his own destiny: 'he was not free to choose his actions. The hour of his death and the manner of his dying had been fated long ago. So had the manner of his life' (Price 1996: 103). When he becomes a god, he is 'shining, quick, lithe, beautiful – but cruel' (297), with the power to kill or cure. Those who have loved him now find him fearsome and treacherous; empathy and human fellow-feeling are curiously alien to him. To be destined to be king and god, or, in the Ghost World tril-ogy, Czar or Czaritsa, God on earth, is a terrible fate.

The title of Robert Leeson's historical novel *Beyond the Dragon Prow* (1973) indicates not only the expected adventurous journeying, but also an endeavour to get beyond stereotypes of the Vikings. Leeson sys-tematically inverts such stereotypes by including diversity of race and physical ability, and advocating social equality, in an internally consist-ent and vraisemblant narrative. Stiglaf is born with one foot 'shortened and twisted' (21). Enduring his disability with fortitude, he is a capable farmer, but he refuses 'to wear a sword, carry a spear, or to train in battle-skills' (31); he does not have it in him to kill a man. Stiglaf is of mixed heritage, his father a black-haired Viking, his mother half-Celt, half-Saxon. The father, Sven Fork-Beard, has made a 'secret pledge' to his wife not to go 'viking', preferring to make the best use of his home territory by clearing forests and tilling the earth.

Stiglaf befriends and seeks out reindeer-herding nomads (Sami in all probability), only to get himself caught in a life-threatening blizzard, from which the nomads rescue him. His return home in hippyish garb, 'wearing the skin-clothes and bright beads of the nomads' (34), might be seen as signifying the subjection of a northern indigenous people to the same spiritual tourism and cultural theft as inflicted upon Native Americans in the west (see Johnson 1995), and Indians in the east (see Mehta 1979) – the latter peaking in the 1970s, the decade in which *Beyond the Dragon Prow* was published. Stiglaf initiates trade with the nomads, and continually consults with a wise old woman who on one occasion enables him to cure some cattle, provoking a mixed reaction from his own people: 'The Skallings looked on Stiglaf with new respect, but also with a little fear' (Leeson 1973: 45).

After fifteen years of peace, Stiglaf's people are persuaded to fight against men 'beyond the southern sea', in North Africa, even though 'one of the oldest men' of the Skallings cannot understand why they should get involved in a quarrel between Christian and Moslem monotheists. The narrative stays with Stiglaf, not the voyagers, who on their return tell Stiglaf that his father has died a hero's death. Stiglaf is 'now fourteen and a man – a fatherless man – a man who must bear all his burdens alone' (48). Stiglaf's cousin gives fighting 'the dark hordes' (51) a repellent moral complexion: 'as the day and the sun rise to triumph over the night and the dark, so have we conquered the dark princes' (52). The cousin has even brought back a black child captive, the mistreatment of whom Stiglaf speaks out against, with the upshot that the child is given to Stiglaf. The captive cannot speak, though she can hear, and she and Stiglaf improvise a way to communicate: 'Often she would take up his hand in hers and with her finger trace the outline of a sign on his palm, and he would do the same in her palm' (60). Stiglaf learns she is called Djamila, she is the daughter of a prince, and she has lost her father as he has lost his. They become constant companions, but rumours against her of poisoning and witchcraft spread, until she is cast on the burning funeral ship of Stiglaf's uncle.[8] In the most thrilling and ingenious episode of the book, Stiglaf jumps on the blazing vessel and saves Djamila, and she in turn cleverly improvises a sail so that 'This dumb girl, whom he had tried to protect, had saved him' (83).

There is no turning back so they sail west to England, a green land of beeches and oaks and outlaws. There they are joined by Guthlac, a wandering smith who is deaf, and Aelwyn, a singing monk who is blind. Aelwyn, like the poet Caedmon as reported by Bede, has set psalms to popular tunes – 'though the one true God has the best words, the old gods have the best tunes' (107). Unfortunately, 'words of love and praise of beer' (ibid.) also slipped out and he decided to leave the monastery. Now, he finds 'true friendship among heathens, after so many years' cold comfort among the men of God' (106). Aelwyn argues that Stiglaf's life has not been determined by fate, but by the young man's own choices, under providence; but Guthlac's challenge – what if providence makes bad things happen? – is not answered. A pacifist message, especially critical of war waged in the name of Christ, the Prince of Peace, is strongly voiced through Aelwyn, as through the old man of the Skellings earlier, and also a woman from Stiglaf's mother's village in

England: 'What did these things mean to us? Christian, heathen, to us it was an old and evil game, one man against another' (130). The rune-inscribed comb that was Stiglaf's mother's and has inspired him to trace her roots also embodies a message of equality and peace: Aelwyn translates the runes as ' "All the teeth of the comb are of the same length," which means that all men are as good as one another' (110), and in the end Stiglaf declares 'let Skalling live with Wealdor folk, like teeth in a comb' (158). Thus the egalitarian, inclusive ideology, agreeable as it may be, is hardly conveyed with subtlety, and Stiglaf and his companions might be regarded as ticking boxes of disability and race too schematically. Even so, in the decades since *Beyond the Dragon Prow* was published, there has not been such a bold experiment in children's fiction in revisioning Heathenism as embracing difference.

* * *

From the children's fiction discussed so far, it is apparent that, in recent years, presenting shamanism as a living tradition in circumpolar cultures seems to have entailed using prehistoric or historic settings. This section concentrates specifically on the depiction of Lapps (Sami) contemporaneously with the time of writing of three children's novels. Christian missionary activity, persecution and conversion, had long since destroyed Sami shamanism, but it is remembered in *The Reindeer and the Drum* (Kerven 1980). *The Twins of Lapland* (Jenkins 1960) preserves something of Sami spirituality, but not shamanism as such. Memories of Sami spirituality and shamanism are conspicuous by their absence from *The Summer of the White Reindeer* (Pohlmann 1965).

Rosalind Kerven's *The Reindeer and the Drum* (1980) is framed as a holiday adventure, in which Anna travels north from Oslo to visit her Lapp relations and helps to rediscover the family's magic drum, hidden about two hundred years previously because 'the missionaries went round burning [drums] because they thought they were wicked' (25). The story also delineates the difficulties of maintaining a nomadic reindeer-herding lifestyle in an era of technological change. Kerven was inspired to research and write her first book by her own travels in Lapland, and by her interest in social anthropology – she is fascinated:

> not just with how other cultures live, but also how they think. I love challenging the preconceptions of our own culture's mindset. Anthropology teaches you that every cultural thought structure has

its own basic premises, and if you accept and believe in these, everything else follows. (Kerven 2005)

The journey north is full of wonder for Anna: 'the silence seemed as magical as the landscape itself. It was almost magic, as if the whole place had been touched by enchantment' (Kerven 1980: 21). Gazing at the Northern Lights and the featureless landscape below causes Anna to lose all sense of time and movement. Reaching the reindeer herders' summer quarters, Anna meets her cousins and their grandmother. Grandma has 'deep-set blue eyes that seemed able to see a long, long way into the distance' (30), maintains the Sami tradition of *yoik* singing, and keeps up 'an endless stream of stories' (40). The cousins value these stories, but the intervening generation is too preoccupied: 'Mum and Dad are too busy worrying about the reindeer to think about the Old Days. But *we* like hearing about it' (17) says cousin Berit.

On a midnight fishing trip with Anna and the cousins, Grandma outlines pre-Christian belief in animism and shamanism:

> The sun, the trees, the mountains, the sea, the rocks: see how full they are with the stuff of life. And the thunder and the wind, and in the darkness of the winter, the silver ball of the moon. Nowadays we learn to love them as God's own creation – but in the time of my great-great-grandfather we knew them differently. Each one had its own spirit, and it was the Holy Men who could enter into their world and speak with them. (Kerven 1980: 46–47)

The Holy Men 'brought hope and healing to our people' (47), Grandma says, and explains the uses of the shaman's drum for divination and soul-journeying. Kerven follows Spencer (1978), an acknowledged source (Kerven 2005), in assuming that most Sami shamans were men, and, while this has been disputed since (Lundmark 1987), it is notable, even so, that the old beliefs are preserved and mediated in the story by a wise old woman.

Anna confesses to having hoped for adventures, and she is not disappointed: she and her cousins secretly go in search of a runaway dog, using an old map, and shelter from a thunderstorm in a cave that has a secret passage. The atmospheric cave, 'heavy with dim, ancestral memories [...] slightly spooky, yet tranquil' (Kerven 1980: 71), contains a shrine consisting of a semicircle of size-graded antlers. The return of the three children is greeted with relief and anger, and the news that Anna's uncle and aunt are thinking of selling the reindeer herd because they are unable to make a living without mechanising, which they cannot afford. This accords with Uncle Matte's opinion, expressed earlier, that 'It's no good having magic drums now. We need technology to keep up a profitable herd' (36). Nevertheless, the whole family goes back to the cave in search of their ancestral Drum. A riddle Grandma's grandfather taught her leads them to the Drum, which Anna and the dog pluckily retrieve from a narrow passage.

The Drum, perfectly preserved in a locked box from a century before Grandma was born, is decorated thus:

> Across the creamy skin, wild red matchstick figures were dancing. There were men and women, reindeer and fish, sledges and trees...
>
> And painted right in the middle, a bear. He was the largest figure of all, with the sun at his right paw, the moon at his left, and a half-circle of tiny stars about his head.
>
> All around the rim of the Drum hung tiny ornaments: trinkets of brass, copper and silver, and smooth white fragments of bone. They rattled softly each time that Berit's hand moved, making a fine, silvery, elfin music. (Kerven 1980: 112)

Grandma will not let cousin Berit play the drum: 'If the Drum carried you into the Land of Spirits, would you know how to find your way? If it showed you all the secrets of your future, would you be brave enough to read them?' (112–113). With Grandma's consent, the Drum is sold to a museum so that the family can afford to mechanise their reindeer herding. Grandma says, 'we've managed without the Drum for two hundred years. But never without the reindeer. And [...] whatever good is a Lapp without his reindeer?' (118). Reindeer nomadism is presented as surviving and adapting to change, whereas Sami shamanism is extinct, but not forgotten. And maybe, Grandma thinks, animistic beliefs could return:

> Everything changes, and yet some things are constant. We've forgotten all about the old spirits and yet, you know, all around us the tundra and the mountains are still alive and waiting for them to come back. (Kerven 1980: 113)

The Twins of Lapland by Alan C. Jenkins (1960) follows half a year in Lapp life, from summer to winter, focusing on the twins Arnas-Andero and Sofi-Marit Nakkilajärvi: reindeer are earmarked, herded and protected; the twins help keep cows, go fishing, and adopt a bear cub. Like

Kerven a generation later, Jenkins depicts Lapp culture as Christianised, while grandparents remember old beliefs, and to an extent still put them into practice. Although the story is entirely set in Lapland and among Lapp people, Jenkins does not share Kerven's anthropological perspective of seeing a culture in its own terms: to say that 'The Lapps are carefree, they live for the moment, and are sometimes rather like children, which of course is a happy state' (83) infantilises Lapps, and is also a twee construction of childhood. Maintaining 'superstitious' practices is regarded as 'backward' compared with the 'up to date' technology the Lapps use for forest management, fishing and reindeer herding (31), though the state is criticised for making environmentally damaging interventions, such as burning land where trees are felled, and planning to flood land to create a hydroelectric plant. The Protestant work ethic is repeatedly and didactically projected onto the Lapps: 'There was never any grumbling in Lapland: life was work and work was life' (22); 'They knew only too well that in this world, especially their Arctic world, nothing worthwhile is won without hard work' (86/88); 'She [Sofi-Marit] knew the fish were food and food was life and life was work and work was happiness!' (89).

Grandfather Ancient-Jouni is a hunter and a storyteller who informs Sofi-Marit about the Lapps' former heliolatry, greeting the sun's spring return with special 'loaves outside their tents and [...] joyful songs' (21). Bears are 'the living symbol of so much Lapp folk-lore and legend' (77) and are referred to by periphrases such as 'Winter-Sleeper' and 'Grandfather-of-the-Hill'. Ancient-Jouni tells of the elaborate rituals that used to be performed, to avoid vengeance from a hunted bear's spirit: the hunters would apologise to the slain bear and tell him 'that it was not they but somebody else who had really killed him' (43), they would enter their tents at the back, and the women would disguise them with alder dye and protect them with brass rings. With the possible exception of a hint of guising or shape-changing when Ancient-Jouni wears on his shoulders 'the bloody pelt of the wolf he had slain' (139), there is no reference to Sami shamanism in *The Twins of Lapland*. What we do get is some persistence of Pagan beliefs alongside Christianity: 'Ancient-Jouni went to church, he took Holy Communion, but he wasn't convinced that the old Lapp gods had gone for ever! He never worked on Thursday in case he offended Thor' (123–124). The Norse god-name Thor is odd in a Lapp context, though there has been contact and influence between these two northern cultures; perhaps the equivalent of Thor would properly be 'the eastern Lapps' great god Tiermes, lord of thunder and weather' (Spencer 1978: 89).

The best example of the coexistence of Christianity with survivals of pre-Christian beliefs and practices in *The Twins of Lapland* occurs when the twins' baby sister is taken to be christened in the Finnish Lutheran church. On the way, the twins' father sings a *yoik*, and it is explained that 'The Lapps like to compose impromptu songs about people or events, particularly when they are out sleighing by themselves' (109). There may be a flavour of Laestadianism, the 'revivalist cult [that] arose in the mid-1800s and [...] appealed to the cathartic group ecstasy of the old religion' (Spencer 1978: 35), in how 'worked up and excited' (Jenkins 1960: 114) some of the Lapp congregation get during the sermon. The baby is given a baptismal reindeer, 'the nucleus of a girl's dowry' (ibid.). Her cradle is adorned with silver charms to ward off spirits and trolls that might replace her with a changeling, and the twins chase off a willow-tit, because it is 'the devil's troll bird' and 'It would have been most ominous if it had perched on the cradle' (110). Possibly because of the long-term fragmenting effect of Christianisation on old Sami beliefs, *The Twins of Lapland* presents piecemeal superstitions, bereft of an underlying belief structure.

The reason for the Evans family to travel from the USA. to Lapland in *The Summer of the White Reindeer* (Pohlmann 1965) is an ecological one: Jay's father is testing whether reindeer moss has been tainted by atomic testing. The focus of the story is Jay finding his identity as a middle child (compare Robson 2001) and as a young man. Jay is envious of the talents of his older sister and younger brother and feels that others are always laughing at him, but he finally proves himself by bravely rescuing a white reindeer ensnared by barbed wire, and thereby makes his father proud. Jay idolises the Lapp boy Heikki, 'absolutely the best boy I've ever known, so far' (132), who is a model of a certain type of masculinity: 'there was something about him that seemed quiet and strong to Jay – something like a man' (29). Heikki is fascinated by Jay's skill at making model aeroplanes, and in the end they cement their friendship, Jay giving the white reindeer earmarked for himself to Heikki, Heikki giving his dog to Jay.

There are the barest traces of spirituality in *The Summer of the White Reindeer*. The nomadic Lapps attend church when they are able, accompanied by their dogs. Jay's mother perceives the Lapp landscape as 'like holy ground, so thick with nature's patient, miraculous work, layer upon layer, season upon season' (64), but there are no indications of traditional Sami belief. 'By the end of the eighteenth century the Christian faith was widely and firmly established in Lapland' (Spencer 1978: 35), so to present pre-Christian Sami spirituality with any degree of credibility authors either have to use the device of grandparents preserving what their ancestors believed for contemporaneous settings, as Kerven and Jenkins do,[9] but Pohlmann does not, or use historical or fantasy counter-historical settings, as with other examples in this chapter.

* * *

Many of the texts considered so far involve contact, and sometimes clashes, between cultures. This motif is all the more prominent in the novels explored in this section. Mette Newth's *The Abduction* (1987), and Celia Rees's *Witch Child* (2000) and *Sorceress* (2002), are set in the 16th and 17th centuries, times of European exploration and colonisation of the Americas. While the European explorers and settlers spark conflict with indigenous cultures, young adult characters are seen to connect across divides of mutual incomprehension and hostility.

Based on Queen Elizabeth I's command to Martin Frobisher to bring back natives from his travels, Mette Newth's *The Abduction* (1987) tells of how the Inuit young woman Osuqo and her betrothed, Poq, a shaman, are captured and brought to Europe. The narrative alternates between Osuqo and Christine, a servant in a God-fearing merchant house, whose father is a sailor on the European ship. While Osuqo and Christine connect across cultures which otherwise share only incomprehension and mistrust, the differences in the presentation of their viewpoints are revealing. Whereas Garamond typeface and the first person are used for Christine, Osuqo is seen through the third person and Helvetica, a clear sans serif typeface which might be taken as implying simplicity and honesty, a romanticising of the Inuit. The Norwegian author may not have wished to presume to narrate the Inuit side of the story in the first person, but the distancing effect of the third person also underlines the European reification of the Inuit – 'They treated Poq and her as if they were objects, not human beings' (85). What is more, the subjectivity and agency entailed by the first person may be seen as a European ideal alien to Inuit culture, though circumstances force Osuqo to recognise that 'Shaman Aua could not help her now. She had to manage alone' (56), and Poq to realise that 'Our ancestors [...] have no amulets to give us, nor magic words. [...] We must fight to free ourselves alone' (62).

Poq is a young shaman who entered into his power through the psychic trauma of his father and brothers drowning in a whale hunt. A footnote explains the role of the *angakoq* (compare Kipling's 'Quiquern' discussed above), of 'master[ing] the difficult art of entering an ecstatic state [... to] guide and help people in daily life, in illness and death' (5).

When the European ship arrives, an older shaman warns 'against having too much to do with the foreigners' (12), and to Osuqo the vessel is 'the sinister black bird from her nightmares' (10), but their kinspeople welcome it for trade. Osuqo and Poq are captured, Osuqo's father is shot resisting. After she had just had her first period and observed the taboos, 'The first day of Osuqo's adult life had become the day her life ended' (23). Osuqo is raped on board, by the captain and others, and nearly dies of blood loss. Poq's shaman song tells her 'the power is yours for all eternity [...] You are us/our suffering and our triumph' (50). To her abusers 'It's just a heathen creature, a wild female animal!' (56), but Christine's father, one of the crew, stands up for Osuqo, 'hardly older than my own daughter' (56), and tends to her. In a storm, Osuqo mistakes Christine's father for an abuser, pushes him away, and he is lost overboard. On realising her mistake and that 'The unknown man must have been the helping spirit Tornaq!' (59), Osuqo despairs.

When the ship disembarks, Christine meets Osuqo's proud gaze: 'I saw deep sorrow, but no fear. I saw a plea for mercy, but not help' (70). Osuqo speaks to Christine's mind: 'Father is dead. He's never coming back' (70) could refer to either's loss. Heinrik, the young man of the house in which Christine is a servant, saves Osuqo and Poq from an angry mob, only to have them imprisoned in his father's house, with Christine their 'warder'. Heinrik's intentions are honourable when he declares that 'as good Christians our first duty is to turns these heathens to God, and it is our duty to let learned men study the customs and ways of the godless' (74), but fails to anticipate the abuses Osuqo and Poq will be put through in the names of science and Christianity. Osuqo escapes into memories: of her little brother, of her grandparents choosing the moment and manner of their death, of the highly ritualised hunting of an enchanted polar bear with 'the same magic power and knowledge as people' (162). To Osuqo, because of her sufferings, the foreigners are 'insane, evil spirits' (88) as she and Poq are to them, but Poq shares with Heinrik a spirit of scientific enquiry:

Now we know that there is a world outside *our* world, with people who look like us but who are not of our race. [...] It's our task to gather all the knowledge we can and take it back to the land of the People. (Newth 1987: 88)

Poq's curiosity is crushed, his pride utterly broken when he and Osuqo are stripped for anatomical drawings, an all too literal version of ethnography. After that, plus being exorcised and forcibly baptised, Poq perceives that 'They've stolen everything! Everything! Our thoughts, our gods, our past. [...] They want to shape us in their own image. They cannot bear that we are different from them' (136).

Heinrik colludes with the exorcism and forced baptism in order to save Poq and Osuqo from execution. Osuqo tries to comprehend in her own terms the attempts to Christianise herself and Poq: 'the foreigner with the stone face [the priest] was some kind of shaman and he was bellowing at them about the foreigners' gods' (130); the Bible contains 'the foreigners' strongest magic words' (132); the crucifix is 'the foreigners' strongest amulet' (ibid.), in which she recognises her own suffering. In her heart she will never relinquish her dedication to her own Gods, the Mother of the Sea and the Father of the Moon. While Osuqo keeps her faith, Christine doubts the faith she is named after. Torturing herself with the pernicious doctrine that disability is punishment for sin, she supplicates God in vain for 'forgiveness for the sins that had made me crippled' (37). After she hears of her father's fate, she cries 'Were you dozing, God, when Father was lost?' (76). Christine's mother, however, is a paragon of a different sort of Christianity than the one with which Christine punishes herself, and the one that persecutes Osuqo and Poq: 'she was the only one – of all the God-fearing people who had surrounded the foreign man and woman – who had been merciful' (157), and she maintains that 'To God, all his children are equal. His mercy and love are just as great towards [...] the familiar and the unfamiliar' (ibid.).

Heinrik's father plans to get Osuqo and Poq off his hands by giving them as a wedding gift to Heinrik's sister's groom, who intends to ill-use Osuqo and let Poq die, so that his skeleton can be shown in universities around Europe. Forced by threats to comply with his father's plans, Heinrik nevertheless resolves to help the captives escape. He arranges for Poq to make a public display of his skill with hunting weapons, and the people take to Poq, but when he is made to fight a maltreated bear, and charms it with song into a merciful death, the fickle crowd turn against him with cries of witchcraft. In the hubbub, Poq and Osuqo flee, taking a kayak out to the open sea.

A 'major starting point' for *Witch Child* (Rees 2000) and *Sorceress* (Rees 2002), Celia Rees reveals, was thinking:

> how interesting it would be if someone who had been accused of being a witch in Europe and risked being hanged for evil [...] then went to live in America where she was revered as "gifted" because of her knowledge of Shamanism. (Rees 2001)

Set in the 17th century, *Witch Child* tells how, after her grandmother is hanged for a witch, Mary Newbury crosses the Atlantic with Puritan settlers and forms a bond with the Native American Jaybird and his Grandfather, despite the surrounding fear and mistrust between settlers and natives. Mary is herself arraigned for witchcraft by the settlers, and flees: *Sorceress* follows her fortunes as she is adopted by Jaybird's people as healer and wise woman, and endures the conflict between invading and indigenous people. The premise is similar to that of *Religion and the Decline of Magic* (Thomas 1971): that there is an anthropological equivalence between Early Modern European folk belief and supposedly 'primitive' cultures such as Native American societies.

Witch Child follows a tradition in children's historical fiction, such as Monica Furlong's *Wise Child* (to which *Witch Child* may pay a titular tribute), of presenting wise women as descended through the female line, needed as healers and midwives, but suspected for their independence and learning by the communities at the edges of which they live (compare Chapter 1 above) – villagers distrust Mary's grandmother as she 'live[s] so well with no man to keep her' (Rees 2000: 29). On the crossing to America, Mary saves a newborn child through knowledge, denying that magic has anything to do with it: 'All I did was clear his mouth and nose so he could breathe' (72). Mary is well aware of the perils of a vocation to healing and midwifery:

> To be a midwife, to be a healer, brings danger. If everything goes well, then all are grateful, but when things go wrong, as they do often enough, well, that is a different matter. Those that heal can harm, that's what they whisper, those that cure can kill. (Rees 2000: 189)

Staring into the sea, Mary discovers she has the gift of scrying. She sees the future of a ship's boy of whom she has grown fond. Mary's foresight could be magical, or rational, based on what the boy has already told her – Rees was conscious of trying to leave interpretation open where magic is involved (Rees 2001). As we have seen before with magical and shamanic aptitudes, Mary's foresight is an unwished-for and terrible responsibility: 'I have seen his past. I have seen his future. I know how death will come to him and I feel the knowledge like a burden' (Rees 2000: 80). As Mistress Hesketh, whom Mary encounters as the latest settlers pass through Salem, says of being a witch: 'Whether 'tis a gift or a curse, I can't tell, but I know 'tis not of our choosing' (110).

It is as if there is a covert witches' network, for Mary's flight to America is facilitated by a mysterious benefactor, 'a most powerful witch', and as the ship sets sail Mary sees 'women in high places, on craggy headlands and jutting promontories, keeping a watch for our passing' (47). And as well as Mistress Hesketh, there is Martha, a Puritan but also a healer wise in matrilineally conveyed herblore, who takes Mary under her wing on the sea crossing and in the colony. It is Martha who encourages Mary to make a quilt, safer and more befitting a woman than writing – 'inky fingers on a girl are very far from natural' (158), Mary is chided by a Puritan Goodwife. The quilt serves to hide Mary's journal, the discovery of which by a 21st-century scholar frames the narrative.

Mary and Martha are among a group making a new settlement, led by the Reverend Johnson, who is dangerously setting himself up as a prophet: 'The people who came here with him almost worship him. They hang on every word he says. His word is God's word and God's word is law' (135). Mistress Hesketh has warned Mary about this, and that the superstitions and fears that folk bring with them are only exacerbated in the new land. Especially frightening is the unknown forest, but not for Mary, since she was brought up 'on the very edge of the forest' (11), at one point before she left England seeing herself in the mirror as a kind of Green Woman (compare Chapter 2 above): 'My hair fell down in thick cords, grey as ash bark, the tips drying to dull gold, the colour of oak leaves in winter' (24). Through the leaves of the New World forest, Mary's and Jaybird's eyes first meet.

As Mary and Jaybird's friendship develops, similarities of belief become apparent, for example with regard to shamanic shape-shifting/power animals, and sacred sites. Mary comes to believe that her grandmother's spirit has followed her in the form of a hare; Jaybird's power animal is the blue jay, his grandfather's the eagle, and Mary's the wolf – Mary's strength of character and her liminality are seen by Jaybird's grandfather in terms of:

> a young she-wolf he knew once. She was fierce, proud and brave but not fully grown into her strength. [...] You want to bow to no-one, but you are young and life on the edge is uncomfortable. (Rees 2000: 166)

There is some similarity between British henge monuments, 'sacred to those who live by the Old Religion' (31), and a rock formation sacred to Jaybird's people. Reverend Johnson and his followers desecrate the latter site by building their Meeting House on it, lending a certain irony to Reverend Johnson's accusation that the natives 'caper and gibber in the forest, carrying on their heathen rites not a mile from God's House!' (203). Mary is far more syncretic when she compares Jaybird's people's sacred cave art with her experiences of both Christianity and the Old Religion: 'I had the feeling of being in a great church, a place filled with spirit, like the Temple of the Winds on Salisbury Plain, heavy with the presence of those who had gone before' (168). To be sure, there is some idealisation of 'the Ecological Indian [who] inhabits an improbable Eden untouched by ignorance, stupidity or greed' (Garrard 2004: 134) in Mary's perception that 'The Indians go lightly in the world [...]. They make their homes from living trees, only taking what they need before moving on to let the land replenish itself' (Rees 2000: 156).

Mary's association with the feared otherness of the natives and her independent spirit catalyse accusations of witchcraft: to Reverend Johnson, the Indians 'are the Devil's instruments, in league with the Evil One himself, intent on driving us from our rightful place in this land' (204), and 'Rebellion is as the sin of witchcraft' (178). In fact, Reverend Johnson's own wife is a woman he saved from being ducked for a witch, only for her to face a life of domestic submission, which prompts Mary to think: 'if I had to choose between the life she'd had and death by drowning, I would choose the latter' (186). Rees is careful to distinguish her fictional Beulah from Salem, but comparisons are unavoidable. Deborah Vane (note the homophony with 'vain') in particular is rather like Abigail Williams in Arthur Miller's *The Crucible* (1953). Deborah wants to make love spells, and comes to Mary for advice, accusing her: 'you talk to the animals. Bend trees to your will. Conjure spirits. Meet with the Indians. Dance naked!' (Rees 2000: 200) – all true, but misconstrued. Mary refuses to have anything to do with it, but Deborah and her cronies go ahead anyway, with a grotesquely garbled version of ritual magic that has nothing to do with Mary's authentic hedgewitchcraft. When a time of freakish weather and afflicted animals follows, the settlers seek a scapegoat. The remains of Deborah's ritual are discovered, but she feigns possession to evade responsibility and put the blame on someone else. The witch-finder is none other than the one who put Mary's grandmother to death. Under cover of the women-only work of a birthing, Martha helps Mary escape.

The sequel to *Witch Child, Sorceress* (Rees 2002), follows Mary's changing fortunes as she flees the Puritan community of Beulah and goes native, consummating her relationship with Jaybird and occupying an important role as healer and wise woman. She finds that Native clothes fit her just right, and remembering the Bible verse 'thy people shall be my people, and thy God my God' (Ruth 1: 16), she feels 'that I had found my people, that I belonged with them' (103). After a number of years, the idyll is broken by the fighting catching up with them: 'Everywhere the English settlers were encroaching, cheating the Indians out of their tribal lands, fencing in hunting grounds. But the trouble went deeper, for the Puritans would brook no difference' (126). Some of those closest to Mary perish. She soul-journeys to meet the spirit of Jaybird's grandfather, White Eagle, in the Cave of the Ancestors, and he advises her to move northwards. *En route*, she rescues an English boy, Ephraim, from the aftermath of a raid, and asserts her role as healer: 'I was a healer and it was my duty to offer my skill to any in need of it. Friend or foe, it did not matter' (165). In the north, Mary falls under the spell of a suave, menacing French privateer, but she is rescued from luxurious captivity by Ephraim and her son Black Fox, only for all three of them to be taken by Mohawks. Expecting to be put to death, they are adopted instead and given new names – Mary is now 'Katsitsaioneh, which means Bringing Flowers' (259). Assisted by a mysterious medicine man, she sets up an isolated infirmary to treat smallpox, and introduces vaccination, a technique she learned from her grandmother. There, on the edge of her adopted community, she heals and teaches healing.

Mary's life story is accessed through the visions of Agnes Herne, or Karonhisake 'Searching Sky', an 18-year-old Native American student of anthropology. Knowing the oral tradition of a woman who 'came out of a storm [...] when the people were sick' and 'helped to heal them and stayed with them, a powerful medicine woman' (44), Agnes connects her visions with the Mary of *The Mary Papers*, and so contacts the academic Alison Ellman, who compiled the *Papers* from a diary found in a quilt (the framing device of *Witch Child*). Agnes's Aunt M enables her to go on a vision quest, after submitting her to a regime of chilly skinny-dipping and chores, which Agnes takes as 'Some kind of testing thing, to do with humbling herself to another and discipline' (85). Agnes is finally judged to be ready when she comes in to the lodge in the forest with a couple of jay bird feathers on her. She experiences shamanic dismemberment and mystical oneness: 'muscles and sinews seemed to be disengaging one from another. There were no limits to her. She was unravelling from the inside, becoming nothing, part of everything' (91–92). The familiar issue of apprenticeship and control is raised by Agnes coming into her medicine power: she realises that 'for the moment she had taken on the role of shaman's apprentice, assistant sorceress, and as such she had to do as she was told' (246–247). Even before she goes to her Aunt, Agnes's initial visions are a compulsion: 'though she had not consciously sought for it, it had come to her anyway. [...] She had to find out what it was and follow. Wherever it took her. Whatever the consequences. She had no choice' (20).

Aunt M's campaigns against museums holding Native American arte-facts 'amassed as ethnic knick-knacks, cultural curios, by collectors who had no idea of their true worth to the people from whom they had been taken' (Rees 2002: 18), and her objections to the wampum belt being 'dishonoured, devalued and disrespected' (271), accord with criticism of the theft and commodification of sacred objects (compare Johnson 1995, Mumm 2002). However, Aunt M's complicity in provid-ing vision quests for outsiders is more controversial, to the extent that Agnes is resistant to participating in 'some kind of cheesy vision quest, like something her aunt might put on for the city folks who came to her for "spiritual development"' (86). Aunt M's eclectic approach to spir-ituality acknowledges the error of homogenising the great diversity of Native American belief and practice while yet at the same time commit-ting that error: in subjecting Agnes to a sweat-lodge ceremony, Aunt M admits it is 'not traditional to the Haudenosaunee' but she is 'not averse to adopting and adapting the practices of the other peoples. [...] She did not see one religion, one nation or one people as having a monopoly on the truth' (Rees 2002: 89).

Emphasising commonality between diverse spiritual traditions is a fundamental premise of *Witch Child* and *Sorceress*, the affinity between Mary's inherited belief system and Native American spirituality again being underlined when Jaybird's grandfather takes her into the Cave of the Ancestors, and she presumes a shared pantheism and animism: Mary's grandmother likewise 'had believed in the holiness of all things. [...] She saw the divine in all things growing' (110). Faced with fellow English people who persecute difference at home and in the American colonies, Mary embraces difference by becoming one with the indigen-ous population, but she flattens difference by observing that Puritan settlers and Native Americans both believe 'in dreams and portents. [...] A time of trial approached and both would look to some great spirit for guidance and blessing. Be it God or Manitou, what did the naming of him matter?' (126). And yet there are limits to this homogenising of spirituality: encountering a Jesuit who yearns for Christ-like suffering, Mary finds 'What he was saying was stranger by far than any beliefs I had come across among the Indians' (203).

Some acknowledgement that it is questionable to call Native American medicine power 'shamanism', and that the term 'shaman' is Siberian in origin, is given by having Jaybird's grandfather White Eagle make a remarkable pilgrimage. First he goes 'north to the land of constant snow' where '[t]hey taught me the proper way to move between worlds, and the secret language of the animals', and then he is taken:

> across the great ice roof of the world to a distant land of forests. The land of the Tungus, who call their holy people *shaman*. I learned much from them. They taught me that true wisdom comes only through suffering. I became as one dead so I could return to life again. I wanted to bring my new knowledge back to my people. (Rees 2002: 113)

White Eagle's experience would seem favour a 'dispersal' model of the spread of shamanism over an 'independent development' model (Hutton 2001: 127), by reversing the direction of diffusion: to enhance his medicine power, White Eagle goes north for authenticity of practice ('the proper way') and then west to the Tungusic shamans. White Eagle is also the Ecological Indian in apocalyptic mode, prophesying unstoppable devastation and sacrilege: 'Soon the forests round about will ring with the white man's axe. His ploughs will tear the land. One day he will hollow even this mountain, taking the stone to build and burn in fires' (Rees 2002: 151).

Sorceress is much concerned with ways of knowing and telling history. Academic history, requiring artefacts and written evidence, is represented by the scholar Alison Ellman, who discovers a wide range of documents and conducts interviews, all of which reveal alternative viewpoints on events subsequent to Mary fleeing Beulah. But for Mary herself, living among the Native Americans, there is a lacuna in the records. The gap is filled by Agnes's other ways of knowing and remembering – oral history, psychic experiences, and a view of history that is cyclic: 'it's not as though time is stretched in a long line [...]. It's more as if it's all of a piece. Past, present, future going round like so' (43).

In the same way Agnes's nascent medicine power is inherited through the female line back to Mary and her grandmother and, by implication, beyond, so too the quilt 'follows the distaff side, the female line' (37). A female production, it also has the function of protecting mother and newborn child. The three phases of the Triple Goddess inform the description of the quilt's descent:

> Ten girls in all had received this inheritance. Ten girls growing from child to woman, each in turn fading from maiden to matron, handing on the quilt, then ageing to crone before death and the grave claimed them and turned them to dust. (Rees 2002: 25)

Alison says, 'the quilt is so central. Everything about it is meaningful. Its history, its discovery, everything' (41), and, while it is a vehicle for the survival of Mary's journal, in *Sorceress* the meaning of the quilt itself is foregrounded. That it is known as the Morse quilt, after an early keeper of it, indicates that there is a code to it, a potential for signification, and indeed 'the motifs [...] were not just a random collection of patterns. They told a story complete with characters' (39–40). 'The designs were strong but simple, like the bead embroidery of Agnes's people' (39), and it is through a comparison with wampum belts (*'gehsweda'*), which 'carry the word, the code, the law' (272), that Aunt M sums up alternative, complementary ways of telling:

> This is how I figure it: you [Agnes], me, Mary, the people in her life, the folk Alison has found out about, Alison herself, we're like beads on this belt. Look at us apart and you can't tell a lot. But put us together and then you can read the whole story. (Rees 2002: 272)

And yet all these ways of telling are not equal: the final, clinching metaphor of the wampum belt is from Native American signifying practices; Alison the historian realises that 'The solution to this, to Mary, did not lie [...] in books, museums and libraries. It lay with Agnes' (190); and Agnes and Aunt M's medicine way is privileged by being the method by which Mary's story is accessed. Alison Ellman's 'Historical Notes' are relegated to an appendix, in the last sentences of which the scholar allows in the unverifiable preternatural: 'As for the father [of Mary]? We have no information about him. I personally believe he *was* the Erl King' (301).

* * *

Cold, ice and snow; reindeer, bears and wolves – all are prominent signifiers in children's fiction of the circumpolar environment of northern peoples. But the signifier *par excellence* is the Aurora Borealis, or Northern Lights. The Aurora Borealis acts as a shifting prism for differing beliefs. For Torak in the *Chronicles of Ancient Darkness*, the Northern Lights are axial to his world view and have, at first, a single and stable meaning – they are

> The First Tree. From the dark of the Beginning it had grown, bringing life to all things: river and rock, hunter and prey. Often in the deep of winter it returned, to lighten hearts and kindle courage (Paver 2006: 217).

However, in *Oath Breaker* (Paver 2008) Fin-Kedinn tells Torak that to the White Fox Clan, the Northern Lights are 'the fires which our dead burn to keep warm' whereas to the Otter Clan, 'the lights are a great reed-bed which shelters the spirits of their ancestors' (Paver 2008: 231). Fin-Kedinn – very much a didactic figure in the series – uses this diversity of interpretation to teach the lesson that nothing is certain in life. Of that he is certain.

In diverse Siberian traditions, the Northern Lights are variously: 'a special world inhabited by those who died in violence' or 'families and friends who had passed out of this world [...] now dancing happily around fires in the heavens' or 'brothers engaged in mock battle in the sky at night [...] who return to earth to sleep during the day' (Riordan 1989: 20). In a number of the novels that have been discussed in this chapter, the Northern Lights constitute a site of struggle between spiritual and scientific outlooks, with a conspicuous pattern, or stereotype, of female characters being associated with the spiritual and male characters with the scientific.

Thus, in the Snow-walker trilogy, the Northern Lights have alternative interpretations in Norse cosmology: 'Some said a giant named Surt made this light; others that it was the walls of Asgard glimpsed in the sky' (Fisher 1995: 26–27). The poet Skapti's scientific explanation is presented, with nudging irony, as unbelievable: 'Skapti believed it was caused by frost in the air, but that was surely poet's nonsense' (27). To Rose in *North Child*, the Northern Lights are 'the way into a whole new land, or into Asgard itself, where Freya and Idun and the thunder god Thor lived' so that she is bemused by her father unweaving the Aurora with a 'logical explanation' when '[t]o me it was sheer magic' (Pattou 2003: 189).

Celia Rees's *Witch Child* presents the widest range of beliefs and ambiguities. When the ship to America drifts way off course to the north, 'lost in an ice-bound wilderness' (Rees 2000: 56), the passengers assume that this must be either punishment for some sin, or else the workings of 'a witch on board, a servant of Satan working some malediction' (57). The appearance of the Northern Lights causes 'many to lapse back to their old beliefs' (60) in magic, though an apothecary, a man of science, who 'has no truck with omens and visions', thinks them to be 'as natural a part of the heavens as the sun and the moon and the stars' (62). To the clergyman on board they are the Celestial City, a sign. But a sign of what? Mary muses:

> My grandmother taught me to read auguries and to me the sign is
> not so clear. The lights spanned the whole of the sky, from east to

west, west to east. Where would the death and destruction fall? On the world we have left, or the one we sail towards? (Rees 2000: 62)

At the climax of *Northern Lights* (Pullman 1995), Lord Asriel controls the Aurora with his alternate world steampunk anbaric technology to open a bridge between worlds. Employing unsubtle but awesome big science to channel the protean Aurora into a phallic, piercing spear of light, Lord Asriel is exploiting what is a new discovery to him, but has long been known by northern witches. For the witches – all female in Lyra's world, unlike our own – 'have known of the other worlds for thousands of years' (187). This accords with beliefs of northern peoples in our world, 'that there are several worlds': 'Each one has a hole in the top of the sky, usually at the foot of the pole star; the shamans slip through this hole when moving from one world to another' (Riordan 1989: 18).

Philip Pullman's Siberian witches 'live in forests and on the tundra [...] Their business is with the wild' (Pullman 1995: 165). They own nothing and have preternaturally long lifespans, and their capabilities include invisibility, prophecy and divination. When it is given to one of Pullman's anticlerical caricatures, the priest Semyon Borisovitch, to rant that 'All things from the north are devilish. Like the witches – daughters of evil!' (105), one can be sure that the trilogy in fact holds northern witches in high esteem. Not only have they always known the reality of alternate worlds that scientists theorise, they also enjoy the unique distinction of having a deity named and taken seriously: Yambe-Akka 'is the goddess of the dead. She comes to you smiling and kindly, and you know it is time to die' (314), and she is Sami in origin (see Ann and Imel 1995).

While daemons in *His Dark Materials* are very amenable to interpretation as Jungian animus and anima projections (see, for example, Hunt and Lenz 2001: Chapter 4), they can certainly also be compared with witches' familiars and shamans' power animals. Shamans and witches are still distinctive in Lyra's world in that they are the only people who can separate themselves, without severance, from their daemons. In *The Subtle Knife* (Pullman 1997), Will's father John Parry, also known as Dr Stanislaus Grumman, is found alive among the Siberian Tartars, practising shamanism. Grumman now has an osprey-daemon, or a totemic power animal, about whom he marvels, 'Can you imagine my astonishment, in turn, at learning that part of my own nature was female, and bird-formed, and beautiful?' (223). Grumman's daemon, like a witch's, can travel far from his body; what makes him a shaman is his ability to soul-journey when in a trance state. He wears the shaman's 'heavy cloak trimmed with feathers' (336), which Will receives on his father's death – taking over his father's mantle, Will inherits shamanic potentials, the background to his ability to leave his daemon behind when he accompanies Lyra into the world of the dead in *The Amber Spyglass* (Pullman 2000).

* * *

Contemporary controversies surrounding shamanism, about dilettante decontextualisation, cultural integrity, personal development and gender, have been addressed by the children's fiction featuring northern shamanism discussed in this chapter. Cultural integrity is maintained against decontextualisation implicitly by placing shamanism in appropriate socio-historical milieux, and occasionally cultural theft and 'weekend' neo-shamanism are overtly criticised, as in *Sorceress* (Rees 2002). While Native American traditions struggle to maintain their integrity, a perceived problem of Anglo-Saxon and Norse shamanism and Heathenism is that they are too exclusive and intolerant. More satisfactorily than Richard Rudgley's (2006) proposed northernised New Ageish mishmash (see Chapter 1 above), Robert Leeson's *Beyond the Dragon Prow* (1973) and Susan Price's *Elfgift* (1995) and *Elfking* (1996) systematically re-vision historical Heathenism as egalitarian and inclusive, though the tolerance does not extend to militant Christianity. Perhaps this exception is understandable, when Christian persecution has long since destroyed Sami shamanism, such that the only options for credibly depicting Sami shamanism in children's fiction appear to be to use historical or fantasy settings, or to have present-day characters preserving attenuated oral folk memories.

Having chosen to concentrate on northern shamanism, it might then appear self-evident and self-fulfilling to say that northern shamanism is spiritually oriented towards the north. But what happens in so many of the texts examined in this chapter is that the protagonists believe that the numinous and the magical are to be found *further* north, and they embark on northward quests accordingly. The Northern Lights particularly act as a prism for beliefs. This northward spiritual orientation could be seen as a distinctive and defining contrast between Paganism and many other religions, which have their origins in the east (from a European and North American perspective) and face that way.

The imposition of notions of personal development, subjectivity and agency onto indigenous shamanism is the trap that fiction for young adults is least able to avoid, fundamentally concerned as it is with adolescent self-realisation. Shamanic apprenticeship in children's fiction may be seen as paralleling young adult struggles with parental and societal control. The apprenticeship paradigm consists of resistance, submission and liberation: the implied ideology being the paradox that only through conformity can individualism achieved, rather a different message from the countercultural claims made for neo-shamanism. Greater independence is only achieved by breaking out of the apprenticeship paradigm altogether, as Ambrosi does in *Ghost Song* (Price 1992) by refusing to be apprenticed despite his gifts, and Shingebiss does in *Ghost Dance* (Price 1994a) by going it alone, untutored. Tensions between (pre)destiny and choice are arguably a characteristically north European preoccupation, from the role of *wyrd* (fate) in Heathenism through to Calvinist predestination, and they suffuse the struggles of fictional apprentice shamans, in a similar manner to Lyra in *Northern Lights* being 'destined to bring about the end of destiny. But she must do it without knowing what she is doing, as if it were her nature and not her destiny to do it' (Pullman 1995: 310).

Claims that shamanism in all or any traditions is a male preserve are highly questionable. Such claims are countered to such an extent by the stories that have been discussed that there is an alternative stereotype of only women practising authentic shamanism, while male shamans tend to be charlatans. There are exceptions, most conspicuously Torak in the *Chronicles of Ancient Darkness* (Paver 2004 onwards), though Renn also has shamanic aptitudes and often shows more wisdom, fortitude and moral consistency than Torak does. A pattern related to the feminisation of fictional shamanism is the association of textile manufacture (such as weaving, patchwork and embroidery) – presented as mostly a feminine domain – with textual practices, as a way of preserving knowledge and shaping destiny (compare Kruger 2001). Moreover, as the shaman experiences alternate realities, and as incoming and indigenous cultures do not share a common language, a profusion of non-verbal signifying practices is connected with shamanism: music, the decoration of drums, the shaman's penetrating gaze, communing with speechless animals... The reflexive irony is that authors represent all these through words, verbalising flights of imagination just as shamans' flights of the soul are narrated to their people.

Depiction of shamanism and indigenous spiritualities has become so widespread in children's fiction that it has been necessary to be more selective for this chapter than when looking at the Green Man (Chapter 2). But as with the Green Man, representations of shamanism, including northern shamanism, in children's fiction look set to continue appearing, possibly to proliferate, so that all that can be offered here is a snapshot of a particular moment. Perhaps one way of looking at further depictions of northern shamanism and spirituality in children's fiction as they appear in future would be to consider them in terms of the controversies explored in this chapter, and of conformity with, or innovative deviation from, the patterns and trends that have been observed.

4
Prehistoric Monuments, Witchcraft and Environmentalism

At the heart of this chapter are the ways in which children's fiction with historical and contemporary settings uses prehistoric monuments (especially but not exclusively standing stones, including megalithic henges) in connection with witchcraft and environmentalism. In this context, there is a wide range of representations of witchcraft, from malevolent, to dualistically split between warring good and evil, to benevolent but persecuted old religion. In novels from the last category, modern Wiccan beliefs and practices are retrojected into historical or time-slip narratives and antiquity is conferred on them by association with prehistoric monuments. Some children's fiction linking megalithic monuments with environmentalism admits modulated debate, but more often a combination of heritage and earth mysteries ideology simply favours rural conservation over any new developments. Frequently, prehistoric monuments are presented as timeless and organic, rather than as human artefacts that could be regarded as intruding into the landscape as much in the time of their construction as tourist developments, new roads and so on in our time. This central discussion of witchcraft and environmentalism is followed by an analysis of the spiritualities projected onto prehistoric monuments in some children's fiction set in prehistory and in the future. The chapter concludes with a celebration of Catherine Fisher's *Darkhenge* (2005), which focuses aspects of the Green Man and shamanism onto a newly discovered prehistoric wooden henge in a psychologically profound story of sibling rivalry and self-discovery. First of all, I look a little more closely at some of the underlying issues, including the gamut of Pagan, New Age, earth mysteries and heritage attitudes to prehistoric monuments.

Charles Butler's typology of 'Uses of Prehistory' is eminently applicable:

(a) Places for Ceremonial and Sacrifice
(b) Living Beings
(c) Machines
(d) Portals to Other Times
(e) Portals to Other Worlds
     (Butler unpublished)

Butler exemplifies each use, and goes on to discuss *Elidor* (Garner 1965) and *Darkhenge* (Fisher 2005) in detail as texts that use Avebury as a portal to other worlds. Incidentally, the Corn Stone/Kerney Stone in Butler's own novel *Death of a Ghost* (2006a) can be seen as a place for sacrifice, a machine ('almost metallic', 12), and a link between different time periods, if not formally a portal. Butler's typology does us the favour of showing that portals are not the only use of prehistoric monuments in children's fiction; in fact, more often than not, the texts considered in this chapter put stone circles and menhirs to other uses. But, staying with portals for the moment, Maria Nikolajeva maintains that 'A much abused variant of the door [aspect of the magic passage fantaseme] seems to be a stone circle, which in Britain is closely connected with belief in the magic and the occult' (Nikolajeva 1988: 79). I would not apply such a moral judgement ('abused') to the relationship between witchcraft and stone circles explored below, though it has to be said that there is no shortage of supernatural thrillers wherein standing stones exert a malign influence, such as Green (1984) and sequels, and Hugh Scott's *The Shaman's Stone* (1988). In the latter, excavating 'Ruggen's Dolmen' near Rollright reawakens an Anubis-like, werewolf-like monster 'too terrible for worship' (Scott 1988: 80–81), which was first summoned by a Neolithic shaman. Scott adds a ley line into the mix, acknowledges 'Francis Hitching's lovely book *Earth Magic* [(1976) which] tells of energy spiralling around many ancient stones' (111), and indulges in woolly mysticism: 'Martha felt that love reigned between the stars, that cosmic wisdom bound the universe in ultimate joy' (105–106).

By referring to Hitching's *Earth Magic* and a ley, Scott is drawing on earth mysteries. Earth mysteries researchers have recast Alfred Watkins's (1925) prehistoric straight tracks as conduits of subtle energy. Tom Graves (1978) sees standing stones as earth acupuncture, and Paul Devereux (1992) has argued that leys are shamanic spirit paths – the colonised discourse of shamanism has become a viral, pervasive colonising discourse. An early and influential text in the modern earth mysteries movement is John Michell's *The View over Atlantis* (1969), which sees earth mysteries as a global phenomenon with a single explanation, perhaps following the earlier 20th-century academic trend, in fields such as anthropology and structuralist linguistics, to impose universal patterns and efface difference. *The View over Atlantis* can be criticised on numerous grounds, as Ronald Hutton (1991) does: for not comparing like with like, for inventing prehistoric sites, for imposing a linearity alien to the prehistoric mind. Yet earth mysteries ideas have a strong inspirational pull; for example, Michell's linkage of ley lines with Chinese *lung mei* or dragon paths has appealed to some writers of children's fiction (discussed below). The yoking of earth mysteries with ecology has made it difficult to relate prehistoric monuments to ecology in children's fiction without invoking earth mysteries, or to debate environmental issues in a nuanced way in this context.

Some Pagans view earth mysteries with suspicion, associating them with that defining imaginary Other of modern Paganism, the New Age: Hutton opines 'that the sort of people they [earth mysteries exponents] condemn, the ' "New Age" cultists, would-be gurus,' etc., are precisely the natural constituency for those who believe in leys' (Hutton 1991: 129); 'Pagans are at least as likely simply to hug a standing stone as they are to approach it with a pendulum or dowsing rod' (Harvey 1997: 158). This can be seen in terms of a dialectic between Butler's first use of prehistory and the third: for Pagans, standing stones are places of ceremonial, spontaneous or scripted, and meditation; for earth mysteries researchers, megaliths are a measurable and manipulatable technology. Some children's texts can be regarded as making a derogatory connection between earth mysteries and the New Age. *Children of the Stones* (broadcast 1977, DVD R2 2002, novelisation Burnham and Ray 1977) has a charismatic leader exploiting the electromagnetic energies of the stones at 'Milbury' (Avebury), an astronomically aligned nexus of ley lines, to convert the villagers to submissive and preternaturally healthy 'Happy Ones'. The children are like a new stage of evolution, pacific and precociously intelligent, but with no will of their own.

In Peter Dickinson's *Healer* (1983), Barry sets out to rescue his friend Pinkie from the Foundation of Harmony. Ten-year-old Pinkie has an otherworldly appearance and manner, and a gift for healing. Fees to attend the Foundation are very high, its meetings are a mixture of revivalism and pseudo-science, and Mr Freeman its leader speaks of 'the new age'. Barry, who himself has a dual personality with an alter ego he calls Bear, sees two sides to Mr Freeman: 'One was a phoney, a crook, a chancer, a loony with a dyed beard. The other was a seer, leader, hope of the world. [...] And they were both wrong' (162). The climactic confrontation at 'Ferriby' stone circle epitomises different attitudes. Mr Freeman projects his New Age philosophy onto the ancient builders, and he wants to buy and commodify the circle: 'He wanted Ferriby for himself. He wanted to own it and use it, in the same way that he owned and used Pinkie' (165). Pinkie is excited and energised by the stones, 'Her skin gleamed. Pale light seemed to be flowing out of it so that it shone like a signal' (163). This estranges Barry – 'He was outside the mystery, if there was one' (167) – even though the Ferriby Circle is a place where he has visions and insights, and has a ritual of walking round touching each stone as an act of identity: 'The process was a way of telling himself who he was: Barry Evans, who came to Ferriby every so often and did this' (78).

Concepts of heritage and conservation of historical monuments inform the association of prehistoric megaliths with witchcraft and environmentalism in children's fiction. Heritage, according to Valerie Krips, 'speaks to a remembrance associated with a sense of the past rather than an experience of or knowledge about it [...] to symbols rather than facts, and to places or sites rather than events' and 'like [imagined] childhood, heritage is closely attached to the mythic' (Krips 2000: 20, 45). Older than memory and history, prehistoric monuments nevertheless accrue memories and histories. As archaeologists often claim, henges – circles of stone or timber surrounded by banks and ditches – in particular 'are an insular British phenomenon [...] The henge phenomenon provides the first evidence for a common cultural tradition that spans all of the British Isles, indicating a sense of cultural, and perhaps religious, unity' (Waddington and Passmore 2004: 66). Thus modern Pagans' attraction to henges can be seen as generating a myth of origin and national identity, in accord with Raphael Samuel's argument that:

> perhaps as a result of the collapse of ideas of national destiny, there is the growing importance of 'memory places' [which are] now called upon to do the memory work which in earlier times might have been performed by territorial belonging. (Samuel 1994: 39)

Modern witchcraft's 'valorisation of historical creativity rather than historical authority' (Purkiss 1996: 40) is especially evident in those children's novels, discussed below, that present megalithic monuments as sacred sites for witches during the 'Burning Times', thereby creating for 20th and 21st century Wicca a historical metanarrative of continuous and authentic native religion surviving from prehistory through the early modern period to the present.

After some notorious reconstructions by antiquarians and archaeologists – Alexander Keiller's vision of prehistoric Avebury leading to destruction of housing in the village, the pebble-dashing of Newgrange – priorities have shifted to conservation. Yet maintaining stasis, as at Stonehenge, involves plenty of engineering, restricting access, and effacing the present to preserve the past into the future. Both past and future are thereby implied to be endless, and national identity is again implicated, as something fixed and permanent. Although ancient monuments can be 'scheduled' and legally protected, it cannot be assumed that their very presence prevents development: witness the incorporation of Callanish XII into a housing estate (see Ponting and Ponting 1984) and Lundin Links into a golf course, and the proximity of Sellafield nuclear power station to the neglected Greycroft Stone Circle (see Cope 1998). Children's fiction that combines prehistoric monuments with environmentalism adds other tactics, such as stones with some sort of consciousness becoming active subjects in their own survival, earth mysteries ecological rhetoric, supernatural intervention, and campaigning child protagonists.

* * *

Penelope Lively's *The Whispering Knights* (1971a) is an early, foundational text for the relationship in modern children's fiction between prehistoric stone circles and both witchcraft and environmentalism. Earlier children's novels use megalithic monuments as settings for adventure stories (Mattam 1959, Russell 1963), or locate them on the other side of portals from the present to past or parallel worlds (King 1963, Garner 1965). Some later texts (considered below) present witchcraft in more subtle ways than Lively's good witch/bad witch dualism, and in any case some readers might prefer the sexy and powerful villain Morgan le Fay to the homely, jam-making and gardening Miss Hepplewhite. Charles Butler (2006b) thinks that heritage and environment are treated in more 'nuanced' ways in Lively's later work, and I would add, and do argue later, that children's novels of the time by other authors (such as Hunter 1970 and Allen 1975a) are also more nuanced in their presentation of issues around environmentalism. The parallel wastelands of Alan Garner's *Elidor* (1965) are ecologies not tied to environmentalism as such, but *The Whispering Knights* follows *Elidor* in using a henge as portal, and in the detail of Morgan's presence interfering with television reception, as the hallows do in *Elidor*.

The Whispering Knights opens with William, Susie and Martha making a witch's brew in a barn reputed to have once been inhabited by a witch. Ingenuity and lateral thinking go into finding the ingredients from the Weird Sisters' words in *Macbeth*. Martha describes William as unboyish – 'He doesn't like the other boys that much. He doesn't like what they do – just fighting and mucking about. He likes doing things with us' (Lively 1971a: 23) – which would seem to be confirmed by his acting as one of three Weird Sisters, but his attitude is that they are conducting a scientific experiment, not a spell, and he invokes the patriarchal authority of his father, a schoolmaster, for the view that: 'There weren't ever such things [as witches], you know. It was just superstition. Trying to blame other people when things went wrong' (8).

This view is overturned by the coming of Morgan le Fay, who is described by Miss Hepplewhite as being opposed to reason and the laws of nature, and as having many forms: 'She is Morgan le Fay, who was Arthur's sister and did all she could to destroy him, and Duessa, and Circe, and the Witch in Snow White, and the Ice Queen, and many, many others' (17). Morgan's existence and defeat depend on belief, which is thinning. 'Walpurgis activities' led by Miss Hepplewhite and transposed from the eve of May Day to an August dusk bring temporary respite. And although Miss Hepplewhite says that 'the sign of the Cross, [...] is losing its power: it has been too much misused' (66), Susie is able at one point to ward off Morgan with a straw cross in the sanctuary of a church. One of Morgan's peaks was when 'she was rampant in the seventeenth century' (153), again overturning William's father's scepticism, but also the myth of the Burning Times which construes kindly healers like Miss Hepplewhite as victims (see Purkiss 1996) – unless, that is, Morgan was embodied not as the witches but as the witch-hunters...

When a new motorway is planned to run nearby the children's Cotswold village, Susie's mother thinks it will be good business for her shop. Her attitude changes when the route is altered to go right through the village, Mr Steel having refused to sell up his factory on the original route, under the influence of his new, young, mink-wearing wife – yes, Morgan. William's father leads the protest, raising a petition and gaining coverage on television and in national newspapers, but it is yesterday's news within a few days. It is Miss Hepplewhite's climactic, time-shift defeat of Morgan at the Whispering Knights stone circle that puts paid to the scheme, but in a morally oversimplified way, as Charles Butler observes: 'the closure of a factory – and by implication the consequent unemployment of all its workers – is celebrated as a wholly satisfactory outcome because it means that the beautiful Sharnbrook valley will be saved' (Butler 2006b: 83). Indeed, although the contemporary setting does not allow Mr Steel to wear a stove-pipe hat, his Rolls Royce, his manor house and his spoilt wife all signify vulgar *nouveau riche* ostentation. The factory and the proposed motorway are intrusions, whereas the human construction of older buildings is effaced when they are presented as homorganic with the landscape: 'The barn lay in the sunshine, the shape of it melting into the shape of the land as though it had not been built there but had simply grown'; Cotswold-stone dwellings seem 'to grow one from another, with cottages huddling companionably together' (Lively 1971a: 29, 59–60). The children like to hear about 'old fashioned times' from Miss Hepplewhite, but her assertion that 'times change. Frequently for the better, I suspect' (51) runs against the story's resistance to change. Earth mysteries ideas are not prominent in *The Whispering Knights*, but neither are they entirely avoided. While old tracks, 'straight as a die' (70, 144), are associated with Stonehenge and the Whispering Knights, the earth mysteries mystification of Alfred Watkins's tracks into subtle and disruptible energy flows is deployed against the new straight track of the motorway when Miss Hepplewhite claims, 'A stretch of road could easily be malevolent – a place where accidents happen' (64; compare the haunted bend in Allen 1973, discussed below).

The Whispering Knights Stones are often described as watching over and guarding the valley; they are on the side of Miss Hepplewhite, the children and heritage, and against Morgan and the motorway development. The children feel an affinity with the stone circle: it is one of Martha's 'very favourite places' (67), subject to a proprietorial and privatised spirituality, as 'the Stones had always been a private place of theirs. [...] hardly anyone visited the Stones' (68). Morgan is averse to the Stones: 'I wouldn't want to go up there, would I? That's a bad place, isn't it, dear?' (95); the children all realise that the peaceful stones and the terrifying Morgan 'are against each other, they are the opposite sides of things' (142). Martha sees the stones move, looking 'like an army getting ready for battle' (141), in accordance with folklore told to William by the school caretaker, the familiar voice of elderly male rural working-class wisdom (compare Tom Hancock in Lively 1971b and Old Tom in Louise 1983, the latter discussed below). In Miss Hepplewhite's showdown with Morgan, the circle closes in to protect the children, and once Morgan is defeated there is the merest hint that the number of Stones has changed: 'William's lips moved, counting. Then he shook himself briskly' (149). Like the Cotswold barn and cottages, the Stones' human construction is effaced, by being described as if they were eternal: 'standing, where they had always stood and perhaps always would stand' (133).

Lively's Whispering Knights are based on the Rollright Stones, which consist of a circle known as The King's Men, an outlier called The King Stone, and the remains of an earlier long barrow known as The Whispering Knights, the name that Lively transfers to the circle. Since Rollright appears, perhaps surprisingly, at least as often in children's fiction as the larger and better known sites of Avebury and Stonehenge, it may be worth pausing to consider why. Accessibility and proximity could be factors: the Rollright circle is compact and lies on sympathetically owned private land; it is on the border of Oxfordshire and Warwickshire, near where Penelope Lively and Celia Rees live; and it could be reached by an outside broadcast crew from London for filming *Doctor Who* in the 1970s. Being less famous than Stonehenge and Avebury may allow Rollright to be treated with more creative freedom, while at the same time the wealth of folklore associated with it can be an inspiration – Lively draws on a number of legends, notably that the Stones are petrified knights that come alive in time of need. Some of Rollright's folklore is recorded on a leaflet available at the site (Flick [no date]), and more is reported by Leslie Grinsell, who observes that 'A larger quantity of interesting folklore has been published of the Rollright Stones than of any other prehistoric site in Britain, thanks largely to the work of Sir Arthur Evans [1895]' (Grinsell 1976: 267).

* * *

It may appear perverse to start this section on Rollright and witchcraft with *Doctor Who and the Stones of Blood* (script David Fisher, broadcast 1978, DVD R1 2002, DVD R2 2007, novelisation Dicks 1980), when it is supposed to be set in Cornwall, and the 'witch'/'Goddess' is an alien criminal whose neo-druidic worshippers are deluded – but bear with me. Rollright was chosen by director Darrol Blake for location filming, and, what is more, the villainous 'witch' may owe something to Penelope Lively's Morgan. The name of Vivien Fay in *Doctor Who and the Stones of Blood* conflates Morgan le Fey (as in *The Whispering Knights* and Arthur's half-sister sorceress in the Matter of Britain) with Vivien, the Lady of the Lake, Merlin's beloved student who imprisons him in an oak. Vivien Fay is also the Cailleach, the '"Hag of Winter." A wise old woman who created stone monuments' (Ann and Imel 1993: 507), who, like Lively's Morgan, has many (Celtic) names: Morrigu, Nemetona, Ceridwen. Terrance Dicks (1980) rather garbles some of these names compared with the broadcast version (similarly, Dicks turns a reference to Cornish fogous, Iron Age underground passages, into a scholar's name as a joke). Despite Miss Fay's cosy heritage cottage 'with whitewashed walls, low ceilings, chintz curtains and comfortable old-fashioned furniture' (1980: 55), she has an air of menace from her first appearance, sudden and silent, wearing a black hooded cloak, at the stone circle. 'I used to be a Brown Owl' (22) she explains humorously – a Brownie leader, but there is also a hint of shape-changing. The ever-present crows and ravens 'are the eyes of the Cailleach' (35), and, dressed in shamanic bird mask and robe, Vivien Fay/the Cailleach nourishes the stones with human blood.

The Cailleach is worshipped by misguided modern druids. Despite Dicks opening the novelisation with comparisons with 'Stonehenge in the days of the Druids [...] in the dark dawn of prehistory' (7, 8), the Doctor and Vivien herself are dismissive of neo-druidism and its association with stone circles. The Doctor says: 'there's not very much to know about the Druids is there? Not that's historically reliable, I mean. Oh, there's the odd mention in Julius Caesar's memoirs, a line or two in Tacitus' (33) and 'I always thought Druids were more or less invented by old John Aubrey, back in the seventeenth century, as a sort of joke' (34). The latter comes close to Stuart Piggott's (1968) explanation that Aubrey, in pioneering the view that Stonehenge was pre-Roman, associated it with the also pre-Roman druids. Vivien's attitude that the activities of the local druidic group are 'all very stagey and unhistoric' (23) serves both to deflect suspicion and yet also to reveal her cynical manipulation of the Cailleach's worshippers. Intriguingly, Leslie Ellen Jones (1998) compares the Doctor with Taliesin and claims that 'The Doctor himself, especially in Tom Baker's portrayal, comes close to the ideal of the riddling, mercurial, scientifically advanced druid' (Jones 1998: 224; compare Vetch in Fisher 2005, analysed below). Leading the druids are Mr De Vries, who lives in the mansion where he maintains an altar, and Martha the High Priestess, whose motivations the novelisation fills in: it is 'a kind of game for her' – she is 'a local schoolteacher [...] the Druid rituals and sacrifices brought some colour into a very dull life' (Dicks 1980: 52, 39). When De Vries announces that 'The Cailleach demands blood,' Martha is bemused: 'She's never demanded human sacrifices before' (39). As with Sutcliff's *Shifting Sands* (discussed below), it is a case of the sacrificer sacrificed, as the moving stones crush De Vries and Martha.

Charles Butler (unpublished) refers to *Doctor Who and the Stones of Blood* as an example of prehistoric monuments as living beings – the stones are Ogri, 'silicon-based – globulin dependent' (Dicks 1980: 60) life-forms, K9 pronounces – but *The Stones of Blood* also ticks all of Butler's other categories. According to the Doctor, henges are astro-archaeological machines, observatories that could be used to calculate eclipses. The stone circle is also a portal – into hyperspace, where a prison spaceship has overlaid the monument since it was erected. Miss Fay/the Cailleach is really Cessair, from planet Diplos in Tau Ceti system, from where the Ogri also come. 'Cessair' is still another Celtic name, 'of the original settler of Ireland, according to the *Lebor Gabala Erenn*' (Jones 1998: 223). She was imprisoned for 'Murder. And the removal and misuse of the Great Seal of Diplos' (Dicks 1980: 115), and is further convicted by the Megara, justice machines, of 'illegal detention of this vessel in hyperspace' and 'Impersonating a religious personage, to wit a celtic goddess' (120), her punishment being petrifaction: 'She seemed to freeze, her body shimmered...and she became a monolith herself, another stone standing between the others' (121).

I tend to agree with the views of other *Doctor Who* fans, that *The Stones of Blood* is a story of two halves: 'The first two episodes are delightfully Hammeresque, but the last half of the story, largely centred on the ship in hyperspace and the Doctor's defence of himself against the Megara, is woeful' (Cornell et al. 1995: 228); 'The first two episodes are wonderfully dark and menacing. Unfortunately, the last two are rubbish, with the Ogri consigned to the background and Tom Baker out-hamming every-one in sight' (Campbell 2000: 58). The problem is not so much with mixing horror with science fiction as with grafting on static courtroom drama. The science fiction does quasi-rationalise away the magic, fol-lowing 'the Frazerian thesis [Frazer 1922] that magic is misunderstood science' (Jones 1998: 222) or Arthur C. Clarke's Third Law: 'Any suffi-ciently advanced technology is indistinguishable from magic' (Clarke 1974: 39).[1]

In *The Witch of Rollright* by Merlin Price (1979), Sarah, 'standing on the verge of adolescence' (3), comes into her powers as a good witch to defeat an evil one. As in Lively (1971a), good and bad witch-craft are straightforwardly opposite poles, though Price didactically defines 'True Wicca'. His research shows in the exhaustive catalogue of Rollright folklore included in the story, with an historical chap-ter in an otherwise contemporary story adding little but repetition. The legends most salient to the plot are: stones as living beings; an Act of Appeasement whereby, according to a book Sarah's father is handily reading, heathen warriors would secretly on the eve of battle 'throw all their valuable tackle, gold plate, jewels and the like, into a lake or a stretch of water to please the spirits' (55); and the association of the 16th-century witch Mother Shipton with Rollright. For there is a present-day Mother Shipton, the last of a female line, who intends to animate a Rollright stone to tell her where to find the Act of Appeasement treasure. Sarah, her brother John and their friend Simon stumble across the plot on a school trip to Rollright and subsequent independent visits, and by being befriended by an incomer to Long Compton, who reckons 'there's something queer still going on in this village...the Old Ways...Witchcraft!' (53). It is through John's determination to disprove the uncountability legend that he notices that a stone has disappeared between visits. Mother Shipton and her followers, 'the Watchers', attempt with Words of Power and *son et lumière* to animate the stone, but the tortured being inside does not reveal the location of the treasure, so the Watchers all the more audaciously remove the Kingstone.

From the outset, Sarah is sensitive to the atmosphere of Rollright, on her first visit discerning a face in the Kingstone. As with the children in *The Whispering Knights*, Sarah senses no malevolence in the stones, but rather she is comfortable among them:

> Sarah however felt no terror at all. It was as if she derived some hidden strength and safety from being surrounded by those stone giants, as if she had been a part of the story for a long time. (Price 1979: 65)

Indeed 'she had been a part of the story for a long time', for, in a series of flashback visions, she sees a girl with her own face in the distant past, 'the true Witch of Rollright' (88) who was defeated by 'the Shipton' but swore to return. Again, as with *The Whispering Knights*, the conflict is age-old, but Price adds a fervent lesson about 'the True Religion':

> Once, at the beginning, there had also been a girl.
>   In those days the Earth Mother had been worshipped throughout the land. But the temptation to use the powers that were given to those who dedicated their lives to Wicca for their own ends had led the Shiptons to corruption. Lust and greed for power had led them from the True Religion. Their worship had become a travesty of the beauty and wonder of the Elder Way and their dealings had turned towards the darker forces of the world.

It was then that the girl had come.
Pure and beautiful.
She had held the true power of Wicca.

(Price 1979: 87–88)

Here we see the savage language of Paganism splitting off from the language of universal prehistoric matriarchal religion, and a bid to give an emollient Wicca, or 'the Elder Way' as the insider phrase has it, a questionable antiquity (compare Hutton 1999). Truth is defined in terms of female reification, a girl who is youthful, pure and beautiful, which is hardly mitigated by Sarah's later flashback of 'the girl with her face [...] a few years from now. Still beautiful, but lined with cares that she as yet did not know. Her voice was gentle and reassuring' (108).

The narrative is distinctly more edgy when it is indicated that Sarah's antagonist, Mother Shipton, could be her double or shadow: 'Sarah was suddenly aware how thin was the dividing line between their two minds. Almost as if at another time it could have been Sarah who stood there, arrogant in the usage of her power' (103). The Kingstone not doing Mother Shipton's bidding, and her ultimate defeat, are down to Sarah's capacity for empathy, and her coming into her own power, subjectivity and agency, as she becomes 'aware at last of who she really was, or who she had become' (104) and shows a 'new dominance' (115). Yet this is only achieved by the spirit of the original good Witch of Rollright conjoining with hers, and by Sarah being subjected to the elemental 'powers of True Wicca' (104).

It comes as some relief to read Elizabeth Arnold's *A Riot of Red Ribbon* (1998), third in the Freya/Gypsy Girl trilogy. Arnold does take a risk by connecting some Romanies – only Freya Boswell and her kin, the story stresses – with stone circles, considering that New Age travellers are more commonly associated with stone circles and that Romanies' 'greatest fear seems to be the intrusion into their lifestyle caused by the modern Traveller' (Arnold 1998: 213, and see Hetherington 2000). *A Riot of Red Ribbon* is given texture by the use of Romanes words and by the narrator Freya's idiolect of alliterative and rhyming compounds, for example: 'spout-steam spurting', 'jelly-belly laugh', 'mutton-mule stubborn-head' (Arnold 1998: 77). The story begins at the Rollright Stones, where 'rules of place and time become a law unto themselves' (2) and Freya finds herself 'in the cross-over time, that moment which is neither waking nor sleeping, living nor dying, that transitory state which seems so pleasant, and yet is the most dangerous of all' (1–2).

Dibby Gran was born at Rollright and feels that the stones are her friends. Mentally impaired by a head injury sustained long ago, Dibby sets off with precocious four year-old gorgio Briar Rose on a journey of independence, self-discovery and growth that begins and ends at Rollright. Freya and her gorgio friend Mary Reed follow watchfully at a distance, using a linking-crystal to keep an eye on Dibby and Briar, though Mary needs the device more than Freya, for Freya can mind-travel, as 'a chime-child, born on Good Friday as the clock struck twelve' (33). The circular journey is also decisive for Freya, because she must choose between her vocation as a choviar, a witch, and romance with Churen Isaacs, a shape-shifting choviar with whom she could produce the greatest ever chime child, but somehow at the expense of her own power. The dilemma is a false one, but common to fictional wise women (compare Bramwell 2005a), a projection of the equally false assumption that, to have a career, women must make sacrifices and cannot have it all; possibly it is also a reflex of the requirement of chastity for the male Roman Catholic priesthood.

Gypsy beliefs are presented in *A Riot of Red Ribbon* as a mixture of Pagan survivals and a syncretic and folkloric relationship with Christianity. When Mary is ill, Freya sees it in terms of Arivell, the god of death, and Moshto, the god of life, contending over her. Freya summons Bastet the Egyptian cat goddess to watch over Briar Rose, and, when Dibby and Briar return to Rollright, Mary sees, through the crystal, that 'The stones are *dancing*, and would you believe it, each stone has the face of a watching cat' (201) – Bastet. Freya describes herself as 'Jesus-muddle minded' (49), and the practice of Christian burial from Romanies is 'like an extra insurance, my mum says' (46). A folktale that Dibby relates has it that Gypsies are always on the move because they forged the nails for Christ's cross, and a spare one, red-hot, pursues them.

Dibby Gran and Briar Rose's peregrination takes in and comments on several prehistoric monuments, including Stonehenge and Avebury. Dibby objects to the static preservation of Stonehenge, which has taken away the strange lights and music, clicking and chatter of the living stones. She opines, 'They put up the wire to save the stones from the people, but the stones *need* the people, just as the people need the stones,' and Briar Rose learns the lesson, 'So it is better to be useful and one day die than to take no risks and live for ever...even for stones' (139). They far prefer Avebury, where they skip round the stones in moonlight. Briar sees through the stones into the past, and hears them talk, and Dibby comments 'I told you they were miles better than Stonehenge [...]. These stones live among the people, loved and protected but *free*' (149). On their return to Rollright, Dibby and Briar walk round touching every stone and celebrate what they have learned about themselves and each other, and Freya and Churen make their choices.

Celia Rees (2006) identifies Rollright as the site for the secret rituals in which Mary's grandmother participates in *Witch Child* (Rees 2000, analysed in Chapter 3, above); association with prehistoric henges confers antiquity and mystery upon the 'Old Religion'. Fleeing the 17th-century witch persecution that claims her grandmother, Mary discovers that great stones are also sacred to Native Americans. The stones that are desecrated by the building of Puritan settlers' Meeting House are described as if they are a striking natural formation, but Native Americans also constructed astronomically aligned 'medicine wheels', the similarities of which with henges could be seen as calling into question claims made for henges being unique to the British Isles.

* * *

I now discuss children's fiction that connects witchcraft with prehistoric sites other than Rollright, from the Channel Islands to the Outer Hebrides and beyond, in historical, timeslip and contemporary narratives. I simply take these stories in chronological order of publication, and, though there is a broad trend of moving from negative or dualistic portrayals of witches to more sympathetic Wicca-friendly depictions, negative stereotypes persist and can reappear at any time. In any case, associative antiquity applies: it is intimated that Wicca-style witchcraft is not a modern invention but an old religion descended from prehistory, and also notably that in the 17th century 'Burning Times' an authentic faith was persecuted.

The eponymous sculpted monolith of Margaret Greaves's *The Grandmother Stone* (1972) is imbued with menace and used by a malicious witch to bolster her power and influence – an unreconstructed portrayal. Philip Hoskyn, aged 15, comes to stay with his grandfather in 17th-century Sark and rescues Marie from bullies who call her 'Witch-brat'. Marie is being brought up by her aunt, the witch Annette Perchon, who lives 'far away from all the village houses' (58) in a ramshackle and squalid hovel. Though Philip's grandfather and the church minister oppose Annette on different grounds, rational and religious, they can both see that the community depends on her. The islanders also bring simple offerings to the Grandmother Stone, for, as Philip's grandfather explains, 'They are of the Church indeed; but in their secret hearts they must have the Grandmother too' (51). Annette is a Miss Havisham figure, embittered by being jilted, and determined that her niece should not fall in love with Philip. Her curses are seemingly effective, bringing death to the woman for whom her lover left her, and to Philip's mother, but both were sick anyway. When Annette tries and fails to kill Philip and Marie with a fall of stones, Philip comments, 'Mistress Perchon has little faith in her own malediction if she must fulfil it by murder' (91). The climax is like a Hammer horror movie. To protect Philip, Marie submits to being made a witch by her aunt, even though, as Philip points out, 'Witchcraft cannot be forced upon you. Only the consenting will could make you a witch as she is' (135). The island populace believes that the Grandmother Stone must be placated to ensure good weather and harvests, and so Annette intends to sacrifice Marie on Midsummer Night. The church elders move the Grandmother Stone from hallowed ground to break its and Annette's power, but Annette squares up to the church minister in a contest over whose god or goddess is greater, like Elijah and the prophets of Baal. The fickle rent-a-mob islanders switch loyalties so that Annette, now described as insane, meets a sticky end. It all amounts to an obvious and unsavoury valorisation of patriarchal rationalism and religion, embodied in Philip's grandfather and the church minister, over the ignorant superstition of the mass and the hysterical, bitter witch. Philip is inducted from adolescent ambiguity – 'Beneath Jacob's teaching, beneath his own daylight disbelief, stirred the superstitions of centuries, the dim imaginings of vast inscrutable forces' (79) – into adult male certainty, when the elders' ruination of the Grandmother Stone breaks its power over him.

To Louisa and her family in *The Witch-Finder* by Mary Rayner (1975), 'Wansbury Ring' (Avebury) is a familiar local attraction where they walk round the henge on outings. But by night, when mother is returning from picking up father from the station, it is a different prospect: the huge Swindon stone is 'leaning towards the road, crouched against it like some enormous animal ready to spring' (22); the stones are ogres to Louise, yet to her mother they are beautiful. Mother is different after a minor car accident at the stones; she becomes *unheimlich*, 'unhomely' indeed: 'She no longer made meals at the proper times' (57) and she leaves her children unsupervised, unwashed and unfed. She seems lost in her own thoughts and hardly leaves the house; it is left open whether this is through a magical shape-change, or whether it is loneliness, depression and distrust of her husband. Louisa senses 'an unfriendly presence throughout the house' (67) and wonders whether both her mother and herself might be developing witchy powers: 'What is my mother? And what does that make me? Who am I? Can I make things happen by thinking them?' (88). 'Witches' daughters [...] were believed to have the same powers as their mothers' (87), reads Louisa in a library book that seems very much based on Margaret Murray (1921) in that it argues 'that witchcraft had been an organised cult, a remnant of some primitive, pre-Christian religion' (Rayner 1975: 86).

An uncanny motif of *The Witch-Finder* is Louisa's application of the playground game paper, scissors, stone to the Avebury megaliths. Paper beats stone – if paper is replaced by burning straw – in the bygone practice of trying to break up the stones with fire. Louisa thinks that the scissors found with the 'barber' buried under a fallen stone were an attempt to ward off evil with iron, which failed because stone blunts scissors. In the end, paper covers stone when her father remembers to give Louisa the paper money he promised her for swimming a length, and her fear of the stones disappears. This happens during a family trip to a carnival, a nice evening out that papers over all the marital tensions. The magical explanation of mother's behaviour is maintained, but cosy motherliness is reasserted, when Louisa stands on her mother's second shadow and mother's stone-like silhouette dissolves and she becomes a 'proper' mother again, 'gentle and warm and full of concern' (125). Thus, although Louisa has been exposed to sympathetic and empowering accounts of witchcraft, more conventional feminine roles are ultimately upheld.

Monica Furlong's *Wise Child* (1987) and *A Year and a Day* (1990), set in 7th-century Dalriada and 6th-century Cornwall respectively, are comparatively early examples in children's fiction of the association of a positive stereotype of wise women with ritual use of megalithic monuments. As will be shown below by examining other texts published more recently, this positive stereotype coexists with, rather than supplanting, the negative ones that persist. Furthermore, as noted in Chapter 1 above, Diane Purkiss (1996) questions just how veracious and empowering the perfect and persecuted 'midwife-herbalist-healer-witch' figure really is. Monica Furlong, in both her children's fiction and her theological writing, satirises and subverts patriarchal Christianity through witches who 'with their herbal remedies and their interest in the rhythms of nature, hark back to earth religion, to a faith not of domination of nature but of harmony with it' (Furlong 1991: 26). Wise Child declares, 'I want to be both a Christian and a *doran* [wise person]' (Furlong 1987: 170), and the ceremonies conducted by *dorans* at stone circles in *Wise Child* and *A Year and a Day* conspicuously resemble Christian vicarious sacrifice and eucharist. In *Wise Child*, at a Beltane gathering of robed and masked *dorans* at a stone circle (Callanish, judging by the description and the journey involved), there are echoes of the biblical story of Abraham and Isaac when Wise Child surrenders herself to be sacrificed, only for a deer (rather than a ram) to replace her. Then, in a eucharistic rite, everyone sips from a silver chalice and partakes of the sacrificial deer's flesh. And in *A Year and a Day*, having undergone a quasi-shamanic sweat lodge ordeal, Juniper is given bread and wine at a ring of standing stones.

Sixteen-year-old school leaver Liz Finlay, in Catherine Lucy Czerkawska's *Shadow of the Stone* (1989), embraces the Granny Kempock monolith overlooking the River Clyde, and wishes with peculiar intensity for an opportunity to sail, with an undertow of yearning for romance. Her wish comes true in Steve, a wiry American come to discover his roots, who takes Liz out in his yacht the *Marie Lamont*. Marie Lamont is also the name of a 17th-century young woman whose ambition to sail was frustrated, and who confessed to being a witch. Extracts from Marie's confession appear at the end of each chapter, and Liz sees through her eyes in the past and is inhabited by her in the present – she is like Liz's double, and when Liz looks at herself in the mirror she wonders, 'Who looked back at her from the mirror? Herself or somebody different? Was that her own face, or not?' (106). The Kempock stone is a marker for fishermen, and 'a silent reminder of older beliefs, older patterns of thought' (39–40). Folklore of witchcraft, sabbath-breaking and petrifaction (compare Grinsell 1976) surrounds it: 'They say that the real Granny Kempock was a wise old woman who could work magic. [...] But she danced on the sabbath and was turned to stone' (Czerkawska 1989: 39). When Marie does not get to sail and is sent into service, she finds comfort in the company of other women with whom she tries to move the Kempock stone, thereby raising a storm that causes her cousin Thomas to be drowned. There is a danger that history will repeat itself. A beach barbecue bonfire evokes for Liz the burning of Marie as a witch, but Liz changes things by saving present-day Tom from drowning and in the process proving her own competence to sail.

Unfortunately, to realise her independence Liz relies heavily upon Steve. He is determined to rationalise Marie's experience – 'What had persuaded her that she was a witch? What had been her state of mind? What had convinced a simple and presumably innocent country girl to make such a disastrous confession?' (92) – and he explains away the devil that pleasured Marie greatly as 'some bad guy who knew he was on to a good thing' (139). At one point, when Liz is possessed by Marie and by hateful motivations, Steve slaps her out of it, and in Tom's eyes, 'the scene he had just witnessed, no matter how shocking, had something passionate and sensual about it' (114). At the end, Steve orders Liz to be her own woman. 'Oh Lizzie, women do it all the time. They like to have a man to rely on, instead of taking responsibility for themselves, the tragedies as well as the triumphs,' he claims (140), and commands: 'don't rely on me to direct your life. Don't exchange one form of slavery for another. Don't make me or any man into a talisman for you' (141). Steve gives Liz a pendant with a Hopi Indian spiral design on it – 'It stands for the feminine principle. The Mother, if you like' (141). Not only is a Native American emblem commodified (compare Chapter 3 above), but also Goddess Paganism colonises Native American symbolism, and Goddess Paganism is in turn appropriated by Steve. Steve tells Liz not to rely on the pendant or anything other than herself, and she sees new possibilities opening up. The cult of the individual and the illusion of the unitary self triumph. And the Granny Kempock stone becomes merely a transitional object when Liz's gran suggests 'Maybe you won't need her quite so much now' (144).

Figurations of witches are all too obviously projections of adolescent male psyche in Tim Bowler's *Dragon's Rock* (1995). When Benjamin goes to stay with Toby's farming family in Devon, there is tension between the two 14-year-old boys, especially over a stone that Benjamin took from Dragon's Rock monolith on a previous visit six years before. The stone must be returned to end Benjamin's nightmares, and to heal the land. To Toby, the vagrant woman who loiters around Dragon's Rock is the frightening, powerful, shapechanging Wild Woman; to Benjamin, she is the mysterious, attractive, empathetic Ione. She is always seen through someone else's eyes, and through her conversations with Benjamin it is the pallid Ione side that is privileged. The overt didactic intent is spelled out clearly and frequently enough: the epigraph quotes Ralph Waldo Emerson, 'That only which we have within, can we see without'; the chip off Dragon's Rock is 'Two-faced [...] One side nice and smooth. The other side you'll cut me' (62); 'it's only evil that sees evil, and good that sees good' (140). But any attempt to generalise about human nature is undone by gendering and dualism – woman is constituted by male gaze and psychic projection, and good and evil are ungraduated binary opposites. And in effect we again have a dualistic formulation of witchcraft, but realised in a single woman, who is a cipher.

Like some texts discussed in the next section, and at least as unsubtly, *Dragon's Rock* yokes ecology to earth mysteries, particularly dragon energy. A crassly literal subterranean dragon is formed by a tunnel and cave. Along with this evident female anatomical image, there is a scattering of serpent and worm similes throughout the book, intriguingly suggesting the dragon is androgynous. In a second-hand bookshop, Benjamin finds 'a work of scholarship for experts' called '*Dragons in Landscape and Legend*' (70) that explains that dragon paths can be manipulated for good or evil and are 'especially powerful at certain points such as [...] standing stones in remote hills or valleys' (71). This piece of exposition also involves a trip to a nearby town and so distracts from the story's otherwise intense and atmospheric unity of place.

Accusations of witchcraft are presented as being motivated by popular misapprehension of independence and difference in Sherryl Jordan's *The Raging Quiet* (2000). Soon after Marnie moves in to an old witch's house on the edge of the vaguely medieval Irish village of Torcurra, her much older husband, who forced her into marriage, dies in a fall, and Marnie grows close to Raven, a young man persecuted by the villagers for his deafness. The sign language Marnie and Raven develop also arouses the locals' fear and suspicion, and, even though Marnie is acquitted of witchcraft, the couple decide to move away. The devout Christianity of Marnie and her mentor, Father Brannan, filter the apparently Pagan elements in the story, such as a midsummer fire festival. Raven is portrayed as a Christ-like wise fool, innocent, unworldly and peripatetic, with a den in a long barrow. When Raven looks to the skies and dances, Father Brannan interprets: 'It could be looked upon as pagan worship of the sun. Though, like you, I tend to think it is his own way of singing psalms' (81). One might see innate nature religion and spontaneous Paganism in Raven 'embrac[ing] the stones, stroking them, sensing their primal force', but Marnie's perceptions remain Christian as she longs to dance with Raven like 'Adam and Eve [...] in newborn Eden' (236).

Trystan Mitchell's illustrated short story *Once Upon a Winter's Turning* (2000) is set in Yewof in Kernow-by-Lyonesse (that is, Fowey in Cornwall) and is a fantasy of village life where everyone has a craft. Standing stones are apprehended mystically, and can help with healing, as can Drew's mother, who is 'a hedgerowmancer, which is a witch and a healer to you and me' (16). Her methods are holistic, addressing both mental and physical health, including the talking cure, and herbal remedies enhanced by positive thought in their preparation. The story passes through a segment of the Wheel of the Year, from the Spring Equinox – 'a good day in the year for special portents and things to be happening' (20) – to Beltane. Drew Widdershins is bored, wishing for something to happen, when he hears three knocks on the door, thrice, and finds 'the Men-an Wrah stone circle from up by Heartsease Tor' (4) hovering outside. He invites the stones in and sings and dances with them, and it is 'as if he and the stones and their music and dance were all mingled together and flowing through the stars, wrapped about the world, flowing through every ocean and dancing from the top of every mountain' (10). Afterwards, he touches each stone and says thank you before they return to the moor. When everybody in the village becomes ill, Drew goes to the Men-an Wrah stone circle and falls asleep against the largest stone. He awakes in a stone circle in Wales, at night under a full moon. There he gathers Healwort (see Figure 4.1), with which he returns: 'His mother dowsed the herb with her amethyst pendulum and smiled' (52). Her Healwort tincture cures the villagers in time for the Spring Fayre and Beltane Banquet – a festival of fire and feast, story and song, music and merrymaking, during which the stones up on the moor 'turn and spiral to the melody as if, by their dancing, they helped to keep the whole world turning' (58).

Figure 4.1 Drew gathers healwort in Trystan Mitchell's *Once Upon a Winter's Turning*

Source: Trystan Mitchell's *Once Upon a Winter's Turning* (Wooden Books 2000, ISBN 1902418212).

Although Anthony Horowitz's *The Power of Five* series (2005 onwards) starts with the titular British henge of *Raven's Gate* (2005) being activated for evil ends, Horowitz makes many moves to avoid insularity. The scenario is a global one in that the Five, teenagers from around the world who have special powers, are supported by a secret international organisation, Nexus, in their battles against the evil Old Ones. The series follows the earth mysteries premise of giving a single rationale for monuments and natural features from diverse times and places: in this case, they are all portals. Thus Raven's Gate in Yorkshire and the Nasca lines in Peru (in *Evil Star*, Horowitz 2006; and see Aveni 2000 for an account of the Nasca lines and theories about them) are gates sealing the Old Ones off from the earth, but through which they threaten to re-enter, given propitious rituals and celestial alignments at 'Roodmas' (Beltane) or the summer solstice. The third book, *Nightrise* (Horowitz 2007), explains that there are also 25 doorways to transport the Five across the world, one of which is a Native American sacred site. As well as getting more psychological and political by having the Old Ones manipulate individual and corporate greed and power-lust, *Nightrise* also includes a Native American medicine woman, again showing how shamanism appears to be becoming a dominant Pagan discourse in children's fiction. Like some other fictional shamans (compare Chapter 3 above), the medicine woman's gender is at first ambiguous, and her power flows through her gaze: 'Only the *shaman*'s eyes were truly alive. They were grey in colour but seemed to shine with an inner strength' (Horowitz 2007: 225). Her medicine bag includes a surgical scalpel, and the efficacy of traditional medicine is scientifically explained: 'Willow bark contains salicylic acid – it's a natural painkiller' (342). Horowitz authenticates by acknowledging the help of two 'elders of the Washoe Indian tribe [who] told me much about their culture and history' (403).

Ecological comment becomes more prominent as the series progresses. The Pan-American Highway is criticised for dissecting the Nasca lines, 'a piece of modern vandalism cutting through a work of ancient art' (Horowitz 2006: 267–268). In *Nightrise*, contemporary apocalyptic ecological rhetoric describes the Old Ones' previous attempt 10,000 years ago to lay waste to the planet – they cut down forests, polluted rivers and 'melted the ice fields in the north and took away the barriers that had been put around the earth to protect us' (Horowitz 2007: 328). The Five, whose individual gifts include precognition, telekinesis, telepathy and healing, could be compared with the adolescents in the 1970s British science fiction television series *The Tomorrow People*, whose traumatic process of coming into their special powers is called 'breaking out', a term Horowitz uses at one point. In both *Nightrise* and *The Tomorrow People* adventure *Secret Weapon* (broadcast 1975, R2 DVD 2003), shady organisations kidnap children with psychic abilities. The first name and trivial gifts of one of these children in *Nightrise*, Indigo Cotton who bends spoons and stops clocks, can be read as satirising the New Age belief in a rising generation of Indigo children, whose traits and behaviours are very broadly defined (as listed in Carroll and Tober (ed.) 1999). Like the Alex Rider thrillers (Horowitz 2000 onwards), *The Power of Five* novels feature disfigured villains – one with a facial birthmark, one with an artificially elongated head, one completely hairless and 'beyond ugly – almost inhuman' – so that this appears to be a common motif to Horowitz's work, not confined to what might otherwise be assumed to be one of the less fortunate James Bond borrowings in the Alex Rider novels. At the front or back of each *Power of Five* book, Anthony Horowitz says that the thinking behind the series is to set fantasy 'here, now, in the real world' – hardly an innovation, but a great tradition exemplified by much of the fiction discussed in this book, not least Susan Cooper's *The Dark is Rising* quintet, with its own (benevolent) Old Ones.

Having surveyed the *Power of Five* series, it is time to look more closely at *Raven's Gate*'s treatment of witchcraft and a stone circle. Matthew Freeman, one of the Five, is fostered by Jayne Deverill (whose surname contains d/evil), who is introduced rising from a tube station while 'sparks from the oxy-acetylene torches flashed and flickered behind her' (Horowitz 2005: 38). She is witch as ice queen, with 'hard, ice-cold eyes and cheekbones that formed two slashes across her face' (39), a *femme fatale* who makes a mugger kill himself. In the earlier version of the story, *The Devil's Door-bell*, the boy is Martin Hopkins (a witch-finding surname) and the villain is Elvira Veronica Irene Lavinia (note the initials) Crow, a fairy-tale hag: 'Her nose was long and thin, and her chin was pointed with a wart on its tip' (Horowitz 1983: 10). *Raven's Gate* fears a different kind of witch, tough woman rather than old woman, but the Dennis Wheatley style storyline is essentially the same: Jayne Deverill is part of a conspiracy to unleash the Old Ones through the Raven's Gate portal that requires Matthew's blood in a black mass, with all the trappings: black candles, black marble altar, the Lord's Prayer recited backwards, and so on. There is no Wicca-friendly revisionism here. The witch Jayne Deverill is punished by a sort of burning – in an acid bath.

A member of Nexus explains Raven's Gate and other stone circles to Matt, taking Stonehenge as an example: 'Some say it's a sort of stone computer or even a magical tape recorder. Some believe it's an observatory and that it can calculate the exact time of a solar eclipse' (Horowitz 2005: 213). Raven's Gate is the original stone circle, but in the Middle Ages it was feared as evil and ground to powder and poured into the sea. Its evil reputation is undeserved, because it was created to seal out the Old Ones when they were vanquished by five children 10,000 years ago; 'The stones are gone, but the gate is still in place' (216). The site is a portal and a place of ritual, but also a kind of machine, for a decommissioned nuclear power station on the site is reactivated by the conspirators. Ingeniously, the control rods are described as corresponding to the standing stones. The crazy scientist in charge of the reactivation and ritual elides nuclear power with nuclear weapons, black magic with witchcraft, and declaims, 'The medieval witch splits throats. The twenty-first century witch splits atoms. Tonight we shall have both' (254). Advanced science is like magic, in accordance with Arthur C. Clarke's Third Law (cited above in the discussion of *Doctor Who and the Stones of Blood*), while witchcraft is pejoratively primitive, as when Matt's first glimpse of 'shadowy figures' round a bonfire reminds him of 'a scene from primitive times' (158).

*   *   *

At a similar time to the appearance of *The Whispering Knights* (Lively 1971a), Mollie Hunter (1970) and Judy Allen (1973, 1975a) took different approaches to linking prehistoric monuments with environmental concerns, and then the BBC children's television series *The Moon Stallion* (Hayles 1978), set in the Edwardian era, associated a welter of legends, myths and ecological rhetoric with Wayland's Smithy and the Uffington White Horse. Judy Allen's first two novels for children are suffused with earth mysteries ideas, something mainstream publishers of children's fiction have since to a large extent eschewed, leaving earth mysteries ecological rhetoric to small and self publishers. Occasionally, prehistoric monuments and environmentalism resurface in the mainstream: William Corlett (1991) and Patrick Cooper (1998) straightforwardly resist tourist developments, the former with earth mysteries admixed, the latter without.

Published a year before *The Whispering Knights*, Mollie Hunter's *The Bodach* (1970) is more sympathetic to a new development. Like the road in Christine Pullein-Thompson's later *The Road Through the Hills* (1988), the hydroelectric dam in *The Bodach* causes Scottish Highlanders to regret the loss of a more simple lifestyle, but also to welcome the benefits of change. At the centre of the narrative is the Bodach ('old man') and ten-year-old Donald Campbell, a shepherd's son, who inherits the old man's gift of Second Sight. The Bodach only resists the flooding of the glen, including his home and a circle of 13 standing stones, until the time is right, in accordance with ancient wisdom and the Wheel of the Year.

Similarly to Alison Fell's *The Grey Dancer* (analysed in Chapter 1 above), which also involves a hydroelectric scheme, *The Bodach* constructs Gaelic racial identity: Gaelic 'is the natural tongue of men of the Second Sight' (Hunter 1970: 17; compare Sutherland 1985), and Donald likes best those of the Bodach's stories 'that spoke of the strange, shadowy beings of the Otherworld – the world of sealmen, kelpies, urisks, and all the other creatures of Highland legend' (Hunter 1970: 43). The Bodach enigmatically but accurately prophesies 'three men coming to this house, and these three men have but one name between them' – the white-haired one 'carries a forest on his back', the red-haired 'carries lightning in his hand', and the black-haired brings death (5). Sure enough, three men called Rory Mackenzie arrive: Rory Ban (the Fair) carries a sack of pine cones, as he will be planting trees; Rory Ruadh (Red Rory) carries a blueprint of the power station, the electricity being the 'lightning'; and Rory Dubh (Black Rory) brings death as the glen will be flooded, though he says 'my work will mean life to other people' (19). For with the development come employment and prosperity, Donald's own family getting a new, modern house and his father a well-paid forestry job. Donald and the other local boys are 'mad with dam fever' (30) and hero-worship the 'tigers', the construction workers.

The Bodach holds out against the dam for a period, using his ability to bilocate, or project a 'Co-Walker', to prevent the flooding of the glen. The stone circle needs to remain unflooded until Beltane (May Day), when every hundred years since prehistory, the Bodach tells Donald, the stones have been recharged by the rising sun, and the man of Second Sight has had his vision renewed. Solar and lunar cycles are coordinated, for this Beltane (solar calendar) occurs at full moon, and there are 13 stones, 'one for every moon-month in a year of the earth's life; and their shape is a circle, which is the shape of the sun' (75). When the Bodach and Donald encounter the *Bean nighe*, the Washer at the Ford, the Bodach takes the slap from her wet washing and knows that his days are numbered and so he wishes to make Donald his successor. In accordance with the apprenticeship paradigm (see Chapter 3 above), Donald has natural aptitudes but is initially resistant to a calling that will ultimately empower him. He has had mountain-top experiences that have convinced him that mountains are alive, and his 'imaginary friend' Bocca – 'the name of an earth-spirit from times so long ago that even the Stone Circle was new when he was old' (74) – is his Co-Walker. Childhood spirituality is privileged in the Bodach's explanation:

> the power to create a Co-Walker exists in the minds of many children. But this power fades, of course, as they grow older, and it is only a man of the Second Sight who can keep it for the whole of life. (Hunter 1970: 72)

The line of seers appears to be all male, rather than the succession of wise women we have more usually seen, and is elective rather than hereditary. With the Bodach sick with pneumonia, and Beltane still approaching, Donald takes over, again preventing flooding before the right time by projecting his own Co-Walker to lead the construction workers a merry dance. On May morning, at the stones which he thinks could be the priests of antiquity petrified, Donald is energised by the rising sun so that he can 'see the vision beyond sight and in his ears was the sound beyond silence' (119). After the Bodach has died and the stone circle has been deluged, Donald resolves to keep the magic alive and find more standing stones elsewhere. And yet the original circle, though it had a short stay of execution, is now lost, so *The Bodach* in the end does not favour preserving monumental heritage.

Judy Allen's first two novels for children are informed by earth mysteries ideas. *The Spring on the Mountain* (1973) features an old straight track, including a menhir, leading to a mountain spring with mystical properties; and in *The Stones of the Moon* (Allen 1975a), a stone circle is 'activated' when a motorway development threatens a factory – the different treatment of the same scenario as Lively's *The Whispering Knights* would seem to be a direct riposte. Watkins (1925) and Michell (1969) are recommended in the afterword to *The Spring on the Mountain*, and referred to in Judy Allen's piece (1975b) on 'Dragon Paths' in the second *Puffin Annual*; in both cases, Allen follows Michell in applying to British ley lines the Chinese concept of *lung-mei* or 'dragon paths' – positive masculine yang lines across high ground, negative feminine yin lines through lowlands, harmonising where they meet (Allen went on to give a psychological, perhaps Jungian, inflection to yang/yin in *The Lord of the Dance*, 1976). Allen appears to have no doubt that 'There really are ancient tracks, like Arthur's Way, all over Britain' (1973: 157) and that 'the truth of Watkins' theory is something which can be tested today by anyone who has access to an Ordnance Survey Map, a ruler and a pencil' (1975b: 40).

The Spring on the Mountain has mystical Peter, rational Michael and sensitive Emma, the peacemaker between the jostling males, staying in the country with a couple who are themselves townie incomers, satirised by Allen for their fantasies of rusticity. Heritage and nimbyism are also mocked in a meeting of the local Preservation Society that Mr and Mrs Myer attend: 'The possibility that the 1.5 per cent of summer visitors who were regularly damaged at [a dangerous] corner might escape unscathed worried the villagers less than the probability that a rather fine Elizabethan house would be destroyed' (Allen 1973: 58). The children find out about Arthur's Way, a ley line connecting a church, a crossroads, a menhir and a mountain peak. The menhir is an 'oddly powerful stone, which seemed to exist in its own time and not in theirs' (98), and Arthur's Way is associated with Grail legend, though the old wise woman Mrs White is more interested in the spring on the mountain at the intersection of yin and yang dragon paths. She wants to divert the stream to a reservoir so that everyone can benefit from the spring's mystical powers.

The three young people undertake the quest on Mrs White's behalf, but are discouraged by a well-spoken tramp who appears younger the closer they get to the source. Aged, mature and young, the three aspects of the man parallel the triple-Goddess attributes of Mrs White, who has over her mantelpiece a triptych that consists of two portraits of herself in youth and middle-age, and thirdly a mirror. The man is revealed to be called Aquarius, the name of the constellation and watery star sign that appears several times in the story and can be linked to the notion that the two-thousand-year reign of Pisces is being replaced by the Age of Aquarius, a well-known belief of the 1970s New Age movement. Young Aquarius warns the children not to drink, nor to divert the spring into the water supply, because 'it's strong medicine, too strong for most' (137), and Mrs White later accepts this outcome. Even though it is clunkingly spelled out that 'there was no clear-cut right or wrong in this Quest, there was no clear-cut good or evil, either' (130), there is moral complexity to the story, not all of it overt. Mrs White's desire to divert the stream democratises spirituality, but does not allow for consent or dissent, whereas Aquarius winning the argument could be seen as a victory for spiritual exclusivity and patriarchy. Although the bogus rusticity of Mr and Mrs Myer is satirised, arguably there is just as much of the urban fantasy of the rural in the village wise woman, the ley and the mystical spring. Certainly Peter's solution to his personal quest to unblock the kink in the track that has created a whirlpool of bad energy, a fearful place where a lynching once occurred, is a fantasy of the rural:

> a great procession from the standing stone to the sea along the old straight track. A procession of life to carry the force along its proper way and to sweep it past the corner that had perverted its power. A procession of as much life as possible – people, children, dogs; a carnival; the children carrying flowers and branches and everyone singing; like all the traditional country festivals there had ever been –. (Allen 1973: 155)

In *The Stones of the Moon* (Allen 1975a), building works for a new motorway activate a stone circle, presented as a conscious machine – a mixture of Charles Butler's second and third uses of prehistory. David Birch's father is called to a Yorkshire community to lead the excavation of a Roman mosaic uncovered by the roadworks. Having previously visited two other stone circles elsewhere, David is keen to seek out the Weeping Stones. He finds them unnerving, 'as if they were in communion with each other [...] an alien community which was somehow conscious in a way he did not understand [...] unimaginably dangerous, just as heavy machinery in action is dangerous' (Allen 1975a: 14), and he receives an electric shock off one of the stones.

Alternative perspectives on environmentalism are to the fore. David is concerned about pollution: he thinks that once people would have given offerings to the river, but now 'all they had to offer it was rubbish, waste, things they didn't want, which clogged its beds and damaged its wildlife and caught in the lowest branches of the trees that bent over its banks' (80) – the group of three and the sprawling right-branching structure give rhetorical force. He encounters local children Jane and Tim Thornby measuring pollution by the textile mill for a school project, and finds that Jane is especially sensitive to the stone circle, and that Tim has a more complicated take on environmentalism. Tim is interested in a career in ecology, but he can see that the pollution from the mill needs to be balanced against the employment it provides, including for his father; similarly, he is conscious that a delay in constructing the motorway means 'men who've been laid off on half-pay' (48); and he rebukes David, 'pollution is lives, pollution is to do with our whole future – it isn't a hobby. [...] think on, and see how you're going to fit people to live without the things they depend on' (100).

The mouthpiece in *The Stones of the Moon* for eclectic and elaborate earth mysteries theories is, like David and his father, an incomer – an 'elderly hippie' called John Westwood. He correctly predicts that 'the mosaic will depict Diana, the Roman goddess of the moon' for he believes that 'this whole area belongs to the moon' (24). Westwood is a pendulum dowser, attuned to earth energies, and he dips into astronomy and astrology, geography and geology, myth and legend to propose that the Weeping Stones have become activated because they belong 'to the moon – and this time of year is governed by Cancer – the Crab – the moon's sign' (31). His explanation of Jane's sensitivity to the Weeping Stones is replete with mystified female stereotypes: the megaliths are 'Calling to all that they own. Calling to white things, to things of the moon – female things, water, all liquid, all people under the sway of the moon, all Cancerian people, like Jane' (70).

Many of the characters are wary of Westwood, for varying reasons. Not surprisingly, David's father, as an archaeologist, calls him 'pathetic', 'a dabbler' who is 'chasing a chimera'. David wonders whether Westwood has become enchanted by forbidden knowledge, 'fairy food'. Tim resents him for filling Jane's suggestible mind with hokum. And Tim and Jane's father 'thinks it's unhealthy for a man of Westwood's age to befriend three youngsters' (61) and suspects him of taking drugs. Westwood does admit to the children that he has taken drugs and still needs them, but he warns that 'illusion blurs the perceptions even while seeming to heighten them' (74) and asserts, 'I will do anything to prevent any one of you from embarking on my foolishness' (75). Shortly afterwards he is arrested, and he doesn't appear again. But David looks through Westwood's notes, and puts the final piece of the theory into place.

Westwood's notes say that the stone circle is activated in high summer to provide water – it 'is a very fine machine to avert drought' (86). However, there is no shortage of water, so why has the circle been activated? David works it out:

> In its day it would have been activated deliberately by the chanting of men's voices – pitched to the exact note to which the stones had been designed to respond.[2] And by pure chance the new plant in the textile mill was reproducing exactly a sound which had not been heard on these moors for thousands of years. (Allen 1975a: 89)

So the mill is to blame, and the motorway earthworks exacerbate the risk of catastrophic flooding: modern development interferes with prehistoric technology. It would appear that Westwood is vindicated, and that

Tim's advocacy of the factory and motorway is overridden. Nevertheless, David can convince no-one of his theory or the need to close the mill, so that the unheeded prophet almost wishes for 'the holocaust that would prove him – and Westwood – right' (105). In the end, there is such chaos that the mill has to stop anyhow, and so the stones are deactivated and disaster averted. Tim remains pragmatic: 'now it's all over it doesn't matter if they hammer those old stones to bits to get rid of their anger. What matters now is to go back to the town and start clearing up' (120), but David and Jane do not want the standing stones damaged. Though Jane does not think the Weeping Stones are bad, David cannot connect with them when he returns to them: 'He was alone, flesh and blood in a community of stone, an alien community which was somehow conscious in a way he could never understand' (122).

The BBC children's television series *The Moon Stallion*, scripted and novelised by Brian Hayles (1978), creator of *Doctor Who*'s Ice Warriors, does not use a stone circle, but links together two other prehistoric monuments: pre-henge Wayland's Smithy longbarrow, and post-henge Uffington White Horse hill-figure. The series is a heady brew of deities and legends, including the Goddess Epona, the Green King, the Wild Hunt, King Arthur and the Golden Bough. Set in 1906, in the midst of the publication of the original 12 volumes of Frazer's great work (abridged 1922), *The Moon Stallion* takes a similarly universalist attitude to myth and legend, emphasising similarities, whereas anthropologists today might be more interested in differences and distinctiveness. *The Moon Stallion* conjoins prehistoric monuments with both witchcraft and ecology.

Archaeologist Professor Adrian Purwell is hired by Sir George Mortenhurze to seek evidence for King Arthur's final battle having occurred in the Berkshire hills. The Professor's daughter Diana's name links her with the Celtic horse Goddess Epona, whose sign the Uffington White Horse is said to be, and whose messenger, the Moon Stallion, is ridden at night by Diana the blind seer. Mortenhurze blames the Moon Stallion for his wife's death in a riding accident and is so obsessed with revenge that he is in thrall to his servant, the groom Todman. Todman is a 'Toadman', a 'warlock' (a term that has no currency among modern Pagans – a male witch is a witch, see Harvey 1997), with crazed ambitions:

> all the secrets of nature will be open to me. I will rule wind and water, earth and fire. I will speak with the beasts and make the very minds of living things serve only me! (Hayles 1978: 119)

He is a horse whisperer, arms himself with talismans, and is highly selective in his interpretations when using horse brasses for divination. As with Hunter (1970) and some later texts (Arnold 1999 and Fisher 1999, discussed in Chapter 1 above), solar and lunar cycles coincide at the climax. At Beltane under a full moon, Mortenhurze follows the Beltane fire to Wayland's Smithy and tries to master the Moon Stallion. Exit Mortenhurze, pursued by Wild Hunt, to fall to his death on Dragon Hill below the White Horse geoglyph. There is no question in Professor Purwell's mind that Beltane is a time of sacrifice, or in Diana's and Todman's minds that Mortenhurze is that sacrifice to Epona, though defiled by Todman's manipulations. Todman challenges the Green King to single combat to replace him as the Goddess's consort, but Todman's tainted, power-hungry motives are his undoing.

Ecological rhetoric first enters the narrative through Diana's father, Professor Purwell, who contrasts 'muscle and sinew against steam and steel, the elegance of nature versus the brute force of industrial progress' (8), but it is most prominent in Diana's midnight encounter with the Green King at Wayland's Smithy, in which she is reminded of 'her father's academic distrust of Science and Industry and their dark, satanic progress' (86). The Green King wears a helmet with horns that 'could have been antlers or even the twisted branches of an ancient tree' (133) and wields, in the broadcast version, what looks very like a replica of the Iron Age Battersea shield; he is a Green Man figure (compare Chapter 2 above) whose arm is 'gnarled and mossy, like the back of an immensely aged tree' (89), who has 'the strength of seasoned oak' (136), and who is known by many names – Wayland, Volund, Merlin. The cyclic and apocalyptic are combined in Diana's visions (in the book)/the Green King's prophecies (on the television): in the 'Wheel of Being' there are cycles of technological development and destruction. Looking forward from 1906 and with the benefit of hindsight from 1978, the First World War and the atom bomb are foreseen. Mechanisation of war will lead to Armageddon, and yet a new cycle will begin: nature will survive and the human species will begin again under the guidance of 'the Dark Rider', the once and future king Arthur, resurrected from Dragon Hill. Despite the note of hope, the vision is fatalistic: there is no indication that humankind can avert the apocalypse.

Although Judy Allen's *The Spring on the Mountain* and *The Stones of the Moon* were reissued millennially in 2000, mainstream-published novels linking earth mysteries with environmentalism have become a rarity, though William Corlett's *The Tunnel Behind the Waterfall* (1991), third in the Magician's House Quartet, is an instance. William, Mary and Alice Constant – whose parents are away doing good deeds in Africa (William blames the famine on global warming, war and greed) – return in the summer holidays to Golden House on the border of England and Wales, to stay with their uncle Jack Green (a Green Man name) and his partner Phoebe Taylor. The Constant children again spirit-walk in the local fauna, and are reunited with the Tudor magician and pendulum dowser Stephen Tyler, who presents alchemy as self-realisation: 'It is our uniqueness that is the gold in us; it is our striving to be the same that is the dross' (237). An alchemical symbol is inscribed on Golden Valley itself: Silver and Golden paths flank an elaborate 'energy line' that runs from a mountain peak, to a gap in the trees, to Golden House's secret room, to a dovecote, to a yew tree, to a standing stone, to Goldenwater lake, to a waterfall with a tunnel and cave behind it, to another gap in the trees and another mountain peak. Old buildings are presented as homorganic with the landscape: a house in the woods is 'covered in creeper and look[s] more like an untidy bush than an actual dwelling' (222).

The idyllic valley is under threat from developers, 'Playco UK', who want 'to introduce the holiday theme park to this country as it has never been seen before. America's Disneyland will pale into insignificance by comparison,' as Jack Green puts it (34). It will have a Wild West Trail, Medieval and Tudor Experiences, a lido resembling 'a Cornish fishing harbour scene' (139) – hyper-reality to which Mary objects, 'I don't want a pretend life' (159). Those who disapprove most are incomers: the visiting Constant children, and Jack and Phoebe. The couple's purchase of Golden House to convert into a quiet country hotel is used as a pretext by Playco to further open up the area to development, though Phoebe complains, 'I can't see how a country hotel [...] is in any way comparable to their vulgar fun fair ideas' (34). However, some locals do not see the difference, and can see the appeal of an increase in activity, trade and employment. At a public meeting, Playco's solicitor acknowledges heritage but takes a revisionist attitude: 'our one real asset is our scenic and historic heritage. But this must be made to pay. We cannot live on our past. We have to make our past into out future' (102).

The time-travelling 16th-century magician Stephen Tyler's views are straightforward. The developers are descendants of his rebellious apprentice: 'Morden is the dark to my light. Wherever there is evil – look for Morden!' (10). Tyler uses the centrality of the standing stone to the energy line that runs through the valley to contrast ancient wisdom with modern exploitation:

> In your time, people harness and destroy; they take and don't give back. They believe that all things are for their personal use. The people I am talking about lived in harmony with their world. They took nothing, expected nothing and harmed nothing. (Corlett 1991: 60)

He blames the development on selfishness and greed, and deploys vengeful, apocalyptic rhetoric: 'He who destroys, shall be destroyed. He who causes suffering, shall suffer' (166). William too blames human greed for a litany of environmental calamities: 'The rain forests are going; the whales and the dolphins are being killed; elephants are murdered for their ivory tusks; the earth is being poisoned; there's a hole in the ozone layer' (240). William certainly thinks globally when acting locally, and act he does. While the adults around them waver, the children persevere. William's courage and cunning in disputing the developers' claim on the land wins the day.

Patrick Cooper's *O'Driscoll's Treasure* (1998) also uses a prehistoric monument to defeat a tourist development, though without overtly invoking earth mysteries. Developers intend to buy Inish na Ri, the Island of Kings, and 'make it into a holiday camp with a golf course and a marina' (12). As in Susan Cooper's later *Green Boy* (discussed in the previous chapter), the island could be seen as playing out in microcosm a global ecological threat. In a Blytonesque adventure including a stray pet and a staircase behind a chimney and other secret passages, the child protagonists of *O'Driscoll's Treasure* discover a carved rock which leads to a long barrow, claimed to be *'the burial chamber of the Munster Kings on the ancient, sacred hill of Inish na Ri'* (71, original italics). An archaeologist visiting the island thinks such important heritage should be conserved, and Inish na Ri is declared a Site of National Importance and thereby protected from development.

Central to the story is Kaia, a New Age traveller from London, who shows an affinity with a standing stone prominent on the island. She is also able to reveal the burial chamber by making the carved stone turn through mystical sympathy. Kaia was befriended by the late Mr O'Driscoll, who claimed 'that he was descended from the old kings of Ireland, that he was the last Irish king' (17). O'Driscoll it was who found the burial chamber and accompanying documentary evidence that the children rediscover. A letter from him exalts *'the sense of Spirit of Place'* (70), which he feels Kaia shares. Indeed Kaia and her companions all respond in the burial chamber to 'a sense of solemnity, like a church – the presence of the past enveloping us' (69). Kaia as a traveller would appear to partake of the 'common structure of feeling' between New Age travellers and earth mysteries exponents that Kevin Hetherington (2000: 128) describes as 'an understanding of the rural landscape as a space full of mystery and discovery and a sense of the countryside as a place of authenticity'.

It is worth looking at a number of small press and self-published stories featuring child protagonists and prehistoric monuments, because of just how overtly earth mysteries ideas are yoked to ecological messages. Shallow or stereotypical characterisation sometimes accompanies this didacticism, and, other than preaching to the converted, such designs on readers may provoke resistance.

The Boy from the Hills by Cara Louise (1983) is a sub-*Stig of the Dump* (King 1963) tale in which a Bronze Age (rather than Stone Age) boy called Kai time-slips into the present and is befriended by a solitary, nature-loving boy, Jamie Geeson. Kai is bemused, frightened and amazed by defamiliarised modern technology, and his ancient wisdom is used to critique environmental damage. The Acknowledgements admit didactic intent: that children will be receptive to earth mysteries writers, and 'perhaps learn to treat this planet with more respect than their immediate forbears have done.' The story starts with Jamie watching fox cubs from an oak tree on Oldstone Hill, and idealising the rural: 'It was all sleepy agricultural land for as far as the eye could see; rich, beautiful and still' – 'only the strings of pylons marching towards the skyline, betrayed the uneasy presence of modern technology' (2), though presumably modern technology would be used on the agricultural land, too. A thunderstorm energises the standing stone on the hill, and Kai comes through – and, as with many of the shamanic figures discussed in the previous Chapter, the power is in the eyes: 'his eyes were the most striking feature of all. They were jet black and alert, gleaming with a strange mixture of wildness, intelligence and mystery, like black coals in the firelight' (4). Gaze is a way of communicating without words, but Kai also goes on to learn English, though Jamie does not bother with Kai's language. They also have a kind of telepathic link, proven in moments of peril, and Kai opens new horizons for Jamie: 'The coming of Kai had made everything different, strange and wonderful. A door had suddenly opened wide on the mysteries of life and a new world lay beyond' (34).

Adult authority figures find out about what they regard as a feral child, and are determined to 'civilise' Kai. Jamie's parents take him in, with the support of a negatively stereotyped, fastidious social worker who considers Kai 'backwards', while he takes 'an immediate dislike to her self-important and condescending manner' (30). Kai is resistant to conventional schooling and objects in a lesson on prehistory: 'People were never sacrificed at the stones and they were more civilised then. They didn't live surrounded by dirty concrete and noisy machines. They understood the world' (60). Supposed primitives are upheld to be more civilised and more environmentally friendly, and from here on the ecological didacticism escalates. The bulldozers clearing land for a new housing estate are depicted as bestial rapists, 'tearing away great chunks out of the green and hurling them aside, revealing the naked earth beneath' (62). Kai objects, 'It's sacred country. It's so close to the stones. You can't!' (61), and both he and the wise villager Old Tom warn of Mother Earth's anger. Yet the development is unstoppable, Earth's vengeance a vague threat. And other sides of the debate are not addressed, such as the need for affordable housing in the country.

As Midsummer draws near, Kai yearns to go to 'the Temple in the West', which Jamie realises is Stonehenge. The whole family go. Kai is incensed by a highly stereotypical American tourist couple (overweight, crass) not treating the Altar Stone with due reverence, but still he is able to observe Midsummer sunset over the Heel Stone. As we have seen in other texts, the human artefact of a stone circle is claimed to be timeless and organic:

> The scene which lay before them was wild, primeval, and could have belonged to any time since the world began. The stones never changed. It could be the end or the beginning of the world. It did not matter to the stones and the sky. (Louise 1983: 68–69)

After again criticising the modern world, including the housing development, and maintaining that 'We lived in peace with the earth but your world has lost much of what we had' (71), Kai returns much as he came, through the standing stone portal on Oldstone Hill in a thunderstorm.

Cara Louise has continued to produce straightforward ecological morality tales with an earth mysteries basis, populated by loners who do not fit in at school, wise old men, and the Goddess. I have selected two of these stories to analyse here. The Goddess is vengeful in *The Lady of the Rock* (Louise 1993). Near where Edward lives is a rock formation in which he sees the figure of a lady: maiden in spring, mother in autumn, hag in winter. But the granite is being quarried for new houses – the rape imagery of the works is all the more graphic than in *The Boy from the Hills*: 'A huge contraption equipped with a great long spike of metal began to bore into the rock, thrusting unmercifully, penetrating deeper and deeper' (13). As Old Seth predicts, 'Ole Mother Earth' gets her revenge: during a thunderstorm, a landslide mercilessly buries all the quarry workers and the owner, a stereotypical villain, dressed in black, overweight, sweaty and greedy. The quarry is abandoned and in time the lady returns.

The earth mysteries appropriation of Chinese 'dragon energy' (Michell 1969), which we have seen in *The Spring on the Mountain* (Allen 1973), also underlies *Annie and the Dragon* (Louise 2006). Feeling bored at St George's Methodist Church, where she has to go because her uncle is the minister, Annie sides with the dragon being slain by St George in a stained glass window. She starts seeing dragons everywhere, and dreams of a dragon in the sky, which spews out the constellation of Aquarius (a New Age touch, compare Allen 1973) and which is also one with the earth. Annie's mentor is Mr Jones, secretary of the village Preservation Society, who explains that the dragon embodies earth energy, with which prehistoric henge builders worked in harmony. St George and the dragon represent 'the new church driving its cold, sharp spear through the heart of the old ways of the earth and the sky' (Louise 2006: 24). Mr Jones says that the Victorian St George's was badly sited, and since then prosperity has declined and weather and harvests have become poorer. He believes that young people like Annie will bring in a New Age: 'I'm an old man now. If the old ways are returning, it's you youngsters who'll inherit their secrets and take them with you into the brand new age of the future' (26). This rediscovery of ancient wisdom is 'the wheel com[ing] round again' (24), complemented by Annie's circular perception of space from a hill-top viewpoint: 'the land spread out below her as far as the eye could see, like some great wheel' (27). She discerns 'a real, living dragon formed by the living land itself' (28), coiled around the hill, with place names corresponding to parts of its body, and St George's 'sitting right on top of the dragon's neck, slowly killing it' (34). Annie dreams of the distant past, when a ring of standing stones stood where the harmoniously sited old church St Catherine's is now, and she sees how the land was renewed by a procession in white robes walking the dragon's path. Annie revives the custom, disguised as a sponsored walk, for, as Mr Jones says, 'People tend to switch off if you start talking about dragons and earth energies' (37). Quite. A thunderstorm ensues, which destroys St George's so that 'the life-giving energies could once again flow freely through the dragon's blood of the land' (43). Unsurprisingly, earth mysteries are used to valorise the old (St Catherine's) over the more recent (St George's Methodist), but the ending is also rather unsavoury in annihilating a named denomination's church.

The Silverberry Tree by Paul Pendragon (1996) is 'an environmental fairy-tale *for all ages*' (86, original italics), an ecological quest fantasy set around 'Silverberry' and 'Silverberry Hill' (Avebury and Silbury Hill) in a parallel pastoral England, tiresomely constructed of ale-houses, feasts, shire horses and Old English sheepdogs. The Foreword acknowledges the influence of *Beowulf*, the sparrow's flight from Bede, the *Bhagavad Gita*, Chief Seattle ('The earth does not belong to man, man belongs to the earth'), and Tolkien – though *The Silverberry Tree* 'is about something more important': environmental destruction. Not only does this show how environmentalist grandstanding can erase literary judgement, it also misses the not uncommon reading of *The Lord of the Rings*, that it is anti-industrial (anti-industrialised warfare in particular).

Accompanied by an anthropomorphic bear called Zappo Zhi, Prince Little Stone and Princess Red Dawn head north on a quest to defeat the evil Morindoor and liberate their daughter Astra, whom Morindoor has turned into a star. Progress is sedate. At Silverberry, Little Stone assures his companions that 'the circles of stone are magic places where no evil may enter' (15), and at Silverberry Hill he communes with the Keystone and discovers that he is the prophesied prince who will unlock the secret of the hill (a variant of the noble warrior *within* Silbury Hill; compare Grinsell 1976). At a feast thrown in their honour, the questers meet Elfriend, a Green Man figure, dressed all in green and with green eyes, who bewails destruction brought by pollution. At last Zappo Zhi, Little Stone and Red Dawn move on, are led astray by a cat barrow-wight, then enter an ancient forest made silent by Morindoor's privations.

The ecological message is spelled out most blatantly in a chapter entitled 'The Great Lesson'. Zappo lectures, 'there are little Morindoors in every man and woman's heart. It is *mankind* who in the end must destroy the greed and destruction within his own heart' (55). The quest is not only to rescue Princess Astra, but to save the planet, an animate and interconnected world in which hurting one thing hurts them all. Continuing abuse of the Earth Queen's gifts will invoke her wrath. After this homily, the companions encounter the stream of the Lady of Lifell, who answers the deepest questions: Red Dawn asks after Astra, Little Stone the meaning of Silverberry Hill – and Zappo for beer and inns along the way. Finally they reach a settlement of Zappo's folk, where they are feasted again, and decide to postpone continuing their northward journey until spring. The lack of urgency does not leave one desperate for sequels, which in any case have not as yet appeared.

In Joanna Vale's *Jessiebelle: The Secret* (2004), 12-year-old Sam Greenwood is sent to discover her roots by staying with her Gran in Avebury, and finds herself having to defeat and redeem the dragon Rego, turned bad by men's aggressive and polluting ways. To streetwise Londoner Sam, her Gran's cottage seems 'to exist in another time frame altogether' (6), and the standing stones around the village belong 'to a time when people did things differently. Life was simpler and shorter then and the land unspoilt' (9). Unlike in London, 'It seems as if everyone down in Wiltshire talks about magick like it's more nat'ral than breathin'' (102). Gran is a wise woman, or 'wizaarde' as she would have it: ' "Witch" is not politically correct these days and I'm converting to New Age' (16). Apart from this odd perception, Gran is a mouthpiece for orthodox Wicca. 'It's part of the pagan way of life to give equal value to the male *and* female aspects of creation,' she says (31), though she predicates the evil that men do on a biological argument: 'If those *horrible* men had to bear new life, they wouldn't treat it so cheaply then' (41). She takes a conventional Wiccan line on Magick (with a capital 'M' and a terminal 'k'), that it is nothing to do with tricks and everything to do with transformation, that it is a neutral medium that can be used with good intent in accord with the natural order, and that 'What you give out always comes back to you threefold' (125). And, in a way that chimes with the views of Starhawk and Margot Adler (see Chapter 1 above), Gran is beginning to perceive the importance of 'risking our comfortable, self-obsessed lives by campaigning and speaking out. We can't make everything better just by using spells' (40).

In no time, Sam has an epiphany. She finds a harp that sings in the breeze as she climbs to the top of Silbury Hill, where she undergoes a mystical rebirth. Like shamanic psychic disintegration and reconstitution, it is 'as if some bits of her that had come loose were being linked together in some way' (13). 'She felt she loved the whole, beautiful, natural world and was connected to it' (ibid.), and she resolves to fight off 'the tree-fellers and the concrete mixers' (14). Other characters change miraculously, too. Sam's mother Maddy is brought healing from mental health problems by Sam's leafy card of a green girl and by a silver ring, engraved with a quarter moon, that comes from Jessiebelle, the unicorn that Sam's experience at Silbury Hill has released from the mound. Maddy repents her treatment of Sam, as does a teacher whom Sam tells to move out of London and become a librarian. Like the conversions, possessions, exorcisms and healings in *Shadowmancer*

(Taylor 2002), it is all too easy and arbitrary, the sudden switches in personality a frustration to any reader expecting character motivation and development. As Sam comes into her powers as 'the next generation witch' (Vale 2004: 105), she finds that her wishes come true and money keeps coming her way – a deplorable prosperity gospel. Sam is determined to find her own path, despite pressures listed at length, and yet she is subjected to Jessiebelle paradoxically ordering her to think for herself: 'you will have to look inside your *self*, come to your *own* conclusions and forge your *own* relationship with something ["the Great Spirit"] you *cannot* prove scientifically is there at all' (51, original italics). Sam's 'real self', it transpires, is 'a very, very old woman; older than Gran even; thousands of years old' responsible for 'nurturing and protecting all the vibrant but fragile new life she knew was buzzing around her' (153).

While connecting witches with prehistoric monuments in children's literature appears to continue to be productive, it is perhaps surprising that, since its peak in the 1970s, the linking of environmentalism with prehistoric monuments in children's fiction has declined or gone underground. I have argued that this has come about because earth mysteries ideology has colonised this area and spiritualised and oversimplified the environmental issues in a manner that has limited appeal. It seems that motifs of shamanism and the Green Man currently respond better to ecological concerns.

* * *

Having considered children's fiction with contemporary, timeslip and historical settings, it remains to examine the spiritualities projected onto prehistoric monuments in a selection of novels set in prehistory and the future. Out of quite a wide choice of children's novels set in Neolithic prehistory, I have chosen two based on the same site and event, but taking some strikingly different approaches to artefacts, beliefs and ritual, and leadership and power. The Neolithic settlement at Skara Brae in Orkney was uncovered by a great storm in 1850; *The Boy with the Bronze Axe* (Fidler 1968) and *Shifting Sands* (Sutcliff 1977) account for its loss in prehistory, and for artefacts found there, notably a broken necklace and some carved stone balls (see Clarke and Maguire 1989). Just as interesting as the belief systems retrojected into prehistory in these two stories is the portrayal of religion and power in a post-catastrophe future in *The Prince in Waiting* trilogy (Christopher 1970, 1971, 1972), in which Stonehenge is a spiritual centre.

Kathleen Fidler's *The Boy with the Bronze Axe* (1968) starts with 13-year-old Kali and her little brother getting stranded on a tidal island. Out of the blue, out of the sea, comes Tenko to rescue them. Both his boat of wood, and his bronze axe, are novelties to the people of Skara. Fidler characterises Stone Age communities as diverse, with new technology diffusing slowly: whereas Kali's people are herders, Tenko's are ostensibly less 'advanced' hunters, and yet Tenko possesses the bronze axe, though his people did not make it; they traded for it. Tenko's ambition is to find out how bronze tools are made. Throughout the story, he proves to be single-minded, inventive and heroic: he dispatches an eagle that has been menacing Kali's people's sheep; he carves out a second log boat from a driftwood tree, and joins it to the boat he came in to make 'the first catamaran to sail the northern sea' (140); and, when the disastrous storm arrives, the few who follow him find safety. The necklace artefact is made by Tenko for Kali; she gets caught by it in the evacuation, and Tenko breaks it to free her.

Tenko has fled from a tribal war in which his father, a chieftain, was killed, and he regards meeting Kali and her brother as the fulfilment of an enigmatic prophecy from 'an old wise man, a priest of his tribe': 'In the great water one will be lost, yet two will be found. Out of this, good will come' (Fidler 1968: 21). Kali's people also have their wise man and repository of the tribe's stories, the benevolent Lokar, remarkably old for the time as Kali's great-grandfather. He repeatedly prophesies the fate of Skara, for example: 'the doom will come to Skara. [...] a cloud that comes out of the sea. [...] a cloud of death. Some it will take, few it will leave' (65) – the repetition, and the inverted object-subject-verb word order in syntactically parallel, semantically contrasting phrases, heighten the portentousness. Lokar's foresight has the benefit of authorial hindsight: 'Skara will vanish in a night but it will not be lost for ever. The same power which overwhelms it will restore it, but not for many, many winters and summers' (166). There is also a kind of knowingness behind Lokar's declaration that 'The Ring of Brodgar belongs to the past and to the future too' (124), in that it can be seen that way in the reader's present as well as in Lokar's, and there may be implied an argument for preservation and perhaps even for continuing ritual use.

The kindly ruler of Kali's people is her own father, Birno. He supervises the quarrying of stone for the Ring of Brodgar, the construction of which is presented as taking many generations. Birno also carves some of the stone ball artefacts as symbols of the Sun, and he is proud of his latest work: 'The carving on it was so deep that the pattern stood out in spikes like a hedgehog. It had taken Birno a whole year to carve, sitting by his fire at nights. The spikes represented the rays of the sun' (121). In a midsummer ceremony at the Ring of Brodgar, prepared for with cleansing, body-painting and fasting, the carved balls and Tenko's axe are used for ritual purposes, held aloft in honour of the (male) Sun God, and a new standing stone is raised. Despite Tenko being able as an outsider to break one gender taboo by training Kali in archery, the ritual at Brodgar confirms the impression of a patriarchal society already given by leaders, spiritual and temporal, being male: as Kali explains to Tenko, 'The women do not walk in the procession. We follow after the men in a crowd. No woman is allowed within the Ring of Brodgar, so we watch from the outside' (115).

When an antagonist of Tenko's argues for sacrificing a human, rather than the expected lamb (see Figure 4.2), Lokar the wise old man retorts: 'The Sun God does not ask for the blood of men' (129) and 'The God of the Sun who speaks to you through me demands obedience and not sacrifice' (132). Fidler rejects the lurid fantasy of human sacrifice at stone circles by having Lokar argue that such an act would break tribal

Figure 4.2 Confrontation at the Ring of Brodgar in *The Boy with the Bronze Axe* by Kathleen Fidler, illustrated by Edward Mortelmans

Source: Edward Mortelmans on page 107 of *The Boy with the Bronze Axe* by Kathleen Fidler (Puffin 1972 ISBN 0140305637).

laws, turn the Sun God against the people, and shatter a long-standing peace (archaeologists assume, through lack of evidence of weapons or fortifications, that Neolithic Orkney was peaceful). Though patriarchal rather than matriarchal, the religion of *The Boy with the Bronze Axe* can be thought of in terms of Ronald Hutton's third language of Paganism, that of a universal prehistoric religious system (see Chapter 1 above). This can be seen in Lokar's pronouncement: 'Our temple will one day be complete, like those temples in far-off lands of which our forefathers have told us. All our tribes are children of the Sun wherever those temples are built' (128).

Rosemary Sutcliff's *Shifting Sands* (1977) seems systematically to invert *The Boy with the Bronze Axe*. The necklace is a man's, the leadership is cruel and arbitrary, and the evacuation is unhurried but most people survive. The story starts with the 1850 storm that uncovers Skara Brae, and highlights the broken necklace, before going back to prehistory with words that synthesise oral storytelling: 'This might have been the way of it. Listen, and I'll tell you' (Sutcliff 1977: 7). The necklace is a mark of the leader Long Axe's authority, and it is an amulet protected by powerful taboo: 'his necklace of animals' teeth that was so sacred that nobody but the Chief could touch it without being blasted by the God-Power in it as though by a lightning flash' (21). Unlike Fidler's separation of seer and leader (a convention followed since, for example Saeunn and Fin-Kedinn in Michelle Paver's *Chronicles of Ancient Darkness* series – see the previous chapter), Long Axe is both Chief and Priest, a dangerous concentration of power in one man. Like *The Boy with the Bronze Axe*, *Shifting Sands* eschews human sacrifice, for Long Axe's belief in it is invalidated twice over.

Firstly, 'Long Axe's father had had the two oldest women of the People strangled and buried under his bed-place' (29) in order to give warning if the sands are going to shift. But the warning does not come from that source; rather, from Moon Eye, a one-eyed seer who is as unheeded as Cassandra. Secondly, when it can no longer be denied that the sands are beginning to shift, Long Axe claims that a human sacrifice is required to appease the Ancient Ones and to save the settlement, but events turn against this and also allow romantic love to triumph. Long Axe's selection of Singing Dog for the sacrifice is very dubiously motivated, since Singing Dog is a much younger rival for the affections of Blue Feather, whom Long Axe intends to have as his third wife. Long Axe's hypnotic power over his sacrificial victim is broken by the in-rushing sand, and then he and Singing Dog fight hand-to-hand until Blue Feather's father, Moon Eye the seer, stabs Long Axe with a bone hairpin. Long Axe flees and his necklace scatters, and thereby his power is broken. Long Axe being 'gored and trampled into red rags by his own herd bull' (85) perhaps makes him the sacrifice – to plot exigency, to Blue Feather and Singing Dog's romantic love, and to Moon Eye replacing him as a more benign Chief.

Like Fidler, Sutcliff divides ritual according to sex, though the women in *Shifting Sands* are not excluded onlookers but have their own ceremony. In the spring, the women dance 'for the Great Mother, that she might make the cattle and sheep have many young, and send fine sons to the People' (17). The Spring Dancing defines the feminine solely in terms of reproduction, and of course that or any sort of female identity would be short-lived if the result were *only* 'fine sons'! Men's role is just as reductive, as hunters: in the autumn, they clash 'together the antlers of deer they had killed in other years, that the Horned One might give them good hunting' (18/20). The seasonality, the divinely sanctioned gender demarcation, and the names of the divinities all suggest a casting back into prehistory of 20th-century Wicca, with the Horned One deriving from the work of Margaret Murray (1921), and the Great Mother, Diane Purkiss maintains, being in origin a 'male fantasy' of female 'identity grounded in the maternal body' (Purkiss 1996: 33).

John Christopher's *The Prince in Waiting* trilogy (1970, 1971, 1972) centres on the Winchester canton of a post-catastrophe feudal and feuding society. Although the catastrophe was a natural one, machines are blamed, and knowledge and use of them are prohibited as blasphemy by the organised religion, 'Spiritism': 'machines were forbidden by the Spirits: anyone building or using one was punishable by death. This by the command of the Seers themselves' (Christopher 1971: 10). Yet the High Seers of Spiritism secretly preserve and develop technology, and the sacred centre of their power is 'the Sanctuary': Stonehenge. Whereas in *Shifting Sands* Long Axe is a manipulative individual whose selfishness does not necessarily compromise the overall belief system, in *The Prince in Waiting* trilogy Spiritism is systemically deceitful. Christianity survives, in an admirable primitive and peaceable form, thriving on persecution, to the bemusement of the dominant militaristic culture.

The trilogy is narrated by Luke, second son of the Prince of Winchester. He attends 'a true Séance', in which 'the Spirits manifested themselves in strange sounds and sights: weird music, fluting high up in the rafters, tinkling bells, lights that moved across the blackness overhead, faces suddenly appearing' (Christopher 1970: 51), and the Spirits of the ancestors answer a stream of petitioners – 'some rebuked, some advised, some comforted' (52). A more private and elevated Séance follows, in which a dead former Prince speaks, and a 'crown of light' descends not on Luke's older brother Peter, but on Luke himself. Luke is the flawed tragic hero in the events that follow, from remarkable initial successes, to abject exile, to triumphant return, though he becomes dehumanised by the technology of war and marred by motives of jealousy and vengeance. Throughout he is subject to the schemes and control of the Seers.

In particular, Ezzard, Seer of Winchester, empire-builds in the name of the Spirits. By his counsel, the previous dynamic equilibrium of warring city states extracting ransom from each other is replaced by annexing, with the ultimate aim of a whole nation under one ruler. Luke knows very well where the power lies: 'our wanting or not wanting was unimportant. The Spirits required it. [...] We had no choice' (119). That the established church, especially Catholicism, is being satirised is signalled by the Seers' monastic garb, and by Luke kissing a High Seer's ring and being catechised into submission:

> 'What is the duty of man?'
> 'To obey the commands of the Great Spirit in all things.'
> 'How is man to know these commands?'
> 'They are revealed by the Spirits through the Seers.'
> (Christopher 1970: 109)

At a low point in his fortunes, Luke obeys Ezzard's command to go to Sanctuary (Stonehenge), a place most people are kept well away from: 'No man would go near, no shepherd graze his flocks in their shadow. It was the place of the High Seers, dread and holy' (149). In a variant of Charles Butler's third use of prehistory, the stones hide machinery (rather than being a machine) – 'a sort of mushroom, made of stone but whiter and less pitted than the bigger ones' (150) used as an intercom, and a hidden bunker full of functioning technology. One of the High Seers explains to Luke that the Seances 'Are trickery, to keep the power of the Seers over men's minds' and that 'Prophecies often fulfil themselves because expectation brings its own results. Where they fail, they can usually be explained away' (153).

Seer Ezzard uses machines for his machinations, such as giving Luke's father faith through hearing his dead wife's spirit speak – an edited tape recording. But Ezzard overreaches himself when his plan to use Luke as his puppet ruler is not succeeding and Luke's older brother Peter is Prince: Ezzard has Peter's wife electrocuted. Peter has Ezzard and the other Seers responsible executed on 'Midsummer Day which the Seers have always called a day sacred to the Spirits' (Christopher 1971: 148). Yet the High Seers show their adaptability and resilience, condemning

Ezzard and replacing him by a calmer and stouter man who eschews Ezzard's more extreme methods but still upholds the High Seers' aim: 'to gain control of all the civilized lands. When their control was complete they thought they could wean men from superstition and back to science' (Christopher 1972: 16).

Throughout the trilogy, a counterpoint to the schemes of the Seers and the militarism of the Princes is provided through the marginalised Christians, regarded by the dominant culture as mad but harmless. This is a radical, primitive Christianity, which regards all people as equal and all life as sacred: 'They opposed the taking of life, even in battle or the execution of murderers, and always made a nuisance of themselves on such occasions' (Christopher 1970: 83–84). When Luke is put in the stocks, the Christians protest vociferously and do not resist when they are made to join him. Through Luke's eyes, the imagery and beliefs of Christianity are defamiliarised: 'It was the wildest fantasy, this story of the maker of the whole universe being born in a stable, living as a man and dying a painful and degrading death' (Christopher 1972: 48). He is bemused by the verse 'All they that take the sword shall perish with the sword' (Matthew 26: 52; perhaps Luke would find 'I came not to send peace, but a sword', Matthew 10: 34, more comprehensible...), and by the contrast between plain and gloomy Christian iconography and the warmth of his brother's Christian wife. The Christians are persecuted to varying degrees – 'in Winchester men despise them, but do not harm them. [...] In some cities they are harried by Seers who have them tortured or killed for refusing to worship the Spirits' (Christopher 1970: 138) – putting them in the same position as the early Church, and as the defiers of the later Church. Luke discovers that the more tolerant attitude of the Welsh monarchy results in better-off Christians, though their numbers are in rapid decline.[3]

*   *   *

There could not be a better novel with which to end this book than Catherine Fisher's *Darkhenge* (2005). It integrates prehistoric monuments with shamanism and the Green Man in a psychologically and mythically complex and coherent narrative. Fisher translates the celebrated Seahenge to Avebury, changing the 55 trees (see Brennand and Taylor 2000) surrounding the central inverted oak to 24, to correspond with the characters of the ogham tree alphabet, according to which the sections of the novel are organised. These moves are indicative of the sophistication of the narrative. Discovering Darkhenge at Avebury heightens the epistemological contest between archaeological science and Pagan mysticism. Ogham script is Celtic, and Fisher draws on her native Welsh mythology, as well as fairy tale and the Persephone myth. As we would expect from her previous work (such as *The Snow-Walker Trilogy*, discussed in Chapter 3 above), Fisher applies myth psychologically, in this case to illuminate the sibling rivalry between Rob Drew[4] and his sister Chloe, who lies in a coma. Life-support machine wires are like roots, roots are like neural synapses; from the outset, when a tree Rob is sketching branches 'like a brain' (5), tree imagery is used neurologically. Darkhenge is a portal into the concentric rings of the Celtic underworld Annwn, and the inner space Unworld of the layers of Chloe's mind. That the ogham tree alphabet is a script relates to the power of language in the story's intensely lyrical texture, in itself a vindication of Chloe's gift for words, which she feels has been eclipsed by Rob's talent for visual art.

It is the character who takes the name Vetch who is both shaman and Green Man. He is the Celtic shaman Taliesin whose arrival is anticipated at the start of the story by a group of Pagans at Avebury. His coming takes the form of Ceridwen's pursuit of Gwion from the *Mabinogion* (also used in Masefield's *The Box of Delights*, see Chapter 2 above) – hawk and swallow, hound and hare, otter and fish, with Rob rescuing the fish that then becomes a man. Vetch sees the central inverted oak of Darkhenge as 'a holy tree, a shaman's tree, lightning-struck, bone-white. [...] an axis, a pole linking this place and the Unworld. It leads inside. To the world within' (137). Vetch accompanies Rob on a shamanic soul-journey through Darkhenge and the seven caers of Annwn, a journey through Chloe's soul, a mixture of encroaching wildwood, sacred landscape, fairy tale, and personal memories. For, as Charles Butler (unpublished) argues, the shamanic soul journey is at least as much Chloe's as Vetch's or Rob's. As his adopted name suggests, Vetch is a Green Man, and he is frequently half-glimpsed merged into the shade of trees. At the climax, when his hands become 'crusted with bark, his nails gnarled and lichened', he is revealed to be a product of Chloe's poesis: '*You made me from the forest, Chloe.* I'm anything your imagination wants me to be' (Fisher 2005: 301, original italics). Other characters in addition to Vetch are greened: the King of Annwn is made from leaves and branches and wears a mask of beech, and the archaeologist excavating the henge, Dr Clare Kavanagh who is also Ceridwen, wears 'a green dress that looked like velvet, and a necklace of berries and seeds' (179).

Rob is confronted with his motives for wanting Chloe to recover, and his hidden desire for her to die. Chloe challenges him, 'So you want me back, do you? Little Chloe. Girly Chloe. You want me back so your life will be perfect again, and tidy, and just like it was' (221). Vetch accuses Rob of wanting Chloe to die, so that 'After a while, all their [his parents'] attention, all their love, would come back to you. It would be just you, and them' (99). Chloe herself is torn between ruling the Unworld or returning to consciousness and making it up with Rob; either way, she wants to make her own decision: 'I'm going to do something that I want to do, decide something all for myself, with no one else telling me' (292). The story ends where it starts: at Avebury, where worlds meet. Though Chloe's storytelling gift is less conspicuous than Rob's visual art, it is shown to be at least as important, for words have interpersonal and transcendent power: 'They're the only way we have of making others understand our lives [...]. While we have them we are never trapped in our own souls, our own skin' (308).

* * *

All language is subject to centrifugal and centripetal forces, according to Mikhail Bakhtin (1981). I would say that these forces are heightened when the discourses of modern Paganism and children's fiction meet, because they share similar conservative and progressive tendencies. Their greatest combined drag is their fantasy of the rural – it would be so refreshing to see urban and cyber Paganism represented in children's fiction. At best, contemporary Pagans and producers and critics of children's fiction have common values of upholding diversity and countercultural subversion. There is, however, a danger that the increasing codification of modern Paganism, though it may have improved wider perceptions of the movement, could bring stronger didactic impulses to bear on children's fiction. Currently there is little sign of this, children's literature having a far more interrogative than inductive relationship to Paganism. A creatively critical dialogue between the two is what this book has observed and perhaps, I hope, extended.

Notes

Chapter 1

1. Published just a couple of years after *Spin of the Sunwheel*, *Sabrina Fludde* by Pauline Fisk (2001) is also set at the turn of the millennium and draws on the same legend associated with the river Severn, of the king shunning his wife Gwendolina driven out in favour of the elf-woman Effrildis and their child Abren. Abren, 'a throwback from a legend, carried down the river through time' (141), is washed up in present-day Shrewsbury (called Pengwerne, its Celtic name, in the novel) and travels to the river's source in Wales to discover her story and identity. Narrative time and space centre on the river Severn, also known as the Sabrina Fludde: time flows 'like the river out of sight' (83); in Pengwerne, 'All human life was here, and all human death. *And the river wove its way between it all*' (127, original italics).
2. Comparable criticisms have been made of science fiction stories in books or on screen that concentrate alien invasions or post-catastrophe scenarios in the English 'home counties'.
3. The Protestantisation of Northern Europe is often associated with disenchantment – see the Dymchurch Flit chapter of *Puck of Pook's Hill* (Kipling 1906), Richard Corbet's poem 'The Wee Folk' and Keith Thomas (1971) *Religion and the Decline of Magic*. Alternatively, Geraldine McCaughrean attributes loss of faery to the First World War in *The Stones are Hatching* (1999) and *Peter Pan in Scarlet* (2006).
4. A notable exception in the case of Spiritualism is Catherine R. Johnson's *Stella* (2002), in which a young black woman living in London in 1898 is empowered by her clairvoyance: 'although I am only sixteen, I have been earning my own living these past five years' (56); Stella is capable of being 'in charge, in control, and solemn as a nun' (72). Having always known that what she does is phoney, a comforting charade in which clients are content to collude, Stella is shocked to experience a supernatural vision of her dead Nana, who herself had insisted that communicating with the dead was not real. Other glimpses of dead loved ones' spirits follow, but this transitional phenomenon is not available on demand at Stella's moment of greatest need, and so she has to act on her own. Stella renounces spiritualism for another career, yet it is left open whether or not she has a real gift.

   Philip Pullman's *The Shadow in the North* (1986) is set in 1878, when 'spiritualism [...] was one of the burning concerns of the time' (38), and the story suggests that two characters – adults rather than adolescents – may possess genuine psychic gifts underneath the sham of conjuring performances. The occasional psychometric perceptions of Alistair Mackinnon, 'The Wizard of the North', rest uneasily with his stage act: 'There are many frauds [...]. But there are some who have a genuine gift for the psychic, and I'm one. And in my profession it's a handicap, despite what you might think. I try not to let the two things overlap. What I do on stage looks like magic, but it's only technique' (30). And Nellie Budd, amidst transparent tricks – the inanity of a dead grocer's preoccupation with cheese, the *son et lumière* of a piano and a tambourine jangling, curtains twitching, a table dancing – has fragmented telepathic insight relating to a case in which Sally Lockhart and Frederick Garland are involved. As Nellie Budd's initials signal they should, they note well her words, and, although Nellie has more connections to the case than are at first apparent, the possibility of her having an authentic gift is left open. By the end, Nellie is 'getting tired of the mediumship game' (283) and is planning to do a mind-reading act with her sister, with whom she does have some kind of psychic link. Sally Lockhart, bereaved of her lover, ends up thinking: 'You couldn't bring people back, despite the spiritualists. All that area of things was a mystery, half fraud and half miracle; better leave it alone and stick to real miracles, like photography' (286).

Otherwise, it would appear that mediums are more common in adult fiction, such as Roberts (1990), Waters (1999), Kingdom (2001) and Mantel (2005). The clairvoyants in these novels are invariably female, they are adolescent or they discovered their ability in adolescence, and ambiguity is maintained as to whether their gift is real or sham. Susan Rowland argues that *In the Red Kitchen* by Michèle Roberts 'uses Jungian theory to both express and interrogate dualism as a founding structure of patriarchy' (Rowland 1999: 125). Rowland regards spiritualism as paradoxical in that 'it can be seen as offering women a powerful cultural role at the price of alienating them from their "speech". The medium in a trance, speaking a voice not her "own" but of the dead, is enacting, to a fascinated public, her exclusion from cultural meaningfulness' (47). Rowland also proposes that 'Jungian psychology could be seen as a medicalised attempt to appropriate spiritualism, part of the drive of science to assert dominance over esoteric discourses [...] it could be argued that Jungian psychology is an attempt by a male-authored patriarchal discourse to submerge and rewrite a multifarious female movement with dangerous potential political energies' (48).

Chapter 2

1. Probably from the Roman god of seasonal change, Vertumnus – compare Vertuminus in Jeffrey Ford's short story 'The Green Word', discussed later in the chapter.
2. Ainsworth enjoys a certain status among Pagan readers, both for representing Herne in *Windsor Castle*, and for his depiction of the Pendle witches in *The Lancashire Witches* (1849).
3. Though of course attitudes to hunting do not divide neatly into pro-hunting countryside and anti-hunting town, such a duality is implied by novels with rural settings in which it is assumed that readers are, like the authors, (sub)urban and anti-hunting.
4. This shapeshifting pursuit derives from the tale of Gwion/Taliesin (in the *Mabinogion*), which has influenced much children's fiction, including T. H. White's *The Sword in the Stone* (1938), and, most recently, Catherine Fisher's *Darkhenge* (2005), which is discussed at the end of Chapter 4.
5. Hill's final chapter on 'The Green Man in Literature' is brief and covers just four texts: Treece (1966), Crossley-Holland (1966), Mooney (1997b) and

Gardam (1998). The last three, among others, are analysed here, but Treece (1966), as an adult novel, is beyond the scope of this discussion. Other adult fiction not considered by Hill includes Amis (1969), Elphinstone (1991) and Kingdom (1998).

6. The legend of the Green Children of Woolpit has also recently been elaborated into a trilogy of novels by Mark Bartholomew (2006a, 2006b, 2007).
7. Melvin Burgess's *The Earth Giant* (1995) may be paying an odd tribute to *The Giant Under the Snow* by apparently systematically inverting it, with a female rather than male giant from the earth who is red rather than green. Numerous other intertextual echoes can be discerned in *The Earth Giant*, with the usual caution that they may reflect a reader's connections as much as a writer's elusive intent: Burgess's giant in a derelict cinema is like the Brogan in the ruined museum (Scott 1989), a long barrow spaceship recalls *Doctor Who and the Daemons* (broadcast 1971), a giant also takes a girl for a ride from her bedroom window in *The BFG* (Dahl 1982), and a character with the same name as early 20th-century socialist miners' leader Peter Lee could be interpreted as an indication of Burgess's political sympathies.
8. There is also a Green Lady in one of Catherine Fisher's earliest children's books, *Saint Tarvel's Bell* (1990), placed in Celtic mythology as the goat-footed, green-robed Glaistig. The Glaistig is a villainous *femme fatale*, 'Beautiful, and deadly' (80), lightning-eyed and emanating a 'sickly perfume' (81).
9. The surnames of Jane Drew and Will Stanton could derive from Stanton Drew, a henge complex in Somerset. The uses of megalithic sites in children's fiction are explored in Chapter 4.
10. The literary tradition of people with disabilities having compensating extra senses goes right back to Tiresias, the blind seer in *Antigone*, and there are many examples in children's literature; the stereotype might be construed as positive, but it is still a stereotype. Diana in *The Moon Stallion* (Hayles 1978; discussed in Chapter 4), Laura in *Spellhorn* (Doherty 1989), and Mercy in *Coram Boy* (Gavin 2000) are all 'blind seers'. Meshak in *Coram Boy* is a visionary *idiot savant* who even as an adult has 'the ways of a child, the thoughts of a child and he could laugh and cry as easily as children do' (Gavin 2000: 182) – it is open to question whether this honours childness or demeans disability. In *Stuck in Neutral* (Trueman 2000), Shawn's seizures are presented as spiritual experiences, and he has an exceptional mind with 'total recall'; the case for Shawn to live does not seem to be predicated on a universal right but on his particular hidden giftedness.
11. N. Roy Clifton's *The City Beyond the Gates* (1972) makes for a curious comparison with Susan Cooper's *Green Boy*. The earlier story also has an environmental message and a green boy, though this green boy is not a resurgent God, he just wears green. Even so, wearing green shows that he is out of step with his hyper-industrialised consumerist society, and more in sympathy with Janey-Ann, who passes through the 'Fence of Unwish' from her pastoral Arcadia into the green boy's barren land and ultimately takes him back with her. Like Cooper, Clifton uses science-fiction narrative devices as an ecological warning about the present: described in defamiliarised and futuristic terms, the green boy's land of 'Fair-Look' depends on fossil fuels and is overpopulated, full of cars, skyscrapers and uniform housing; flowers

are artificial, food is tasteless, and televisions ('Forgetters') numb the mind. Fair-Look's God, the Giant, and his priesthood demand taxes: deaths on the road, and a tithe of the population dying of disease before the age of 20. Evading and challenging the authorities is the Stranger, a loin-cloth-wearing, stern but laughing prophet like Gandhi or Jesus. Clifton's ecological message is tinged with Christianity, 'All the trees of the field shall clap their hands' (Isaiah 55: 12) being quoted towards the end of the novel.

Chapter 3

1. I have previously compared Margaret Mahy's *Alchemy* (2002) with Bohm's theory (Bramwell 2005b). 'Nanuak' is close to 'Nanook', a Sami word for white bear (according to Pattou 2003: 73), and certainly it would be appropriate for the world-soul to be associated with the creature which is so central to Arctic cultures.

2. Sedna is also mentioned in Rudyard Kipling's 'Quiquern' (discussed above): 'Now Sedna is the Mistress of the Underworld, and the Inuit believe that every one who dies must spend a year in her horrible country before going to Quadliparmiut, the Happy Place, where it never freezes and the fat reindeer trot up when you call' (Kipling 1895: 143). Compare '*Sedna now rules Adlivin, the place where souls go after death*' (Ann and Imel 1993: 386).

3. When Chingis sets Safa free, he feels 'so tiny, like a single stitch in the mass of embroidery covering his bedspread, like that single stitch undone' (Price 1987: 72). The comparison is effective in expressing Safa's new experience in terms of a significant artefact of his previous severely bounded existence, but then the simile is deftly extended to the end-focused 'undone', conveying his confusion. Whereas the Czar's labyrinthine palace is as unfamiliar to most readers as it is to Safa, the world outside is the reader's world, but seen afresh, defamiliarised: 'the clamour, glamour and clutter of *our* world' (128, my italics). 'He was not surprised to see a house on legs' (74) because he has not learnt to refuse to see what is categorised as unreal.

   The relation of textile to textual practices and gender arises again (compare the discussion of Pattou (2003) and Rees (2000) in this chapter). Though there is no indication of who produced the embroideries which furnish Safa's chamber, his imprisonment in the tower parallels the confined life of the (usually female) needle-worker, the scenes depicted provoking in him curiosity about the wider world. His maid converts textile to text, the embroideries inspiring her to tell him 'stories about knights and their horses of power; about forests and rivers, about fire-birds and singing-birds and princesses' (Price 1987: 45). What is more, in Russian folk belief embroidery has the power of a spell: 'Birds and lions, flowers, horses and fantastic trees, all the magical symbols of fertility and nature were a kind of incantation in thread against evil spirits' (Massie 1980: 198).

4. The magic of song is prominent in the Finnish epic *Kalevala* (Kirby (tr.) 1907). Väinämöinen puts the upstart Joukahainen down with magic songs. Lemminkäinen scatters his opponents by singing, he sings an ice-bridge together in order to cross a snow-pond, and he betters the Lord of Pohjola in a duel of song magic. Lemminkäinen and Väinämöinen display other shamanic characteristics as well: the former is dismembered, and reassembled

by his mother applying nectar; and the latter travels to Tuonela, the realm of the dead, and back, and can also shapeshift.

5. The Arabic trader is Ibn Fadlan, and the relevant passage is:
    They led the girl to an object they had constructed, which looked like the frame of a door. She placed her feet on the extended hands of the men, who raised her above her framework. She uttered something in her language, whereupon they let her down. Then again they raised her, and she did as before. Once more they let her down, and then lifted her a third time. Then they handed her a hen, whose head she cut off and threw away.
    I inquired of the interpreter what it was she had done. He replied: 'The first time she said, "Lo, I see here my father and mother"; the second time, "Lo, now I see all my deceased relatives sitting"; the third time, "Lo, there is my master, who is sitting in Paradise. Paradise is so beautiful, so green. With him are his men and boys. He calls me, so bring me to him."' (Crichton 1976: 37)
    Crichton's book is an elaborate literary joke, as he confirmed 16 years after it was first published, in an afterword added in 1992. The first three chapters really are a translation of Ibn Fadlan, but the rest is Crichton's own invention, a version of the Beowulf story complete with fake academic critical apparatus.

6. John Webster, *The Duchess of Malfi*, Act IV, Scene II, lines 215–218a.
    Duchess: I know death hath ten thousand several doors
        For men to take their Exits: and 'tis found
        They go on such strange geometrical hinges,
        You may open them both ways

7. Similarly, the Lia Fáil at Tara acclaimed the High King of Ireland, and the foot-shaped petrosomatoglyph at Dunadd did the same for the king of Dalriada.

8. Leeson draws the same source, Ibn Fadlan, as Susan Price does in the Ghost World trilogy, as noted above.

9. Lee Kingman (1972) does likewise: Matti says, 'my grandmother said *her* grandmother said [spirits] lived in rocks and trees' (21).

Chapter 4

1. Terrance Dicks returns to stone circles in *The Circle of Death Incident* (1997). Narrator Matt Stirling, who has a gift of prescience, and his sceptical father, 'Professor James Stirling, head of the Scientific Research Institute's Department of Paranormal Studies' (9), investigate strange goings-on at Stonehenge. Attitudes to druidism, and to the functions of stone circles, are similar to those in *Doctor Who and the Stones of Blood*: Professor Stirling asserts that 'Stonehenge has got nothing to do with druids' (13), and Matt advocates that Stonehenge is 'a kind of Neolithic computer that could be used to predict eclipses of the moon' (16). Matt also deduces that ley lines are flight-paths for UFOs – contrast Paul Devereux's (1982) argument, which does connect UFOs with megalithic monuments, but regards UFOs as manifestations of earthly geophysical phenomena – 'planetary ectoplasm'. In *The Circle of Death Incident*, Stonehenge is a beacon and hyperspatial portal

for malevolent aliens, and Matt and his father must prevent an obsessive archaeologist from activating it. Dicks escapes the insularity of henges by the earth mysteries manoeuvre of treating dissimilar monuments of different ages from around the world as part of a single mystery and a single solution, in this case that aliens created and continue to visit ancient sacred sites. As 'The Unexplained' series progresses, Dicks varies the premises and so moves away from a one-size-fits-all explanation. For example, *The Mafia Incident* (Dicks 1999) makes no mention of aliens, but associates witchcraft with a classical Sicilian temple. An ambitious young mafioso gains power at full moon from a Dianic cult represented by an old woman and her grand-daughter. He is warned that the power could destroy him, that 'Few can bear the full burden of the Goddess's Power' (Dicks 1999: 8), and sure enough it causes a breakdown, for 'He was arrogant and proud, but inside he was weak' (91).

2. Research into archaeoacoustics has grown in recent years; see Devereux (2001), Watson (2007).

3. The religious schema of *The Prince in Waiting* trilogy might be compared with that of Susan Price's Mars trilogy (Price 2005, 2006, 2008). Price's future has Classical and Norse Paganism as organised religions, with the former more established and conventional like Spiritism, and the latter more radical and egalitarian, like *The Prince in Waiting* trilogy's primitive Christianity. In the second volume of the Mars trilogy, *Odin's Queen*, religious and political satire is evident in the figure of Zeuslove Thatcher, reactionary archpriest of the Church of Mars, who is inflamed by Odinstoy championing slaves and proclaiming that Mars will have its own goddess, Mother Mars. The Mars trilogy, like other fictional depictions of mediumship (see Chapter 1 notes), maintains tension between genuine gift and sham: Odinstoy can work an audience and is skilled at cold reading, she tricks the faithful to please them and for her own purposes, but some 'coincidences' cannot be explained away, and she is a genuine believer in 'the treacherous God' Odin.

4. The surname Drew reflects that he is an artist, and, as it is also used for characters in *The Dark is Rising* sequence, may be a tribute to Susan Cooper.

Bibliography

Primary Texts

Ainsworth, William Harrison (1843) *Windsor Castle* (London: Henry Colburn).
Ainsworth, William Harrison (1849) *The Lancashire Witches* (London: Henry Colburn).
Allen, Judy (1973) *The Spring on the Mountain* (London: Jonathan Cape).
Allen, Judy (1975a) *The Stones of the Moon* (London: Jonathan Cape).
Allen, Judy (1976) *The Lord of the Dance* (London: Hamish Hamilton).
Allen, Judy (1988) *Awaiting Developments* (London: Julia MacRae).
Allen, Judy (1990a) *The Great Pig Sprint* (London: Julia MacRae).
Allen, Judy (1990b) *The Dim Thin Ducks* (London: Julia MacRae).
Allen, Judy (1991a) *The Cheap Sheep Shock* (London: Julia MacRae).
Allen, Judy (1991b) *The Long-Loan Llama* (London: Julia MacRae).
Amis, Kingsley (1969) *The Green Man* (London: Cape).
Andersen, Hans Christian (1846) *The Snow Queen* (London: Walker, 1988. Translated and introduced by Naomi Lewis, illustrated by Angela Barrett).
Arnold, Elizabeth (1998) *A Riot of Red Ribbon* (London: Mammoth).
Arnold, Elizabeth (1999) *Spin of the Sunwheel* (London: Egmont).
Asbjørnsen, Christen and Moe, Jørgen (1849) 'East of the Sun, West of the Moon' in *East of the Sun, West of the Moon: Old Tales from the North* (London: Folio, 2000. Translated by Sir George Dasent and illustrated by Kay Nielson), pp. 11–30.
Banks, Lynne Reid (1992) *The Magic Hare* (London: HarperCollins, 1993).
Bartholomew, Mark (2006a) *Whispers in the Woods* (Blackburn: Eprint).
Bartholomew, Mark (2006b) *Chaos in the Cathedral* (Blackburn: Eprint).
Bartholomew, Mark (2007) *Swords in the Summer* (Blackburn: Eprint).
Bawden, Nina (1973) *Carrie's War* (London: Gollancz).
Bowler, Tim (1995) *Dragon's Rock* (Oxford: Oxford University Press, 2002).
Bradley, Marion (1982) *The Mists of Avalon* (London: Michael Joseph, 1983).
Browne, Anthony (1995) *Willy the Wizard* (London: Julia MacRae).
Burgess, Melvin (1995) *The Earth Giant* (London: Andersen).
Burnett, Frances Hodgson (1911) *The Secret Garden* (London: Folio, 1994).
Burnham, Jeremy and Ray, Trevor (1977) *Children of the Stones* (London: Transworld).
Butler, Charles (1998) *Timon's Tide* (London: Orion).
Butler, Charles (2006a) *Death of a Ghost* (London: HarperCollins).
Caldecott, Moyra [Olivia Brown] (1989) *The Green Lady and the King of Shadows: a Glastonbury Legend* (Glastonbury: Gothic Image).
Carpenter, Richard with May, Robin and Horowitz, Anthony (1990) *The Complete Adventures of Robin of Sherwood* (Harmondsworth: Puffin).
Christopher, John [Christopher Youd] (1970) *The Prince in Waiting* (London: Hamish Hamilton).
Christopher, John [Christopher Youd] (1971) *Beyond the Burning Lands* (London: Hamish Hamilton).

Christopher, John [Christopher Youd] (1972) *The Sword of the Spirits* (London: Hamish Hamilton).

Clifton, N. Roy (1972) *The City Beyond the Gates* (Ontario: Scholastic, 1977).

Cooper, Patrick (1998) *O'Driscoll's Treasure* (London: Andersen, 2004).

Cooper, Susan (1973) *The Dark is Rising* in *The Dark is Rising Sequence* (Harmondsworth: Puffin, 1984), pp. 177–356.

Cooper, Susan (1974) *Greenwitch* (London: Chatto and Windus).

Cooper, Susan (1977) *Silver on the Tree* in *The Dark is Rising Sequence* (Harmondsworth: Puffin, 1984), pp. 585–786.

Cooper, Susan (2002) *Green Boy* (London: Bodley Head).

Corlett, William (1991) *The Tunnel Behind the Waterfall* (London: Bodley Head)

Cresswell, Helen (1995) *Stonestruck* (Harmondsworth: Viking).

Crichton, Michael (1976) *Eaters of the Dead: The Manuscript of Ibn Fadlan, Relating His Experiences with the Northmen in A.D. 922* (London: Random House, 1997).

Crossley-Holland, Kevin (1966) *The Green Children* (London: Macmillan, 1972. Illustrated by Margaret Gordon).

Crossley-Holland, Kevin (2000) *The Seeing Stone* (London: Orion).

Crossley-Holland, Kevin (2001) *At the Crossing-Places* (London: Orion).

Czerkawska, Catherine Lucy (1989) *Shadow of the Stone* (Glasgow: Richard Drew).

Dahl, Roald (1982) *The BFG* (Harmondsworth: Puffin, 1984).

Datlow, Ellen and Windling, Terri (ed.) (2002) *The Green Man: Tales from the Mythic Forest* (New York: Viking).

Dickinson, Peter (1983) *Healer* (London: Gollancz).

Dicks, Terrance (1980) *Doctor Who and the Stones of Blood* (London: W. H. Allen).

Dicks, Terrance (1997) *The Circle of Death Incident* (London: Piccadilly. 'The Unexplained' series).

Dicks, Terrance (1999) *The Mafia Incident* (London: Piccadilly. 'The Unexplained' series).

Doherty, Berlie (1989) *Spellhorn* (London: Hamish Hamilton).

Druitt, Tobias [Diane Purkiss and Michael Dowling] (2005) *Corydon and the Island of Monsters* (London: Simon and Schuster).

Elphinstone, Margaret (1991) 'Green Man' in *An Apple from a Tree* (London: The Women's Press), pp. 1–72.

Fell, Alison (1981) *The Grey Dancer* (London: Collins).

Fidler, Kathleen (1968) *The Boy with the Bronze Axe* (Edinburgh: Oliver and Boyd).

Fisher, Catherine (1990) *Saint Tarvel's Bell* (Singapore: EPB).

Fisher, Catherine (1993) *The Snow-Walker's Son* (London: Bodley Head).

Fisher, Catherine (1995) *The Empty Hand* (London: Bodley Head).

Fisher, Catherine (1996) *The Soul Thieves* (London: Bodley Head).

Fisher, Catherine (1999) *The Lammas Field* (London: Hodder).

Fisher, Catherine (2002) *Corbenic* (London: Red Fox).

Fisher, Catherine (2005) *Darkhenge* (London: Bodley Head).

Fisk, Pauline (2001) *Sabrina Fludde* (London: Bloomsbury).

Furlong, Monica (1987) *Wise Child* (London: Gollancz).

Furlong, Monica (1990) *A Year and a Day* (London: Gollancz).

Gardam, Jane (1998) *The Green Man* (Moreton-in-Marsh: Windrush. Illustrated by Mary Fedden). 'The Green Man' first appeared in Gardam, Jane (1997) *Missing the Midnight* (London: Sinclair Stevenson).

Garner, Alan (1963) *The Moon of Gomrath* (London: Collins Lions, 1990).

Garner, Alan (1965) *Elidor* (London: Collins).

Garner, Alan (1976) *The Stone Book* (London: Collins).

Gavin, Jamila (2000) *Coram Boy* (London: Egmont).

Geras, Adèle (2000) *Troy* (London: David Fickling).

Geras, Adèle (2005) *Ithaka* (London: David Fickling).

Golden, Christopher and Holder, Nancy (1998) *Buffy the Vampire Slayer: Child of the Hunt* (New York: Simon and Schuster).

Gordon, John (1968) *The Giant Under the Snow* (Harmondsworth: Puffin, 1978).

Grahame, Kenneth (1908) *The Wind in the Willows* (Bristol: Parragon, 1993).

Greaves, Margaret (1972) *The Grandmother Stone* (London: Methuen, 1980).

Green, Roger J. (1984) *The Fear of Samuel Walton* (Oxford: Oxford University Press).

Halam, Ann (2007) *Snakehead* (London: Orion).

Haley, Gail E. (1979) *The Green Man* (New York: Charles Scribner's Sons, 1980).

Hayles, Brian (1978) *The Moon Stallion* (London: Mirror Books).

Horowitz, Anthony (1983) *The Devil's Door-bell* (London: Patrick Hardy).

Horowitz, Anthony (2000) *Stormbreaker* (London: Walker).

Horowitz, Anthony (2005) *Raven's Gate* (London: Walker).

Horowitz, Anthony (2006) *Evil Star* (London: Walker).

Horowitz, Anthony (2007) *Nightrise* (London: Walker).

Hughes, Thomas (1857) *Tom Brown's Schooldays* (Barcelona: Fabbri, 1992).

Hunter, Mollie (1964) *The Kelpie's Pearls* (London and Glasgow: Blackie).

Hunter, Mollie (1970) *The Bodach* (London and Glasgow: Blackie).

Jenkins, Alan C. (1960) *The Twins of Lapland* (London: Cape).

Johnson, Catherine R. (2002) *Stella* (Oxford: Oxford University Press).

Jones, Diana Wynne (1975) *Dogsbody* (London: Macmillan).

Jones, Diana Wynne (ed.) (1994) *Fantasy Stories* (London: Kingfisher).

Jordan, Sherryl (2000) *The Raging Quiet* (London: Simon and Schuster).

Kernaghan, Eileen (2000) *The Snow Queen* (Saskatoon, Saskatchewan: Thistledown).

Kerven, Rosalind (1980) *The Reindeer and the Drum* (London: Abelard-Schuman).

King, Clive (1963) *Stig of the Dump* (Harmondsworth: Penguin, 1985).

Kingdom, Will [Phil Rickman] (1998) *The Cold Calling* (London: Transworld).

Kingdom, Will [Phil Rickman] (2001) *Mean Spirit* (London: Bantam).

Kingman, Lee (1972) *The Meeting Post* (London: Franklin Watts, 1985 revised).

Kipling, Rudyard (1895) 'Quiquern' in Kipling, Rudyard (ed.), *The Second Jungle Book* (London: Pan, 1975), pp. 131–154.

Kipling, Rudyard (1906) *Puck of Pook's Hill* (London: Macmillan).

Lawrence, Louise (1981) *The Earth Witch* (London: Collins, 1982).

Leeson, Robert (1973) *Beyond the Dragon Prow* (London: Collins).

Lewis, C. S. (1950) *The Lion, the Witch and the Wardrobe* (London: Collins, 1989).

Lively, Penelope (1971a) *The Whispering Knights* (London: Heinemann).

Lively, Penelope (1971b) *The Wild Hunt of Hagworthy* (London: Heinemann).

Louise, Cara (1983) *The Boy from the Hills* (Glastonbury: Earth Mysteries Enterprises).

Louise, Cara (1993) *The Lady of the Rock* ([n.p.]: Cara Louise Books, 2007).

Louise, Cara (2006) *Annie and the Dragon* ([n.p.]: Cara Louise Books, 2007).

Mahy, Margaret (2002) *Alchemy* (London: HarperCollins).

Manning-Sanders, Ruth (1976) *Scottish Folk Tales* (London: Methuen, 1986).

Mantel, Hilary (2005) *Beyond Black* (London: Fourth Estate).

Masefield, John (1935) *The Box of Delights* (London: Heinemann, 1985).

Masson, Sophie (2006) *Thomas Trew and the Hidden People* (London: Hodder).

Masson, Sophie (2007a) *Thomas Trew and the Horns of Pan* (London: Hodder).

Masson, Sophie (2007b) *Thomas Trew and the Flying Huntsman* (London: Hodder).

Mattam, Donald (1959) *Standing Stone* (London: Epworth, 1960).

McCaughrean, Geraldine (1999) *The Stones are Hatching* (Oxford: Oxford University Press).

McCaughrean, Geraldine (2006) *Peter Pan in Scarlet* (Oxford: Oxford University Press).

Miller, Arthur (1953) *The Crucible* (Harmondsworth: Penguin, 1968).

Mitchell, Trystan (2000) *Once Upon a Winter's Turning* (Presteigne: Wooden Books).

Molesworth, Mrs [Mary] (1877) *The Cuckoo Clock* (Harmondsworth: Penguin, 1988).

Mooney, Bel (1997a) *The Green Man* (Bath: Barefoot Books. Illustrated by Helen Cann).

Mooney, Bel (1997b) *Joining the Rainbow* (London: Mammoth).

Newth, Mette (1987 in Norway as *Bortførelsen*) *The Abduction* (London: Simon and Schuster, 1989. Translated by Tiina Nunnally and Steve Murray).

Pattou, Edith (2003 in the USA as *East*) *North Child* (London: Usborne, 2006).

Paver, Michelle (2004) *Wolf Brother* (London: Orion).

Paver, Michelle (2005) *Spirit Walker* (London: Orion).

Paver, Michelle (2006) *Soul Eater* (London: Orion).

Paver, Michelle (2007) *Outcast* (London: Orion).

Paver, Michelle (2008) *Oath Breaker* (London: Orion).

Pendragon, Paul (1996) *The Silverberry Tree: The Adventures of Zappo Zhi Book I* (Chelmsford: Little Stone Productions).

Phillips, Ann (1984) *The Oak King and the Ash Queen* (Oxford: Oxford University Press).

Pohlmann, Lillian (1965) *The Summer of the White Reindeer* (Kingswood: World's Work, 1966).

Price, Merlin (1979) *The Witch of Rollright* (London: Rex Collings).

Price, Susan (1986) *Odin's Monster* (London: A and C Black).

Price, Susan (1987) *The Ghost Drum* (London: Faber and Faber).

Price, Susan (1992) *Ghost Song* (London: Faber and Faber).

Price, Susan (1994a) *Ghost Dance: The Czar's Black Angel* (London: Faber and Faber).

Price, Susan (1994b) *Foiling the Dragon* (London: Scholastic).

Price, Susan (1995) *Elfgift* (London: Scholastic).

Price, Susan (1996) *Elfking* (London: Scholastic).

Price, Susan (2001a) *The Bearwood Witch* (London: Scholastic).
Price, Susan (2001b) *The Wolf-Sisters* (London: Hodder).
Price, Susan (2005) *Odin's Voice* (London: Simon and Schuster).
Price, Susan (2006) *Odin's Queen* (London: Simon and Schuster).
Price, Susan (2008) *Odin's Son* (London: Simon and Schuster).
Pullein-Thompson, Christine (1988) *The Road Through the Hills* (London: Hodder and Stoughton).
Pullman, Philip (1986, as *The Shadow in the Plate*; revised 1988) *The Shadow in the North* (London: Scholastic, 1999).
Pullman, Philip (1995) *Northern Lights* (London: Scholastic, 1998).
Pullman, Philip (1997) *The Subtle Knife* (London: Scholastic, 1998).
Pullman, Philip (2000) *The Amber Spyglass* (London: Scholastic, 2001).
Rayner, Mary (1975) *The Witch-Finder* (London: Macmillan).
Rayner, William (1972) *Stag Boy* (London: Collins).
Rees, Celia (2000) *Witch Child* (London: Bloomsbury).
Rees, Celia (2002) *Sorceress* (London: Bloomsbury).
Richemont, Enid (1999) *The Enchanted Village* (London: Walker).
Roberts, Michèle (1990) *In the Red Kitchen* (London: Methuen).
Rowling, J. K. (2003) *Harry Potter and the Order of the Phoenix* (London: Bloomsbury).
Russell, Ivy (1963) *Children of the Islands* (Edinburgh: Nelson).
Scott, Hugh (1988) *The Shaman's Stone* (London: Andersen Press).
Scott, Hugh (1989) *Why Weeps the Brogan?* (London: Walker).
Sewell, Anna (1877) *Black Beauty* (London: Gollancz, 1987).
Starhawk (1993) *The Fifth Sacred Thing* (New York: Bantam).
Stinton, Judith (1983) *Tom's Tale* (London: Julia MacRae).
Sutcliff, Rosemary (1977) *Shifting Sands* (London: Hamish Hamilton).
Sutcliff, Rosemary (1986) *The Roundabout Horse* (London: Hamish Hamilton).
Taylor, G. P. (2002) *Shadowmancer* (London: Faber and Faber, 2003).
Tolkien, J. R. R. (1975) *Sir Gawain and the Green Knight, Pearl and Sir Orfeo* (London: Allen and Unwin, 1979).
Tomlinson, Theresa (1989) *Summer Witches* (London: Walker).
Tomlinson, Theresa (1993) *The Forestwife* (London: Julia MacRae).
Tomlinson, Theresa (1998) *Child of the May* (London: Julia MacRae).
Tomlinson, Theresa (2000) *The Path of the She-Wolf* (London: Red Fox).
Tomlinson, Theresa (2002) *The Moon Riders* (London: Random House).
Tomlinson, Theresa (2006) *Wolf Girl* (London: Random House).
Treece, Henry (1966) *The Green Man* (London: Bodley Head).
Trueman, Terry (2000) *Stuck in Neutral* (London: Hodder, 2001).
Vale, Joanna (2004) *Jessiebelle: The Secret* (Banbury: Haveluck).
Waters, Sarah (1999) *Affinity* (London: Virago).
Wayman, Vivienne (1975) *Panchit's Secret* (London: Abelard-Schuman).
Webster, John (1623) *The Duchess of Malfi* (London: A. and C. Black New Mermaids, 1987).
Westall, Robert (1991) *Yaxley's Cat* (London and Basingstoke: Macmillan).
White, T. H. (1938) *The Sword in the Stone* in *The Once and Future King* (Glasgow: Collins Fontana, 1988), pp. 7–208.
Yolen, Jane (1995) *The Wild Hunt* (San Diego: Harcourt Brace).

Secondary Sources

Adler, Margot (1986 rev. edn.; first pub. 1979) *Drawing Down the Moon: Witches, Druids, Goddess-Worshippers, and Other Pagans in America Today* (New York: Penguin, 1997).

Ahlbäck, Tore (ed.) (1987) *Saami Religion: Based on Papers read at the Symposium on the Saami Religion held at Åbo, Finland, on the 16th–18th of August 1984* (Åbo: The Donner Institute for Research in Religious and Cultural History).

Allen, Judy (1975b) 'Dragon Paths' in Bicknell, Treld and Webb, Kaye (ed.), *The Puffin Annual Number Two* (Harmondsworth: Penguin), pp. 39–41.

Anderson, William (1990) *Green Man: The Archetype of our Oneness with the Earth* (London: HarperCollins).

Ann, Martha and Imel, Dorothy Myers (1993) *Goddesses in World Mythology* (New York: Oxford University Press, 1995).

Appleyard, Joseph (1991) *Becoming a Reader* (Cambridge: Cambridge University Press, 1994).

Armitt, Lucie (1996) *Theorising the Fantastic* (London: Arnold).

Atkinson, Jane (1992) 'Shamanisms Today' in *Annual Review of Anthropology*, Vol. 21, pp. 307–330.

Aveni, Anthony F. (2000) *Nasca: Eighth Wonder of the World?* (London: British Museum).

Bakhtin, Mikhail (1981) *The Dialogic Imagination* (Austin, Texas: University of Texas Press. Edited by Michael Holquist, translated by Caryl Emerson and Michael Holquist).

Bakhtin, Mikhail (1984) *Problems of Dostoevsky's Poetics* (Minneapolis: University of Minnesota Press. Translated by Caryl Emerson).

Barker, Eileen (1989) *New Religious Movements: A Practical Introduction* (London: HMSO).

Barry, Peter (2002, second edn.) *Beginning Theory* (Manchester: Manchester University Press).

Basford, Kathleen (1978) *The Green Man* (Cambridge: D. S. Brewer, 1998).

Berger, Helen A. (1999) 'Witches: The Next Generation' in Palmer, Susan J. and Hardman, Charlotte E. (ed.), *Children in New Religions* (New Brunswick, NJ: Rutgers University Press), pp. 11–28.

Beyer, Peter (1998) 'Globalisation and the Religion of Nature' in Pearson, Joanne et al. (ed.), pp. 11–21.

Bohm, David (1980) *Wholeness and the Implicate Order* (London: Routledge, 1994).

Bowman, Marion (2000) 'More of the Same? Christianity, Vernacular Religion and Alternative Spirituality in Glastonbury' in Sutcliffe, Steven and Bowman, Marion (ed.), pp. 83–104.

Bramwell, Peter (2002a) 'The Spirit of the Land: Puck of Pook's Hill' in the *Kipling Journal*, Vol. 76, No. 302, June, pp. 20–27.

Bramwell, Peter (2002b) 'Opening The Box of Delights' in *Children's Literature in Education*, Vol. 33, No. 2, June, pp. 117–129.

Bramwell, Peter (2002c) *The Magic of Susan Price's 'The Ghost Drum'*. Dissertation presented in part fulfilment of the requirements of the MA in Children's Literature of the University of Surrey, September.

Bramwell, Peter (2005a) 'Feminism and History: Historical Fiction – Not Just a Thing of the Past' in Reynolds, Kimberley (ed.), pp. 108–123.

Bramwell, Peter (2005b) 'Fantasy, Psychoanalysis and Adolescence: Magic and Maturation in Fantasy' in Reynolds, Kimberley (ed.), pp. 141–155.

Brennand, Mark and Taylor, Maisie (2000) 'Seahenge' in *Current Archaeology* Vol. 16, No. 11, pp. 417–424.

Butler, Charles (2006b) *Four British Fantasists: Place and Culture in the Children's Fantasies of Penelope Lively, Alan Garner, Diana Wynne Jones, and Susan Cooper* (Lanham, Maryland: Scarecrow).

Butler, Charles (unpublished) 'Children of the Stones: Prehistoric Sites in British Children's Fantasy, 1965–2005.'

Cameron, Geo (1997) *Spiritual Crisis in Early Irish Literature and Later Folk Life.* Submitted for the Award of MSc in Celtic Studies, University of Edinburgh, September. http://www.celticshamanism.com/alt_thesis.html (accessed 4/7/02).

Campbell, Mark (2000) *The Pocket Essential Doctor Who* (Harpenden: Pocket Essentials).

Carpenter, Humphrey (1985) *Secret Gardens: The Golden Age of Children's Literature* (Boston: Houghton Mifflin).

Carroll, Lee and Tober, Jan (ed.) (1999) *The Indigo Children: The new kids have arrived* (Carlsbad, CA: Hay House).

Clarke, Arthur C. (1974, revised edn.) *Profiles of the Future: An Inquiry into the Limits of the Possible* (London: Gollancz).

Clarke, David and Maguire, Patrick (1989) *Skara Brae: Northern Europe's Best Preserved Prehistoric Village* (Edinburgh: Historic Scotland, 1996).

Cope, Julian (1998) *The Modern Antiquarian: A Pre-Millennial Odyssey through Megalithic Britain* (London: HarperCollins Thorsons).

Cornell, Paul et al. (1995) *Doctor Who: The Discontinuity Guide* (London: Virgin).

Crossley-Holland, Kevin (1980) *The Norse Myths* (London: Deutsch).

Crowley, Vivianne (1996) *Principles of Paganism* (London: HarperCollins).

Crowley, Vivianne (1998) 'Wicca as Nature Religion' in Pearson, Joanne et al. (ed.), pp. 170–179.

Davidson, H. R. Ellis (1964) *Gods and Myths of Northern Europe* (Harmondsworth: Penguin, 1990).

Devereux, Paul (1982) *Earth Lights* (Wellingborough: Turnstone).

Devereux, Paul (1992) *Shamanism and the Mystery Lines* (London: Quantum).

Devereux, Paul (2001) *Stone Age Soundtracks: The Acoustic Archaeology of Ancient Sites* (London: Chrysalis Vega).

Drury, Nevill (2000 rev. edn.; first pub. 1989 as *The Elements of Shamanism*) *Shamanism: An Introductory Guide to Living in Harmony with Nature* (Shaftesbury: Element).

Eliade, Mircea (1964) *Shamanism: Archaic Techniques of Ecstasy* (Princeton: Princeton University Press, 1974).

Evans, Arthur J. (1895) 'The Rollright Stones and their Folk-Lore' in *Folk-Lore*, Vol. 6, No. 1, March, pp. 6–51.

Fairclough, Norman (2001, second edn.) *Language and Power* (Harlow: Pearson Longman).

Fitch, Eric L. (1994) *In Search of Herne the Hunter* (Chieveley: Capall Bann).

Flick, Pauline S. ([no date]) 'The Rollright Stones' (Chipping Norton: The Printing House).

Ford, Paul F. (1994, fourth edn.) *Companion to Narnia* (San Francisco: HarperCollins).

Foss, Karen A. et al. (1999) *Feminist Rhetorical Theories* (Thousand Oaks, CA: Sage).

Frazer, Sir James (1922, abridged) *The Golden Bough: A study in magic and religion* (Ware: Wordsworth, 1993).

Furlong, Monica (1991) *A Dangerous Delight: Women and Power in the Church* (London: S.P.C.K.).

Gamble, Nikki (2002) 'An Interview with Kevin Crossley-Holland'. http://improbability.ultralab.net/writeaway (accessed 7/1/03).

Garrard, Greg (2004) *Ecocriticism* (London and New York: Routledge).

Glob, P. V. (1966) *The Bog People: Iron-age man preserved* (London: Faber and Faber, 1969. Translated by Rupert Bruce-Mitford).

Goldthwaite, John (1996) *The Natural History of Make-Believe* (New York and Oxford: Oxford University Press).

Goodin, Robert E. (1992) *Green Political Theory* (Cambridge: Polity).

Graves, Tom (1978) *Needles of Stone* (London: Turnstone).

Grinsell, Leslie V. (1976) *Folklore of Prehistoric Sites in Britain* (Newton Abbot: David and Charles).

Harvey, Graham (1995) 'Heathenism: a North European Pagan Tradition' in Harvey, Graham and Hardman, Charlotte (ed.), pp. 49–64.

Harvey, Graham (1997) *Listening People, Speaking Earth: Contemporary Paganism* (London: Hurst).

Harvey, Graham (2000) 'Boggarts and Books: Towards an Appreciation of Pagan Spirituality' in Sutcliffe, Steven and Bowman, Marion (ed.), pp. 155–168.

Harvey, Graham and Hardman, Charlotte (ed.) (1995 as *Paganism Today*) *Pagan Pathways* (London: Thorsons, 2000).

Hay, David with Nye, Rebecca (1998) *The Spirit of the Child* (London: HarperCollins).

Hetherington, Kevin (2000) *New Age Travellers: vanloads of uproarious humanity* (London: Cassell).

Hill, Peter (2004) *In Search of the Green Man* (Chieveley: Capall Bann).

Hitching, Frances (1976) *Earth Magic* (London: Cassell).

Hollindale, Peter (1988) 'Ideology and the Children's Book' in *Signal*, Vol. 55, pp. 3–22.

Hollindale, Peter (1997) *Signs of Childness in Children's Books* (Stroud: Thimble).

Hopkin, Michael (2002) 'The shaman and his exobrain' in *The Guardian*, 19/1/02.

Hultkrantz, Åke (1991) 'The Drum in Shamanism. Some Reflections' in Ahlbäck, Tore and Bergman, Jan (ed.), *The Saami Shaman Drum: Based on Papers read at the Symposium on the Saami Shaman Drum held at Åbo, Finland, on the 19th–20th of August 1988* (Åbo: The Donner Institute for Research in Religious and Cultural History. Translated by John Skinner), pp. 9–27.

Hunt, George (1994) 'Authorgraph No. 89: Susan Price' in *Books for Keeps*, Vol. 89, November, pp. 16–17.

Hunt, Peter and Lenz, Millicent (2001) *Alternative Worlds in Fantasy Fiction* (London: Continuum).

Hutton, Ronald (1991) *The Pagan Religions of the Ancient British Isles: Their Nature and Legacy* (Oxford: Blackwell).

Hutton, Ronald (1996) *The Stations of the Sun: a history of the ritual year in Britain* (Oxford: Oxford University Press).

Hutton, Ronald (1999) *The Triumph of the Moon: a history of modern pagan witch-craft* (Oxford: Oxford University Press).

Hutton, Ronald (2001) *Shamans: Siberian Spirituality and the Western Imagination* (London: Hambledon and London).

Jamal, Michele (1987) *Shape Shifters: shaman women in contemporary society* (Harmondsworth: Penguin).

Jennings, Pete (1998) *The Norse Tradition: a beginner's guide* (London: Hodder).

Johnson, Myke (1995) 'Wanting to be Indian: when spiritual searching turns into cultural theft' in Pearson, Joanne (ed.) (2002), pp. 277–293.

Johnston, Rosemary Ross (1995) 'The Special Magic of the Eighties: Shaping Words and Shape-Shifting Words' in *Children's Literature in Education*, Vol. 26, No. 4, pp. 211–217.

Johnston, Rosemary Ross (2002) 'Childhood: A narrative chronotope' in Sell, Roger D. (ed.), pp. 137–157.

Jones, Leslie Ellen (1998) *Druid – Shaman – Priest: Metaphors of Celtic Paganism* (Enfield Lock: Hisarlik).

Jones, Mervyn (1982) *The Sami of Lapland* (London: Minority Rights Group).

Jones, Nicolette (2007) Review of *Outcast* by Michelle Paver, in *The Sunday Times*, 16/9/07.

Jones, Prudence (1995) 'Pagan Theologies' in Harvey, Graham and Hardman, Charlotte (ed.), pp. 32–46.

Jones, Prudence (1998) 'The European Native Tradition' in Pearson, Joanne et al. (ed.), pp. 77–88.

Jones, Raymond E. (1997) *Characters in Children's Literature* (Detroit: Gale).

Kabbani, Rana (1986) *Europe's Myths of Orient* (London: Macmillan).

Kenin-Lopsan, Mongush (1997) 'Tuvan Shamanic Folklore' in Balzer, Marjorie (ed.), *Shamanic Worlds: rituals and lore of Siberia and Central Asia* (New York: M. E. Sharpe), pp. 110–152.

Kernaghan, Eileen (2002) 'Revisiting the Snow Queen': Eileen Kernaghan interviewed by Casey Wolf. http://home.portal.ca/~lonewolf/kernaghan.html (accessed 10/8/02).

Kerven, Rosalind (2005) Personal correspondence, 18/1/05.

Kirby, W. F. (tr.) (1907) *Kalevala* (London and Dover, NH: Athlone, 1985).

Krips, Valerie (2000) *The Presence of the Past: Memory, Heritage, and Childhood in Postwar Britain* (New York and London: Garland).

Kruger, Kathryn Sullivan (2001) *Weaving the Word: The Metaphorics of Weaving and Female Textual Production* (Selinsgrove: Susquehanna University Press).

Lovelock, J. E. (1979) *Gaia: a new look at life on earth* (Oxford: Oxford University Press, 1989).

Lundmark, Bo (1987) 'Rijkuo-Maja and Silbo-Gåmmoe – towards the question of female shamanism in the Saami area' in Ahlbäck, Tore (ed.), pp. 158–169.

Lycett, Andrew (1999) *Rudyard Kipling* (London: Weidenfeld and Nicolson).

MacDermott, Mercia (2003) *Explore Green Men* (Loughborough: Heart of Albion Press).

Maclellan, Gordon (1995) 'Dancing on the Edge: Shamanism in Modern Britain' in Harvey, Graham and Hardman, Charlotte (ed.), pp. 138–148.

Marples, Morris (1949) *White Horses and Other Hill Figures* (Stroud: Alan Sutton, 1981).

Massie, Suzanne (1980) *Land of the Firebird: The Beauty of Old Russia* (London: Hamish Hamilton).

McCrickard, Janet (1990) *Eclipse of the Sun* (Glastonbury: Gothic Image).

Mehta, Gita (1979) *Karma Cola* (London: Jonathan Cape, 1980).

Merivale, Patricia (1969) *Pan the Goat God: his myth in modern times* (Cambridge, Mass: Harvard University Press).

Michell, John (1969) *The View over Atlantis* (London: Sphere, 1973).

Mumm, Susan (2002) 'Aspirational Indians: North American indigenous religions and the New Age' in Pearson, Joanne (ed.), pp. 104–131.

Murray, Margaret (1921) *The Witch-Cult in Western Europe: A Study in Anthropology* (Oxford: Clarendon Press).

Nikolajeva, Maria (1988) *The Magic Code: The use of magical patterns in fantasy for children* (Stockholm: Almqvist and Wiksell International).

Nikolajeva, Maria (1996) *Children's Literature Comes of Age: toward a new aesthetic* (New York and London: Garland).

Nikolajeva, Maria (2000) *From Mythic to Linear: Time in Children's Literature* (Lanham, MD and London: Scarecrow).

Nikolajeva, Maria (2002) 'Growing up: The dilemma of children's literature' in Sell, Roger D. (ed.), pp. 111–136.

Partridge, Christopher H. (2001) 'Pagan Fundamentalism?' in Partridge, Christopher H. (ed.), *Fundamentalisms* (Carlisle: Paternoster), pp. 155–181.

Pearson, Joanne (ed.) (2002) *Belief Beyond Boundaries: Wicca, Celtic Spirituality and the New Age* (Aldershot: Ashgate in association with the Open University).

Pearson, Joanne (2002a) 'The history and development of Wicca and Paganism' in Pearson, Joanne (ed.), pp. 15–54.

Pearson, Joanne (2002b) 'Witches and Wicca' in Pearson, Joanne (ed.), pp. 133–172.

Pearson, Joanne et al. (ed.) (1998) *Nature Religion Today: Paganism in the Modern World* (Edinburgh: Edinburgh University Press).

Pentikäinen, Juha (1987) 'The Saami shamanic drum in Rome' in Ahlbäck, Tore (ed.), pp. 124–149.

Philip, Neil (1981a) *A Fine Anger: A critical introduction to the work of Alan Garner* (London: Collins).

Philip, Neil (1981b) 'Garner and Shamanism' in *Labrys*, Vol. 7, November, pp. 99–107.

Philip, Neil (1989) 'The Wind in the Willows: The Vitality of a Classic' in Avery, Gillian and Briggs, Julia (ed.), *Children and their Books* (Oxford: Oxford University Press), pp. 299–316.

Philip, Neil (1997) 'England's Dreaming' in *Signal*, Vol. 82, January, pp. 14–30.

Phinn, Gervase (1998) *The Other Side of the Dale* (London: Michael Joseph).

Piggott, Stuart (1968) *The Druids* (London: Thames and Hudson, 1989).

Ponting, Gerald and Ponting, Margaret (1984) *The Stones around Callanish* (Callanish: G. and M. Ponting).

Price, Susan (2002a) www.susanprice.org.uk (accessed 26/4/02).

Price, Susan (2002b) Personal correspondence, 24/5/02.

Purkiss, Diane (1996) *The Witch in History* (London and New York: Routledge).

Purkiss, Diane (2000) *Troublesome Things: a history of fairies and fairy stories* (Harmondsworth: Penguin).

Raglan, Lady [Julia] (1939) 'The Green Man in church architecture' in *Folklore*, Vol. 50, No. 1, March, pp. 45–57.

Rees, Celia (2001) 'Celia Rees Interview' by Book Wholesalers, Inc. http://www. bwibooks.com/news1.php (accessed 28/7/01)

Rees, Celia (2006) In conversation, 11/11/06.

Reynolds, Kimberley (ed.) (2005) *Modern Children's Literature: An Introduction* (Basingstoke: Palgrave Macmillan).

Riordan, James (1989) *The Sun Maiden and the Crescent Moon: Siberian Folk Tales* (Edinburgh: Canongate).

Robson, Pam (2001) *The Middle Child in Children's Literature*. Dissertation presented in part fulfilment of the requirements of the MA in Children's Literature of the University of Surrey, September.

Rowland, Susan (1999) *C. G. Jung and Literary Theory* (Basingstoke: Macmillan).

Rudgley, Richard (2006) *Pagan Resurrection* (London: Century).

Rutherford, Ward (1986) *Shamanism: the foundations of magic* (Wellingborough: Thorsons).

Said, Edward (1978) *Orientalism* (New York: Pantheon).

Sainsbury, Lisa (2005) 'Childhood, Youth Culture and the Uncanny: Uncanny Nights in Contemporary Adolescent Fiction' in Reynolds, Kimberley (ed.), pp. 124–140.

Samuel, Raphael (1994) *Theatres of Memory Volume 1: Past and Present in Contemporary Culture* (London and New York: Verso).

Schama, Simon (1995) *Landscape and Memory* (London: HarperCollins).

Sell, Roger D. (ed.) (2002) *Children's Literature as Communication* (Amsterdam and Philadelphia, PA: John Benjamins).

Simoncsics, Pal (1978) 'The Structure of a Nenets Magic Chant' in Diószegi, Vilmos and Hoppál, Mihály (ed.), *Shamanism in Siberia* (Budapest: Akadémiai Kiadó), pp. 387–402.

Somby, Ánde (1995) 'Joik and the theory of knowledge'. http://www.uit.no/ ssweb/dok/Somby/Ande/95.htm (accessed 1/9/02).

Sommarström, Bo (1987) 'Ethnoastronomical perspectives on Saami religion' in Ahlbäck, Tore (ed.), pp. 211–250.

Spencer, Arthur (1978) *The Lapps* (Newton Abbot: David and Charles).

Stephens, John (1992) *Language and Ideology in Children's Fiction* (London: Longman).

Stephens, John (2003) 'Witch-Figures in Recent Children's Fiction: The Subaltern and the Subversive' in Lucas, Ann Lawson (ed.), *The Presence of the Past in Children's Literature* (Westport, CT: Greenwood), pp. 195–202.

Stephens, John and McCallum, Robyn (1998) *Retelling Stories, Framing Culture: traditional stories and metanarratives in children's literature* (New York and London: Garland).

Stewig, John (1995) 'The Witch Woman: A Recurring Motif in Recent Fantasy Writing for Young Readers', in *Children's Literature in Education*, Vol. 26, No. 2, June, pp. 119–133.

Sutcliffe, Steven and Bowman, Marion (ed.) (2000) *Beyond New Age: Exploring Alternative Spirituality* (Edinburgh: Edinburgh University Press).

Sutherland, Elizabeth (1985) *Ravens and Black Rain: The Story of Highland Second Sight* (London: Transworld, 1987).

Svenson, Rig (1998) *Pierced by the Light: Viking Gods, Runes, and 21st Century Teutonic Magic* (Coalville: Flying Witch).

Thomas, Keith (1971) *Religion and the Decline of Magic* (Harmondsworth: Penguin, 1985).

Thomson, Stephen (1998) 'Substitute Communities, Authentic Voices: the Organic Writing of the Child' in Lesnik-Oberstein, Karín (ed.), *Children in Culture: Approaches to Childhood* (Basingstoke: Macmillan), pp. 248–273.

Thomson, Stephen (2004) 'The Child, The Family, The Relationship. Familiar Stories: Family, Storytelling, and Ideology in Philip Pullman's *His Dark Materials*' in Lesnik-Oberstein, Karín (ed.), *Children's Literature: New Approaches* (Basingstoke and New York: Palgrave Macmillan), pp. 144–167.

Thubron, Colin (1999) *In Siberia* (London: Chatto and Windus).

Todorov, Tzvetan (1970) *The Fantastic: a structural approach to a literary genre* (New York: Cornell University Press, 1995. Translated by Richard Howard).

Versluis, Arthur (1993) *The Elements of Native American Traditions* (Shaftesbury: Element).

Waddington, Clive and Passmore, Dave (2004) *Ancient Northumberland* (Wooler: The Design Desk).

Watkins, Alfred (1925) *The Old Straight Track* (London: Sphere, 1974).

Watson, Aaron (2007) http://www.monumental.uk.com/site/research/index. html, accessed 2/6/08.

Yovino-Young, Marjorie (1993) *Pagan Ritual and Myth in Russian Magic Tales: a study of patterns* (Lewiston, NY and Lampeter: Edwin Mellen).

Index

Note: Page numbers in **bold** denote illustrations.